THE UNTAMED FORCE

THE UNTAMED FORCE

J. A. Springs

WRITING
FOR THE
WORLD
PRESS

since
2021

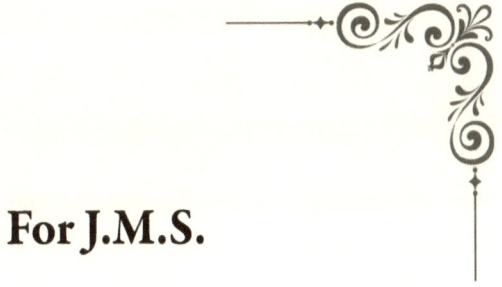

For J.M.S.

P relude

The two shadows, like unseen puppeteers, ensnared the girl, holding her captive in a dreadful tableau. A heavy silence hung in the air, pregnant with anticipation, as a darker mass, another sinister shadow, advanced towards her with ominous intent. His motives were unmistakable; he sought possession of her body, indifferent to whether she acquiesced willingly or resisted vehemently. Her feelings mattered not to him; his sole focus lay in the perverse act he was poised to commit, craving the ecstasy of the impending release. The prospect of her screams held no deterrent for him.

Meanwhile, Aaron occupied a desolate corner of the room, though "stood" hardly described his posture. Leaning against the corporeal form of the fourth shadow—a curvaceous silhouette resembling a woman with ample breasts and full hips—he felt the soft contours of the feminine shape pressed against him. Yet, such sensual details paled in significance, overshadowed by the urgency of the terror enveloping him.

His desperate desire to aid the redheaded girl collided with an overwhelming sense of helplessness. Fear, the relentless emotion dominating the moment, rendered him impotent. As the scene unfolded, fear became more than a mere abstraction; it manifested as a palpable force, paralyzing Aaron and leaving him incapable of intervening in the impending tragedy.

A piercing shriek reverberated through the room, accompanied by the swift motion of a hand, drawn back and then unleashed with monstrous force. The darker mass, now consumed by anger, delivered a backhand that propelled the girl violently across the room. The brutality unfolding left Aaron unable to avert his gaze, grappling with the incomprehensible ruthlessness. Whatever this entity was, it defied the bounds of humanity; it couldn't be human.

Caught in the aftermath, Aaron locked eyes with the redheaded girl. In that moment, he sensed an imaginary plea in her gaze, as if she were begging for assistance. Yet, there was no vitality in those eyes—only emptiness. *A sickening thud had echoed through the once-silent space, followed by the swift snap of breaking bones. Crumpled against the wall, she now lay on the floor, a trace of blood lingering at the corner of her mouth.*

Aaron's heart raced, a visceral realization settling in. She was gone. The accusatory stare of those lifeless eyes haunted him. Then, a terrible scream shattered the air, emanating from the dark mass of hatred that loomed in the room with him.

A macabre cascade commenced, as blood permeated every surface. It poured relentlessly from the ceiling, the walls becoming tearful conduits for the crimson tide. The floor, once solid beneath Aaron's feet, transformed into a treacherous terrain, slick with the thick, hot fluid. The shadows, once ominous companions, vanished into the horror unfolding.

Now alone, Aaron stood amidst this gruesome scene with the lifeless girl. Her dead eyes fixated on him, their vacancy seeming to emanate from a void. A haunting smile adorned her lifeless face, sending a shiver down Aaron's spine. In response, he couldn't contain the primal scream that erupted from deep within him, echoing in the blood-soaked chamber.

1

I n the oppressive darkness of the room, Aaron awoke, drenched in sweat and convulsing with such intensity that it threatened to propel him from his bed. His chest rose and fell in erratic spasms, his heart pounding against his ribs as if seeking escape. The turmoil within him teetered on the brink of a scream, a sonic manifestation that could rouse the entire household from their slumber. It was the recurring nightmare, an unwelcome visitor haunting him since his tenth birthday. Though it had vanished during his seventeenth year, the respite was short-lived, and now it returned with vivid, disturbing details that tested Aaron's resilience beyond his capacity.

Attempting to quell his shattered nerves, Aaron took deliberate, deep breaths. Gradually, the rhythmic inhalations helped, restoring a semblance of normalcy to his frantic heartbeat. As he sat up, he surveyed the room with a vacant expression mirrored in his mind. It wasn't a search for anything specific; he needed reassurance of his surroundings, a grounding in reality.

The room retained the inky darkness from when he drifted into slumber. An uneasy feeling crept over him as he surveyed the shadows, a discomfort exacerbated by the lingering residue of his recent nightmare. The darkness now held an unsettling weight, a consequence of the vivid images that still clung to his mind. Reluctant to confront the obscurity, he postponed the task of illuminating the room, opting instead to allow his thoughts to settle into some semblance of order. Besides, the darkness, though palpable, didn't obscure the room entirely; he could discern the familiar outlines of his surroundings.

His gaze shifted to the side, and his orientation slowly returned. Seated on his own bed, in his own room, he found reassurance in the familiar features—a dresser against the opposite wall, the closet door beside it, and his small desk with a computer next to the bed. The darkness, it seemed, hadn't veiled the room entirely. It offered just enough visibility for him to confirm that he was alone in this shadow-laden space.

Aaron shook his head vigorously, a futile attempt to dispel the haunting remnants of the horrendous dream. Despite its futility, he persisted, the act serving as a ritual of reassurance. As a result, his heartbeat gradually returned to a rhythm more aligned with normalcy, reinforcing the tangible reality of his existence within the confines of his own room.

Determined to extricate himself from the bed, he attempted to swing his legs over its edge, only to find an unexpected hindrance. A glance downward unveiled the culprit—a tangled mass of sheets ensnaring his feet. He lifted his legs, liberating them from the constricting embrace of the linens, and let them dangle over the bed's edge. The realization dawned that the sheets had likely contributed to the sense of restraint he felt. It would have been a plausible explanation, a comforting lie, if not for the bitter truth that he had known for a month—the recurring nightmare, each iteration more vivid and lurid than the last. Desperation coursed through him, and he would have sacrificed almost anything to free himself from its relentless grip.

Rising from his bed, Aaron extended his limbs in a stretch, attempting to alleviate the tension that lingered in his muscles. It was clear to him that returning to sleep was a futile endeavor. Casting a wistful gaze back at his abandoned bed, a longing for the elusive rest tugged at him, yet he quickly dismissed the idea of reentering its confines. The clock on the nightstand caught his attention, revealing the early hour of five forty-five in the morning. With school on the horizon, he resigned himself to being awake for a substantial stretch of time, a reality he acknowledged with a sigh.

In a deliberate motion, he bent down and laced up his running shoes. Dressed in a t-shirt and shorts, he was mentally prepared for what lay ahead. Aware of the therapeutic power of his routine, especially when faced with insurmountable problems, he harnessed his thoughts. Running became his refuge, a familiar remedy for quandaries lacking clear solutions. As the morning unfolded, he would navigate the labyrinth of his contemplations one stride at a time.

Years ago, Aaron had meticulously mapped out a running course—a coping mechanism born from the relentless grip of recurring nightmares. Initially, he shared with those few who cared that running was a remedy for his inability to return to sleep, and while partially true, the deeper reality was that it provided a respite from the haunting dreams. The act of placing one foot in front of the other, persisting despite chest pains and leg cramps, diverted his mind from the nightmares that plagued him.

The course, not overly challenging but far from easy, acted as a natural deterrent, causing most to abandon the run before completion due to its demanding nature. Winding through his block, traversing the park at the outskirts of the residential area, and extending almost to the fringes of downtown, the route covered a substantial four miles. Upon doubling back, he'd find himself back at his starting point—his parents' house, concluding an arduous eight-mile circuit. Remarkably, Aaron would conquer this challenging course in approximately an hour and a half, maintaining a pace of nearly six minutes per mile. The rhythmic pounding of his footsteps served as both a physical and mental escape, allowing him to outrun not just the distance but the haunting echoes of his nightmares.

Aaron made it a point to check in on his younger brother, Michael, before embarking on his morning run. Some days, he would find Michael eagerly waiting in his own bed, a testament to his admiration for Aaron. These instances usually occurred when Aaron managed to sleep in until after six thirty. Michael harbored a deep affection for his older brother, often aspiring to emulate him in every way.

However, on this particular morning, Michael remained peacefully asleep. Aaron, not disappointed, understood the dynamics of running with his younger brother. Despite their comparable endurance levels, the inherent sibling rivalry fueled a friendly competition. Michael had a knack for pushing Aaron to run faster than usual, defying the odds with an uncanny ability to bring out the best in his older brother. In those rare instances when Michael emerged victorious, they completed the challenging eight-mile route in precisely an hour—an accomplishment that spoke volumes about their shared determination and the friendly rivalry that fueled their runs.

Silently descending the stairs, Aaron slipped out the front door with ninja-like precision, careful not to disturb anyone in the still-slumbering house. As he surveyed the road ahead, contemplation veiled his expression, acknowledging the physical toll the impending run would exact on him. The mere act of embarking on this run was already diverting his thoughts away from the lingering nightmare.

Commencing with a leisurely pace, Aaron felt the gradual release of tension as his tight muscles began to yield to the rhythmic cadence of his strides. By the time he reached the seventh mile, the sun's gentle ascent over distant hills marked the horizon. As he neared his house for the final stretch, the sun was now visible, casting a warm glow on the landscape. Exhausted and drenched in sweat, Aaron ascended the front porch, his worn and battered body a testament to the physical exertion he had endured.

The tactic had worked; the nightmare no longer tormented him. Instead, the searing pain in his lungs and the burn in his legs emerged as the prevailing sensations, a trade he welcomed to escape the clutches of haunting dreams.

"You can't keep running from your problems, son. You need to face them square ahead," came the gravelly voice, unmistakably Aaron's father.

Startled, Aaron lifted his gaze from the foot of the stairs, where he was attempting to soothe his aching muscles and burning chest. His father's presence on the porch had eluded him as he ascended. If his heart wasn't already racing, the sudden appearance would have triggered it, adding a pulse of fright to his already accelerated beats.

John, Aaron's father, stood at the stair's summit, casually leaning on the rail and puffing on his pipe. The realization hit that his father must have observed from the window in the living room as Aaron rounded the corner up the street. This likely prompted him to emerge precisely when Aaron reached the stairs. John's eyes exuded a composed coolness, a gaze that not many dared to confront. Aaron, like many others, preferred not to linger too long beneath its penetrating scrutiny.

John nonchalantly shrugged, pivoting to reenter the house.

"You been having them dreams again haven't you? No need to answer, I can see it all over you, you always ran in the morning when the dreams came."

Pausing, John stood with his back partially turned to Aaron, a contemplative expression clouding his features. It seemed as if he harbored an unspoken desire to convey something more, but he chose restraint. The unspoken words lingered, transforming into a respectful silence rather than voiced truths.

"Get up stairs and get yourself cleaned up. Your momma's in the kitchen making breakfast." With that directive, John strolled into the house, the lazy puffs from his pipe trailing behind. Aaron complied with his father's instructions.

In no time, Aaron found himself seated at the breakfast table downstairs, eager to eat and swiftly depart from the house. "No need to linger where you're not needed," his father's words echoed in his mind, and today, he had no desire to be near his father—especially with school looming ahead.

Taking his place at a prepared plate, Aaron observed his mother, Emma, approaching from the stove.

"Good morning, baby. Would you like some more grits?" she asked with a warm smile, her gaze fixed on her first-born.

Emma's love wrapped around him, refusing to let go—a quality that rendered her the most beautiful woman in the town of Ionia and John the luckiest man in town to have her. They had met when John worked down south in Georgia one summer, falling in love, getting married, and eventually bringing her back to his hometown. Despite the passing years, her thick southern accent persisted, a charming relic of her heritage.

"I'm okay, Momma," Aaron reassured, "I'll just finish what's on my plate now; I need to hurry because I don't want to be late for school."

Responding with another warm smile, Emma bent down to plant a kiss on her son's forehead. She swiftly navigated around the table, replenishing John's plate with more food before settling down to her own breakfast. Not bothering to inquire if Michael desired seconds, Emma knew he'd decline—his modest appetite rarely led to a cleaned plate.

Gazing across the table at Aaron, Emma broached a more probing question, "Are you having those nightmares again, Aaron?" Her concern echoed in the inquiry, a sentiment noticeably absent from his father.

Aaron hesitated, torn between the truth he didn't want to share and sparing his mother unnecessary worry. Her propensity for concern was one of her defining qualities—she reveled in worrying about everyone. Looking over at his father engrossed in the newspaper, Aaron couldn't help but harbor thoughts of his apparent indifference. 'Nice of you to ask too, dad, it's not like you care about me or anything like that,' Aaron mused internally.

"Boy," John's voice interrupted Aaron's thoughts, causing him to nearly jump out of his chair. The fear that his father had somehow heard his inner musings flashed across Aaron's face. "That Baker girl came by here looking to see you. She's standing out back, waiting on you. I think she wants to walk with you to school."

The words from his father barely registered before Aaron found himself on his feet, swiftly making his way toward the back door of the house. Rounding the breakfast table, he paused briefly to plant a gentle kiss on his mother's cheek. "I'm alright, Momma. I'll be fine."

Passing by his father, Aaron considered briefly the notion of kissing him on the cheek but thought better of it. The prospect of displaying such a gesture of love felt uncertain, their relationship lacking that level of intimacy. They had seldom shared such moments before. Deciding against it, Aaron proceeded to leave and retrieve Sara from the back porch.

Michael trailed closely behind, grabbing his own school bag and shadowing his brother's lead. They both exited through the back door, aiming for the cut between their house and the next, onward toward the street and school.

On the back porch, Sara awaited them, radiating her customary beauty. Midnight black hair secured in a ponytail, with a few stray strands gracing her back, she greeted Aaron with a sweet smile. As she began to speak, an unexpected force yanked her off the porch, leaving her unable to voice even a modest protest at the abruptness of the situation. Aaron had grasped her hand and was leading her away.

"Why didn't you come in for breakfast, Sara?" Aaron inquired as they strolled past the sides of both his and her house.

Sara nonchalantly shrugged her shoulders, expressing her indifference to waiting outside for Aaron, regardless of the duration. With her hand securely in his, Aaron glanced down at their entwined hands, tightening his grip slightly. Sara responded with a smile, reciprocating the gesture with a gentle squeeze.

Slowing his pace, Aaron took a moment to marvel at her beauty—the elegance of her smile and the tenderness of her love—as they leisurely walked down the street.

"I didn't need to eat breakfast," Sara spoke in her soft voice. "I already ate at home. I didn't want to bother your parents this early in the morning with having to provide me breakfast, even though they would have."

Aaron felt a slight surprise at Sara's considerate gesture. She was aware of how his parents felt about her; they loved her. In fact, Aaron sometimes entertained the thought that his parents loved her more than they loved him, but he knew that wasn't true. While they treated her as one of their own, it wasn't favoritism—it was an acknowledgment of the unbreakable bond between the two.

MICHAEL gestured down the street opposite to the one they were walking on. Despite his brother's attempt to draw attention, Aaron continued forward, maintaining an unwavering pace. Undeterred, Michael quickened his steps, positioning himself in front of Aaron.

Coming to an abrupt halt, he emphatically pointed back down the street they had just traversed.

Silence prevailed as Michael refrained from speaking, a trait that had long become familiar to his family. Teachers may have found it infuriating, but within the family circle, it was nothing new. While Michael possessed the ability to communicate fluently, he chose silence unless absolutely necessary. In the present moment, speaking didn't fall under that category.

"I know which way we gotta go to get to school. Sara and I aren't going that way," Aaron asserted, glancing down at his displeased brother. "You go ahead and go to school; we'll be there soon."

Intent on continuing, Aaron found his path blocked as Michael stood resolute, refusing to yield. Michael grounded himself, spreading his feet as though firmly rooted in the earth.

"Go ahead, Michael. Go on."

When Michael persisted in his refusal to move, Aaron released Sara's hand and lifted his younger brother by the shoulders. Turning Michael towards the school's direction, Aaron delivered a swift, albeit not overly rough, boot to his backside, prompting him to start moving.

Michael suppressed his anguished protest and adopted a measured pace toward school, intermittently casting a resentful glance over his shoulder. While physically unharmed, his wounded pride lingered. His admiration for Aaron was boundless, and all he desired was to emulate his elder brother. However, Michael harbored a particular aversion to the time Aaron spent with Sara; jealousy welled up at anyone who seemed to take his brother away.

Turning his attention back to Sara, Aaron interlocked his fingers with hers. They both pivoted, retracing their steps in the original direction. Sara sensed they weren't heading to school immediately, and that suited her just fine. Her sole wish was to maximize her time with Aaron, especially since they hadn't seen each other over the weekend. Her parents had taken her along to visit her aunt.

Sara shifted her gaze toward Aaron, her view limited by the angle. Even with just a portion of his profile visible, it sufficed. She admired the determined look in his eyes and the playful smile that lingered at the corner of his lips, ready to reveal itself to the world.

His brown, tousled hair danced in the wind, mirroring what hers would have done if not neatly confined. Despite the bustling morning traffic on the street, no one paid much attention to the two adolescents walking away from their high school. The time for their morning classes had not yet arrived, and they both understood that they would reach there soon enough.

"Aaron," Sara started sympathetically as they strolled down the street, "I saw you running this morning. Are you having those nightmares again?"

Aaron eased his pace, coming to a stop. He turned to gaze into Sara's sparkling blue eyes, certain that he could confide in her without judgment. "Yeah, I had one this weekend while you were at your aunt's house. I didn't want to tell you, but I should have known you would find out anyway."

Neighbors since birth, Aaron and Sara had grown up together, navigating every school year side by side. During their eighteen years of life, a profound love and trust had solidified, undeniable to anyone who witnessed it. Their parents, the Bakers and the Smiths, acknowledged and even encouraged their close bond, realizing that attempts to separate them would prove futile. Initially resistant, the parents had tried when the two were fourteen and began showing signs of recognizing the opposite sex, but nothing could sever the unbreakable connection between Aaron and Sara.

Their intimacy led to an understanding that surpassed even what their parents knew in some aspects. Sara could sense when Aaron was troubled—a connection forged over the years.

Aaron increased his pace, realizing they needed to reach their destination before time slipped away and school beckoned. Turning at the corner street, they headed towards an abandoned gas station halfway up the block. This spot had become a makeshift clubhouse for local teenagers. While parents were aware of the place, there was little cause for worry. It served as a preferable hangout, preventing the kids from engaging in reckless behavior elsewhere and potentially getting into trouble.

The youngsters of Ionia seldom found themselves entangled in serious trouble. While not a small city, it wasn't among the largest. Crime, for the most part, was a rarity here. Occasional incidents included some minor disturbances and the sporadic speeding ticket, leaving the police with little else to occupy their time.

Choosing a discreet entry, Aaron and Sara slipped through a loose board at the back of the building. They avoided the front entrance, the usual point of access for others. The interior near their entry point was dimly lit. Broken windows at the back had been boarded up, leaving the space a bit shadowed. A few chairs were scattered haphazardly, accompanied by a worn-out couch salvaged from the street. Newspapers lay strewn on the floor, and a dozen or so empty beer cans congregated near an overflowing trash can. Despite these remnants, the place maintained a relative cleanliness. Remarkably, it even boasted a functional bathroom and electricity.

Little did the frequent patrons realize, the conscientious parents had ensured the facility remained well-lit, each parent taking turns covering the modest monthly expense, never exceeding twenty dollars. Chaperoning the activities of the adolescents wasn't necessary; the kids limited their use to weekends, and police patrols routinely checked the premises to ensure everyone dispersed and headed home by midnight. On weekdays, the police conducted checks to prevent vagrancy.

Guiding Sara to a bench along the distant wall, away from the entrance, Aaron assured them privacy. They steered clear of the front, eliminating the risk of being observed through the unbroken windows. Sara settled onto the bench, delicately placing her hands in her lap. Looking up at Aaron standing above her, she silently wished for him to join her, understanding his underlying nervousness. This marked their first moment alone in over a month.

Aaron wrestled with the desire to share the unsettling dream that had plagued his sleep the night before. Initiating a few steps away, he abruptly returned, only to be met by Sara's gentle grasp as she reached up and took his hand. Pausing in his pacing, Aaron stood, allowing her touch without any interruption.

"Tell me about the dream, Aaron," Sara urged softly.

Running his free hand through his hair, Aaron eventually settled down beside Sara and began recounting the details of the disturbing dream. Despite his morning run, the nightmare lingered, and he felt perturbed.

"It's different this time. I can recall more details now," he confessed, lifting his gaze from their intertwined hands.

"There's also a darker feel to it," he added, hesitating as he searched for words to convey the ominous atmosphere, finding language inadequate for the task.

"This time, I actually remember the details of the dream," he reiterated, his voice soft.

When the nightmares initially plagued him, Aaron couldn't recollect any details about them. This persisted for years, leading his parents to seek the help of specialists to no avail. The dreams persisted, recurring with unwavering regularity. Commencing at the age of ten, they haunted him once every three days for months, ceasing just shy of his sixteenth birthday. Periods of respite, lasting a month or so, peppered the eight years of the recurring nightmare, yet the relief was always fleeting.

Aaron's shoulders slumped slightly as he resigned himself to share the details with Sara. "It started with me and some girl in a park here in town. The next thing I remember is being in a room somewhere with her screaming, and I couldn't do anything about it. There was this dark creature present, and it harmed her in a way that I can't quite remember, and then there was blood."

Sara gasped audibly, prompting Aaron to cast a concerned glance her way. Once assured she was fine, he continued sharing the details of the nightmare, recounting what he could remember.

As Aaron started narrating the dream again, his voice gradually lowered, almost to a whisper. Sara struggled to discern some of the descriptions until she leaned in, almost close enough to have her forehead touching his. "There was so much blood. I didn't know what to do... I couldn't help her," Aaron whispered, his voice winding down as the emotions stirred by the story took their toll.

Sara gently stroked his cheek and planted a kiss on his forehead, the barest inches from her own. She then took his listless hand in hers and looped his other arm around her trembling waist. "Do you remember anything about the park or any details about the room?" she inquired.

When Aaron indicated he didn't recall details about these aspects, Sara pressed on. "Do you remember anything else about the girl?"

Aaron jerked his head up abruptly, anxious to assure Sara that it wasn't her. He yearned to convey that she wasn't the girl, but uncertainty held him back. Drawing her close to his chest, he enveloped her in a tight embrace.

"No," he declared emphatically, "No, let's not talk about this anymore. I haven't seen you for two days, and I missed you. I just want to focus on us right now and let all the problems of the world slip away."

Aaron kissed her passionately—not a simple peck on the lips, but a deep and lingering embrace. His tongue danced in and out of her mouth, seeking hers. He ran his hands fervently across her body, tracing down her sides. His touch sent prickly shivers up her spine, and her blood raced through her veins. She could feel the pulse of her heart against her chest, the drumbeat resonating relentlessly in her ears. Finally, he ran his hands up her legs, lifting the soft material of her dress to her slender waist.

Sara welcomed his kisses, parting her lips. She arched her back and spread her legs to accommodate his exploring hands. This moment marked only a partial culmination of their love, a fleeting instant etched into both their memories. It served as a brief respite for the intense longing Aaron felt for her. He recognized that he could only indulge in exploring the softness of her flesh before their private time expired, and they needed to proceed to their designated place in school.

The passion had steadily built up over the two days of separation and the preceding week when they couldn't find moments alone together. Soft kisses and light touches proved insufficient to quench this growing fervor. Only the momentary release of excess energy, this abandoned interlude, fulfilled their mutual desire for each other.

Aaron attended promptly to Sara's needs, realizing that his own desires would have to wait for another time. Sara, understanding and willing, would have reciprocated, but Aaron held back, focusing solely on pleasuring her in that moment. His skilled fingers and probing tongue swiftly extinguished the fire burning within Sara. He chose to let his own desires subside naturally, not wanting to force anything or allow Sara to feel used. His love for her prevented him from compromising her well-being.

Sara stood, positioning herself between Aaron's legs. Gently wrapping her arms around his neck, she pulled him into her embrace. Her legs felt weak and unsteady, the passionate spark now extinguished. She would have gladly remained in that position, relying on Aaron's support to prevent her from falling. Lifting his head, Aaron kissed Sara gently on the belly before pulling himself to his feet.

He offered her a tender smile, taking her into his arms briefly before they turned to leave.

"I missed you, Sara," Aaron confessed.

Sara nodded slowly. "I know," was all she said. It was enough.

2

The eagerly anticipated prom was just around the corner, a culmination they had eagerly awaited since the commencement of their senior year. Now, a mere day away, it loomed on the horizon. Five months had elapsed since the memorable day at the club, and Aaron presently found himself seated at the foot of Sara's bed. His gaze was fixed on her, observing her leisurely pacing back and forth across the room.

Sara's bare feet made a muted sound against the cold wooden floor, cushioned by the luxurious cream-colored carpet that extended from beneath her bed. This particular rug, designed as an area rug, didn't span the entire floor but served the essential purpose of preserving warm little piggies from turning cold once they left the confines of the bed.

Aaron observed her in silence, finding satisfaction as she passed in front of the lamp on her dresser. The play of light revealed the translucence of the nightgown she wore. It was an unspoken pleasure, considering his normal teenage inclinations—his occasional inability to sleep through the night notwithstanding. For now, he had no intention of asking Sara to cease her pacing.

Earlier in the day, Sara had called and invited Aaron to her house for the evening, a request made after their return from school. True to his commitment, he showed up in less than a minute after their phone conversation. He wouldn't have missed it for the world; being by the side of the girl he loved was exactly where he wanted to be.

Besides, he had a suspicion about the topic she wished to discuss. It was likely either the upcoming prom or the college acceptance letter, a matter her mother had mentioned as he entered the house.

Sara's distress was palpable, evident enough for Aaron not to overlook. Her pacing persisted, and at times, she resorted to chewing on her fingernails—an observable bad habit that left him wondering where she had picked it up.

"Sara, would ya slow down and tell me what's bothering you? You're making me dizzy." Aaron's exasperation grew as her ceaseless motion continued. Ten minutes had elapsed since he entered the room, and she showed no sign of stopping.

Contemplating the situation, Sara felt the temptation to maintain her pacing but recognized it wouldn't resolve the issue at hand. Shifting her gaze past Aaron's shoulder to the other side of the bed, she noticed a letter on the nightstand. It had arrived while she was at school, and she had read it just moments before calling Aaron over. The contents of that letter fueled her apprehension, and the burden of keeping its contents to herself weighed heavily. With a deep breath, her shoulders rising and falling with exertion, she knew that delaying the revelation wouldn't make it any easier.

"I received a letter from the college today," she began, taking a moment to peer into Aaron's eyes, attempting to gauge his reaction. His expression remained neutral, and she found it challenging to discern his thoughts. It felt akin to deciphering a brick wall, given Aaron's impassive demeanor—a mask of patience as readable as a plain white wall. Undeterred, she pressed on, recognizing the need to provide more information to elicit a response.

"I got accepted. I'll be able to start the fall semester as soon as summer is over."

That was only part of what she intended to share. The news causing her distress remained unspoken—the revelation that her acceptance placed her in a school miles away from where Aaron had been offered a full athletic scholarship. As she opened her mouth, poised to disclose the complete information, Aaron stood in front of her, gently placing his finger on her lips.

"I know, Love, I know. Just sit down and relax," Aaron said, guiding her around him and settling her onto the bed. Seating himself beside her, he curled his leg underneath, positioning himself to face her. Aaron marveled at how well he understood, solely from her mannerisms, that she was contemplating turning down the college acceptance just to be with him halfway across the state. The depth of their mutual understanding was truly remarkable.

"You don't have to turn down your acceptance to Dale College," Aaron assured. A spark lit up in Sara's eyes at his words, and without further elaboration, she sensed that they would be attending college together.

"I turned down the athletic scholarship at State and decided to take up Dale on their offer instead," Aaron disclosed.

Sara felt a mixture of surprise and happiness at his decision to forgo the scholarship at State and join her at Dale. Yet, as the realization sank in, she grasped the magnitude of what Aaron was sacrificing just to be with her. While she wouldn't have been able to attend State due to financial constraints, her current situation involved a partial academic scholarship and several grants to help alleviate the burden of hefty tuition. With some financial prudence and a decently paying after-school job, she believed she could manage.

Aaron lacked the same financial flexibility. State had granted him a full ride, and it was a necessity. College expenses were beyond his means, and the athletic scholarship from State held the promise of more significant rewards, potentially paving the way for a professional career in sports, unlike being a student athlete at Dale College.

He observed Sara's silence for a few seconds and anticipated her thoughts.

"It wouldn't do to have you going all the way to Dale without me. Besides, Dale has a pretty good athletic department. I'm not trying to go into professional sports or anything. I just wanted the scholarship so I could get some smarts out of it," Aaron intentionally used poor grammar to emphasize his point. "Dale offered me the same full ride as State did yesterday. I called them not more than an hour ago accepting that offer."

A joyful squeal erupted from Sara, causing Aaron to clap his hands over his ears in response. Sara, teary-eyed with happiness, no longer had to fret about Aaron attending a distant school or struggling to afford college.

She was poised to embrace him, intending to pull him onto the bed for some playful wrestling and tumbling, where accidental touches might transpire. However, her plans were interrupted by her mother's voice calling from down the hall.

"Still up here, Aaron?" Norma inquired. "You know how late it is, and the prom is tomorrow. You two can see each other then." Her voice gained volume as she approached the bedroom door, providing ample warning in case they were engaged in any inappropriate activities.

Sara's mother gently rapped her knuckles on the door twice before entering her daughter's bedroom. Upon seeing them sitting on the bed, she smiled. "You better get yourself home before you worry your mom, Aaron. Sara will be here when you wake up in the morning; she ain't gonna disappear."

Aaron rose from the bed and planted a quick kiss on Sara's cheek. Passing by Mrs. Baker, he repeated the gesture, kissing her on the cheek as well. She embraced him, offering a warm hug before playfully ushering him out of the room. As Aaron made his way down the hall toward the stairs, the sounds of laughter and giggles

reached his ears. Evidently, Sara had shared the news about school
with her mom.

EXITING the Baker house through the back door, Aaron found
the backyard seamlessly connected to his own. The houses were only
separated by a small hedge, which he effortlessly jumped over,
bypassing the conventional route. A big grin graced his face. Tonight,
nothing would impede his swift movements—not on this evening,
on the brink of the prom and just after revealing to his girl that they
could attend college together.

Stopping a few feet short of the back porch, Aaron detected
a faint noise emanating from the vicinity and couldn't discern its
origin. The yard was shrouded in darkness, the streetlights out front
failing to penetrate the obscurity at the rear of the houses. Squinting
his eyes, he allowed them to adjust, directing his attention toward
the source of the sound that had caught his attention.

Aaron heard the sound once more, this time before his eyes
could fully adjust to the darkness, preventing him from identifying
what had caused it. As his vision clarified, he recognized the source
of the noise—a creaking rocking chair on the back porch. It was his
father, seated there as his mother had set him out to enjoy the night
air before putting him to bed.

Three months earlier, John had fallen victim to a hit-and-run.
Though fortunate to survive, Aaron didn't perceive it as luck. His
father had lapsed into a coma for three days, emerging a changed
man upon waking. However, the change wasn't for the better. John
no longer afforded Aaron the opportunity to act without immediate
condemnation for any perceived failure, whether Aaron could
complete the task or not.

Aaron hesitated, contemplating avoiding his father altogether by going around the house to the front door. He preferred not to see him, but before he could act on that inclination, his father's voice rang out.

"Who is that? That you, Aaron? What cha doing sneaking around out here, don't you know I could have killed you with this shotgun?"

Aaron wasn't concerned about being shot with a shotgun, as the weapon didn't actually exist. However, his father couldn't grasp that fact, his mind slightly delusional from the coma. The doctors had warned that it would only worsen, and there was no room for false hope. Comprehensive tests indicated irreversible brain damage, foretelling John's eventual descent into a catatonic state, rendering him no better than a vegetable.

Aaron remained frozen in place, contemplating whether ignoring his father would allow him to slip away once the delirium took hold again. The unpredictable nature of his father's lucidity was often marked by the use or omission of names.

"I see you there, boy. You can't ignore me all night," John barked, his rough voice cutting through the darkness. "Get over here in the light so I can see you better."

Aaron discreetly moved to the side, trying to avoid the meager light seeping through the glass pane in the back door of his house. Even though the illumination was weak, it revealed more than Aaron wished to confront. The accident and subsequent surgeries had disfigured his father's once handsome face. A patch of hair was missing on his head, a testament to the car's impact. The affected side was slightly deformed, marking the origin of a scar that traversed John's face, across his jaw, and ended just below his chin. Even in the dim light, Aaron saw enough.

"What do you want," Aaron asked with a sarcastic drawl, eager to bring this chance encounter to a swift end. He had already deduced that nothing good could come of it. The pungent scent of alcohol emanated from his father's pores, noticeable even from the ten feet that separated them.

John's hand twitched involuntarily, another symptom of the damage to his brain and central nervous system. "Come closer so I can see you, boy."

Despite his reluctance, Aaron hesitated for a moment before moving. He didn't want to witness more of the damage inflicted on his father. Avoiding the stark reality, he respected his father even in his current condition, regretting his earlier sarcastic outburst.

He loved his father and wished that none of this had ever happened to him. What Aaron desired most was for his father to express his love verbally, a sentiment that would have meant more to him than anything else in the world. Although his father had shown love somewhat reluctantly, he never vocalized it.

Aaron took slow steps forward, mindful of the diminishing distance and the porch rail being the only barrier between them. Despite his father's reduced mobility, Aaron continued to close the gap cautiously.

The accident had made his father unpredictable. There were instances when his mother had to mediate in potential conflicts between Aaron and his father, situations that had the potential to escalate into violence.

John was aware that his son, Aaron, harbored wariness toward him, a sentiment that had persisted for many years. After the accident, he realized how seldom he had the clarity of mind to express his feelings to his son. Throughout Aaron's upbringing, John had intentionally kept a distance, avoiding getting too close or expressing too much love, fearing the inevitable loss. Now, faced with the aftermath of the accident, he found himself incapable of holding Aaron in his arms and expressing care and love. The ability to communicate on that level had slipped away. John felt a slight flare of temper, but he maintained tight control, recognizing that he was on the verge of revealing a truth to his son that he was hesitant to voice.

John made a decision, realizing that it was high time to express his care for his son. He whispered quietly, "I don't know why I didn't tell you this sooner." Aaron took another reluctant step forward, eager to hear what his father had to say.

"You don't deserve any of this. We should've warned you a long time ago about the girl. We should've told you about this damn town... everything that happens in it happens for a reason, son." John paused, hinting at a desire to share more, but his attention was diverted by someone emerging from the back door of the house.

As John turned, Aaron glimpsed his father's left eye—glassy and still, unsettling to look at. Leaning over, John revealed the right side of his face, marked with scar tissue from reconstructive surgery, now visible in the light.

John acknowledged that he wouldn't have the time to convey everything he wanted to say. With careful choice of words, recognizing the urgency, he leaned toward Aaron and whispered conspiratorially, "Don't you forget about those dreams, they're a warning to you. You keep your eyes open, boy, and don't let them—"

John's words were cut off, just as he expected.

"You hush now, John," Emma cooed, standing in the doorway. "You're scaring the poor boy half to death with your crazy talk." She smiled sweetly at Aaron, as though he were a child needing reassurance and receiving it in the subtlest gesture. Emma had overheard some of her husband's words to Aaron and stepped in to prevent him from revealing too much.

Emma was determined to shield her son from the town's sad history and curse for as long as possible. She walked over to John and draped a blanket around his shoulders. "It's time you got to bed,

John." Assisting him out of the chair and onto his feet, she took charge of guiding him.

"You gotta tell him, Emma. He got a right to know the truth. Them dreams is a warning," John spoke harshly, his speech slurred from alcohol consumption and jaw damage. Spittle dripped from his mouth with each word, rendering him childlike and weak. Despite his feeble resistance, Emma led him through the door and up the back stairs to their bedroom, settling him into bed for the night.

Aaron felt more than a little confused. His father had been rambling, a behavior Aaron had never witnessed before to this extent. Though he couldn't comprehend most of his father's words, some were unnerving. It seemed to Aaron that there was more left unsaid, deliberately kept from him.

Entering the kitchen, Aaron took a seat at the table. His mother joined him shortly thereafter. His immediate instinct was to inquire about his father's cryptic talk, but he anticipated that his mother's response would veer off into a different subject, leaving his original question unanswered.

"Have you eaten yet, Aaron?" she asked in her matronly voice. "There're leftovers in the fridge. Go ahead and make yourself a plate. You need to eat to stay strong." Emma sat down next to Aaron, placing her warm and caring hands on his. The look in her eyes made Aaron blush, despite himself.

"I'm fine, Momma. I ate at Sara's house," Aaron said softly, smiling. His spirits were lifted, dismissing his father's ranting as effects of alcohol. His thoughts returned to Sara. He kissed his mother on the cheek as he stood up and made his way out of the kitchen, heading to his own room for some sleep.

EMMA lingered in the kitchen for a moment, finding solace in the warmth of her family despite the recent tragedies that had befallen them. However, this tranquility was short-lived. An ominous sensation pervaded the room, casting a dark shadow that draped across the space. Emma felt its unwelcome presence settling upon her, causing discomfort. The joints in her bones responded with aching pain, a familiar response to the cold.

The once cozy warmth in the kitchen dissipated, replaced by an unexplained chill that Emma couldn't ignore, especially when she discerned the peculiar behavior of the shadows. They seemed to awaken, exhibiting restless movements akin to a troubled sea. Initially, Emma dismissed it as her overactive imagination, desperately clinging to the notion that it was mere trickery. Yet, a deep-seated knowing in her soul contradicted that belief.

Subconsciously shivering, Emma realized it wasn't the room's temperature that elicited this response. A profound awareness settled in as she recognized the manifestation of an otherworldly presence in the shadows.

Emma had only heard tales of its presence and had never before been in its chilling embrace. However, encountering this entity once was sufficient to etch an indelible mark on her soul. The memory lingered, haunting her, and she harbored no desire for a repeat experience. Emma would have welcomed death over the terror that this visitation brought.

In an attempt to dispel the foreboding atmosphere, Emma found herself addressing the shadows in the room, seeking reassurance. "John's words—out there, he didn't mean nothin by them. It was the alcohol talking, that's all. He was unaware of what he was saying, is all," she called out, attempting to reason with the unseen presence that seemed to envelop her surroundings.

In the solitude of the room, Emma's words hung unanswered. Another wave of chill coursed through her, an icy presence that triggered a shiver—deep-seated, cold enough to freeze even on the hottest summer day. It traced a path down her spine, leaving a tingling sensation in her limbs. Emma wasn't physically cold; it was an instinctive reaction to the entity sharing the room with her, an unnatural presence residing in the shadows. Positioned at the far end of the kitchen, it seemed to intensify with each passing second.

A faint breeze swept through the room, causing the glass in the cupboard doors to rattle and setting the kitchen door into a slow swing. It was an unsettling draft, unwelcome within the confines of a house. Emma nearly jumped out of her chair when the back door slammed shut, heightening the eerie atmosphere that had taken hold. The legs of the chair skittered to a halt on the linoleum kitchen floor when it finally settled.

Summoning every ounce of strength within her, Emma confronted the encroaching presence. "You leave Aaron and the Baker girl alone, you hear me. The Baker's have given you what you wanted and you got no reason to take Sara away just cause she's sweet on my Aaron."

Her gaze darted anxiously from one corner of the room to another, searching for the elusive entity. Eventually, Emma turned her attention to the darkest part of the room, anticipating the appearance of the mysterious visitor. Without a sound, no breath or the soft rustle of movement, the entity materialized in the shadows, seizing Emma's undivided attention. She stared at the figure before her in a mix of dread and fascination. It had taken on the form of a little girl.

The young girl appeared to be no older than ten or eleven, her blond hair partially gathered within a blue silk ribbon, allowing the unbound strands to flow gently over her shoulders. Clasping her tiny hands before her belly, she kept her gaze lowered, concealing the fair blue eyes that radiated from her cherubic face. Her attire consisted of a simple white dress with an empire bodice, adorned with a baby blue silk sash cinched in a bow at the middle of her back.

As she spoke, the doors on the cabinets shuddered, and the glass panes within threatened to shatter. Without lifting her head to meet Emma's gaze, the young girl's lips remained sealed, her mouth seemingly not responsible for producing the uttered words. "Don't presume you can tell me what to do."

Emma sensed it was the little girl who spoke, an intuition without clear explanation. Her courage waned, dwarfed by the overpowering presence in the room. It dissipated like steam from a boiling pot, vanishing as swiftly as it had materialized. When Emma spoke, her voice emerged feeble and inconsequential, uncertain if it could carry the weight of her intended words.

"I only meant to say that you already have what you want from the Baker's. Norma and Leon done give you their first-born. I didn't mean to imply nothing by it that you couldn't do as you please. Do you want to take away Sara?" Emma's voice, pitifully frail and lacking conviction, seemed to fall upon unheeding ears.

A prolonged silence ensued, and Emma received no response. As the seconds ticked by without an answer, a new sense of dread crept over her.

"Did you come for my Aaron?" Emma's attempt to query the entity standing before her felt feeble, and she thought her own voice sounded pathetic.

"You forget who I am. I don't answer to you." The voice that replied was childlike—innocent and sweet-sounding, yet devoid of kindness. This wasn't a child in a white Sunday dress with a neatly tied blue sash around the waist, showcasing the edges of a large bow from behind her elbows. "What is my name?" Sweet malice tinged her voice.

Emma remained silent.

The little girl lifted her gaze, revealing stunning ice-blue eyes that stood in stark contrast to her alabaster skin. Those eyes ensnared Emma in their piercing gaze, trapping her within their depths. It felt as if her entire world was laid bare before those eyes, capable of exposing every hidden fear, every secret.

"What's my name?" the little girl repeated.

"P-Pre... Pre... Precious," Emma stammered.

"I am Precious. I am the Forgotten Child of Ionia. I am the Dark Daughter of Ionia."

Emma slowly stood up from her seat. She was keenly aware of the nature of the apparition before her. She also knew she didn't want to be in such close proximity to it. As she attempted to step back, she suddenly found herself face to face with Precious. In the blink of an eye, Precious had closed the six-foot distance between them. Emma never saw her move.

"Sit down, bitch," Precious hissed vehemently. Her face contorted with anger—brows furrowed, a malicious smile playing on her lips, and her bright blue eyes colder than arctic ice.

Emma dropped into the chair like a stone. The chair she landed on almost skidded out from under her, nearly causing her to tumble to the floor.

"Listen to me," Precious said, venom dripping from every word, "You will shut that old, fat bastard of a husband of yours up. I don't want to hear him say another word to Aaron. Do I make myself clear?" Precious waited for a response that was slow in coming.

Emma nodded, her head bobbing up and down like a wooden marionette.

"Aaron is mine. I need him, and I'll take him when I'm ready," Precious smiled.

She reached out her hand and stroked Emma's cheek, wiping away a tear that had somehow fallen. Precious looked forlornly at the tear as she took her hand away from Emma's face. Her face relaxed from the hideous look it held before as she looked at the tear as if she had lost something in it. She tore her eyes away from her fingers and wiped them on her dress. Precious' touch on Emma's face had been so soft and gentle, a complete contrast to the thing that she appeared to be at times.

Precious turned and walked away towards the shadows. "Save your tears. The first born, before all others, are mine; that was the promise that I spat through the flames as I burned, and I won't change that now."

Emma watched the little girl disappear into the shadows as if her small form were one of them. When she knew that she was finally and truly alone, she flung her hands to the table and dropped her head to her forearms. She began to sob uncontrollably. It took about an hour for her to gather herself together enough to go upstairs and play at being asleep. Unbeknownst to her, she never saw her youngest child, Michael, slip up the steps before her and retreat to his room. This was the first time that she had ever met Precious, and she hoped that it would be the last time ever in her life that she would have to be in her presence again.

3

Father Gordon found himself seated at his desk, engrossed in the task of crafting his sermon for the upcoming Sunday. However, the work proved more time-consuming than he initially anticipated. Setting his pen down, he reclined in his chair, massaging his temples in an attempt to overcome the writer's block that had impeded his progress. Despite his efforts, the mental obstacle persisted.

Frustrated by the unforeseen challenge, Father Gordon acknowledged that the sermon wasn't progressing as smoothly as he had hoped. Leaning back, he contemplated the nature of such impediments to clear thinking. Reflecting on the lack of choice in encountering these mental hurdles, he grappled with the persistent blockage that disrupted his otherwise lucid thoughts.

Realizing that further productivity was elusive at the moment, Father Gordon decided to abandon his efforts. Rising from his chair, he stretched his limbs before navigating toward the sanctuary. Exiting his office through the side door, purposefully attached for this very convenience, he found himself on the path leading directly into the heart of the church. The alternative door in his office opened into a hallway, connecting to various other offices, and served as a circuitous route leading to the sanctuary's entrance at the front of the church.

Father Gordon surveyed the sanctuary before making his way toward the pulpit. Engaging himself in the tasks of his faith, he meticulously arranged the sacred articles along the railings and tables, refusing to tolerate any semblance of disorder within the church.

Despite his outward busyness, Father Gordon recognized that he was merely going through the motions. He had, in fact, inspected the sanctuary just two hours prior, ensuring every element was in its designated place, a routine check preceding his attempt to compose the Sunday sermon. However, a mysterious force lingered, contributing to the writer's block and clouding his otherwise clear thinking. An uneasy feeling settled within him, disrupting his focus and concentration. Father Gordon acknowledged his state of distraction, understanding its impact on his ability to immerse himself fully in his tasks.

Unsettling events besieged the town, pulling Father Gordon's attention away, particularly the enigmatic presence of Precious. He had fervently entreated heaven, seeking solace for the troubled city, his congregation, and his own soul, yet the answers remained elusive. Undeterred, he persisted in his prayers.

Fatigue weighed heavily on him, raising doubts about his endurance in the ongoing struggle. Amidst weariness, he questioned the purpose of his fight and whether it bore any fruit. The memory of congregants gazing up at him from their pews, receptive to the divine teachings he imparted, served as a source of strength. It buoyed him, offering sustenance during moments of spiritual lowness.

Ceasing his activities, Father Gordon realized that merely rearranging the sanctuary offered little respite from the underlying issues. Returning to his office in silence, he felt compelled to record his thoughts in his journal. Hoping that this act might bring solace to his troubled soul and facilitate the completion of his sermon, he would immerse himself in the act of writing again.

If this introspective exercise proved insufficient, he contemplated ending the day's work, seeking solace in the familiar embrace of the Good Book awaiting him at home. Within its pages, he would revisit the words that had initially called him to a life of service and devotion.

Closing the door behind him with a soft click, Father Gordon reentered his office. His eyes scanned the room until they settled on the window. Making his way there, he stood and gazed across the church lawn at the majestic trees gracing the clearing. Soft lights illuminated the green expanse, dispelling the encroaching darkness. The view provided a moment of solace, allowing him to reflect on the beauty of nature and the myriad wonders God had crafted on this Earth. In their diversity, these creations prompted him to pause and contemplate.

Turning away, he walked toward his desk. Retrieving his journal, he settled into his chair, ready to put pen to paper and capture the swirling thoughts within him.

"It never ceases to amaze me how I can still find beauty in the simplest of things. Through the passing years, I've grappled with making sense of the tumult around me. Delivering the Word in this place becomes a challenge amid the chaos. In my perspective, this sanctuary stands as a beacon, breathing life into our town. It seems to be the linchpin preventing the town from succumbing to despair. In the midst of adversity, this church nurtures the flame of hope in our hearts, affirming that our reality, though grim, is undeniably real. Sometimes, I ponder if our aspirations for change border on the unrealistic, questioning if we're deceiving ourselves into expecting a brighter future."

"One of the challenges we confront is the yearning for change to improve our circumstances. Change doesn't materialize in isolation. It demands something from us—boldness. For change to take root, a crucial step is required. A choice must be made, and that choice needs unwavering commitment. Perhaps our stumbling block lies in our hesitance to make that definitive choice. Time is of the essence; without a decisive choice, improvement will remain elusive."

Father Gordon scrutinized the words he had penned, a sense of shame creeping in as doubts clouded his mind. In this town devoid of peers, he longed for someone with whom he could share his fears and misgivings. However, entrusting such confidences to a parishioner risked compromising his ability to preach to them impartially. It seemed unfair to burden another soul with his innermost thoughts, so he chose the solace of his journal, a non-judgmental companion for his reflections. Yet, the journal offered no guidance or advice on how to proceed.

Regarding the Holy Church, they were well aware of the town's issues but chose to turn a blind eye. Sending Father Gordon back to his birthplace, they hoped he could leverage his understanding of the situation to instigate change. Expecting support from that specific quarter proved futile—a reality he had to come to terms with.

4

Katherine shifted in bed, moving from her stomach to her back. Her head dangled over the bed's edge, and her red hair cascaded just inches above the floor. Rubbing her eyes with the back of her hands, she attempted to dry the tears prompted by the sunlight streaming through the open drapes. Emitting a soft groan, she lamented not closing the drapes more tightly the night before. The prospect of getting up didn't appeal to her just yet.

She adjusted her head to catch a glimpse of the clock on the nightstand—fifteen minutes past ten. The early hour didn't align with her inclination to rise, but she had plans to meet her girlfriend at her house in less than half an hour. Their destination: the mall. The purpose of this outing was for her girlfriend to get her opinion on the boys they'd encounter. It was a way to fill the idle hours of summer. At eighteen, she was gearing up for college in the fall, and the desire to savor every moment before the academic hustle took over was paramount. Surveying the local mall for attractive guys seemed like a fitting pastime to wile away the days of summer.

She tossed the blankets off her legs, but they clung stubbornly, resisting release. After a brief struggle, she persuaded the covers to relent and moved towards her bedroom door, making her way downstairs. The foster parents were, as usual, absent from view. As she progressed through her senior year of high school, their presence in her life dwindled. For Katherine, this was a welcome development. While she liked and cared for her foster parents, she had always been a loner, a disposition that suited her just fine. The decreasing frequency of their interactions was in harmony with her preference for solitude. Her foster parents had long recognized that Katherine was self-sufficient and valued her independence. They offered her a home, love, and the space she desired once the affectionate gestures were received.

To outsiders, their small family might have appeared peculiar, given their individual idiosyncrasies. However, despite their eccentricities, they found a way to make the family dynamic function. A steadfast tradition for them was sharing dinner together, a ritual none were willing to disregard or alter. Katherine acknowledged their absence, surmising that her foster parents were likely perusing antiques at a flea market, a weekend activity they enjoyed but one that held little appeal for her.

Descending the stairs, Katherine was met with the chime of the front doorbell. Quickening her pace, she welcomed the early arrival of her girlfriend, Mindy. This deviation from their usual schedule meant an early start to their mall outing. As Katherine swung open the weighty wooden door, there stood Mindy, clad in a short skirt and tank top. A floppy hat perched casually on her head, complemented by gaudy sunglasses. Strapped to her feet were sandals, showcasing impeccably painted red toenails that glinted in the late morning light. Katherine couldn't contain her excitement, emitting a joyful scream before stepping outside to envelop her friend in a warm hug. In the process, Mindy's hat toppled off, allowing her brunette hair to cascade down from its loosely tied bun.

"Easy there, girl," Mindy teased, "you're gonna give me a heart attack."

Katherine was about to respond when she glanced up and noticed someone she'd rather avoid. Making his way up the driveway from Mindy's parked car was none other than Scott.

"Hi, Scott," Katherine greeted with evident disdain. Mindy turned to glance at Scott, who had halted just before reaching the front step. It was apparent that the feeling was mutual – Scott seemed as delighted to see Katherine as she was to see him.

"Why'd you bring the boyfriend?" Katherine inquired of Mindy.

"I wish you two would be nicer to each other. I don't know why you two don't get along," Mindy responded, her tone exasperated, high-pitched, and nasally. She took hold of Katherine's arm and guided her into the house.

"Why don't you like my boyfriend, Kate?" Mindy persisted.

Katherine rolled her eyes; it was a question Mindy had posed numerous times before. She didn't want to answer it now, and she certainly didn't want to entertain it later.

"He's alright. Don't worry about it," she replied, effortlessly masking the truth.

She glanced back over her shoulder in Scott's direction, shooting him a glare with her eyes. The reason why she didn't like Scott was something she couldn't share with Mindy. Revealing the truth would jeopardize their friendship, and that was a consequence she wished to avoid.

On a night when Mindy was away on one of her frequent trips with her parents, Katherine and Scott attended a party with no intention of anything more. However, alcohol played its part, leading to some roughhousing that resulted in an indiscretion they both regretted. Despite Katherine's desire to come clean when Mindy returned the following week, Scott persuaded her against it. He argued that disclosing the incident would only strain her friendship with Mindy and complicate his relationship with her.

He assured Katherine that he could handle a breakup if Mindy chose to end their relationship over what had transpired. However, he expressed a strong desire not to tarnish Katherine's friendship with Mindy, recognizing the precious nature of the bond between the two girls. Despite being just a kiss, albeit a long and passionate one, they both acknowledged their mistake and deeply regretted it. It was a lapse in judgment they would have to live with. Katherine found it challenging to determine which decision was worse: putting themselves in a compromising position initially or choosing to conceal the truth from Mindy.

Unhappy with both the unfortunate incident and the subsequent lie to her friend, Katherine felt compelled to make a difficult choice to preserve her friendship with Mindy. Knowing that Mindy would likely place the blame on her, Katherine found herself in an even more challenging situation as she realized she was developing feelings for Scott. Faced with the dilemma of being unable to have both Scott and maintain her friendship with Mindy, Katherine opted to distance herself from Scott as a way of compensating for her conflicting emotions.

Scott entered the house, closing the door behind him, and cast a disapproving glance at the two girls engaged in conversation in the foyer. His gaze shifted to Katherine's outfit, and an immediate disapproval crossed his face.

"Don't you think you should change, Kate?" he remarked.

Interrupting their conversation, Mindy and Katherine turned their attention to Scott. Defiantly, Katherine faced him, placing her hands on her hips.

"What's wrong with the way I'm dressed?" she demanded, failing to see any issue with her attire. Firmly asserting her right to dress as she pleased in her own house, she made it clear that Scott's opinion held little weight in that regard. She felt if he didn't like it, he could leave.

Scott's eyes traveled up and down, and for a moment, he found himself speechless. Katherine sported a diminutive camisole, barely concealing the upper part of her stomach. The thin satin material struggled to contain her ample breasts. As for her lower half, referring to it as panties would be a generous overstatement. The skimpy satin clung to her buttocks like a second skin, hanging low on her hips. Scott stole one more glance before turning away, overwhelmed by embarrassment and the desire to look longer. He continued into the kitchen, unable to endure the impact her attire was having on him. The last thing he wanted was to reveal his physical reaction.

Mindy found amusement in Scott's reaction. She had no doubt what Katherine's dress—or lack there of—was doing to her boyfriend. Smiling, she redirected her attention to Katherine, understanding she needed to alleviate Scott's discomfort, as entertaining as it was to witness him in such a state.

"You should get dressed. I don't want my boyfriend getting any ideas," she giggled.

Katherine hesitated before deciding not to say anything. Being underdressed didn't bother her; she was comfortable with nudity and would have confidently strolled around the house in such a state if her parents weren't insistent on her wearing something. If they had been home, she would have thrown on a robe to cover up.

While Katherine chatted with Mindy, her back turned to the kitchen, Katherine could see over Mindy's shoulder as Scott covertly glanced at her attire. Uncomfortably, she realized she was enjoying his looks. Katherine kissed Mindy on the cheek, excusing herself to get dressed for their outing.

Shortly afterward, Mindy settled into the passenger seat of the compact car, engaged in lively gossip with Katherine. The trio had departed not long after Katherine changed into an outfit equally as alluring as her sleepwear. Her long, tan legs peeked out from beneath an ultra-short denim skirt. The shoulder strap of the seatbelt intersected with the tank top she wore, causing her breasts to slightly spill over the fabric.

"I heard Brian's interested in you," Mindy shared cheerfully.

Katherine was not paying much attention to her words. Instead, she kept glancing ahead, catching Scott's eyes in the rearview mirror. He sought to gauge her reaction to the mention of Brian's name, aware that she openly admired Brian.

"I don't think I want to see him this weekend. He's a little pushy, and besides, he's still with Cheryl," Katherine lied. She was privy to the gossip mill and knew before others that Brian and Cheryl were no longer together, possessing such information sometimes even before the subjects of the rumors themselves, laughingly.

Mindy giggled and smiled, saying, "You should know; you keep up with everything. How do you stay so current?"

Katherine smiled in return, maintaining the mystery of why she was always ahead of the gossip curve. Her secret was closely guarded. A friend she had known since childhood. This friend started as an imaginary companion, persisting into her adulthood. Katherine trusted this friend more than anyone else in the world and was determined to keep this special relationship a secret, even from her closest friend, Mindy.

Scott's voice, crisp and clear, cut through Katherine with its deep, husky masculine tone as he spoke over his shoulder. "You're lying, Kate. I spoke with Brian last night. He and Cheryl have been broken up for nearly a week now, and she's already seeing somebody else."

Katherine crossed her arms, her gaze fixated angrily out of the window, and her bottom lip poking out. "Okay, I lied. I knew that. I just don't think it will work with him. He's too..." She paused, searching for the right word, "clingy," she finally declared, waving her hand dismissively in the air.

Katherine turned just in time to catch Scott's eyes in the mirror again. He wore a knowing look on his face.

You're lying again, he mouthed, ensuring Mindy wouldn't see him intone the words. I'm sorry, he added silently.

He was right about her lying again, but she wasn't going to admit it. She knew why she wasn't interested in Brian anymore. The reason was driving the car. She couldn't help herself. That one night had been more than she could handle, and now it was getting worse. If she didn't distance herself from her best friend's boyfriend soon, she felt that she might do something to jeopardize her best friend's trust in her. As she considered the situation again, it occurred to her that having someone to distract her would be beneficial. She decided it would be better to start seeing Brian.

"Mindy, can you call Brian and ask him to meet us at the beach later on this afternoon?" Katherine requested.

Mindy nearly jumped out of her seat; she was so happy. She quickly pulled out her cell phone and placed the call. Everything was neatly arranged, and soon enough, the early evening found them leaving the mall and walking along the beach as two happy couples. They joined a circle of friends who had started a bonfire on the beach, sitting beneath blankets, engaging in conversation, kissing, and playfully fondling each other before calling it a night and heading home.

Mindy sat in the back seat with Katherine, at Katherine's insistence. She couldn't trust herself with Brian being near her after drinking as much as she had. She didn't think their relationship should go much further than it already had until they had been dating a little while longer. She had been correct in her thinking that she needed someone to distract her from Scott. Brian was handsome, blond, and tall. His muscular build was sexy, and Katherine found herself wanting him a lot more than she wanted Scott.

Katherine nestled her head on Mindy's shoulder, and they talked about nothing in particular. Katherine remembered something that she hadn't told her friend yet, something she really wanted to discuss with her.

"Mindy, I heard from a relative last week. She's my great aunt."

"I thought that you were an orphan?" Mindy said questioningly.

"I thought I was too, but obviously I'm not. This letter came in the mail last week, and now I suddenly have a great aunt. She wants me to visit her in Ionia next summer," said Katherine groggily. She was a little inebriated, and it was beginning to show.

Mindy brushed Katherine's long red hair out of her face and kissed her on the forehead. "Ionia is a long way from Saxton, but it's what you've always wanted, isn't it? To finally meet someone from your real family."

Katherine shrugged her shoulders while simultaneously attempting to nod her head.

"Yeah, but I don't know. I can't imagine what she's like. I don't know what kind of person she is and why she waited so long to get in touch with me."

Katherine lifted her head and looked into her friend's eyes. There were tears welling up in the corner of Katherine's eyes, and she could see the same thing mirrored in Mindy's eyes.

Mindy's tears were of joy thinking of how her friend had always wanted to know her real family. She had no idea that Katherine would take this knowledge so hard and be so disturbed about it when she finally got the chance to meet them.

"Why did she wait so long?" Katherine sniffled. "She said she didn't want to confuse me in the letter. She said I was better off with my foster parents but now she says it's time for me to come home. I don't know what to do."

Mindy placed her hand on top of her friend's head and gently lowered Katherine's head back to her shoulder.

"It's alright to have doubts, Kate. I'm happy for you that you've finally heard from someone in your real family, but I can't tell you what to do. Only you can make that decision. Remember, I'll always be here to support you, no matter what."

Katherine looked toward the front of the car and caught Scott looking at her through the rearview mirror again. He smiled gently. She winced as she thought once again about the real reason she was about to start dating Brian – so that she wouldn't long for Scott and end up hurting her best friend in the process.

"Go see your aunt," he mouthed, encouraging her as a concerned friend. He too knew of her longing to know where her real family was and who they were.

Scott understood her feelings towards him, and he cared for her deeply, but he recognized that a romantic relationship between them wouldn't be feasible. His love for Mindy was too profound to let go, and he couldn't bear to hurt either of them. He fervently wished he could undo that one night he and Katherine shared, a mistaken kiss that brought them closer than necessary.

Katherine returned his smile. Despite their past mistakes, he remained a steadfast friend. She recognized his efforts to guide her towards Brian when he called her out on her lies earlier that day. Scott wanted her happiness, and she appreciated that.

WHEN Katherine arrived home, her parents were already there, seated in the living room, enjoying glasses of wine and engaged in a quiet conversation. As she approached the door, her father intercepted her, preventing a potential mishap as she navigated the smooth flooring. Detecting the scent of alcohol on her breath and noting her unsteady movements, he didn't react with anger or raised voices. Instead, he acknowledged her condition.

Sensing that she had been drinking, he gently guided her inside, keenly aware of her lack of coordination. Without uttering a word, he supported her to prevent any potential falls.

He cradled his daughter in his arms, carrying her to her bedroom. Once there, he let her inside to undress and change for bed while he waited outside the door. When she was prepared, he returned, gently tucking her into bed. A soft kiss on her forehead accompanied a tender gesture of brushing aside her long, curly red locks to ensure he wouldn't end up with a mouthful of hair.

He remained unperturbed, as did her mother, who waited patiently in the hall, observing with a gentle smile. They wouldn't harbor any resentment in the morning either. They recognized her as a teenager, relishing the summer between high school and college.

Reflecting on his own youth, her father acknowledged having engaged in similar revelry. While his daughter wasn't prone to coming home intoxicated, this marked the first time he witnessed her in such a state. He disapproved of it, yet he planned to discuss the matter with her in the morning. His intention was to ensure she comprehended the associated risks and would take precautions, such as reaching out to him if she needed a safe way home.

"I won't make this a habit, Daddy," Katherine assured.

"I know, Katie," he responded gently, planting another kiss on her forehead.

Exiting the room, he closed the door softly behind him. Katherine had already drifted into slumber before her parents descended the stairs.

Katherine awoke the next morning, still grappling with the aftermath of her night on the beach. Sunlight streamed through the curtains, casting a warm glow in the room. Attempting to sit up, she emitted a loud groan, her head pounding with the effort. It was only the second time in her life that she had indulged in alcohol, and now she understood why she could never be a serious drinker—morning-after discomfort was too much to bear.

Glancing at the clock, she noted the time: eight-thirty in the morning. Despite her desire to go back to sleep, the realization struck her that it was an unattainable luxury. Just as she began to acclimate to the new day, a familiar voice reached her ears. It wasn't her parents or friends; it was her secret companion.

"Good morning, Red," chirped the little one, affectionately using the nickname she had coined for Katherine.

Across the room, Katherine spun around and spotted her diminutive friend perched in the rocking chair nestled in the corner. With an eagerness that momentarily eclipsed her throbbing head, she leaped out of bed. The oversized shirt she wore, a relic from her father, served as a tangible reminder of his enduring love. Although the shirt extended below her knees, posing a tripping hazard, Katherine paid it little heed in her haste to embrace her tiny companion. The little one reciprocated the gesture, leaping from the chair straight into Katherine's waiting arms.

"My beautiful Katherine, how are you?" inquired the little one.

Katherine couldn't contain her joy, teetering on the brink of tears. It had been an extended period since she last laid eyes on her diminutive friend. "I'm fine. Where have you been? I've missed you terribly." Katherine tenderly set her friend down and perched on the edge of the bed, her feet casually curled beneath her. The discomfort from the previous night's revelry momentarily slipped from her thoughts.

Seated gracefully on the floor before Katherine, the little one's dress gently billowed around her, and she gazed up at Katherine with love in her eyes. "Oh, my dear, I'm sorry I had to go. I had things I had to do. I couldn't come and see you when I wanted to. I missed you so terribly, but now I'm here, and everything will be alright." The little one reached up and took Katherine's hands into her own small ones. "Tell me about him."

Katherine felt a pang of confusion. There hadn't been anyone but Brian, and that had happened just last night. How did her little friend already know? However, she swiftly dismissed the thought.

Her little friend knew more than she ever revealed. She was the reason Katherine stayed abreast of gossip and knew so much about what was going on.

"I met him last night. I had known him since we began high school, but he always had a girlfriend," Katherine began. She would have said more, but her little friend interrupted her.

The little one shook her head in the negative. "He's not the one I'm talking about. Tell me about the one that you love. The one named..." she stopped and looked up at the ceiling, as if trying to pluck the name from a source that hid up there. "Scott."

Katherine was taken aback. She hadn't expected to hear that name, especially not knowing that her best friend was dating him. "I don't love Scott. He's Mindy's boyfriend. There's nothing between us."

The little one smiled knowingly. "You can't lie to me, Red. I know more about you than you do. Remember, I've known you all your life, and I've watched over you all that time. Your mind may lie to you, but your heart shows me the truth of the matter."

Katherine smiled. It had been foolish for her to attempt to mislead her little friend. Her little friend was right; she did love Scott, but she couldn't have him. He belonged to another. "You're right," said Katherine sheepishly. Her cheeks burned a hot red, complementing her red curly hair. "But nothing can come of it. He belongs to another, someone I care about also. As much as I'd like to be with him, I can't hurt her."

It was Katherine's little friend's turn to smile now. "If you want him, you only have to ask, and I will assist you in any way I can. You can be with him if you want."

Katherine actually considered the proposition for a moment before her conscience told her not to do it. Her body ached for his touch again. She could feel the shivers racing up and down her spine. If she had been standing, she was sure that her knees would have given up from under her. It was too tempting. She couldn't do it, though; her best friend's feelings meant too much to her.

"I daren't ask you. I know that you can make it happen, but I won't. I love Mindy too much to hurt her," Katherine said.

With a thoughtful tilt of her head, the little one observed Katherine from a different angle, a moment of silent contemplation passing between them. A radiant smile graced her face, casting a warm glow across the room. Katherine couldn't help but feel a sense of familiarity, as if the little one held a significance beyond the ordinary, prompting Katherine's imagination to toy with the idea of her being an angel.

"Well chosen, Kate," spoke the little one, her voice carrying a certain wisdom. "But there's something else on your mind. What is it?"

In an instant, Katherine recalled the news she had shared with Mindy the night before. A surge of excitement propelled her to unleash a torrent of words, eager to divulge her secret and share the wonderful news with her enigmatic friend.

"I believe you should seize the opportunity to visit your great Aunt; Ionia is a town you'll likely find enjoyable," she suggested. After a momentary pause, she asserted with emphasis, "I am confident you'll have a great time, and don't fret—I'll be right there beside you, ensuring your safety," her little friend assured, cheeks lifting in a smile. "After all, I am your guardian angel."

In the blink of an eye, Katherine leaped off the bed, enfolding her diminutive companion, the guardian angel, in a tight embrace.

DOWNSTAIRS, the aroma of breakfast wafted through the air, beckoning Katherine into the warmth of the kitchen. Her guardian angel's ethereal presence had vanished, leaving behind a lingering sense of reassurance. Joining her parents at the breakfast table, she was greeted with smiles and warmth.

"Morning, sweetheart," Irene, her mother, chimed, pouring coffee into a mug. "How was your night?"

Katherine took a seat, trying to mask the remnants of a headache with a smile. "It was fun, Mom."

Her father, Kirk, chuckled knowingly. "Fun enough to come home a bit... merry, I'd say."

Katherine's cheeks flushed as she recalled her inebriated state. "Yeah, well, maybe a bit too much fun."

Irene's concern softened her features. "Honey, you know we just worry about you. It's a parent's job."

"Absolutely," Kirk added, nodding. "We were young once too, you know. But we want you to be safe."

Katherine nodded, grateful for their understanding. "I know, Dad. It won't happen again."

The conversation shifted to a more serious note, both parents sharing advice about responsible drinking and being cautious in unfamiliar situations. Katherine listened attentively, her agreement underscored by the discomfort of her hangover and the realization that she didn't enjoy the effects of excessive drinking.

"Yeah, I get it," she said, rubbing her temples. "I don't like feeling like this the next day, and being drunk isn't as fun as they make it out to be."

Her parents exchanged glances, a mix of concern and relief on their faces. Irene reached across the table to pat Katherine's hand. "We just want you to be safe, sweetheart. Drinking responsibly is one thing, but we worry about the consequences."

Katherine nodded, appreciating their genuine concern. "I know, Mom. I'll be more careful."

Kirk grinned. "That's our girl. And you can always call us if you need a ride, no questions asked."

As the breakfast conversation continued, Katherine reflected on the genuine care her parents displayed. Despite the lecture, she understood their perspective and silently vowed to be more mindful in the future. The warmth of family, combined with the remnants of her guardian angel's comforting presence, created a sense of security that lingered even after the breakfast plates were cleared away.

After the last dish was dried and put away, Katherine found herself lost in thought. Her Aunt's invitation echoed in her mind, a gentle call to visit a part of her life she hadn't explored. As she wiped down the kitchen counter, the decision weighed on her, contemplating the prospect of connecting with her biological family.

Turning to her parents, she broached the topic cautiously. "Mom, Dad, I got that letter from my Aunt in Ionia. She wants me to visit."

Irene and Kirk exchanged glances, their supportive demeanor unwavering. Irene, hands in the soapy water, looked at Katherine. "Sweetie, we'll support whatever decision you make. Do you think you'll be comfortable going to visit your biological family?"

Katherine paused, her hands still in the dishwater. She gazed at her parents, grateful for the unconditional support they consistently offered. "You know, you guys have always been my real family. But I've always wondered about where I was born, who my parents were and all that. Maybe it's time to understand where I come from."

Her parents nodded in understanding, expressing their unwavering love. "No matter what, Katherine, you're our daughter," Kirk affirmed, a reassuring smile on his face.

Irene added, "You've always had a place here with us, and we'll be here for you no matter what."

Feeling their warmth and support, Katherine felt a surge of gratitude. "Your support makes the decision easier. I'm going to go, Mom, Dad."

Their eyes lit up with understanding and pride. "That's wonderful, sweetheart," Irene said, reaching over to give Katherine a reassuring hug.

Kirk chimed in, "We're proud of you for making this decision, and we'll be right here when you get back."

With a newfound resolution, Katherine headed back upstairs to her room. The weight of the decision lifted as she appreciated the unshakable foundation her parents provided. As she entered her room, she felt a sense of peace and readiness for the journey that lay ahead. Closing the door behind her, she took a moment to reflect before preparing for the next chapter in her life—one that promised new connections and a deeper understanding of her roots.

5

Aaron lay in that blissful period of slumber right before you lose awareness of the world, the room enveloped in a tranquil darkness disrupted only by a faint glow from the street lamp outside, casting a subtle luminescence through his bedroom window. The quietude of the night cradled him, but his peaceful repose was interrupted by an unexpected tapping sound.

Instinctively, he opened his eyes, initially attributing the noise to a tree branch lightly rapping against his window. Ready to drift back into the arms of sleep, he was jolted awake by the persistent tapping.

Tap... tap... tap.

A realization dawned on him. 'Not a branch,' he mused, his curiosity aroused. Stirring from his comfortable haven, Aaron rose from his bed, a determined look in his eyes. He ambled towards the window, the one facing the side of the house, bypassing the second one that offered a view of the silent street and the front facade of the house.

In the dimness, Aaron discerned a silhouette standing adjacent to the house. Despite the obscurity shrouding her features, he instantly recognized her. It was Sara. Her presence spoke volumes—sleep eluding her, seeking solace in his company rather than wrestling with the night alone. Fortuitously, he felt he was on the verge of confronting that recurring nightmare and welcomed the distraction.

With swift determination, Aaron navigated the distance from his room to the back door, ready to ease Sara's evident unease. As he swung the door open, Sara stood framed in the entrance, resembling a frightened field mouse cornered by a cat.

Leading her up to his room, both moved with calculated steps, conscious of the need for silence, avoiding any disturbance that might disturb the nocturnal tranquility. Sara clutched her housecoat tightly, a visible shield against the perceived vulnerability.

In unspoken agreement, they tread softly, cautious not to rouse Aaron's slumbering parents. The late hour demanded discretion, and the duo understood the futility of waking the household amidst the hushed symphony of the night.

Aaron, cautious and perceptive, stole a glance down the hallway, his senses attuned to both sight and sound. The quietude of the house reassured him; no inadvertent witnesses to their clandestine meeting. Once convinced of their solitude, he closed the door with a soft, deliberate motion.

In the center of the room, Sara stood, a subtle tremor coursing through her. Patiently, she waited until Aaron turned his attention toward her, his gentle smile fading as he noticed her shivering.

"Are you cold?" Aaron inquired, the realization of the chilly night seeping into his consciousness. Winter's grasp might be loosening, but the nights still retained a briskness, especially for someone who had been outside before seeking refuge in his room. The question, though well-intentioned, hung in the air with a tinge of obviousness. She had obviously been outside for some time before he woke up and let her in.

Closing the distance, Aaron gently gathered the folds of Sara's housecoat, cocooning her in its warmth. His arms encircled her in a protective embrace. Sara endured this tender moment briefly, but with a gentle push, she parted from him, allowing the housecoat to cascade to the floor, revealing her vulnerability.

Aaron found himself rendered speechless, his mind racing, struggling to articulate the whirlwind of thoughts within. Sara, in all her beauty, stood before him. Clad in a light blue, sheer camisole, delicate spaghetti straps draped over her shoulders. The camisole, skimming the top of her hips, offered only a modest veil over the matching bikini panties beneath.

Sara drew nearer to Aaron, a proximity that blurred the lines between them, her breasts delicately grazing his chest. The contact sent a surge of warmth through Aaron's veins, a natural response to the enchanting presence of Sara.

With a gentle touch, Sara placed her hands on his hips, seeking balance as she rose on the tips of her toes to bestow a kiss upon his lips. Their eyes locked, and Sara felt herself succumbing to the pull of desire. After a fleeting moment, she initiated the unspoken dance, lifting Aaron's t-shirt over his head with a subtle ease. Assisting him out of his shorts, she guided him towards the bed.

Effortlessly, Sara drew back the sheets, creating an invitation for Aaron to join her. Hesitation found no foothold as he willingly followed her lead. Any resistance he might have harbored melted away in the face of their shared longing and unspoken connection.

Aaron enveloped her in his arms, finding a seamless connection. It was a union that felt tailor-made, as if she had been crafted expressly to be held in his embrace. Her response was immediate—she purred softly, a kitten surrendering to comfort, melting in his arms like ice yielding to the sun. Sara's fingers curled, delving deeply into Aaron's hair.

Passion echoed in Sara's voice as she gazed into Aaron's dark eyes, entreating him, "Make love to me, Aaron. I'll chase away your bad dreams while you fulfill my desire for you."

Aaron acquiesced to Sara's fervent plea, a silent understanding passing between them. In the quiet hours that followed, they would find peaceful repose, slumbering through the night. Yet, in this moment, Sara sought solace in Aaron's presence, a sanctuary from the intricacies of both their worlds.

Aaron hesitated, his desire tempered by a need for understanding. There was a reluctance to dive straight into intimacy with Sara until he unraveled the reasons behind her abrupt late-night visit.

"What's going on, Sara? Why this sudden urgency?" he inquired, searching for clarity.

Nestling her face into Aaron's shoulder, Sara remained silent, unwilling to speak immediately. Aaron waited patiently, sensing her reluctance and giving her the space to gather her thoughts.

"I was scared of losing you. I didn't know how I'd cope if we were separated by school. The fear of being forgotten if we weren't together consumed me," Sara finally confided, her vulnerability echoing in the quietude of the room.

Gently disentangling himself, Aaron moved Sara far enough away to meet her eyes.

"We've been together since childhood. The thought of being apart from you has never crossed my mind since the day I realized how much I loved and needed you in my life. You are the center of my world," he reassured her with sincerity.

Leading Sara to a sitting position on the bed, they settled down side by side. Aaron's tone softened as he continued, "You worry too much, Love. You are my anchor, making life more manageable. I can't fathom living a single minute without you, Sara." His words carried a quiet assurance, an unspoken commitment to the enduring bond they shared.

Sara nestled onto Aaron's shoulder, tilting her head to meet his cheek with a tender kiss.

"I appreciate your reassurance. I just didn't anticipate the school thing hitting me this hard," she admitted, lowering her gaze. "And, I know you've been holding back. That nightmare has been bothering you, and you haven't shared how much it's been stressing you out."

Aaron began to pull away, a hesitancy in his movements, but Sara swiftly reached out, encircling her hand around his waist, urging him to stay close.

"Stay right here. Keep talking," she insisted, desiring a continued closeness.

Aaron smiled ruefully. "I didn't want to worry you anymore than you'd already been. You've been dealing with your own difficulties and I didn't want to add to that. I saw how the school issue was bothering you and I was working hard to get accepted to Dale with you." His words unveiled a silent struggle to shield Sara from additional burdens, even as they navigated their individual challenges.

"Well, I'm glad that it worked out," Sara remarked, edging even closer to Aaron, a feat that seemed almost impossible given their already intimate proximity. "Now, tell me what's going on."

Aaron cleared his throat before addressing her concern. "The nightmares intensified, especially during the whole process of getting into Dale."

Doubt flickered in Sara's eyes as she regarded him.

"I'm serious," he assured her. "They hadn't gotten any worse than they've always been. It was just the added stress of worrying about you that made things harder for me. I'm okay now since I got into Dale and told you. Now that you've gotten through your own troubles, mine are seeming to be easier to deal with." His words carried a mixture of vulnerability and relief, an unspoken acknowledgment of the healing power of shared burdens.

Accepting Aaron's explanation, Sara leaned in to seal their understanding with a kiss. Aaron reciprocated, matching her passion. As they finally parted from the embrace, Sara gazed into Aaron's eyes.

"Will you make love to me now?" she asked, her request carrying a sense of vulnerability.

"Of course I will, Love. You didn't even have to ask," Aaron responded with sincerity.

For the next hour, Sara and Aaron surrendered to the intimacy of each other's arms, a shared connection that quenched their thirst for closeness and reassurance.

THE following morning, Emma stirred first, planting a gentle kiss on her husband's cheek as she left the bed. She observed with a quaint smile as he stirred in his sleep, managing to express his love for her.

Moving silently down the hallway on slippered feet, Emma made her way to Michael's room and then to Aaron's. A quiet sentinel in the morning, she checked on them, ensuring their well-being. Upon reaching Aaron's room, she paused. The room retained a dimness that obscured details, yet Emma couldn't help but notice a discarded robe on the floor.

Examining the bed more closely from the doorway, Emma squinted to discern details. Upon closer observation, she realized there were two people nestled in the bed. Ready to rouse them, she hesitated as recognition dawned – it was Sara lying beside Aaron. Opting not to disturb their slumber, Emma decided to let them continue resting. She pulled the door back slightly and retraced her steps, leaving it partially open in her haste.

An hour later, Aaron jolted awake, initially attributing it to the phone ringing. However, it wasn't the phone that had disrupted his sleep; it was the distant sound of his mother's voice calling his and Sara's names, inviting them to breakfast. Gazing beside him, he found a drowsy Sara waking up as well.

"Aaron," Emma's voice rang from downstairs, "are you and Sara coming down for breakfast?"

Aaron, still grappling with the remnants of sleep, struggled to find his words. Blinking away the grogginess, he managed, "Uh, we'll be down in just a few, Mom."

Hastening out of bed, Aaron pondered on an excuse to offer his parents about Sara's presence. Despite being eighteen, he knew he needed to navigate this situation delicately. While John and Emma would have readily permitted Sara to spend the night in the guest bedroom, the explanation for her being in his bed this early in the morning seemed a conversation he wasn't ready to broach.

By then, Sara had managed to shake off her drowsiness. However, uncertainty hung in the air. "What time is it, Aaron?" she asked nervously.

Aaron glanced at the clock, astonished to find it was nearly nine o'clock. Sara couldn't help but register the time as well. "Didn't you set the alarm?" she inquired, a hint of hysteria threading through her voice. The realization hit her like a shock – they were meant to be up by a quarter to six so she could head home before anyone woke up. With no spare clothes and the prospect of wearing last night's outfit downstairs, embarrassment painted her cheeks a vivid red.

"I set the alarm and closed the door," Aaron quickly explained, his heart racing, a wave of nausea threatening to overwhelm him.

Choosing to sidestep the implications, Sara redirected her attention to more practical matters – finding something to wear. Panic wouldn't be productive. Aaron, too, contemplated the same issue as Sara, swiftly arriving at a solution. In a blur of motion, he crossed the room to his dresser, retrieving a pair of shorts and a shirt from his closet. With a casual toss, he sent them in Sara's direction, seamlessly beginning to dress himself.

Sara slipped into the shorts, only for them to cascade down to her ankles. "They're too big," she whispered urgently, wary of anyone overhearing. Grasping the shirt Aaron provided, she pulled it over her head. Though the length almost drowned her, her bosom lent it a graceful flow over her body.

Having completed his own dressing, Aaron observed Sara. The short-sleeved shirt seemed to suit her, its loose fit allowing her to effortlessly pull off a shirt-dress look, the length just enough to be worn as a dress.

"This will have to do," Sara declared, surveying herself in the mirror on Aaron's dresser. Content with the makeshift outfit, she began heading towards the door until Aaron interrupted her with a cough.

"Ahem," Aaron cleared his throat, drawing her attention.

Turning to face him, Sara noticed something dangling from his finger. "Don't you think you'll need this little item too?" Aaron quipped, wearing a playful smirk on his face.

Sara swiftly snatched her panties from Aaron's hand and pulled them on. "You are so bad," she teased, completing her dressing. "Let's go before I jump your bones again."

As they made their way to the door, Sara had barely reached it when an involuntary squeak escaped her. She went darting down the hall, Aaron's mischievous pinch on her butt prompting the sudden reaction.

Sara ambled into the kitchen, a tad behind Aaron. The prospect of presenting herself to Aaron's parents at this early hour, clad in borrowed attire, made her wish she could simply vanish. Uncertain about what to anticipate, both she and Aaron found themselves navigating uncharted waters.

Emma greeted her eldest son with a sweet smile upon his entry into the kitchen. Standing on her toes, she peered around Aaron's shoulder, catching sight of the slender young girl clinging to the back of his shirt, akin to a lost child.

"Good morning, young miss," greeted Aaron's father casually. John didn't even lift his gaze from the morning paper. "What are you two doing today, Aaron?"

Stunned by the question, Aaron hesitated before finding his words. The next voice to break the silence was Sara's.

"We were thinking about going up to the lake today and spending some time there," she offered.

She gracefully sidestepped Aaron and approached his father, apparently deeming the situation acceptable after spending the night. Leaning over, she planted a kiss on John's cheek. "Good morning, Mr. Smith," she greeted warmly. Sara then made her way to the stove, where Emma awaited, and melted into the welcoming embrace that enveloped her.

Observing this, John gestured for his eldest son to take a seat at the table, right next to his brother, Michael. Michael maintained a neutral expression, glancing between Aaron and Sara.

Emma led Sara to an empty spot near Aaron. "Oh now, you hush up, John. Them two kids can take care of themselves." She placed a plate of food in front of each of them. "Eat up."

John's smile, a rare occurrence, graced his face. "Emma, you know as well as I do that Sara is the best thing that ever happened to that boy," he declared, gesturing toward his son. "Thank God he's got her, just like I got you, or else he and I wouldn't know what to do with ourselves." Putting down his morning paper, he turned to Michael. "Don't you worry none, Michael. We'll find a pretty, young girl to attach yourself to as well." He chuckled gently at his own jest.

Michael laid down his fork and pushed his plate aside, having barely touched his food. "I can find one on my own," he uttered somberly. Standing up, he scanned the faces in the kitchen, maintaining the usual neutral expression he wore. "I have to go now, excuse me," Michael stated before exiting the room.

With that one statement, the atmosphere in the kitchen underwent a dramatic shift. It felt as if all the energy had been drained from the room with Michael's departure. Aaron scanned the faces in the room, seeking eye contact with anyone, hoping that a small connection would somehow alleviate the tension. John, however, picked up his paper again and resumed reading, steadfastly avoiding eye contact with anyone. Sara seemed to be busy with her own plate.

Emma was the first to react, attempting to ease the tension in the kitchen. She placed her hands on Sara's shoulders, turned her around, and nodded toward her plate of food. She did the same for Aaron.

"You two eat up. You've got a long day planned, and you need your energy." Emma moved gracefully to the stove, finding something to do to keep herself busy, a skill that consistently amazed Aaron.

Emma glanced over her shoulder toward the kitchen table and its occupants, focusing her attention on Sara. She scrutinized what Sara was wearing.

"That shirt you're wearing, Sara, where did you get it? It looks a lot like a shirt that I got for Aaron not too long ago."

Sara glanced at Aaron, who suddenly found his breakfast very intriguing, avoiding eye contact with her. A wide grin almost prompted a laugh from him, so he quickly stuffed a forkful of food into his mouth to smother any emerging laughter and, in the process, nearly choked.

Sara gave Aaron an elbow to his ribcage. "I got it quite recently," Sara said slyly, never taking her eyes off Aaron. He had quickly recovered, but he still refused to look at her. If he had met her gaze, he wouldn't have been able to control his laughter. Sara, however, didn't find anything funny about the situation. She continued to eat, occasionally pausing to glare at Aaron as he sat at the table.

They both finished eating rather quickly and got up to leave. Emma called Sara to her and gave her yet another hug. As she held Sara in her arms, she whispered into her ear.

"Next time, dear, bring a change of clothes with you just in case." Emma kissed Sara on her cheek and turned around to start cleaning the kitchen.

Aaron noticed his mom whispering into Sara's ear, causing her to blush intensely. She turned bright red. After they left the kitchen, he asked Sara what his mom had said, only to be ignored as Sara struggled to hide her face. Each time he inquired about his mom's words, Sara turned red from head to toe, blushing uncontrollably.

IONIA, despite its modest size, couldn't accommodate a large international airport. Katherine's plane, with just one aisle and two seats on either side, reflected the city's limited aviation infrastructure. The terminal consisted of a single large building, underscoring the airport's compact nature. Despite these constraints, air travel to and from Ionia was still possible.

Katherine's aunt had arranged her travel, which involved a flight from a major airport on the west coast to a smaller plane for the journey to Ionia. Katherine couldn't help but speculate about the expense of such arrangements. She surmised that flights on smaller aircraft to Ionia must have been comparably pricey, if not more so, than her ticket on a major airline from the west coast.

As one of the few passengers on the flight, Katherine emerged from the small terminal to be promptly flagged down by an older woman, whom she correctly assumed to be her aunt. With red hair mirroring her own and a smattering of freckles adorning her cheeks and nose, the woman bore a striking resemblance to Katherine.

A warm smile graced Katherine's lips as she approached her aunt with enthusiasm. She was immediately enveloped in a comforting hug, a gesture that melted away any lingering uncertainties she had harbored during her journey. Initially unsure of what to expect upon reaching her destination, Katherine found herself reassured by her aunt's genuine warmth, dispelling the last vestiges of anxiety that had accompanied her.

"Hi, Katherine. I'm so glad you could make it," Megan greeted warmly.

Katherine's voice faltered as she began to respond, a lump forming in her throat. After a brief pause, she managed to articulate her thoughts. "Hi, Auntie. I'm glad to be here. I'm happy to see you."

Megan stepped back, still holding Katherine by her shoulders, and observed her niece closely. She scanned Katherine from head to toe, struck by the striking resemblance to her brother and her late friend Diana. Katherine was the spitting image of her mother, but her hair color and freckles were unmistakably reminiscent of her brother Bryant.

"I know that this is probably overwhelming for you, discovering you have living family and traveling all this way to see them. Let's head home and get you settled in. Once we're there, I can answer any questions you may have." Megan gave Katherine another quick hug before turning towards the waiting vehicle behind her. A man approached from the opposite side of the car, opening the door for them to get in. Katherine was taken aback by her aunt's car and driver but chose not to comment. With so much already on her mind, she filed this detail away to ponder later.

The journey to her aunt's house passed quickly. Situated on the outskirts of town, the airport's proximity meant a short trip. Megan remained mostly silent, allowing Katherine to absorb the passing scenery. Lost in thought, Katherine stared out the car window, drinking in her surroundings and trying to acclimate herself to the area.

As they approached the house, Katherine couldn't help but notice its size. Among the few residences in the area, it stood out as one of the largest. Each house occupied a sizable plot of land, reminiscent of manor estates found in the Deep South. The car pulled up onto a crushed gravel driveway, halting in front of the imposing house. Megan and Katherine disembarked from the vehicle.

"Don't worry about your bags. Jeffery will bring them in. Let's go inside and relax so I can get to know my niece better," Megan suggested warmly.

Katherine nodded, feeling a bit overwhelmed by everything that had transpired. Going along with her aunt's suggestion seemed like the path of least resistance. It was easier to accept the situation and go with the flow rather than resist.

In no time, they found themselves settled in the living room. A maid appeared, offering them drinks and a small tray of cheeses, fruit, and crackers.

"Help yourself to some iced tea and snacks," Megan encouraged.

Katherine offered her aunt a grateful smile and decided to accept the offer. She hadn't eaten much since the previous night, her nerves getting the better of her upon meeting her blood relative. Selecting something from the tray, she nibbled while her aunt began to speak.

"I'm sorry it took so long to reach out to you," Megan said, her tone tinged with sadness.

Katherine paused, her nibbling halted as she turned to look at her aunt. She was at a loss for words. A whirlwind of questions swirled in her mind. How long had her aunt known her whereabouts? Why hadn't she come for her after her mother's death? Countless inquiries jostled for attention, but Katherine couldn't seem to organize her thoughts enough to voice any of them.

"I need to tell you about your family—both on your father's side and your mother's side," Megan began solemnly.

Katherine had gleaned the basics of her family history from the letters exchanged with her aunt. She knew her father was Megan's brother and that her mother had a sister, but beyond that, she was in the dark. Anxious anticipation filled her as she waited for Megan to elaborate.

Megan observed Katherine's tense demeanor, sensing her eagerness for more information. She was determined not to disappoint her niece and intended to share everything she knew. There was nothing she wished to withhold.

"My parents' ways are... well, let's just say, outdated," Megan began, setting down her cup and fixing Katherine with a meaningful gaze.

"I must apologize for them first. They were the primary reason things turned out the way they did with you. Your mother was my best friend, and she came from a less affluent family than ours. She fell in love with my brother, and they began dating while they were in high school. When she became pregnant, she confided in him, and he, in turn, informed our parents. But they refused to acknowledge his paternity and pressured your mother, Diana, to undergo an abortion."

Katherine absorbed Megan's revelations with a mix of apprehension and dismay. Learning about her family's history wasn't bringing her the comfort or closure she had hoped for. Instead, it was unraveling a tangled web of emotions, stirring up feelings of rejection and abandonment.

The weight of Megan's words settled heavily on Katherine's shoulders. She couldn't shake the feeling of being unwanted by one side of her family, a realization that only compounded her existing struggles with feelings of loss and anger over her mother's death at her birth.

As she grappled with these newfound revelations, Katherine couldn't help but question her decision to seek out her aunt and delve into her family's past. The more she learned, the less enthusiastic she felt about uncovering the truth about her father and grandparents on that side of her lineage.

Megan sensed the somber atmosphere engulfing the room and hastened to dispel the rising tension. "My parents wanted Diana to abort you, but unfortunately, my brother wasn't swayed either way," she explained earnestly. "I'm not here to justify his actions or his stance in all of this. I want you to understand that I stood by your mother's decision to keep you wholeheartedly, but as a young bystander, there was little I could do to influence the outcome. I offered as much support to your mother as I could, encouraging her to stay strong and to keep you."

Her words carried a weight of sincerity, an attempt to convey her solidarity with Katherine's mother during a tumultuous time. Megan hoped to bridge the gap between the past and the present, offering insight into her role in supporting Diana's choices, despite the limitations she faced.

Megan's voice wavered, her gaze shifting to her folded hands resting in her lap. "Your mother had wanted to leave Ionia," she disclosed softly, the weight of regret evident in her tone. "I tried to persuade her to stay, but she was adamant about getting away from everything that was happening here. She mentioned having relatives in California, a place where she could seek refuge." Megan paused, a hint of bitterness tainting her words. "It wasn't until nearly a decade after your birth and her passing that I discovered the truth."

Katherine cleared her throat, grappling with a complex mix of emotions. She recognized it wasn't fair to harbor resentment toward her mother for leaving her home and ultimately passing away during childbirth. Similarly, she understood it wasn't fair to hold her aunt accountable for revealing the truth about her family history later in life. Despite this, she couldn't deny a sense of gratitude for her aunt's efforts to bridge the gap in her understanding of her past.

"So... do I still have relatives here in Ionia other than you? Other than Dad and my grandparents?" she inquired softly.

Megan's smile was tender. "Your grandparents—my parents—passed away a few years ago. Your father no longer resides in this state. He's become a senator and is now based in Washington, D.C."

Megan hesitated, preparing to share the news with Katherine about her remaining relatives in the city. Yet, she couldn't predict how Katherine would react—whether with tears or joyous celebration. Mentally bracing herself, Megan stood ready to offer comfort, whatever Katherine's response might be.

"You still have an aunt and two cousins who are alive," Megan finally disclosed.

"What are their names?" Katherine inquired.

"Your other aunt's name is Emma, and your cousins are Aaron and Michael. They don't live too far from here. Of course, in a small city like this, nowhere is really too far from anywhere else."

"Can I—" Katherine began as Megan started speaking.

"Do you want to—" Megan interjected.

The two of them burst into laughter.

"Do you want to meet them?" Megan asked again.

"Yeah," Katherine replied after a moment's pause, her smile brightening. "I think I'd like that very much."

Megan rose from her seat and approached Katherine, coaxing her out of her chair and enveloping her in a loving hug.

"We can make that happen. Soon. Don't worry."

In her aunt's embrace, Katherine let her emotions flow freely. It had been a long time since she'd dared to hope she'd meet anyone from her real family, and now that dream was coming true. Not only that, but the possibility of meeting even more relatives in the near future filled her with anticipation. She eagerly looked forward to it.

Megan escorted Katherine to the room she would occupy during her stay in Ionia, ensuring she was settled before departing to arrange a meeting with her aunt and cousins.

Over the following week, Katherine had the opportunity to meet her aunt Emma and her cousin Michael, but Aaron remained elusive. He and Sara had ventured to the nearby lake to cherish some time together before their impending high school graduation and departure for college—a plan they had long anticipated. While Katherine harbored a slight disappointment over missing out on meeting Aaron, she found solace in the cherished moments spent with her aunts and cousin Michael.

Departing for home, Katherine felt content with her decision to visit the aunt she had previously only known through letters and occasional phone calls.

6

Sara waited patiently, her gaze drifting between her watch and the clock adorning the library tower. With each passing minute, her frustration grew, Aaron's tardiness gnawing at her nerves. He was never late—always the punctual one. Yet today, he was fifteen minutes overdue, and the worry crept in. Lately, he'd been distant, disappearing for runs, a telltale sign that something troubled him.

Throughout the school year, their academic success had been commendable, boasting a combined GPA just above 3.9, though Sara's slightly edged past Aaron's—a reflection of her extra dedication. Yet, amidst their achievements, Aaron's behavior had shifted. He'd begun departing their apartment earlier, opting for solitary runs, leaving Sara to wonder about the secret burden he carried. She had her suspicions, but his silence left her guessing.

Sara understood that whatever weighed on Aaron was significant, realizing its potential to jeopardize his performance in the upcoming finals. Despite her concern, she maintained composure, refraining from pressing him with questions. Experience taught her that Aaron would eventually confide in her; their bond was built on trust, after all. Yet, she sensed a change this time, a heightened intensity in his struggles, perhaps fueled by the recurring nightmares.

Just as Sara contemplated the time once more, Aaron emerged, sprinting towards the library steps, his figure glistening with sweat, breaths labored. A pang of worry mingled with admiration for his relentless determination. "Why does he always push himself so hard?" she pondered silently. "Doesn't he realize the toll it takes? But then again, maybe that's his way of battling the demons within." Sara's empathy surged, wishing she could alleviate his suffering, wishing there were a solution beyond mere words.

Aaron halted a step below Sara, hands on his knees as he doubled over, gasping for air in ragged breaths, on the brink of hyperventilation. Despite his current state, his prowess as a runner was undeniable; his relentless training had rendered him unmatched on the track team, a formidable force in longer distance races.

Observing him with a detached gaze, Sara patiently awaited his recovery. She couldn't help but notice his physique—lean, athletic, slightly larger than his peers. Aaron's weight, just over one hundred and ninety-seven pounds, surpassed the average for marathon runners, yet it was evident that every ounce was sculpted muscle, his six-foot frame boasting a less than average percentage of body fat.

For the first time in her life, Sara found herself pondering how she managed to capture the attention of someone as undeniably attractive as Aaron. Battling with low self-esteem, she perceived herself as only moderately appealing. Were it not for Aaron's unwavering insistence, his daily affirmations of her beauty echoing in her mind, she might not have held herself in such esteem.

Moreover, the attention she received from classmates who made passes at her offered a semblance of validation, though Sara harbored this information, wary of Aaron's reaction. She refrained from disclosing these encounters, fearing his potential anger, oblivious to the fact that Aaron was already privy to these advances.

A broad smile illuminated Sara's face, not solely because of the man below her on the step, but because she understood the foundation of their relationship. Their bond was woven with immeasurable love, a force that transcended their imperfections.

Their lives were anything but flawless; they clashed like fire and water, yet beneath it all, their love endured.

Despite her shyness, Sara refused to be steamrolled by Aaron; she held her ground, unwilling to yield. Aaron, on the other hand, recognized when he had overstepped, readily conceding when in the wrong—a scenario that unfolded more frequently than naught. However, despite their occasional conflicts, he harbored no intent to inflict pain upon Sara, knowing that such an act would shatter him. Their love, though tested, remained steadfast, anchoring them through life's tumultuous seas.

Despite everything, Aaron's tardiness persisted at fifteen minutes past their agreed meeting time. Sara clenched her jaw, seething with frustration, yet remained silent. She understood the turmoil he faced, but his delay meant their dinner plans would likely be further delayed while he cleaned up.

This evening held significance for both of them—a rare moment of overlap between their work and school schedules, a precious opportunity to share time together. Their days were consumed by obligations, leaving only fleeting moments in the evenings to connect, moments they treasured deeply.

Despite the challenges of juggling work and school, their bond endured, strengthened by the moments they stole away for each other. Each shared instance became a cherished memory, a testament to their enduring love amidst life's chaotic demands.

Aaron straightened his posture, his breath gradually steadying. No longer gasping for air like a drowning man, he now resembled someone who had sprinted for survival, evading street thugs. Sara marveled at his swift recovery, contrasting it with her own slower pace. Wiping sweat from his brow, Aaron attempted a smile, though it faltered, failing to deceive Sara, who stood before him, arms crossed, her gaze unwavering, a testament to her stubbornness.

Sensing Sara's simmering displeasure, Aaron recognized the urgent need to address the situation before facing her wrath later—or perhaps even sooner. Meeting her unyielding gaze, he realized the gravity of his oversight. The recurring dream had resurfaced with intensified force, intruding upon his time with Sara for the first time. Judging by Sara's stern expression, he understood that such lapses in presence would not be tolerated again.

"I'm sorry, Sara," Aaron began, his tone contrite.

"Don't give me that. You know better than that. You know I know you better than that," Sara retorted, her voice tinged with anger. "Why don't you just tell me what's going on? I've waited patiently long enough. It's time for you to spill the beans. Is it the dream?"

Aaron's gaze fell to the ground, conceding silently to her astute observation. She knew him inside out, a fact that neither could deny after spending countless hours together. Their connection ran deep; they could anticipate each other's thoughts, even complete each other's sentences. Comfortable in each other's presence, they could relish the silence for hours, their understanding unsettling to their friends at times. Their bond transcended physical proximity; they could synchronize decisions effortlessly, even without verbal communication, a phenomenon that often left others bewildered.

Aaron met Sara's gaze, weariness evident in his eyes. Despite his exhaustion, the nagging problem persisted, haunting him relentlessly. Behind his eyes lurked the horror of his nightly ordeal, a constant companion he couldn't shake off no matter how far he ran. The issue loomed large in his mind, an inescapable presence.

"There's something happening to me," Aaron confessed, his voice heavy with vulnerability. "I feel lost in the dark. Alone."

Sara sensed Aaron's pain, prompting her to envelop him in a comforting embrace. "You are not alone, my love. I'm here with you, if only you'll let me in," she whispered tenderly, her arms offering solace. Pausing, she pressed a kiss to his forehead, despite the layer of sweat. "And please, open up your damn mouth and talk to me," she finished politely.

Aaron chuckled wearily, unable to refute her words. She was always right. "That dream feels too real now. Every time it visits, I'm transported back, feeling the presence of the unknown lurking in the shadows. Sometimes, it's almost welcoming. But I'm scared, Sara. I don't know what to do," he confessed, his vulnerability laid bare.

Sara gently cupped Aaron's cheeks, coaxing him to meet her gaze. He had averted his eyes while speaking, but she sensed a flicker of something hidden deep within him—an enigmatic presence that seemed poised to surface. It was a mixture of darkness and mystery, both captivating and unsettling. For a fleeting moment, she felt the urge to look away, but just as quickly as it appeared, the moment passed, leaving behind only the familiar sight of the man she adored.

"We can weather this storm together. We always have," Sara reassured him, her voice steady with determination.

Aaron smiled, enfolding Sara in his arms, finding solace in her embrace as they confronted his fears together, preparing to tackle whatever challenges lay ahead.

"Ew!" Sara exclaimed, feigning disgust. "Get off me, you sweaty beast," she added, her voice laced with playful affection. They shared a moment of laughter before making their way back to their apartment, where Aaron could freshen up. Despite the interruption, they still had a few precious hours to spend together before the demands of work and classes resumed the next day.

They dined at a decent restaurant, mindful of their tight budget as full-time students and part-time employees. Occasionally, they indulged in splurges, like tonight, when the occasion warranted it. Despite their financial constraints, they relished the opportunity to savor a delightful meal and each other's company. Aaron's charm and wit entertained Sara, who, though she may have heard his stories countless times before, listened with grace, her beauty radiant in the soft glow of the restaurant.

Returning home, Aaron found himself captivated by the sparkle in Sara's eyes, his desire for her intensifying. As they walked, his hand occasionally wandered from her waist to her buttocks, met with a playful protest from Sara, who tolerated his advances with a mixture of amusement and anticipation. She knew she would capitalize on his good mood once they reached the privacy of their apartment. The thought of not making it to the bedroom before their passion reached its peak didn't concern her; she welcomed the intimacy wherever it found them.

Aaron slept like the dead that evening, utterly exhausted from his run and the time spent with Sara after they returned home. The troubling dream had spared him, allowing him a night of deep rest. Rising well before his alarm, he was surprised to find Sara perched on the edge of the bed, engrossed in a phone call. His slumber had been so sound that he hadn't even heard the phone ring. Catching snippets of her conversation, he realized she was talking to her parents.

"Yes, I'll pass on the message," Sara assured, pausing briefly to listen. "We'll be back home as soon as our finals are over next week... Of course, Mom... I'll let him know you send your love... He's doing fine... Yes, don't worry, I'll tell him... We'll see you soon. Love you... Bye."

Sara ended the call and shifted her gaze away from Aaron, lost in her own thoughts. Aaron remained still, feigning sleep, though he had merely opened his eyes, waiting for her to speak. He sensed her need for space, understanding that something weighed heavily on her mind, yet he refrained from pressing for details, opting to give her the time she needed.

Softly, Sara broke the silence. "That was my mom," she murmured, her voice barely above a whisper.

Aaron remained patient as Sara gathered her thoughts. It was evident that something troubled her deeply, and while he longed to know, he recognized the importance of allowing her to share at her own pace.

Finally, Sara turned to face him, slipping under the covers and nestling against his chest, seeking solace in his embrace. Aaron enveloped her, feeling the slight tremor in her body. With a gentle squeeze, he offered her comfort, silently conveying his unwavering support and strength.

"Your mother isn't doing well," Sara started, her voice heavy with concern. "Your brother is doing everything he can to support her. He even moved back home, but she's still slipping away."

After delivering the news, Sara fell silent, and Aaron remained still, his mind swirling with worry for his mother. Yet, amidst his concern, he prioritized Sara's well-being, recognizing the impact the news might have on her. He waited patiently, allowing her the space to articulate her thoughts in her own time.

When Sara spoke again, her voice was barely audible, almost lost in the quiet of the room.

"My mom said your mother gave up on life after your father died," Sara continued, her voice tinged with sorrow. "She secluded herself, refusing to see anyone or leave the house. When my parents finally visited her, they could see she wasn't going to last much longer. The doctors believe she may only have a month or two left. It's like she's lost the will to live."

Aaron understood where Sara's thoughts were leading, her unspoken intentions clear to him. "We'll speak to our teachers tomorrow," he affirmed, anticipating her desire. "We'll request early exams so we can return home. With our grades, they're likely to grant our request. We can be there as soon as the exams are over."

Aaron harbored a truth he couldn't deny, a reality shared by both him and Sara. He longed to abandon all responsibilities, to pack their bags and depart immediately. Yet, the weight of his obligations to his studies and his future tethered him to their current situation. Despite the grim prognosis from the doctors, he clung to the hope that his mother would still be there in two days, allowing him precious time by her side in her final moments.

Sara's assurance that his mother had a few more months left offered a lifeline of hope amidst the despair. Aaron knew he had to hold onto that hope, for it was the only thing that could sustain him until he could be with his mother again.

Aaron and Sara spent the remainder of the morning wrapped in each other's embrace, finding solace in their closeness. As the time came for them to depart, they gathered their belongings and made their way to class.

Aaron's initial assumption about the teachers proved incorrect. Instead, Sara took the initiative to speak to her professors about the possibility of early exams, paving the way for Aaron to do the same. Despite the gravity of their situation, their professors made a compassionate decision. Recognizing their exemplary academic performance, they waived the need for final exams, allowing their coursework from the semester to speak for itself. With well wishes for the future, they bid Aaron and Sara farewell, urging them to return for the next semester fully prepared.

Reuniting at their apartment, Aaron and Sara packed a few essentials, intending to return home to Ionia as soon as circumstances allowed. Opting to retain their apartment for their eventual return, they left their belongings behind and set off that afternoon.

KATHERINE'S school year had commenced on a rocky note. While her academic performance remained commendable, her lack of enthusiasm for her studies began to manifest itself by mid-semester. Sensing her waning interest, Katherine made a bold decision—to temporarily step away from her educational pursuits and explore a different avenue that intrigued her.

Having been approached by a photographer to model, Katherine found herself drawn into the world of fashion and photography. Surprisingly, she quickly garnered attention and acclaim from various magazines, propelling her into a new realm of opportunities. This unexpected turn of events provided Katherine with a newfound sense of purpose and direction, albeit temporary, as she navigated this exciting new chapter in her life.

Katherine's uninhibited nature proved advantageous as she ascended to the ranks of a top lingerie model for a prominent magazine. The prospect of this new career path appeared both thrilling and lucrative, promising rewards both financially and aesthetically. Immersed in this exhilarating world, Katherine reveled in her newfound success. However, her relationship with her boyfriend, Brian, began to unravel shortly after her second magazine feature hit the shelves.

Their bond had flourished since their high school days, a whirlwind romance that continued into their shared college experience. It seemed as though fate had intervened to unite them, and Katherine had never been happier. Brian embodied all the qualities she admired in a partner—kindness, gentleness, and unwavering love. Prior to her modeling venture, he had been a steadfast source of support and encouragement.

As Katherine's modeling career gained momentum, her time with Brian dwindled. Photo shoots consumed her schedule, leaving her increasingly isolated during their supposed moments together. Brian's absence became glaringly apparent, his excuses feeble and unconvincing. Nights meant for intimacy were replaced by his drunken stupor, their physical connection reduced to fleeting and unsatisfying encounters. The breaking point arrived when Katherine sacrificed lucrative opportunities to prioritize quality time with Brian, only to be met with disappointment.

Frustration boiled within Katherine as she waited for Brian's belated arrival. What was intended to be a few days of cherished togetherness had spiraled into nearly half a day of unexplained absence. Ten long hours slipped by without a single call or explanation from Brian. It was a betrayal of trust, a stark realization that her sacrifices were met with indifference. Katherine seethed with anger, feeling as though she had given everything for their relationship while receiving little in return. All she desired was his presence and support, yet even this modest request seemed beyond his capacity to fulfill.

Katherine's heart sank as she heard the door creak open, revealing Brian stumbling into their apartment, clearly intoxicated and disheveled. Suppressing her mounting anger, she watched silently as he tossed his keys onto the coffee table, oblivious to her presence as he trudged past her towards the kitchen. Returning with a bottle of beer in hand, he slumped into the comfort of his favorite chair.

Summoning her courage, Katherine addressed him with a fragile tone, her emotions threatening to overwhelm her. "Brian," she began tentatively, "where have you been? I've been waiting for you all day." The tears welled in her eyes, her voice quavering with suppressed emotion. "Dinner has been ready for hours, and I thought we had plans to spend the afternoon together."

Brian met Katherine's gaze with a mixture of defiance and indifference, his posture slouched in the chair as he shrugged dismissively. "And?" he retorted, his tone dripping with disdain. "What do you want me to do, I'm late."

Katherine felt a surge of frustration and hurt, but she fought to maintain her composure, swallowing back the sob threatening to escape. "Where were you?" she asked, her voice tinged with plaintiveness.

Brian's response was brusque, his movements clumsy as he gestured with his free hand, the bottle of beer still tightly grasped in his other. As the liquid sloshed onto the carpet, he scrambled to prevent further spillage, taking a swig from the bottle with a careless air. "I've been out drinking with the boys. Got a problem with that?" he replied, his words tinged with defiance.

"We were supposed to have this weekend together, just the two of us. We hardly ever get to see each other," Katherine pleaded, her voice laced with disappointment. "I told you about this weeks ago."

Brian's laughter echoed through the room, his drunken slur cutting through the air. "Why would I wanna go out with you?" he jeered, his words dripping with contempt. "I don't wanna be seen in public with no whore."

Katherine felt the weight of his words like a physical blow, her heart sinking in her chest. The room spun as her knees weakened, forcing her to sink onto the couch to steady herself.

"A whore?" she repeated, her voice barely above a whisper, disbelief and hurt evident in her tone.

"Yeah, you heard me. Whore!" Brian's voice rose with each word, his agitation palpable. His grip on the bottle tightened, his knuckles turning white with the strain. If his hold had been any stronger, he might have crushed the bottle's neck.

Gesturing wildly with his left hand, he punctuated his words with erratic movements, splashing beer onto the floor with each swing. Katherine, sensing the escalating tension, rose from her seat and moved away to avoid getting splattered.

"Every guy on campus talks about you. They done seen more of you than I have," Brian spat out, his anger simmering beneath his words. "Do you know what they ask me? Do ya? Huh, huh?" When

Katherine remained silent, he continued, his voice growing more heated with each word.

"They ask me if ya do bachelor parties, they ask me if ya strip and where, they ask me to have ya come by wearing so and so, soes they can see it in real life instead-a in a book. They wanna see what ya tits look like not covered by your arm. They say ya gotta nice ass and ask how it feels to squeeze it. Should I go on? Huh? Should I?" Brian slurred.

Katherine felt a surge of heat flood her body, her own anger rising in defense of Brian's accusations. "Why don't you tell them to fuck off?" she retorted sharply.

Brian's face contorted into a malicious sneer. "They ask me how much would I take to let ya fuck em."

If Katherine had been closer to Brian, she would have slapped him across the face. But her fury rendered her momentarily immobile. She didn't dare move any closer to him, fearing what she might do if she did. She wanted to hurt him as deeply as he had hurt her with his words.

"Ya done let everybody in the world see what ya got. Ya ain't got no secrets left, whore!" Brian's words cut through the air like a knife.

"I've only been with you and..." Katherine stopped herself before mentioning the name of the other person she had been involved with. She refused to acknowledge the almost-affair with Scott.

Even in his inebriated state, Brian's memory would likely retain the name she mentioned, a fact that he might exploit out of spite, especially considering his current demeanor. "One other person," she finished, her voice firm. "That doesn't make me a whore. I am a professional model. I don't prostitute myself out to porno magazines and work in strip clubs so that ham fisted jackasses like you can squeeze dollar bills between my ass cheeks."

Katherine summoned her righteous anger, directing it squarely at Brian. "Fuck you, Brian; if you can't handle what I do then get your sorry ass out of my life and out of my house. I don't want to see you ignorant ass again."

Brian remained seated, his laughter echoing through the room, tears streaming down his face from the force of his amusement. "Who the hell do you think you are? Get off your high horse and go shake your ass for a dollar, bitch."

Katherine reached her breaking point. She felt something inside her shatter, a pain unlike any she had ever experienced before coursing through her. "Get out!" she screamed, her voice piercing the air with raw fury.

Brian rose from his seat, advancing menacingly toward Katherine. With a cruel twist of his hand, he upended the bottle, dousing Katherine with its contents. "Screw you, bitch."

Katherine stood frozen, drenched in beer, her mind reeling as she struggled to process what had just happened. Anger simmered beneath the surface, but it was overshadowed by a profound sense of humiliation and worthlessness. Brian's callous act had extinguished the flames of her rage, leaving her feeling utterly defeated.

Tears threatened to spill from Katherine's eyes, but she held them back, paralyzed by shock and disbelief. However, her attention quickly shifted as she noticed the look of pure terror etched on Brian's face. It was as if he had seen a ghost, his eyes wide with fear and his body trembling uncontrollably.

In a surreal moment, Katherine watched as Brian's fear manifested physically, his bladder betraying him as he visibly wet himself. The sight left her speechless, a mixture of disbelief and disgust washing over her.

A surge of newfound strength coursed through Katherine's veins, dispelling the cloak of shame that had engulfed her moments before. With a swift and decisive motion, she struck out at Brian, sending him crashing to his knees. He whimpered like a wounded animal, his cries piercing the tense silence of the room as he scrambled away on all fours, his escape frantic and unsteady, leaving chaos in his wake.

As the adrenaline ebbed away, Katherine collapsed onto the sofa, her body trembling with the aftershocks of her outburst. Tears streamed down her cheeks unabated, the weight of her emotions too heavy to bear alone. In the midst of her despair, she felt a gentle touch upon her head, followed by small arms enveloping her in a comforting embrace.

A soft, soothing glow suffused the room, casting a warm light upon Katherine's tear-streaked face as she found solace in the embrace of a loved one, their silent presence a beacon of hope in her moment of darkness.

Her friend emerged from the shadows, a comforting presence materializing out of thin air. "It's alright, Kate. I'm here. I won't let that bad man hurt you ever again," the little one reassured her, their voice laced with determination.

Had Katherine been more attuned to her surroundings, she might have detected the ominous undertone in her friend's words, as well as the darkness lurking within those innocent eyes.

For what felt like an eternity, Katherine clung to her friend as if her life depended on it, finding solace in their embrace. It took an hour before she regained a semblance of calmness, her tumultuous emotions gradually subsiding under the comforting presence of her guardian angel. Locking eyes with her celestial companion, Katherine found a newfound sense of peace washing over her, dispelling the turmoil that had gripped her moments before.

"You need to be with the ones who love you," the guardian angel advised gently.

Katherine sniffled, wiping away a stray tear. "My parents are in Europe and won't be back for a few weeks yet."

Her guardian angel shook her head. "I'm not talking about them. Go and see your aunt in Ionia; I'm sure she'll be happy to see you again."

Katherine mulled over the suggestion. The more she considered it, the more appealing the idea became. She yearned to escape from Brian, from school, from her job— and the furthest place from it all was Ionia. Without hesitation, she packed her bags, determined to leave before dawn broke the next day. Although her aunt didn't pick up when she called, Katherine left a message, undeterred in her resolve to put distance between herself and her troubles.

7

Down the hallway, a subtle rustling echoed, punctuated by the hushed scrape of expensive shoes against the cold, stone floors. The soft swish of luxurious fabric accompanied the deliberate steps of a man moving down the dimly lit corridor. He showed no urgency in his gait, possessing an abundance of time at his disposal. The echoes of his footfalls reverberated through the empty expanse, fading into the dampness of the stone walls.

Clad in attire seemingly out of place in this environment, the man paid it no heed. Eventually, he arrived at a grand pair of weathered wooden doors. Thick layers of dust coated them, adding an unnecessary aura of antiquity to their already aged appearance. Rarely utilized and scarcely needed, these doors had remained untouched for quite some time. Indeed, this occasion marked the first physical use they would see in many years.

Entering the room, he eased the doors shut behind him, the soft click resonating in the spacious interior. Before him sprawled the room, furnished with weathered yet inviting pieces arranged around a central fireplace. Flames danced within, casting an unexpected warmth that seemed to beckon to those seeking solace from the chill. However, comfort was a notion foreign to this particular space.

Candles scattered throughout emitted a soft, flickering glow, rendering additional illumination unnecessary. The occupant of the room, indifferent to such trivialities, neither required nor desired the presence of light. It wasn't merely avoided but rather regarded with disdain, deemed an excessive indulgence.

Surveying the room, the man's gaze came to rest uneasily upon the solitary figure within. "Why do you linger, Precious? Does the boy's blood not sing to you?" he inquired with a lazy drawl, his voice carrying an illusory warmth that belied its true nature. With each word he uttered, he wove a subtle enchantment that permeated the space.

"Do you not perceive the alluring aroma of his sweat, even in the depths of your sanctum?" he continued, his words a delicate dance that swirled through the air.

A hiss echoed from the fireplace as smoke billowed forth, ignited by the sap within the heated log. The sudden burst of flames illuminated the chamber, casting light upon the figure of the young girl seated in the shadows across from the man.

Precious remained steadfast in her refusal to meet his gaze as she spoke, her disdain for him palpable. "How dare you interrogate me, Marcus?" she retorted, her tone dripping with contempt. "That is not your prerogative. I am the leader of this coven, not you. If you require assistance in rediscovering your place, I would be more than willing to provide it."

"I do not intend to offend you, Precious," Marcus stated, his conviction ringing hollow. "I simply seek clarity on the wisdom of delaying the consumption of this young soul. As you know, he is a firstborn of this town, and your decree to them mandates the offering of their firstborn to you."

"You are merely reiterating what I am well aware of. Who are you to remind me of my obligations?" Precious interjected furiously. "You, who have only trodden this earth for a little over a century, a mere demon of insignificant stature, daring to spy on me. I have existed since the dawn of time."

Precious knew Marcus harbored the misconception that she claimed the firstborn of select generations for her own ends. However, the truth differed; while it remained that some firstborn in Ionia met untimely demises, this was not her doing. Unfortunately, such distinctions were lost on others. Her promise of old had been made in haste and anger.

She contemplated rising from her seat to confront the interloper for his audacious interruption. However, she deemed such an action beneath her, unworthy of expending her energy.

"It was I who made the pact with the townsfolk all those years ago," Precious declared, her voice escalating in both intensity and volume. "They continue to pay for the sins of their ancestors, even when my hand plays no part in their demise."

Her anger surged, manifesting in her words as she continued, "My curse devours their succulent flesh and drains the marrow from their bones while they are still wet. Your esteemed Master cannot boast such claims."

Despite her impassioned outburst, Precious's anger served as a mere venting of frustration rather than an accurate reflection of the situation. She had no intention of revealing the truth of the matter to Marcus.

As Precious pondered her past words and the ancient promise she had made to the townspeople, memories of that fateful day resurfaced—the day she stood bound to a post, enveloped by crackling flames. She realized the weight of her utterance, spoken amidst the searing heat, but it was never her true intention. She had never actively sought the lives of the town's firstborn, yet they perished nonetheless, despite her efforts to prevent it. Trapped within the confines of that promise, she grappled with the harsh reality that, whether she willed it or not, she bore responsibility for the deaths of countless firstborn children of Ionia.

Abandoning her initial decision to remain seated, Precious gracefully slid from the chair, her simple Sunday dress adorned with a baby blue satin ribbon shimmering in the flickering firelight. Her pale skin radiated an ethereal glow, while her once-human eyes transformed into a menacing shade of charcoal black, slowly igniting into a fiery red hue. Her altered appearance might have seemed amusing under different circumstances, yet the sudden dread that gripped anyone who beheld her dispelled any notion of amusement. For upon closer inspection, it became evident that she was far more than the innocent little girl she appeared to be—she was something altogether different, something beyond the realm of mere humanity.

With a composed demeanor, Precious turned on her heels to face him, her words dripping with ancient authority. "I am as ancient as Old Scratch himself, and I could obliterate you in an instant if not for the fact that you hold a peculiar fascination for me," she remarked, employing the archaic Southern nomen.

"Your insolent demeanor will swiftly lead to your downfall if you dare to question my intentions again," she warned, her tone laced with a subtle menace.

However, Marcus remained undeterred, his arrogance blinding him to the danger before him. Foolishly, he continued to voice his thoughts, oblivious to the true nature of the entity he faced. Despite spending years in her presence, he remained ignorant of her true identity and power.

Marcus knew all too well who his true master was, and it certainly wasn't this presumptuous angel confined within the guise of a child. He had willingly departed from the depths of hell, opting instead to observe the actions of the angelic entity trapped within the innocent form.

As for why the lord of hell would permit such a minor creature free rein was beyond Marcus' concern. His loyalty lay solely with his true master.

Marcus' allegiance belonged to a being known by myriad titles, including The Father of Lies, The Master of Sin, and The Bringer of The Destruction of Innocence. However, he was less famously recognized by his angelic appellation, Samael, but instead by his Latin designation, Lux-lucis ferre, meaning Light Bringer—Lucifer.

In Marcus' estimation, Lucifer would not tolerate anyone exhibiting the behavior Precious displayed, yet Samael took no action against her. Precious remained an enigmatic anomaly that Marcus monitored closely out of sheer curiosity regarding her intentions for lingering in the mortal realm. Though he regarded her with disdain, Marcus harbored no genuine fear of her, as he had never witnessed her full power during the years he had observed her. Indeed, he remained ignorant of her true nature.

"You truly push the limits of Samael's patience and pose a threat to his servant," Marcus remarked, his tone dripping with sarcasm as he uttered her name. "Your audacity knows no bounds, Kafziel."

"What schemes do you concoct that keep you tethered to this insignificant town? Why do you persist in the mortal realm?" he inquired, his disdain evident. "You watch over the human lineage as though tending to a herd, observing their offspring as they propagate like livestock. What purpose does it serve?"

Precious refrained from disclosing her entrapment in her current form to Marcus. Instead, she pivoted towards him, fixing him with a pointed stare. "I will not tolerate the utterance of my angelic name from your venomous lips again," she declared firmly.

Marcus offered a smile in response, acknowledging her directive. In heaven, Kafziel was recognized as the angel of Tears and Solitude, as well as the Speedy one of God.

It was evident to Precious that Marcus sought to goad her into a confrontation, a confrontation he desired but his master avoided. Marcus yearned for the opportunity to confront Precious himself, to test her mettle and gauge her power. He awaited her response eagerly, eager to ascertain her resolve and strength. It didn't take long for her to oblige.

Precious's hand lashed out with precision, though it made contact with nothing but the empty air—an intentional maneuver, yet the potency of her power remained palpable. It served as a stark wake-up call for Marcus, propelling him across the room like a mere rag doll caught in a tempest. He collided with the far wall of the chamber, landing in a disheveled heap, far from the comforting warmth of the fireplace. Precious harbored a fleeting desire to exert her own physical strength to toss him there, rather than relying on the mere flick of her hand.

Before the dust stirred by his abrupt flight had a chance to settle, Precious closed the distance, reaching his side in an instant. She loomed over his prone form, a menacing figure against the backdrop of his finely tailored suit. In one swift motion, she leaned in, her fingernails scoring deep, blood-gushing lines across his too-perfect face, before he could even muster a feeble defense.

Marcus let out a piercing scream, writhing in agony as Precious's assault ravaged him. "Consider yourself fortunate that I spared your eyes, demon," she seethed, her breaths coming heavy with anger, the bubbling rage barely contained beneath her porcelain skin. "Never utter my true name again. Never raise your voice in my presence. Never question my authority, or I will obliterate you."

Slowly, Marcus rose to a sitting position, then struggled to his feet, careful to avoid any inadvertent contact with Precious as he clumsily regained his balance. Despite towering over her in stature, he harbored no illusions that his physical dominance intimidated her. It was merely a facade. Precious's display of power left no doubt in his mind—she possessed a strength far greater than his own. He was no fool to underestimate her prowess after witnessing such a demonstration.

With a smirk, Marcus regained his composure, leisurely brushing the dirt from his suit as he attempted to maintain an air of indifference, though inwardly he still reeled from the onslaught. Standing tall, he bowed deeply at the waist, his movements fluid yet calculated. "Your commands will be duly noted, Precious," he acquiesced, meeting her gaze with a sense of deference. "I shall depart from your presence now, if it pleases you."

Precious half-turned, allowing her hair to cascade down her shoulders as she returned to her seat. As she moved, her wings unfurled from her back, resembling the darkest of ravens' plumage, their smoothness akin to silk. Bathed in the flickering firelight, they exuded an aura of fierceness and power, their feathers appearing as though dipped in blood. Envy clawed at Marcus's insides as he gazed upon them. He lacked wings, and he knew he would never possess such a magnificent appendage. It was only then that he realized Precious's true nature—she was still an angel, albeit fallen, while he remained a mere demon, and a lesser one at that.

Precious was keenly aware of the fear she instilled in Marcus, and she relished in that understanding. With a flicker of satisfaction, she folded her wings back against herself, causing them to vanish into the ether before settling back into her seat.

Her attendants, fellow angels who had once followed her into rebellion, gathered around her, offering solace and seeking to soothe her ire. Paziel, Thaniel, and Lazuriel hovered nearby, attending to her needs as she gradually calmed herself following the confrontation.

MARCUS begrudgingly acknowledged his entanglement with Precious, though he harbored no satisfaction in it. Dealing with her was an ordeal he found intolerable, a realization that now weighed heavily upon him. Ideally, he would have preferred to avoid any association with her altogether, but such desires were incongruent with his objectives in the mortal realm.

As evening descended, Marcus found himself standing in a park, surrounded by the gentle sway and soft rustle of tree tops in the breeze. Under different circumstances, it would have been a tranquil scene, but his mind was far from serene.

He lingered there, awaiting something or someone, using the calm surroundings to temper the storm of emotions stirred by his recent confrontation with Precious. Despite his efforts, curses escaped his lips, their venom failing to assuage the anger boiling within him. Yet, he begrudgingly accepted that there was little else he could do but endure it.

Marcus contemplated seeking refuge elsewhere when he sensed a sudden shift in the atmosphere. The surroundings fell eerily silent, the wind halting its gentle sway, and the evening insects ceasing their chorus. As darkness enveloped the surroundings, Marcus discerned the presence of another, someone unexpected and undeniably more powerful.

"Hello, Marcus," spoke Samael.

"M-Master," Marcus stuttered in astonishment.

"I am not your master. Why have you come here, demon?" Samael inquired softly, his voice carrying a weight of authority.

Marcus felt his head spinning, his thoughts in disarray. He had ventured into the mortal realm without explicit permission, a decision that now filled him with dread at the prospect of incurring Samael's wrath.

"I-I came... I came to monitor Kafziel," he confessed, his words hesitant yet truthful. It seemed futile to deceive Samael.

Samael regarded Marcus with a knowing gaze, understanding that there was likely more to his presence in the mortal realm than he had disclosed. However, he chose not to reveal his skepticism to Marcus, opting instead to maintain an air of tacit acceptance.

"Are you suggesting you're acting in my best interests?" Samael questioned softly, his attention momentarily diverted to his nails, as if searching for a distraction.

Marcus lowered his head in deference. "Yes. My only aim is to serve you. I arrived to monitor this angel upon learning of her presence in the mortal realm."

"Did you believe I was unaware of her descent from heaven all those years ago?" Samael inquired, his tone betraying a hint of amusement.

"I didn't mean to overstep my bounds. I wasn't aware of your knowledge of her presence. My only intention is to understand her motives for remaining here after all this time," Marcus explained cautiously. Summoning the courage, he met Samael's gaze, finding no immediate cause for concern in his eyes. There was no indication of impending wrath or the threat of destruction.

"I was prepared to inform you the moment I uncovered any pertinent information. Currently, she remains confined within the same mortal vessel she inhabited before her demise," Marcus added hastily, as if seeking validation or forgiveness for his actions.

Marcus was confident that Precious remained oblivious to his knowledge of her entrapment. He guarded this secret closely, having gleaned it through meticulous observation of her unguarded moments. He considered the possibility of leveraging this information against her at a later time, should the opportunity arise.

"Demon, you would do well to heed my counsel. She is beyond your jurisdiction and far superior to you. You are not equipped to handle her, but since you are here of your own accord, do what you want; within reason," Samael advised sternly.

Samael pivoted on his heels, striding purposefully into the enveloping darkness that surrounded them. "I have other matters to attend to. Remain here if you want," he instructed, his voice fading into the shadows.

Marcus lowered himself into a deep bow. "Very well," he replied dutifully.

With a silent departure, Samael vanished into the obscurity, his steps guided by no particular destination. He departed, mindful of the lingering impact his presence would have on Marcus, curious to observe the demon's next course of action.

Samael possessed the power to obliterate the demon with barely a thought, erasing its existence as effortlessly as swatting a fly. By daring to leave the confines of Hell without Samael's explicit sanction, the demon had committed a transgression deserving of annihilation. Yet, Samael refrained from immediate retribution, aware that the demon lacked the capability to threaten his sister, even in her weakened state.

For Samael, the priority lay in uncovering his sister's intentions. He needed to ascertain whether he would be compelled to intervene against her actions, potentially safeguarding both Heaven and Hell from her machinations. Though such intervention did not align with his fundamental purpose, it remained a responsibility he willingly bore as his own.

Aware of his Father's ongoing practice of exiling angels from the heavenly realm, Samael considered it his duty to oversee these fallen brethren—his siblings—who had incurred their Father's punishment.

Despite his own, easily considered as exile, and the task of watching over the sinners of the mortal realm, Samael's love for his siblings and Father remained steadfast. Even in the face of his severe job of punishment for transgressions, he harbored no resentment.

Although he acknowledged the slim chances of re-entering the heavenly realm, Samael remained resolute in his commitment to maintaining the balance between Heaven and Hell. This responsibility, along with the task of redeeming sinners, constituted his penance.

One thing troubled Samael: he was certain that his Father knew of Kafziel's activities. He debated whether it was his right to intervene and disrupt her plans. Similarly, he was aware of his sisters and brother—Paziel, Thaniel, and Lazuriel—acting behind Kafziel's back, yet he hesitated to intercede. It seemed beyond his jurisdiction. Choosing to bide his time, Samael opted to observe and wait for the heavenly realm's response, wondering if his Father would finally take action.

Samael was convinced that without intervention, matters would reach a tipping point, disrupting the balance he worked to maintain. He refused to let that happen. With an idea taking shape, he contemplated a plan that would grant him some control over the situation without inviting interference. This plan revolved around a certain young man who had captured Kafziel's interest.

8

Sara felt exhaustion seep into her bones as she took the wheel for the final stretch of their long journey home. Meanwhile, Aaron's restlessness became increasingly evident, his anxiety palpable with each passing mile. His incessant fidgeting and complaints about the duration of the trip threatened to fray Sara's last nerve. However, she remained composed, redirecting her energy toward maintaining their course.

Upon arrival at their destination, Aaron bolted from the car, his mind preoccupied with thoughts of his mother's well-being. In his haste, he fumbled for the key to the front door, only to realize it was nowhere to be found. Frustration bubbled within him, manifesting in clenched fists and muttered curses, until Sara calmly approached and produced the elusive key, a silent testament to her unwavering patience and foresight."Here it is," Sara declared, her voice weary but laced with a hint of amusement as she produced the key from her pocket.

Aaron's expression soured at his own forgetfulness, yet he found solace in Sara's reliability. She had a knack for remembering the details he often overlooked. While he excelled at seeing the bigger picture, he tended to overlook the finer points. Grateful for her assistance, he accepted the key with a subdued expression of gratitude.

Stepping into the dimly lit house, they were met with an atmosphere that felt almost suffocating. The air seemed heavy with neglect, the darkness enveloping the space like a shroud. The only sound permeating the silence was the faint murmur of a television set emanating from the living room. Aaron made a beeline for the source of the noise, only to nearly stumble over his brother Michael's outstretched leg as he lay sprawled across the recliner, obstructing the doorway.

Aaron approached his brother with the intention of rousing him from his slumber, but his attention was immediately diverted by the sight of his mother lying motionless on the couch. Hastening towards her, he knelt by her side, his heart sinking at the sight before him. Her breathing was shallow, her cheeks gaunt, and her once vibrant spirit seemed drained from her emaciated frame. She appeared not merely unwell, but on the brink of death.

At the sound of Michael's feeble voice, Aaron turned, his concern deepening as he took in his brother's exhausted appearance. Michael's words were laden with weariness, a stark reminder of the toll their mother's illness had taken on him.

"Is that you, Aaron? Have you finally come home?" Michael inquired weakly.

Realization dawned upon Aaron as he observed his brother's haggard state. It was evident that Michael had been deprived of sleep, his weary eyes reflecting the toll of his vigil by their mother's side. Glancing towards Sara, Aaron noticed her standing in the doorway, her hand pressed to her mouth in a futile attempt to stifle her rising emotions.

Michael struggled to rise, his weakened state evident as he faltered in his attempt to stand. With a determined effort, he managed to ascend halfway before his strength failed him, and he began to slump towards the floor. Sara reacted swiftly, intercepting his descent and providing him with the support he needed to remain upright.

"Take him upstairs, Sara," Aaron instructed, delegating the task of guiding Michael to his room and ensuring he rested. "Get him to bed. I'll tend to Momma. Michael needs rest before his condition worsens any further."

As Sara assumed more of Michael's weight, Aaron hesitated, torn between assisting Sara with her burden and attending to his ailing mother. However, his devotion to his mother prevailed, anchoring him to her side despite his desire to aid Sara. Sensing his inner conflict, Sara intervened decisively, urging him away from her and compelling him to focus on his mother while she handled Michael's ascent alone.

Taking a seat in the chair beside the couch, Aaron positioned himself close to his mother. Her eyelids fluttered briefly before she awakened, registering his presence beside her. In the short span of time he had turned to assist his brother, she had slipped back into slumber.

"Don't worry yourself none about me, Michael," Emma murmured, her words a whisper.

Aaron shook his head, a wave of despair washing over him, threatening to engulf him entirely. "Momma, it's me, Aaron. I've come home to take care of you." A solitary tear traced a path down his cheek.

With Aaron's assistance, Emma struggled to sit up, her frail frame finding stability with his support. "Oh, my darling boy, it is you. I thought you was never gonna make it home to see me."

"I'm here now, momma. Like I said, I'm going to take care of you," Aaron reassured her.

Tears welled in Emma's eyes as she reached out, her withered hand coming to rest on her first-born son's cheek, stroking it tenderly. "You've gone and gotten so much bigger. Your poppa woulda been so proud of you," she said, her voice heavy with weariness.

Aaron pondered his mother's words, uncertain of how his father might have responded to their current situation. Emma shifted on the couch, inadvertently allowing a strap of her shift to slip from her shoulder. Aaron reached over to readjust it, noting with concern the frailty of her form.

"What happened to you, momma?" Aaron inquired gently.

Emma's gaze drifted momentarily, lost in thought. "That little girl, she come by here and talks to me more often now. I got no problem with her just wantin to talk and all, but it's what she wants from me..." Emma's voice trailed off, her eyes welling with tears once more. Despite her frail state, tears struggled to form, bringing to attention her dehydrated condition.

Aaron listened attentively, waiting for his mother to elaborate on her cryptic statement. However, he was taken aback when her next words veered in an unexpected direction.

"I can't give you up, I just can't," Emma cried out desperately, her words tinged with confusion.

Aaron felt a pang of bewilderment. Emma was in distress and struggling to reconcile the visits from both Katherine and Precious. She was unable to distinguish between the two encounters and Aaron had no idea of who the two visitors were either. He had never met Katherine and didn't even know about Precious's existence.

"What are you talking about?" Aaron asked, his brow furrowed in confusion. "You're not making much sense."

Emma suddenly leaned forward, startling Aaron to the point where he nearly jumped from his chair. She grasped his face tightly with both hands, her grip uncomfortably firm.

"Your poppa told me things about the town. He told me what was going on with the town folk around here," Emma murmured, her voice strained with urgency. "The little girl, you can't stop her. She ain't human, Aaron. You gotta get out of here while you still can. Michael and I can't do nothing for you."

Emma's sudden shift in demeanor unsettled Aaron. He watched as her eyes began to lose focus, a sense of foreboding creeping over him. Leaning in closer, she spoke in hushed tones, her words laden with resignation.

"I'm gonna die soon; it's to be expected. Getting old, real fast."

Aaron felt a knot form in his stomach. It was clear to him that Emma's mind was clouded by confusion and delirium. She was rambling, uttering words that seemed to come from a place of distress and disorientation. He knew he had to find a way to snap her out of this lethargy, to make her see reason amidst the haze of her thoughts.

Emma's abrupt halt in speech sent a shiver down Aaron's spine. Her previously labored breathing escalated into rapid, ragged gasps, mirroring the panicked rhythm of a trapped animal. Her eyes darted around the dimly lit living room, fixating on the shadows in the corners with meticulous scrutiny. Aaron couldn't shake the feeling that she was on the verge of a full-blown panic attack.

Concerned, Aaron scanned the room for any sign of danger, but found nothing amiss. The space was devoid of life, save for himself and his distressed mother.

Then, unexpectedly, Emma let out a gasp, her hands flying to her chest in a desperate clutch. "You stay away from him. He's my boy and you can't have him," she cried out, her voice tinged with desperation. Aaron's heart clenched with fear at her words. "He's mine and..."

Before Emma could finish her sentence, she was overcome by a fit of gagging. Her eyes rolled back, and her hands clenched tightly across her chest in a grip of agony.

"Momma!" Aaron's scream pierced the air as he reached out for his mother, but she pushed him away with surprising force, sending him sprawling onto his back. By the time Aaron scrambled to his feet, she was already on the move, heading toward the kitchen. He watched her closely, his gaze fixed on the side of her face as she paused in the doorway, her eyes widening in fear at something unseen in the kitchen.

Aaron's heart raced as he rushed after her, but he wasn't quick enough to prevent her fall. With a sickening thud, Emma collapsed to the ground, her body descending in slow motion as if weighed down by an unseen burden. Aaron dropped to his knees beside her, cradling her head in his lap as her thin, sweat-dampened hair clung to her face.

Emma's breaths came in shallow gasps, each one a struggle against the inevitable. Aaron couldn't bear to accept the truth, clinging desperately to hope even as he felt it slipping away.

"I love you, son," Emma whispered faintly, her words a final testament of her love before her breaths grew weaker and weaker.

Tears stung Aaron's eyes as he fought back a scream of anguish, his grief threatening to consume him. Suddenly, a voice broke the silence from the kitchen behind him, a voice unfamiliar yet chillingly familiar.

"Goodbye, Emma," said Precious.

9

Father Gordon hesitated at the top of the staircase leading to the church basement, his apprehension palpable. He lingered there, unwilling to descend further into the unknown depths beneath the church. The fear gnawed at him, a relentless presence that dictated his next course of action. Thus, he resolved not to venture down to the wide double doors marking the entrance to the final chamber of the labyrinthine underground.

There would have been little purpose in proceeding anyway; those ancient doors had remained sealed for nearly two centuries, untouched by mortal hands since their installation. Despite occasional visits to the library below, Father Gordon felt no inclination for further research today. The task of finding a solution to the town's plaguing dilemma held little allure. Instead, he chose to retreat to his office, seeking solace in the quiet refuge it provided. There, he would commit his thoughts to his journal, a steadfast companion in times of uncertainty, anchoring him when all else faltered.

Turning the knob on the oak door, Father Gordon pushed it open slowly, his mind already engaged in crafting the words destined for paper and posterity. However, his thoughts scattered upon catching sight of the unexpected visitor awaiting him in his office. There she stood, seated behind his desk, a knowing expression adorning her features. It was evident she had perused his journal, left carelessly on the desk and opened to his latest entry.

"That was quite the read, Robert," Precious remarked, her tone carrying a hint of amusement as she approached him.

Reacting instinctively, Father Gordon made the sign of the cross, his hand tracing the familiar path from his forehead to his chest and across his shoulders.

"I haven't granted you the privilege of familiarity with me," Father Gordon asserted weakly, attempting to muster courage in the face of Precious's presence.

Precious merely smiled, finding amusement in Father Gordon's feeble display of defiance. Standing at the corner of the desk, she exuded an air of innocence that belied her true nature. "Very well, Father. Shall I address you as such? Perhaps you'd like to play the role of my father?" she replied sarcastically.

Father Gordon chose to ignore her taunt, his frustration simmering beneath the surface before he managed to regain his composure. "You have no right to be here. Why don't you return to where you belong, in the depths of hell? I fail to comprehend why God permits you to inflict the pain and suffering upon this town, but if I had the authority, I would consign you to the fiery pits where you rightfully belong."

Precious approached him with measured steps, her movements almost silent against the polished hardwood floor. However, she halted abruptly, maintaining a distance from Father Gordon; his presence was as repulsive to her as hers was to him. Contemplating her next words, she questioned whether it was worth the effort, knowing he could never comprehend her perspective.

"Do you have any idea what it's like for me to be here? I'm trapped in this absurd form, confined to a place where I'm no closer to God than I was in heaven," Precious spat, her disdain evident in her tone. She despised the necessity of explaining such fundamental truths to him.

Her gaze drifted into the distance, as though she could perceive something beyond Father Gordon's comprehension. Turning her head, she gazed out the window, her focus shifting between the outside world and the internal musings of her mind. With a tilt of her head, she appeared to be attuned to voices that eluded Father Gordon's perception.

"I hear them now, Father," Precious began, her voice soft and tinged with sorrow. "Their voices are muffled and indistinct, but I still hear them. I've never truly been severed from them, only deprived of the joy of being among the Choir of Angels, basking in the light of God." Her words carried a weight of longing.

Suddenly, she turned to face Father Gordon, her gaze piercing through narrowed eyes. "And then you and yours came along and took the only thing we ever had. You don't deserve Him. You're imperfect and frail," she exclaimed, gesturing wildly with her arms. Desperation etched across her delicate features. "You turn away from Him when all is well, only to come crawling back on your knees, begging for help when things stray even slightly from your pleasure," she accused, her arms folding tightly across her chest. "I despise you."

Father Gordon instinctively recoiled, his retreat mirroring the involuntary step forward Precious took in her impassioned speech. Fear gripped him tightly, a rational response considering Precious's reputation for wreaking havoc upon the town for centuries. He knew he stood little chance against her, whether her intentions were driven by malice or a twisted sense of benevolence—though he could hardly count on the latter.

As Precious made her way towards the door, Father Gordon edged sideways, eager to put as much distance between them as possible. He watched warily as she exited his office, her presence leaving an unsettling aura in her wake.

Precious's parting words trailed after her as she walked away, her voice laced with contempt and arrogance. "Keep scribbling in your journal, Father. It won't change a thing. Your feeble attempts are futile. My knowledge far surpasses yours, and I have witnessed the ebb and flow of existence from the beginning. You are but a fleeting mortal, insignificant in the grand scheme of things. Your wisdom pales in comparison to mine."

Father Gordon listened to her fading laughter as she made her exit, the sound of her footsteps echoing down the corridor in stark contrast to her sinister amusement. He sank heavily into his chair, the weight of her words lingering in the air like a dark cloud. Though tempted to pray, he hesitated, knowing the futility of his pleas. Yet, he couldn't help but offer up the same desperate prayers, pleading for deliverance from Precious's malevolence. Before he could utter a word, he reached for his journal, determined to document the encounter as a testament to the ongoing struggle against the forces of darkness.

I am left perplexed by the recent encounter with Precious. It marks the first time she has revealed herself to me, and I can't shake the disconcerting mix of emotions it stirred within me. There's a haunting allure to her beauty, yet it's overshadowed by an innate sense of fear and apprehension. Despite an inexplicable pull toward her, I am acutely aware of the danger she represents. She embodies a force beyond human comprehension, one that has wrought havoc upon our community time and again.

As I reflect on this unsettling encounter, I'm at a loss for where to even begin. How does one confront a being of such malevolence? How can we rid ourselves of her insidious presence? These questions weigh heavily on my mind, lingering like a dark cloud over our small town. Precious lurks beneath the church, biding her time until the opportune moment to unleash her destruction upon us all.

The decision of our town's founders to allow such an abomination to take root beneath the House of God remains a perplexing enigma. While I cannot fathom their rationale, their choice stands, and I am powerless to reverse it. The mere thought of venturing into the dark depths below, where Precious resides, fills me with dread. I recall my predecessor mentioning that Precious's body was interred beneath the church, a desperate attempt to confine her to sacred ground and prevent her from plaguing us further. However, it's evident now that this measure proved futile.

AS Father Gordon diligently cleaned the sanctuary of the church, the sound of the doors opening startled him. The memory of Precious's unsettling visit earlier left him on edge, causing him to jump at the unexpected noise. Ceasing his task, he turned to see who had entered. Given the late hour, he hadn't anticipated any visitors, and he was certain he had secured the doors before starting his chores.

"Who's there?" he called out, his voice echoing through the empty space.

A soft sigh filled the air, but when Father Gordon glanced towards the doorway, there was no one in sight. Frowning, he cautiously approached the front doors, only to freeze in his tracks as a voice called out, halting his movement.

"There's no need to go and look, Father. I am here," came a deep voice from the shadows.

Father Gordon turned to see a man seated alone in the front pew of the sanctuary, facing away from him towards the pulpit. Unable to discern the man's features from this angle, Father Gordon felt a sense of unease at the mysterious visitor's presence.

Approaching cautiously, Father Gordon couldn't shake the perplexity of how the man had bypassed the locked doors and his own vigilance to reach the front pew undetected. As he drew closer, he began to discern the man's appearance more clearly. With shoulder-length dark hair and impeccably clean attire, the man exuded an air of sophistication that afforded Father Gordon a measure of reassurance amidst his uncertainty.

"What can I do for you this evening? The church isn't open to supplicants at this time, although I won't turn away those who need to find their own way to worship," Father Gordon remarked, his tone a blend of courtesy and caution.

The man turned around to face Father Gordon, revealing a striking handsomeness that caught Father Gordon off guard.

"I don't need to worship or pay homage, Father. Not now. Maybe some other time," the man replied, his words carrying an air of casual indifference.

Father Gordon took a seat beside the man on the pew, grappling with a mix of curiosity and wariness towards this enigmatic stranger. There was something about him that seemed to transcend mere appearance, yet Father Gordon couldn't quite pinpoint what it was.

Father Gordon extended his hand in greeting. "I'm Father Gordon. I don't believe I've seen you around town before. How can I assist you?"

"You can call me Samael." The man, now identified as Samael, returned the gesture with a smile.

Father Gordon returned the smile, maintaining a polite demeanor. "How may I be of service to you, Samael?"

Samael leaned back in the pew, crossing his legs comfortably. His gaze swept over Father Gordon, assessing him with a calculating stare.

"I've been pondering some questions lately, particularly about the concept of sin."

"I'll do my best to provide some insight."

Samael appeared lost in thought for a moment, then continued with his inquiry. "Do you really believe you understand the nature of sin?"

"I believe I have a grasp on it," Father Gordon replied after a brief pause.

Considering Father Gordon's response, Samael pressed on. "Is enduring tribulations without hope of relief considered a sin?" Samael posed the question.

Father Gordon took a moment to contemplate before responding. "I don't believe suffering without relief is inherently sinful. It's the infliction of suffering on others by an individual that I would consider sinful."

"I may not entirely agree with that perspective, but let's proceed with our discussion," Samael said thoughtfully. "I view sin as any action that goes against the will of Father."

Father Gordon found Samael's literal reference to God as his father peculiar, but he chose to accept it without further scrutiny.

"Indeed," Father Gordon replied. "Sin, as Augustine of Hippo posited, is 'a word, deed, or desire in opposition to the eternal law of God himself.' It's often considered a transgression of Christian theological principles."

"Hmm, interesting perspective, but what are your thoughts on a celestial being committing a sin?" Samael inquired.

Father Gordon pondered for a moment before responding, "The only instance I know of is Satan, who committed the sin of blasphemy by seeking to replace God."

Samael chuckled softly. "I believe that's oversimplifying a complex issue. But let's save that discussion for another time." He adjusted his position to face Father Gordon more directly. "So, if angels can indeed sin, would it be considered a sin to kill one who has fallen?"

Father Gordon raised his hand to his chin, deep in thought. "I'm not entirely convinced. While killing is indeed a sin, it's typically in reference to human life. Angels, being immortal celestial beings, might not fall under the same category. Besides, angels are believed to be invincible."

"I can assure you, Father, that angels can be harmed," Samael interjected. "Objects infused with celestial power can injure them, and celestial items crafted by or for the Father have the potential to kill them."

"Assuming that's true," Father Gordon mused, "why would anyone even contemplate killing an angel? They are messengers of God, after all."

Samael countered Father Gordon's question with one of his own. "Consider this: Satan, thought of by some as an angel and a messenger of God, is now the embodiment of evil. If given the chance to rid the world of such malevolence by killing Satan, would you take it?"

Father Gordon deliberated for a moment before responding, his thoughtful pause indicating the weight of his contemplation. "I hesitate to label Satan as inherently evil. Cast out of heaven and tasked with ruling over hell as a punisher of the wicked, his role may be more complex than mere malevolence. However, this is a philosophical quandary that may warrant deeper examination by individuals more versed in theological matters than myself."

Samael chuckled softly. "A deftly crafted response, Father, but you sidestepped the question."

"I'm not certain if I could bring myself to do so, nor do I believe it's within my moral compass to condone such an action. However, I wouldn't pass judgment on anyone faced with such a dire decision," Father Gordon admitted, exhaling heavily.

Samael reflected on the dialogue exchanged between him and Father Gordon, finding resonance in the man's responses. He found himself in general agreement with the sentiments expressed, each answer resonating with his own thoughts to some degree.

Expressing gratitude for the conversation, Samael bid Father Gordon farewell as he rose from his seat to depart.

Samael glanced back just once, before leaving, thinking to himself, "I believe that is an interesting man. I'll have to clear some things up for him when I see him again."

10

Over the next week, Aaron found himself juggling three demanding responsibilities. First and foremost, he was dedicated to supporting his brother Michael through his recovery from the recent ordeal of having assumed the role of caregiver for his mother, whose illness, leading to death, had remained a mystery. Amidst these challenges, Sara, devastated by the sudden loss of Emma, relied heavily on Aaron's support. Yet, perhaps the most emotionally taxing duty weighing on Aaron's shoulders was arranging the funeral for his beloved mother.

Despite the weight of his obligations, Aaron remained steadfast by Michael's side, attending to his needs with unwavering dedication. However, Michael's recovery progressed slowly, marked by a persistent silence that lingered between the brothers. Despite Aaron's constant presence, Michael remained withdrawn, his gaze often fixed on the sprawling oak tree outside his window for most of the day, lost in contemplation.

Aaron attempted to initiate conversation with Michael, hoping to involve him in the funeral preparations. However, his efforts were met with silence and indifference. Michael steadfastly avoided Aaron's gaze, as though pretending his presence would vanish if ignored long enough. Aaron couldn't shake the feeling of being somehow at fault for his brother's aloofness.

Meanwhile, Sara sought solace within the confines of their home, channeling her grief into domestic tasks. She busied herself with household chores, from laundering linens to tidying the house and preparing meals for their small family. Despite her parents' well-intentioned suggestion to relocate to their home until Michael's recovery, Sara politely declined, opting to remain with the brothers during this trying time.

Norma and Leon grasped the situation. They comprehended their daughter's love for Aaron and her desire to remain close to him, despite their own wish to have her at home. They also recognized Aaron's need for his brother Michael to recover in a familiar and secure environment, which home provided. It saddened them deeply that the boys had lost both parents in such a short span of time.

Yet, one concern weighed heavily on their minds: Sara's future without Aaron. Norma and Leon pondered the inevitable challenges she would face. They were acutely aware of the town's peculiar circumstances and the burden each family bore. In Ionia, birth and death were intrinsically linked to the town; leaving was not an option. Every resident, born into the town's legacy, was bound to its fate, unable to escape the consequences of their forefathers' pact.

Each night, nestled in Aaron's embrace, Sara sought answers about the day his mother passed away. She craved every minute detail, every uttered word, and every action taken.

As Sara persistently questioned Aaron, he began to sense her probing for something more profound. He suspected she was onto a clue that had eluded him. Night after night, he patiently recounted the harrowing events, hoping Sara would uncover the missing piece. Yet, despite his earnest retellings, she remained silent about her thoughts, leaving Aaron in suspense.

The night preceding the funeral, Sara broached a question she had not previously posed. "What did your momma mean when she said, 'Your poppa told me things about the town'? Was there something he confided in her that he never shared with you?" she inquired.

Aaron pondered her question for a moment before responding. "I'm not sure. We've both been here our whole lives, and I can't think of any secret my poppa might've disclosed to momma that we wouldn't already know," he admitted. "This town isn't exactly vast. You know how hard it is to keep anything under wraps here. Heck, word got out about us sleeping together within the first week it happened, and we didn't breathe a word of it."

Can you describe the little girl you mentioned seeing in the kitchen when your momma passed away?" Sara inquired.

Aaron was taken aback by her request, but he complied, racking his brain to recall the details of that unsettling moment. Despite the fleeting nature of his glimpse, the memory remained vivid in his mind, etched with eerie clarity. The girl's presence had left an indelible mark, her enigmatic demeanor lingering like a haunting specter.

"It was a little girl with curly, blond hair cascading down to her waist. She appeared to be around ten years old," Aaron recounted, his voice tinged with uncertainty as he retraced the image in his mind's eye. "She wore a white dress adorned with a baby blue satin sash tied elegantly around her waist. The bow was situated at the small of her back, although I couldn't have seen it directly," he admitted, acknowledging the peculiar detail that seemed to defy explanation.

"She had a delicate beauty about her, yet there was an aura of..." Aaron paused, grappling for the appropriate term to encapsulate the unsettling vibe the girl had exuded. Casting a glance into Sara's attentive gaze, he sensed her anticipation, her curiosity hanging palpably in the air.

"She exuded malevolence," Sara interjected, providing a succinct characterization of the unsettling aura surrounding the girl.

Aaron nodded in agreement, grateful for Sara's articulation of the elusive sentiment he had struggled to convey. "Exactly. It's like she wasn't outright evil, but there was something... off about her," he elaborated, gesturing vaguely as he searched for the right words to encapsulate his impression.

Sara nodded, her understanding evident as she absorbed Aaron's explanation. "I get what you're trying to say," she reassured him, her expression earnest as she processed the significance of their conversation.

"I recall hearing tales of a ghostly presence haunting the town, reportedly that of a young girl," Sara mused, her thoughts racing as she connected the dots between Aaron's account and the local lore. "Based on your description, it's entirely possible that she's the one. I intend to look into the archives at town hall, sift through the old papers, and unearth any information pertaining to this mysterious girl," she declared with determination.

Aaron slumped wearily, the weight of his exhaustion and despondency palpable in the heavy air surrounding him. Every movement seemed like a Herculean effort, each breath a struggle against the suffocating burden pressing down upon him.

Sara, attuned to Aaron's inner turmoil, sought to offer solace in the face of his anguish. "Don't worry about it, love. It wasn't your fault," she reassured him, her voice a gentle balm to his troubled mind. "You couldn't have stopped it even if you had come home earlier. She was going home to heaven regardless," she murmured, enfolding Aaron in a tender embrace.

Leaning into Aaron's side, Sara sought to provide a physical manifestation of her support, intertwining their arms as she nestled her head against his chest. "You don't have to face this alone," she whispered softly, her words a soothing melody amid the discord of Aaron's thoughts. "We'll tackle this together, once the funeral has passed. You don't have to worry about doing this on your own."

Aaron felt a wave of relief wash over him at Sara's reassurance, dispelling the fleeting notion of abandonment that had momentarily clouded his thoughts. Grateful for her unwavering support, he pulled her closer, their bodies entwining in a silent testament to their bond. With whispered declarations of love lingering in the air, they surrendered to the tender intimacy that enveloped them.

As dawn broke, the somber procession to the funeral began, drawing mourners from every corner of the community. The church, usually a beacon of hope and solace, now stood as a backdrop to the collective grief that gripped the town.

As Aaron and Sara entered the sanctuary of the church, they followed Michael's lead toward the front pews, where their seats awaited. Sara's hand found Aaron's, a silent gesture of solidarity amidst the somber atmosphere. Yet, as they walked, Aaron couldn't shake the sense of unease he felt from Micheal that permeated the air.

Michael, several strides ahead, walked with purpose, his pace quickening with each step. His determined gait seemed to signal a desire to distance himself from his brother and Sara.

Sara glanced at Aaron, her brow furrowing with concern as she sensed Michael's deliberate attempt to create distance between them.

Aaron hesitated for a moment, his gaze flickering between Michael's retreating form and Sara's concerned expression. Despite the growing rift between them, he couldn't bring himself to abandon his brother, not when he felt the need to console him most.

With a sigh, Aaron quickened his pace, closing the gap between himself and Michael. As they reached the front pews, Michael took his seat with a stiff nod, his gaze fixed straight ahead, resolute in his silence.

In the front pew, Aaron and Michael sat side by side, their presence reflecting the depth of their loss. Sara remained by Aaron's side offering her unwavering support and comfort amidst the sea of mourners. She reached for Aaron's hand, offering a silent reassurance that they were in this together, no matter the obstacles they faced.

Together, they braced themselves for the solemn ceremony ahead, united in their determination to honor his mother's memory.

As the congregation settled into their seats, the grief hung heavy in the air. Aaron glanced around the sanctuary absently, taking in the solemn faces of their fellow mourners, each grappling with their own loss.

The absence of a few familiar faces, such as the sheriff and local government officials, served as a poignant reminder of the demands of duty that often eclipsed personal sorrow. Despite their physical absence, their condolences echoed through the halls of the church, conveyed through heartfelt phone calls, sympathy cards, and floral tributes.

Sara's presence by Aaron's side was a silent acknowledgment of her role as a cherished member of his family, transcending the boundaries of tradition. Beside him, Sara squeezed his hand, her touch a silent reminder of the strength they found in each other. In the hushed reverence of the church, her place in the front pew was not a matter of debate but a testament to the depth of her connection with Aaron and his family.

The chapel exuded an atmosphere of solemnity and reflection as Father Gordon led the congregation through the customary rituals and prayers for the departed. Amidst the reverent silence, Aaron seized a moment to survey the gathered mourners again, his gaze sweeping across the sea of faces assembled to honor the memory of his mother. He survey had more purpose now.

Aaron's attention was drawn to the figure of a young girl seated towards the back of the chapel. Her fiery red hair caught the dim light, her presence sending a shiver down Aaron's spine. His heart skipped a beat as his eyes fell upon what he thought of as a familiar figure.

He tore his gaze away, his heart pounding in his chest as he struggled to shake the feeling of uncertainty. Disbelief washed over him, threatening to engulf him in a tidal wave of dread. For a fleeting moment, he was transported back to the depths of his nightmares, the vivid memory of the redheaded girl haunting his waking thoughts.

Sara, ever perceptive to his emotions, noticed the sudden shift in Aaron's demeanor and the incredulous expression carved upon his face. Concern etched into her features as she leaned closer to him, her voice a gentle whisper amidst the solemnity of the service.

"What's troubling you, love? What did you see?" Sara inquired, her eyes searching his for answers.

Aaron's response was a hesitant murmur, his words tinged with uncertainty and a hint of fear. "I... It's nothing, really. Just a fleeting thought, that's all."

He refused to entertain the notion, unwilling to admit to himself the possibility of the girl's presence. The distance between them rendered any attempt at identification futile; he couldn't definitively discern whether she was the same girl from his haunting dreams.

Turning his attention back to the pulpit, Aaron willed himself to focus solely on the service, determined to banish all thoughts of the enigmatic redhead from his mind. Yet, despite his efforts, his thoughts drifted inexorably back to the unsettling dream that had plagued him.

As Father Gordon's voice droned on, Aaron found himself slipping into a state of drowsiness, his consciousness succumbing to the pull of sleep. He struggled against the encroaching darkness, but it proved to be a losing battle. Before he knew it, he had succumbed to slumber.

Abruptly, he jolted awake, a surge of adrenaline coursing through his veins as he realized he had dozed off. Though his movement went unnoticed by all but Michael and Sara, Aaron's heart pounded in his chest, his senses heightened by an inexplicable sense of unease. In that moment of wakefulness, the memory of his dream flooded back with startling clarity, the image of the redheaded girl and the sinister presence that pursued her etched vividly in his mind. It was the same malevolent figure he had encountered in the aftermath of his mother's death—an eerie connection that sent shivers down his spine.

In the depths of his dream, Aaron was startled by the sound of a little girl's laughter. It echoed through his subconscious, a mocking reminder that the pieces of his unsettling puzzle were falling into place, yet remained frustratingly enigmatic. Long before the laughter reverberated off the chapel walls, he sensed its taunting presence in his mind, a disconcerting precursor to the tangible manifestation.

Frantically scanning the room, Aaron sought the source of the laughter, his senses on high alert. Its reality dawned upon him—this was no mere dream, but an intrusion into his waking consciousness.

"Stop it! Stop laughing! Who are you? How dare you interrupt at a time like this?" Aaron's voice echoed through the chapel, laden with a mix of fear and indignation.

Startled, Father Gordon paused mid-sermon, his gaze drawn to Aaron's outburst. Bewildered murmurs rippled through the congregation, oblivious to the unseen specter that tormented Aaron's senses.

Sara rose from her seat, her hand gently restraining Aaron's arm as she assessed his distress. Michael, standing beside them, cast a disdainful glare that cut through Aaron like a knife. Despite the gravity of the situation, Michael's animosity remained palpable, a silent testament to their fractured relationship.

"What's wrong, Aaron?" Sara's voice, intended as a whisper, carried an unintended edge of urgency. "You don't look well. Let's leave, get some rest. They'll understand, everyone here cares about you."

Unbeknownst to them, Michael's understanding was a distant hope. Aaron, still reeling from the encounter, found himself unable to articulate a response. Sara's guidance was a lifeline, leading him away from the unsettling scene. His mind, consumed by the echoes of laughter that only he could hear, struggled to reconcile the cruel reality of the entity's torment.

In the rear pew, as Aaron had feared, sat the redheaded girl from his nightmares. Her gaze bore into Aaron's with an unsettling mixture of sadness and accusation as Sara guided him toward the chapel doors. Michael observed the scene with a mixture of disdain and impatience, his arms folded tightly across his chest, his foot tapping with agitation. His resentment toward his brother simmered beneath the surface, exacerbated by Aaron's disruptive outburst during a service meant for honoring their late mother's memory.

11

After the funeral, Michael returned home and checked in on Aaron. He cast a look filled with unabashed scorn in Aaron's direction. "Come sit with me, Michael," Aaron called out, hoping to bridge the growing distance between them. However, Michael merely turned his back and walked away, leaving Aaron feeling rejected and disheartened.

Sara proved to be a tremendous support, unlike Michael. She made sure Michael stuck to his meals, ensuring his health didn't suffer. Spending ample time around the house, she lent a hand to the brothers and attempted to facilitate communication between them.

"Sara, could you please pass the salt?" Aaron asked, extending his hand towards the condiment on the dining table.

"Sure thing, Aaron," Sara replied, handing him the salt shaker with a warm smile.

As Michael entered the room, Sara's gaze shifted to him, concern evident in her eyes. "Hey, Michael, dinner's ready. You should eat something," she urged gently, hoping to coax him into joining them at the table.

Michael grunted in acknowledgment but made no move to take a seat, instead opting to retreat to his room without a word.

Sighing softly, Sara exchanged a knowing glance with Aaron, silently acknowledging the challenge of reaching out to Michael amidst his silent resistance.

Days passed with Michael maintaining a resolute silence towards Aaron and Sara. However, one morning, as Sara and Aaron sat at the kitchen table enjoying breakfast together, a steaming plate of food awaited Michael.

"Care to join us?" Aaron extended the invitation with a pleasant tone, gesturing to the empty chair.

Michael lingered in the doorway, his jaw clenched so tightly that the muscles stood out prominently. The tension in the room noticeably thickened as Michael's gaze bore into them with an intense, simmering hatred. His eyes seemed to smolder with unspoken animosity, casting a shadow over the once-inviting atmosphere.

Aaron felt a twinge of unease as he faced his brother's simmering anger. He couldn't fathom what had triggered such intense animosity, especially when he couldn't recall any wrongdoing on his part.

"What's eating you?" Aaron's voice held a hint of frustration, his own emotions starting to rise. "I haven't done a damn thing to deserve this treatment from you. It's about time you spill whatever's been festering inside instead of sulking around like a wounded animal."

Michael's demeanor was palpably hostile, his face flushed with pent-up fury. If looks could kill, Aaron would have been six feet under. With measured steps, Michael closed the distance between them, his presence looming over Aaron like an impending storm.

"Why should I bother explaining myself to you?" Michael's voice dripped with resentment, his words laced with pent-up frustration. "I don't even want you here anymore. You abandoned us when we needed you most. You weren't around when Poppa needed you, and you barely showed up when Momma was struggling."

His accusatory gaze shifted to Sara, his anger not solely directed at Aaron. He felt as though Sara had stolen something precious from him long ago—a piece of his brother's heart. She had taken Aaron away from him, leaving Michael feeling abandoned and resentful.

Turning back to Aaron, Michael's anger flared with a fury barely restrained by a thin leash. "You chose her over me years ago," he accused, his finger jabbing toward Sara with deliberate condemnation.

But Michael wasn't finished. With each step into the room, he closed the distance between himself and Aaron, his emotions spilling over. "You left me behind, always living in your shadow, craving just a scrap of attention that never came!" A solitary tear traced a path down his cheek, his voice thick with emotion. "I loved you, but you only had eyes for yourself and her. You loved yourself and her more than anyone else in this house," Michael's accusation hung heavy in the air.

Aaron seethed with anger, his frustration bubbling to the surface. He vividly remembered how only Sara had been able to provide solace during those relentless nightmares, while his parents and Michael had failed to be able to offer any comfort. Despite their efforts, nothing had helped alleviate the torment haunting his sleep. It had always been about himself, consumed by the relentless grip of his own psyche.

"How dare you?" Aaron's voice rang out, his tone laced with indignation. "What do you know about who I love or don't love? I gave you everything I had, poured out every ounce of brotherly affection I could muster, and what did I get in return? Nothing but endless demands and expectations. Poppa never cared about me; I was nothing but a disappointment to him. And Momma," Aaron's voice rose, nearly reaching a crescendo, "she was so preoccupied with painting the world in shades of optimism through rose colored glasses for me and fussing over you that she never even noticed my silent cries for attention."

His words echoed off the kitchen walls, charged with pent-up resentment and years of unspoken grievances. Aaron's outburst hung heavy in the air, a stark reminder of the simmering tensions that had long plagued their fractured family dynamic.

In a sudden surge of emotion, Aaron rose from the table, his movements hurried and erratic, causing the chair to topple over with a loud clatter. His anger blazed hotter than he had ever felt before, a fiery inferno consuming his senses. His vision clouded with red, a swirling maelstrom of rage and despair swirling within him, threatening to overwhelm his senses.

"I needed someone, anyone," Aaron's voice trembled with the intensity of his emotions, each word a raw expression of his inner turmoil. "And the only person who was ever there for me, who cared for me unconditionally, who understood the darkness that consumed me night after night, was Sara." He cast a glance back at Sara, his eyes brimming with gratitude and affection. "She was my anchor when I was drowning in the suffocating embrace of Poppa's so-called love. She was my beacon of light when Momma was too lost in her own fears to guide me."

With a sudden pivot, Aaron turned to face Michael, his gaze piercing and unwavering. The abruptness of his movement startled Michael, who recoiled slightly at the intensity of Aaron's stare. "I'm not letting her go, not for you or anyone else," Aaron declared, his voice steady despite the storm raging within him.

Aaron swiftly dodged Michael's swing, narrowly avoiding the intended blow aimed at his jaw. Reacting instinctively, he pushed Michael to the floor, asserting his dominance as he stood over his fallen brother. Michael, fueled by fury, struggled to rise, his eyes ablaze with unchecked rage, his movements betraying his intent to retaliate. Before Michael could regain his footing, Aaron forcefully knocked him back down to the ground, ensuring he remained subdued.

"Get out of my house!" Michael's voice reverberated through the room, laced with venomous hatred. "I want you gone, and don't you dare come back!"

Aaron's brow furrowed in disbelief at Michael's audacity, momentarily taken aback by the sheer intensity of his brother's anger. It was clear that Michael had mistaken their positions, perhaps blinded by his own fury. "I could argue that this house is rightfully mine, being the oldest," Aaron retorted, his voice tinged with a mixture of frustration and resignation. However, he quickly dismissed the notion, realizing it was futile to reason with Michael in his current state.

Backing away cautiously, Aaron distanced himself from his brother, a palpable tension hanging in the air between them. "I'll be gone within the hour," Aaron stated firmly, his tone resolute. "And you can rest assured, Michael, you won't ever have to see me again." With those words hanging heavily in the air, Aaron turned on his heel and strode purposefully towards Sara so he could get out of the kitchen, leaving behind the shattered remnants of their fractured relationship.

Aaron gently took Sara's hand in his own, offering her a reassuring squeeze as he led her out of the kitchen, leaving behind the tumultuous scene with his brother sprawled on the floor. Together, they gathered their meager belongings, a silent acknowledgment of their abrupt departure from Aaron's home. With resolve in his heart, Aaron vowed silently that he would never set foot in that house again for as long as he lived.

As they made their way to Sara's parents' house, Aaron's mind buzzed with a whirlwind of emotions. Anger, betrayal, and a profound sense of loss simmered beneath the surface, mingling with the comforting presence of Sara by his side. He found solace in her unwavering support, a beacon of light in the darkness that threatened to consume him.

Upon their arrival, Sara took the initiative to explain their unexpected presence to her parents. With attentive ears and empathetic hearts, Sara's parents listened intently, offering a comforting presence to Aaron in his time of need. Without interruption, they allowed Sara to share their story, her words a testament to the depth of their bond and the challenges they faced.

Once Sara had finished recounting their ordeal, her parents offered a few quiet words of solace to Aaron, their expressions filled with compassion and understanding. With a gentle pat on the shoulder and a reassuring smile, they left the young couple to themselves in the living room, granting them the space they needed to process their emotions and find strength in each other's arms.

"Try not to dwell on what your brother said, Love," Sara's voice was gentle, a soothing balm to Aaron's troubled mind. "He's still grieving the loss of your mother, and he's struggling to cope with it."

Aaron shook his head, a furrow forming between his brows as he contemplated Sara's words. He couldn't bring himself to fully accept her reasoning. Deep down, he harbored his own suspicions about his brother's outburst, both verbal and almost physical. Despite Michael's grief, Aaron couldn't shake the feeling that there was more to his brother's anger than just mourning their mother's passing. Michael's accusations seemed disjointed, lacking any logical explanation.

He sighed, frustration etched on his features as he grappled with the complexity of his brother's emotions. Michael knew better than anyone how much Aaron cared for him. From the moment Michael graduated high school, Aaron had urged him to join him at Dale College, yearning for their close bond to endure beyond the confines of their childhood home.

"I'm done worrying about them—my Momma, my Poppa, and my brother. It's all in the past now. You're the only thing that matters to me, and I'll do whatever it takes to keep you by my side," Aaron whispered, his voice filled with determination.

Turning to Sara, Aaron gently cupped her face in his hands, savoring the warmth of her touch as she placed her hands atop his. He felt a rush of affection as she pressed her lips to his fingertips before guiding his hands to her own lips. Leaning in, Aaron pressed his lips fervently against hers, igniting a fiery passion that enveloped them both.

KATHERINE hesitated at the edge of the sidewalk, her gaze fixed on the figure slouched on the front steps across the street. Michael sat there, his shoulders hunched with a burden she couldn't quite decipher from this distance. She knew this was her chance to approach him, to finally extend the olive branch she had been carrying in her heart since her last visit to this neighborhood.

Yet, fear gripped her, a familiar sensation that seemed to shadow her every step. She remembered Aunt Emma's comforting presence, her warm smile, and the stories she told about Katherine's mother. But now, faced with the reality of her absence and the weight of her own unresolved past, Katherine found herself frozen in place.

Katherine had ventured to the house to pay her respects to the brothers after the funeral, yet as she approached the front door, the sound of their heated argument stopped her in her tracks. Voices raised in discord echoed through the neighborhood, clear even from the porch where she stood. Hesitating, she lingered in the shadows, unsure if she should intervene or retreat.

Eventually, she opted for the latter, deciding to seek another opportunity to connect with her cousins when tensions were less fraught. Stepping back onto the sidewalk, she cast a lingering glance toward the house before turning away, the weight of their unresolved conflict heavy on her heart.

It was only moments later that she caught sight of Michael emerging from the front door, his posture tense with anger as he settled on the front step. Katherine observed him from across the street, a mixture of concern and hesitation swirling within her. She knew she should approach him, offer comfort or assistance, but fear held her back, rooted to the spot as she watched him stew in his emotions.

Michael remained unaware of her presence, lost in his own thoughts. The morning sun cast long shadows across the street, painting the scene in a soft, golden hue. The tension from the earlier argument with Aaron lingered in the air like an unspoken truth, and Katherine couldn't help but feel a pang of sympathy for her cousin.

Taking a deep breath, she mustered her courage and stepped off the sidewalk, crossing the quiet street toward the house. Toward Michael. As she approached, she noticed the furrow in his brow, the tightness in his jaw, signs of the turmoil raging within him.

"Michael," she called out softly, her voice barely a whisper in the stillness of the morning.

Startled, Michael lifted his head, his eyes widening in recognition as he took in the figure standing before him. Katherine felt a rush of relief wash over her as she saw the flicker of familiarity in his gaze.

"Katherine?" he exclaimed, rising from his seat with a mix of surprise and curiosity. "What are you doing here?"

She swallowed the lump forming in her throat, the weight of her words heavy on her tongue. "I... I wanted to see you and Aaron," she admitted, her voice trembling slightly.

Michael looked back at the house and frowned. His gaze returned to Katherine. A flicker of sadness passed over Michael's features, his eyes clouding with memories of happier times. "Aaron's not here," he said quietly, his tone tinged with regret. "And I'm not sure when he'll be back."

Despite the disappointment gnawing at her heart, Katherine pressed on, determined to bridge the gap between them. "I'm sorry about this morning," she said, gesturing vaguely toward the house. "I heard the argument..."

Michael's look of surprise was short lived. He sighed, a weary expression crossing his face. "It's complicated," he admitted, his voice tinged with frustration. "But I shouldn't have lashed out like that. It's just... Sara..."

Katherine waited for him to say more but he didn't. Her heart going out to him, she asked instead "is Sara his girlfriend?"

Michael just nodded in the affirmative.

"It must be difficult, having her come between you and Aaron," she murmured sympathetically.

A pained expression flickered across Michael's features, and Katherine could see the turmoil roiling beneath the surface. She reached out a tentative hand, placing it gently on his arm in a gesture of comfort.

"It's okay," she said softly, meeting his gaze with empathy. "Families argue sometimes. We'll figure it out together."

Michael's eyes softened at Katherine's words, gratitude evident in his expression. He appreciated her presence more than he could articulate. Despite the chaos swirling around him, there was a sense of calm with her being near.

"Thank you, Katherine," he murmured, his voice tinged with sincerity. "I don't know what to do. Right now, you're a welcome distraction."

A small smile tugged at Katherine's lips, warmed by his gratitude. "I'm sorry we've got to see each other again under these circumstances though," she said to him, her voice filled with condolence.

They stood there for a moment, a silent understanding passing between them. In that brief exchange, Katherine felt a connection deepen, a bond forged in shared struggles and unspoken support.

As the morning sun climbed higher in the sky, casting its warm embrace over the quiet neighborhood, Katherine and Michael found solace in each other's company. Together, they sat on the stoop and faced the uncertainties of the future, drawing strength from the ties that bound them as family.

Michael shifted uneasily on the front step, a sense of discomfort settling over him as he grappled with the role of host. It felt awkward to leave Katherine sitting outside without offering anything, a feeling compounded by the urge to extend an invitation into the house. Yet, a glance in Katherine's direction gave him pause, her demeanor suggesting a level of contentment with the current arrangement.

"Um," Michael began tentatively, his hand running through his hair in a gesture of uncertainty. "Would you, uh, like to come in? Maybe for a drink or something? Coffee, perhaps? Since it's still morning..."

His gaze flickered to the front door of the house, a silent invitation lingering in his words. Yet, as he considered the implications of his offer, a pang of guilt washed over him. The remnants of breakfast remained untouched on the dining table, a stark reminder of the rift between him and Aaron.

Katherine's warm smile eased some of his apprehension, her acceptance a welcomed relief. "Sure, I'll have some coffee," she replied graciously, her gratitude evident in her tone.

Michael couldn't help but feel a surge of relief at Katherine's enthusiastic response. Together, they rose from the front step and crossed the threshold into the house, their shared familial ties beginning to forge as they entered the familiar space.

Pausing in the living room, Katherine's gaze swept over the room, her eyes lingering on the familiar surroundings. It was here that she had first met her aunt Emma, her mother's sister, the connection to a family she had long been estranged from. Memories flooded back, a bittersweet mix of longing and regret.

In the quiet of the room, Katherine found herself recalling that first visit. She was drawn to the photographs filling the photo album, snapshots of moments frozen in time. Images of her mother, captured in her youth, stared back at her, a reminder of the bond they had never shared.

A dull ache throbbed in Katherine's chest, a pain born from the absence of a mother's love. She couldn't help but wonder what might have been, what memories they might have forged together if fate had been kinder. Yet, even in her absence, Aunt Emma had offered solace and guidance, filling the void left by her mother's untimely passing.

The weight of solitude settled upon Katherine as she stood in the living room, a pang of loss piercing through her momentarily. With Aunt Emma now gone, she couldn't help but feel the stark reality of her isolation, her only remaining ties to family being her cousins Aaron and Michael, along with her aunt from her father's side.

These somber reflections led her down the path of contemplating her relationship with a father she had never known. From what she had gleaned from Aunt Megan, it was a relationship marred by indifference, a father who had chosen to remain absent from her life. The bitterness of regret lingered, but Katherine resolved to forge her own path, free from the shadow of a man who had failed to fulfill his paternal duties.

Her musings were interrupted by Michael's return, the aroma of freshly brewed coffee wafting through the air as he offered her a cup. Grateful for the distraction, Katherine accepted the gesture, the warmth of the mug comforting in her hands as they settled down to continue their visit.

Taking a deep breath, Katherine pushed aside the weight of her grief, focusing instead on the present moment. She had come here seeking connection, seeking closure, and she wouldn't let the past hold her back. With Michael by her side, she felt a glimmer of hope, a sense of belonging that she had long yearned for.

And though Aaron's absence loomed large, overshadowing their reunion, Katherine couldn't help but feel hopeful. In the midst of turmoil, she felt comfortable in Michael's presence, a reminder that family were stronger together.

Savoring the rich, nutty flavors lingering on her palate, Katherine cradled the warm mug in her hands, finding solace in the comforting embrace of the coffee. Her gaze drifted to the dark liquid swirling within, lost in the mesmerizing dance of its surface.

As her thoughts meandered, they inevitably returned to Aaron. The intensity of the argument she had overheard between Michael and Aaron lingered in her mind, a weighty reminder of the rift between them. The desire to finally meet her cousin had been abruptly thwarted, her hopes dashed when both Aaron and Sara had slipped out of the house unnoticed.

The memory of their heated exchange left Katherine hesitant to broach the subject with Michael, reluctant to delve into the specifics of their disagreement. Yet, her resolve remained unshaken, her determination to connect with her living relatives unwavering. She longed to bridge the divide, to forge bonds with those who shared her blood, despite the obstacles that lay in her path.

"I came by hoping to meet both you and Aaron," Katherine murmured, her voice barely audible as she maintained her focus on the coffee cup cradled in her hands.

Michael emitted a low grunt, a flicker of discomfort crossing his features at the mention of his brother. "I don't think that's possible now," he responded with a nonchalant shrug.

"Yeah, I kind of gathered that from what I heard," Katherine replied, her tone tinged with understanding.

The silence that ensued hung heavy between them, pregnant with unspoken implications. For several minutes, neither dared to break the quietude, opting instead to nurse their respective beverages in solemn contemplation.

Finally, Katherine set her coffee cup aside, fixing her gaze thoughtfully on Michael. "Do you have any idea why he had that outburst at the church?" she inquired, her curiosity piqued.

Michael shook his head in response, a gesture laden with uncertainty. "I have no idea," he admitted, his voice trailing off momentarily as he sifted through memories of his brother's behavior that day. A furrow creased his brow as he contemplated possible explanations.

"I think it might have something to do with the nightmares," he mumbled to himself, the words slipping out unintentionally into the air.

Katherine's interest was piqued by Michael's cryptic statement. "He has nightmares?" she inquired, her tone laced with concern.

Meeting Katherine's gaze, Michael's surprise was evident, his realization dawning belatedly that he had inadvertently spoken aloud. With a sigh, he acknowledged the slip, knowing that the cat was now out of the bag.

"Yeah, he's had them since he was a child," Michael confessed, his voice tinged with empathy. "The recurring kind. He rarely talks about what they actually consist of, but it's apparent when he has them."

"Is there nothing that can be done to—" Katherine began, her voice trailing off as she broached the subject.

"We've tried everything. The only thing he can do is try to run to get over the effects of the dream the next morning," Michael interjected, his tone tinged with resignation.

"Oh. Is that so," Katherine replied, her words laced with understanding as she lapsed into thoughtful silence once again.

As Michael grappled with his own emotions, he found himself yearning for companionship, a desire to stave off the loneliness that crept in with Aaron and Sara's absence. The memory of his mother, whose presence had once filled every corner of the house, lingered like a bittersweet echo, a reminder of the void left in her wake.

Yet, despite the company Katherine provided, Michael couldn't shake the discomfort that gnawed at him. The topic of conversation, though rooted in concern for his brother, struck a nerve. Anger simmered beneath the surface, a remnant of the unresolved argument that still hung heavy in the air.

While his love for Aaron remained unwavering, Michael wasn't ready to confront the lingering tension between them. For now, he sought solace in silence, a temporary reprieve from the turmoil that churned within him.

"If you're just here to see Aaron, you'll probably have better luck going next door to Sara's house to see them," Michael suggested, his tone tinged with a hint of resignation.

Katherine shifted uncomfortably, her gaze instinctively darting in the direction of the neighbor's house, though the view was obstructed by the wall. It was a reflexive response to being given direction, even if she couldn't actually see the house from where she sat. Yet, upon further reflection, she dismissed the idea.

The thought of venturing to the neighbor's house felt daunting, a step too far outside her comfort zone. Despite her status as a relative, she already felt out of place showing up unannounced at Michael's doorstep. The idea of intruding on strangers only added to her unease, reinforcing her decision to remain where she was.

"Well, I guess I'll just have to wait until a later day to meet him," Katherine offered with a weak smile, her disappointment evident despite her attempt at optimism. Rising from her seat, she signaled her readiness to depart, and Michael, picking up on the cue, accompanied her to the door.

As Katherine stepped out onto the porch, Michael waved her off, a pang of longing tugging at his heart as he watched her disappear down the street. His thoughts drifted toward the potential for a closer relationship with his cousin, a prospect that filled him with both anticipation and uncertainty.

Left alone once more, Katherine couldn't shake the feeling of incompleteness that lingered within her. While she had cherished the brief moments spent with Michael, the absence of Aaron left her longing for more. With a sigh, she made her way through the morning sunlight toward Aunt Megan's home, her hopes of meeting Aaron deferred yet again to another day.

12

At the town's edge lay a vast lake, a familiar sight to Aaron and Sara from their high school days. It was here, in the waning days after graduation and before college beckoned, that they often found solace. As the sun dipped low, its final beams danced upon the water's surface, casting a mesmerizing display of fiery hues. Above, the wind whispered through the treetops, a mournful melody that seemed to disregard the lower reaches, leaving them cloaked in heavy humidity. Beneath the canopy, insects sought refuge, forming a dense cloud near the water's edge, while leaves rustled softly, adding to the symphony of nature's whispers.

At the lake's edge sat a solitary figure, her bare feet skimming the water's edge. Like a statue carved from stone, she remained unmoving, her long hair hanging limp, weighed down by the dampness of the air. Her white dress, now stained by the clammy earth, draped loosely around her frame, unnoticed by its wearer. In this moment of solitude, there was no concern for appearances, no one to judge the state of her attire. She sat in silent contemplation, her thoughts as deep as the waters before her.

Gazing across the water, Precious seemed transported to another realm, mesmerized by the shimmering light. Her fingers absently traced the contours of her neck and chest, searching for something long forgotten. Before she even heard or saw him, she sensed the presence of the person intruding upon her solitude. Without surprise, she identified him as Marcus, even before he settled beside her in the mire.

Precious turned slowly to face her guest, her demeanor belying any residual anger as she spoke to him. "What brings you here, Marcus?" Her thoughts for the unwanted company by her side did not come through in her remarks.

Looking into his eyes, she saw that his attention was straying, and she became aware that her dress had slid up onto her lap, exposing more of her legs. Still, she had given it little thought up until now, the minutiae irrelevant in her detached mood at the moment. Her features showed a hint of disdain, which she did not try to hide.

Marcus couldn't help but be drawn to the milky white expanse of Precious's legs peeking out from beneath her dress. His demonic instincts stirred within him, craving the youthful flesh before him. The perverse nature of his origins whispered temptations, urging him to indulge in the pleasures of the mortal form. Yet, despite the tantalizing prospect, Precious remained resolute in her detachment, unwilling to succumb to Marcus's desires.

With a silent determination, Precious decided she would endure an eternity of searching for what she wanted in the world rather than allow Marcus to lay a hand on her. Slowly, she lowered her legs until they met the damp ground, pulling her dress down to conceal them from Marcus's gaze.

Marcus's eyes drew upward slowly without a hint of trying to conceal what he had been doing. "What were you reaching for, Precious?" Marcus's inquiry broke the silence, his voice tinged with curiosity.

Precious glanced down at her hands, reflecting on the locket that once rested against her chest, a tangible connection to her mortal past. Now lost, its absence left an ache within her, though she refused to acknowledge it, even to herself.

"What do you want, Demon?" Precious's inquiry carried a sharper edge this time, as she sought to elicit a more direct response from Marcus. Meeting his eyes, she noted the lingering lust within them, though it seemed tempered, barely discernible.

Marcus's voice, smooth yet dissonant, resonated like silk dragged over cement as he replied. His features, usually composed, contorted into a smile that appeared fragile, as if molded from delicate plaster. "I came to offer you my company, Precious," he stated, his gaze sweeping the surroundings in search of a suitable spot to settle. Opting to remain squatting rather than dirty himself in the muck near the shore, Marcus seemed mindful of maintaining a semblance of decorum despite his true nature. The oppressive humidity already wreaked havoc on his pressed suit, and the mud had marred his shoes; he couldn't afford further damage to his attire.

"I don't need your company," Precious declared, her voice firm as she turned away from Marcus, fixing her gaze once more on the tranquil expanse of water. Yet, the serenity she once found in its depths seemed elusive now, shattered by the presence of the demon beside her. Though she yearned for solitude, she begrudgingly acknowledged that even Marcus provided a welcome distraction from her inner turmoil.

Sensing Precious's mood, Marcus discerned her desire for companionship without the need for supernatural insight. Recognizing an opportunity to glean information, he resolved to remain by her side, coaxing out the motives that had drawn her to this desolate spot. In his quest for knowledge, he probed gently, aware of her natural reticence, hoping to uncover the secrets she harbored.

"Why do you meddle with these humans?" Marcus's inquiry cut through the silence, his tone laced with curiosity and perhaps a hint of judgment.

Precious paused, contemplating Marcus's question. Initially inclined to question his motives, she ultimately decided to divulge the truth, weighing the consequences of her disclosure. After all, there was little Marcus could do to impede her plans. "I don't meddle; I wait," she clarified, her voice steady despite the gravity of her words. "I seek the descendants of Rachael and Elbert, the progenitors of this form I inhabit. Their bloodline holds the key to recreating this vessel. It may appear human, but it harbors a lineage crucial to my existence. This body, now lifeless, binds me unwillingly. I seek liberation, but it eludes me."

Locking her bright blue eyes with Marcus's dark gaze, Precious couldn't help but feel a flicker of amusement at the fire she imagined simmering behind his eyes. A smirk danced across her lips as she entertained the notion of extinguishing that flame at a whim, a reminder that Marcus posed less of a threat than he might have believed.

"To free myself from this vessel, I require a host of identical bloodline," she explained, her voice tinged with a hint of satisfaction at the prospect. "For generations, I've monitored the descendants of this body's lineage, patiently awaiting the right moment. Once the chosen child is born, I can usurp their spirit, claiming the body as my own. With a living vessel, I'll possess the strength of my celestial origins, unshackled from this stagnant, lifeless form."

Yet, Precious withheld a crucial detail from Marcus, a detail that hinted at her true intentions. What she didn't reveal was her ultimate plan: to use the newfound freedom of a living body as a springboard to reclaim her place among the angels, to ascend once more to the heavens she once called home.

Marcus absorbed Precious's revelations in silence, his mind churning with newfound knowledge. With a deliberate motion, he rose from his squatting position, striding purposefully to the edge of the clearing they occupied. Meanwhile, Precious gracefully stood, her gaze following Marcus's movements with a sense of detached interest. As she rose, the earth relinquished its hold on her attire, leaving her pristine and untouched by the muck.

Lost in contemplation, Marcus's attention drifted away from Precious for several minutes. His gaze wandered upwards, entranced by the avian ballet playing out among the branches, illuminated by the soft glow of dusk filtering through the canopy. Eventually, his path circled back to where Precious stood, bathed in the fading light reflecting off the tranquil surface of the lake.

Approaching silently from behind, Marcus enveloped Precious in an embrace, his arms encircling her petite waist. However, instead of finding solace in his touch, Precious recoiled, a shudder of revulsion coursing through her. Swiftly extricating herself from his grasp, she sidestepped out of his reach, leaving Marcus standing alone, his arms empty and his intentions unfulfilled.

Marcus remained unfazed by Precious's rejection, his desire for her flesh only heightened by her avoidance. "Why seek mortality once more? Isn't that what led to your predicament in the first place?" he queried, his tone tinged with curiosity.

Precious's laughter, sudden and sharp, pierced the tranquil air of the clearing, causing nearby creatures to scatter in alarm. "You fail to comprehend," she retorted, her voice carrying a note of frustration. "In this mortal shell, I am imprisoned. My essence tethered to this plane, unable to transcend. But with a new vessel, I can break free from this existence."

Despite her conviction, Precious hesitated, grappling with the urge to reveal her true aspirations to Marcus. She longed to return to the celestial realm, to once again bask in the glory of God's presence. The desire to reclaim what she had lost centuries ago burned within her, an unquenchable longing that she dared not reveal to her demonic companion.

Marcus's understanding crystallized into clarity. The pieces of the puzzle fell into place before him, a revelation unfolding without the need for Precious to spell it out. Kafziel, the fallen angel, remained barred from heaven as long as Precious's soul remained tethered to her mortal form. However, once she reincarnated into a new body, born of the lineage of Rachael and Elbert, she would once again walk the earth in the flesh, free from the spectral existence that bound her.

The intricacies of Precious's plan unfolded in Marcus's mind. She required the genetic duplicates of Rachael and Elbert, the biological parents of her current vessel, to facilitate the rebirth of Precious. Once the cycle completed, Precious's soul would vacate the borrowed body, allowing its original inhabitant to reclaim their rightful place.

A gnawing sense of unease crept over Marcus as he pondered the implications of Precious's scheme. Something felt amiss, a nagging doubt lingering just beyond reach. Yet, in that moment, he couldn't pinpoint the flaw in her plan. Resolving to seek counsel from his master, Marcus realized the gravity of the knowledge he now possessed, understanding the need to convey his findings without delay.

With Precious falling into a contemplative silence, it became evident that she had said her piece. As she wandered off into the woods, her desire for solitude hung palpable in the air. Marcus, sensing her need for space, wasted no time lingering. Once Precious vanished from view, he wasted no time in departing, his destination clear: to report back to his master.

SAMAEL materialized at the lakeside picnic area just as Marcus wandered aimlessly, lost in thought, his mind elsewhere as he ambled without paying heed to his surroundings. From the shelter of the trees, Samael observed, having silently witnessed the exchange between Marcus, the demon, and Kafziel by the water's edge, their obliviousness to his presence absolute.

His thoughts turned to Marcus's blatant display of desire towards Kafziel, his hands even daring to touch his celestial sister. The sight stoked a simmering anger within Samael, yet he exercised restraint, cognizant of the demon's utility in the unfolding events. Resolved, Samael decided to grant Marcus a temporary reprieve, allowing him to fulfill his purpose before exacting retribution. Two compelling reasons fueled his decision: Marcus's unauthorized intrusion into the mortal realm years prior without Samael's sanction, and the audacious actions witnessed mere moments ago.

Samael's focus shifted back to the pair as they parted ways. Kafziel lingered by the water's edge, her gaze fixed on the tranquil surface, while Marcus, lost in thought, wandered unwittingly in Samael's direction. As the sun's rays danced on the water, Samael understood what captivated Kafziel's attention. He could almost hear the celestial choirs echoing their praises to the Father. Despite feeling the pull of longing to join them, he resisted, mindful of his assigned duty.

Meanwhile, Marcus continued his aimless stroll, his hand absentmindedly grazing his chin as his gaze trailed along the path. Unaware of Samael's presence, he ambled closer, his mind preoccupied with inner musings. It wasn't until Samael's voice pierced the air that Marcus jolted to a stop, startled by the sudden interruption.

"Hello, Marcus," Samael greeted in a nonchalant tone, devoid of emotion.

Marcus glanced at Samael, then quickly cast a glance over his shoulder, checking if Precious had spotted them. It was evident he was anxious about being seen.

Samael's smile was cryptic. "Don't worry. Kafziel is oblivious to our presence. She's..." He paused, searching for the right words. "Lost in thought," he finally settled on.

The reassurance seemed to ease Marcus's concern, but the unexpected encounter with Samael still left him uneasy.

"What brings you here, master?" Marcus asked, his tone deferential as he dipped his head in respect.

Samael fought the urge to reprimand the demon. He knew Marcus's deference stemmed from fear of annihilation, not genuine respect.

"Save your false respect," Samael dismissed with a wave of his hand. "Regarding Kafziel, what were you doing there, and what had you so preoccupied that you failed to notice my presence until you were almost upon me?" he inquired.

Marcus recalled Precious's hand gesture towards her neck, her cryptic words, and his subsequent musings on its significance. He deliberated on how much to reveal, but upon meeting Samael's gaze, he realized full disclosure was necessary. There was no point in attempting to deceive the being before him.

"I was conversing with..." Marcus hesitated, recalling Precious's reluctance for him to use her celestial name. However, Samael had no such hesitation. Resolving to refer to her by the name she had chosen, he continued, "I was speaking with Precious, attempting to discern her intentions. She has resided in this town for centuries, and I was intrigued."

As they strolled onward, Samael's hands remained clasped behind his back, his focus drifting to the verdant canopy of trees enveloping them. Speaking over his shoulder, he inquired, "And what have you gleaned of Kafziel's intentions?"

"Precious aims to liberate herself from the vessel confining her," Marcus revealed, keeping a measured distance behind Samael, his gaze fixed on him. "She awaits the emergence of a suitable vessel from the living bloodline of the body she currently occupies, intending to transfer her essence into it."

Samael fell silent for a brief moment, his mind swirling with thoughts as he pondered the weight of this crucial revelation. There was a lingering sense of something elusive, a puzzle piece that refused to slot into place. He had long been aware of Kafziel and her coven's activities, yet had chosen to overlook their machinations for centuries. It was only recently, prompted by a mysterious pull towards Ionia, that he had felt compelled to investigate why a demon from Hell would take an interest in the affairs of the city. Upon his arrival, he had uncovered the truth behind Kafziel's prolonged presence in the town and the inexplicable string of deaths plaguing its inhabitants.

But something didn't quite add up. While Kafziel appeared to be unrelated to the deaths, they bore the unmistakable mark of supernatural origins. And the presence of Marcus, the demon, only added another layer of mystery. After all, Marcus had only been in Kafziel's company for a mere fifteen to twenty years.

Samael mulled over the revelation that Kafziel sought a suitable vessel for her essence to inhabit. It struck him as unnecessary, for in his understanding, her existence was immutable, transcending the bounds of mortal vessels. He came to an abrupt halt, nearly causing Marcus to collide into him, as his thoughts began to coalesce. If he set aside the enigma of the deaths, only one pressing question remained: What was Kafziel's true purpose? Marcus had provided a clue, and recent observations had furnished further insight into her intentions.

Turning to face Marcus, Samael remained silent, his gaze piercing as he contemplated the demon before him. As the pieces of the puzzle fell into place, one thing became abundantly clear: Kafziel had to be stopped. Though details regarding the vessel she sought remained elusive, Samael was resolute in his determination to prevent her plans from coming to fruition.

Samael's gaze shifted upward, his expression clouded with frustration. "Tch," he uttered in disdain, realizing that no solace or aid would be forthcoming from the celestial realms. He harbored doubts that heavenly intervention could thwart the impending catastrophe he foresaw.

While he harbored no desire to obliterate Kafziel, he recognized the necessity of halting her designs. Yet, confronted with her unique status as neither living nor dead, and her angelic nature, Samael found himself bound by the constraints of divine mandates. Contemplating the dilemma, he surmised that traditional methods of dealing with angels were ineffective against Kafziel. He paused, pondering the potential solution.

It dawned on him that, while celestial weaponry could dispatch an angel, such an outcome was not his desired outcome for Kafziel. Her current form, existing in a liminal state between celestial and mortal, posed a unique challenge. However, Samael conjectured that the proximity of something closely related to the undead vessel she inhabited might render her temporarily mortal, susceptible to mortal intervention.

Samael's lips curled into a knowing smile, satisfaction gleaming in his eyes as he discerned a potential solution to the looming crisis. Yet, despite this revelation, uncertainty lingered, shrouding his thoughts in a veil of ambiguity. His mind drifted back to the enigmatic priest, who had shown signs of unease in the presence of Kafziel. Perhaps the clergyman held key insights that could aid in the execution of his plan. However, Samael harbored reservations about revealing his connection to Precious, opting instead to dispatch Marcus to convey the crucial information discreetly.

As for himself, Samael turned his attention to four individuals within the town whose auras bore the unmistakable mark of celestial influence. Two young men and two young women. It was time to delve deeper into their backgrounds, unraveling the tangled threads of fate that bound them to this unfolding drama.

LATER that evening, Marcus found himself seated in Father Gordon's office, though he hadn't traversed the threshold conventionally; he simply... materialized. Father Gordon's startled reaction was swift, his abrupt movement sending an old chair clattering to the floor as he stumbled backward, seeking support against the bookcase that lined the wall. His fingers grazed the weathered leather bindings of the books, scrambling for purchase to steady himself amidst the unexpected intrusion.

"How did you get in here?" Father Gordon's voice trembled with a mix of surprise and fear, his heart racing to keep pace with the sudden turn of events.

A smirk curled across Marcus' lips, smooth and calculated. He couldn't help but savor the fear emanating from Father Gordon like a tangible aura, but his purpose here lay elsewhere. He had consulted with his master and had been tasked with speaking to Father Gordon.

"Sit down, Father Gordon," Marcus said, his tone casual and inviting.

Father Gordon remained suspicious, his fear lingering like a stubborn shadow. He realized that as long as Marcus was in his office, his unease would persist. After a few moments of controlled breathing, Father Gordon managed to regain his composure enough to retake his seat. "How did you get in here?" he inquired, his voice tinged with suspicion.

Marcus's eyelids drooped lazily as his hands lifted in a nonchalant gesture, tilting his head to the side. "Does that really matter?" he countered, his tone still guarded.

Father Gordon's eyes narrowed in response, and in an instant, a pungent odor filled the room, overwhelming in its intensity. Recoiling at the stench of noxious brimstone, Father Gordon stared hard at Marcus. "Are you a demon?" he asked slowly, the realization dawning on him, accompanied by the unsettling thought of why he kept experiencing these unexpected supernatural encounters.

"I won't hurt you. That's not why I'm here," Marcus reassured, his voice unnervingly pleasant. "I came to talk to you about... Precious."

"This is holy ground, demon!" Father Gordon shot back, his astonishment evident.

Marcus remained unperturbed, finding amusement in Father Gordon's assumption that he couldn't set foot on church grounds. "Wherever man resides, evil lurks. In the brightest light, shadows linger. The potential for darkness exists within each and every one of you. There can be no light without darkness, and you, of all people, should understand that," Marcus explained calmly. "Every doubt you've ever harbored has created an opening to exploit. No matter how devout you may be, you cannot deceive or outmaneuver anyone with your falsehoods. When you attempt to deceive, you're merely stepping into my domain, my territory, my realm."

Father Gordon harbored doubts, his skepticism fueled by the questionable source of the information before him. Yet, he couldn't ignore the unsettling truth that the being known as Satan often intertwined his deceit with elements of truth, albeit twisted to suit his agenda. Half-truths, he knew, were as insidious as outright lies, capable of inciting conflict and chaos.

"You lie," Father Gordon asserted plainly, though uncertainty gnawed at him.

Marcus chuckled lazily, his demeanor unruffled. "You don't believe that," he countered. "And why would I need to deceive you? What purpose would a lie serve me in this moment?"

Father Gordon felt his conviction waver under Marcus's scrutiny. It was evident in his demeanor, impossible to conceal. His emotions lay bare on his face, a transparent reflection of his inner turmoil.

"Don't worry, Father Gordon, I didn't come here to tempt you, or to 'corrupt your soul," Marcus said, punctuating his words with air quotes, then continued, "as much as I would enjoy it. I came to pass on information," he added casually, his gaze drifting out the window.

When he spoke again, his voice dropped to a whisper, a harsh, rasping whisper that seemed to echo with the crackling of hot coals. The words, imprinted on him by his master, flowed from his lips as if compelled. Father Gordon's gaze remained fixed on Marcus's reflection in the window, studying his features intently.

"That... entity known as Precious is an abomination, as much to you as to me. Removing her from existence would be in your best interest," Marcus continued, his control returning as he adjusted his suit jacket with casual precision. He shrugged and turned back to face Father Gordon, a smile playing at his lips.

"And how in the world am I supposed to make that happen?" Father Gordon asked sarcastically. "Am I just supposed to 'pray' her away? If that's the case, the inhabitants of this town have been doing that for eons, and look at the results," he added, gesturing around him with exaggerated motions to emphasize the lack of change.

"Seek something that she has lost and place it in her undead hands. The mark of something loved, lost, and cherished while she was alive will bring her back to life. You can finish her then," Marcus explained.

"That still doesn't make sense. How is that supposed to work?" Father Gordon pressed.

Marcus met his gaze with indifference. "I'm just relaying a message. It was revealed to me by someone that in order to kill her, she needs to be in some form of mortal vessel. He suggested that something significant from the girl's life might aid in the process."

It was the last thing Father Gordon heard from Marcus before the demon flashed a malignant smile and vanished in a puff of acrid, noxious smoke, tinged with the scent of wormwood and sulfur.

Father Gordon found himself adrift in a sea of confusion. His senses told him the demon had been real, yet his rational mind insisted it couldn't be true. What puzzled him most was why he had been given this information in the first place.

Why now? Why couldn't the demon deal with Precious himself? After some time lost in contemplation, Father Gordon realized he wouldn't find answers alone. Resolving to revisit the questions later, he turned to his journal, intent on capturing his thoughts for further reflection.

13

The sun had long set after cast shadows across the city. Early evening found Aaron and Sara settled onto the couch in the living room of Sara's house, recapping the morning's turmoil. Aaron's expression was troubled, his brow furrowed with the emotions evoked during the unresolved conflict. Sara lay up in Aaron's arms while reclining on the couch.

"So, what was that between you and Michael this morning?" Sara asked over her shoulder. Her voice was gentle, probing, as she reached out to grasp Aaron's hand in hers.

Aaron sighed heavily, his gaze fixed on some distant point beyond the window. "I don't know, Sara. He just blew up out of nowhere. I don't even know where to begin trying to figure out what he was angry about."

Sara listened intently, her heart aching for both Aaron and Michael. She knew the dynamics of their relationship well, the unspoken tensions that simmered beneath the surface. "Do you think he's upset because of... us?" she ventured cautiously.

Aaron's shoulders tensed at the mention of their relationship, his fingers tightening around hers. "I don't see why he would be. Michael's always been supportive of us, hasn't he?"

Sara bit her lip, her thoughts racing as she struggled to find the right words. She turned away from Aaron and down at her lap. She sighed heavily. She knew there was more to Michael's outburst than met the eye, a deeper longing for connection and understanding.

"Maybe it's not about us," she suggested softly. "Maybe Michael just feels like he's been... left behind."

The words hung heavy in the air between them, laden with unspoken truths and painful realizations. Sara could feel the pressure of Michael's accusation pressing down on her, accusing her of stealing Aaron away.

But she couldn't bring herself to accept that narrative, couldn't bear the thought of being the cause of rift between the two brothers who meant the world to her. "I know you love him, Aaron," she said quietly. "But maybe... maybe he just needs more of your time."

Aaron recoiled at the suggestion, his jaw set in stubborn defiance. "I can't, Sara. Not after what he said to me this morning. I won't be guilt-tripped into spending time with him."

Sara's heart sank at Aaron's resolute refusal, the divide between them widening with each passing moment. She knew the path ahead would be fraught with challenges and difficult decisions, but she also knew that she couldn't bear to see Aaron torn between his loyalty to his brother and his love for her.

Sara and Aaron sat in silence, each lost in their own thoughts, grappling with the weight of the choices that lay ahead.

"Why not?" Sara finally asked, breaking the heavy silence that hung between them.

Aaron shifted on the couch, his restless energy palpable as he rose to his feet. Sara watched him pace the length of the living room, her concern growing with each restless step he took. Finally, he turned to face her, his expression troubled.

"I don't know," Aaron admitted, his voice heavy with uncertainty. He ran a hand through his hair, the gesture betraying his inner turmoil. "There's just so much going on right now. With Mom's passing and the funeral... It's been overwhelming." Aaron began pacing again.

Sara listened intently, her empathy evident in the gentle curve of her lips. "What else, Aaron?" she prodded gently, reaching out to touch his hand as he passed by.

Aaron hesitated, his gaze dropping to the floor as he struggled to put his feelings into words. "It's just... everything," he confessed, his voice barely above a whisper. "I feel like I'm drowning, Sara. And I don't know how to make it stop."

Sara nodded. She pulled him closer.

"There was that..." Aaron began, his voice trailing off into silence as he struggled to find the right words.

"What?" Sara prompted, her curiosity piqued. She leaned forward on the couch, her eyes searching his troubled expression.

"I heard her," Aaron murmured so softly that Sara almost didn't catch it.

Sara's heart ached at the pain evident in Aaron's voice. She wanted nothing more than to be his rock, his unwavering support in times of need.

"I'm here for you. You can tell me what's on your mind," Sara reassured him, her voice gentle and comforting.

Aaron took a deep breath, steeling himself before he spoke again. "I heard her laughter during the wake service."

Sara's brows knitted together in confusion. "Whose laughter did you hear? I don't recall hearing anything like that."

"It was the little girl," Aaron revealed, settling back down beside Sara. "The same little girl that I thought..." His voice trailed off, a reminder that he hadn't yet shared the full extent of his experience with Sara.

"When Mom collapsed in the house after we got home, I saw a little girl in the kitchen," Aaron admitted, his tone heavy with the weight of the memory.

Sara recoiled slightly, her hand instinctively coming to cover her mouth in shock. While she had complete faith in Aaron's honesty, the thought of a spectral presence in their home was unsettling.

Sara eagerly requested more details from Aaron, who readily provided them. Afterwards, she took a moment to process his descriptions and words. Memories of their childhood in the city of Ionia flooded back to her, tales of eerie occurrences whispered among children. Stories they had once dismissed as mere fiction now seemed to hold a grain of truth.

Turning to Aaron, she suggested, "Perhaps we can unearth more information about this somewhere."

Aaron pondered their options for a moment.

"Let's try searching through old records at city hall to see if the stories we heard as children are true or not," Sara proposed.

"That sounds like a good idea," Aaron agreed. "We can start tomorrow morning."

Sara enveloped Aaron in a comforting embrace, feeling his tension melt as he rested his head on her shoulder. She held him close, as if shielding him from the world's turmoil. Tenderly, she kissed the top of his head, silently reassuring him of her unwavering presence.

"Just let go for now. We'll tackle everything one step at a time," Sara whispered soothingly.

After a while, Aaron felt a sense of calm settle over him, knowing Sara would be there when he woke. Reluctantly, he bid her goodnight, grateful for her comforting presence. As Sara headed to her room, he settled onto the couch, resigned to spending the night there. Despite her parents' insistence on separate sleeping arrangements, Aaron found solace in knowing Sara was just a room away.

THE following morning, Aaron resolved to shift his focus away from his troubles. He recalled Sara's suggestion of visiting the town hall to search through old records and newspapers for any mention of the mysterious little girl. The idea resonated with him; he was eager to delve into this enigmatic puzzle and uncover the truth behind the unsettling mystery.

Meanwhile, Sara made the decision to accompany Aaron to the town hall. She pointed out to him that her background in archaeology and history studies could prove beneficial. Years of conducting research in the school library had honed her skills in navigating vast archives and uncovering hidden gems of information. She assured Aaron that she knew where to look and what to search for amidst the sea of records they were bound to encounter. Recognizing the wisdom in her words, Aaron readily agreed. He felt a sense of relief knowing that her expertise would be a valuable asset in their quest for answers, realizing he was stepping into unfamiliar territory and could use all the help he could get.

The town hall's records division proved to be impressively comprehensive. Given the tight-knit nature of the small community, access to these records was readily available to all who sought it. The rooms beneath the town hall building were open to anyone, inviting visitors to peruse the historical archives at their leisure. Sara wasted no time in beginning her search, heading straight for the microfiche containing the local newspaper archives.

Years ago, in a stroke of foresight, the local newspaper had taken to preserving back issues on microfiche, leaving a copy available in the town hall's records room. Sara settled in front of the microfiche reader, the soft hum of the machine filling the room. She scrolled through the archived newspapers, her eyes scanning the pages for any mention of the elusive little girl. After an hour of this, she realized that she would have to concentrate her search more. There was too much information for her to sift through efficiently.

Someone had meticulously cross-referenced the contents of these papers into a searchable database on the computer. Alongside the newspaper articles were the birth and death census records from the local hospital, creating a comprehensive repository of the town's history. Sara believed that she would gather information more effectively by using the computer first to sort through the information. With this in mind, she moved and seated herself at the computer terminal, her fingers poised over the keyboard as she formulated her query.

With a few deft keystrokes, Sara entered her request, hoping for a straightforward search result. However, the computer's response was far from what she had anticipated. The screen filled with a flood of results, displaying hundreds of articles spanning centuries. The dates ranged from the town's founding in the early 1700s to the present day, a staggering array of information that seemed incongruous with the town's modest size.

Beside her, Aaron leaned in closer, his gaze fixed on the screen as he took in the overwhelming volume of data. The realization dawned on both of them that this seemingly quiet town held secrets far beyond what they had imagined. Sara glanced at Aaron, her eyes reflecting a mixture of determination and intrigue. She knew they had their work cut out for them, but she was more determined than ever to unravel the mysteries hidden within these records.

"That can't be right," Sara exclaimed, a healthy dose of skepticism coloring her voice. "There are far too many deaths of young girls here. It's more than what could be explained by simple accidents, diseases, or birth defects."

"You're absolutely right," Aaron concurred, his brow furrowing in confusion. "Those numbers seem off. Maybe try running the search again. Perhaps there was a mistake in the criteria you entered."

Sara nodded, though she knew her search criteria had been accurate. Still, she indulged Aaron's suggestion and entered the query once more. Perhaps a keystroke error had slipped by her, or some other glitch had occurred. Anything seemed more plausible than the staggering results displayed before them. For the numbers to be accurate, the town's population would have to nearly double.

The computer whirred for a few moments before presenting the same unsettling information once again.

"There it is," Sara confirmed, her voice laced with disbelief. "All the girls between the ages of birth to five or ten... but it's just too many, even for a town of this size. Something doesn't add up."

"Maybe we should narrow it down to just one specific day," Aaron suggested, a furrow forming between his brows. "And we should include male children in the search too. Does the computer have any reference numbers for the fifteenth of July from ten years ago?"

Sara nodded, her fingers flying across the keyboard as she retrieved the requested information. "Yes," she confirmed, her voice tinged with a note of determination. She recited a series of numbers, and Aaron quickly jotted them down in a nearby notepad.

"The microfiche files are on the other side of the room," Sara continued, gesturing over Aaron's shoulder to the rows of filing cabinets. He turned to glance in the direction she indicated, mentally preparing himself for the task ahead.

"Are you going to be able to find the one you need?" Sara's voice was filled with concern, and Aaron felt a gentle pressure on his arm as she reached out to stop him from leaving just yet. Her touch was warm and grounding, a reassuring presence amidst the mounting uncertainty.

"Why that particular date, my love?" Sara inquired, a playful glint in her eyes as she turned to face Aaron.

Aaron's smile was mischievous as he leaned in to kiss her lightly on the cheek. Before she could react, he playfully pinched her on the butt, eliciting a surprised yelp from Sara.

"Ouch," Sara exclaimed, though the pinch was more teasing than painful, a fact that Aaron was well aware of.

"On the fifteenth of July, ten years ago, I realized for the first time that I would always love you and that I would be with you for the rest of my life," Aaron revealed, his voice filled with warmth and sincerity.

Sara felt her heart swell with emotion, a lump forming in her throat as tears threatened to spill from her eyes. "That's so sweet," she murmured softly, her voice barely above a whisper.

"Thank you," Aaron replied, his eyes lingering on her for a moment before he tore himself away, leaving her at the computer. With a determined stride, he made his way to the rows of microfiche files on the other side of the room.

"I'm just going to sit here and try a few more searches. I'll catch up with you over there in a few minutes," Sara called out to Aaron's retreating figure.

With a sense of morbid curiosity, Sara typed in a new search criterion, using her own family name to see if any of the unusually high number of child deaths had occurred within her own lineage. She felt a strange compulsion to uncover the truth, to reassure herself that her family had been spared from such tragedies.

The results appeared on the screen quicker than she had anticipated, and they revealed a stark reality that left her reeling. Her initial naivety shattered as she scanned the names and dates before her. She had been convinced that the numbers were skewed, that her loved ones could not have been affected by such inexplicable occurrences. How wrong she had been.

Each entry seemed to confirm the unthinkable. Every branch of her immediate and extended family tree bore the burden of loss, with nearly every aunt, uncle, cousin, and distant relative having experienced the death of a child. It didn't make sense. Many of her relatives had only ever mentioned having one child, leaving Sara bewildered by the grim statistics laid out before her. How could this be possible?

An idea sparked in Sara's mind, prompting her to type in a new series of commands. The screen flickered, displaying the details she sought. Shock rippled through her as she scanned the results—an obituary column with both of her parents' names listed. Her heart raced, her mind reeling at the revelation. As far as she knew, she was an only child. Her parents had never mentioned any other siblings.

"Aaron, there's something here that I think you need to see," Sara called out, her voice quivering with disbelief.

Aaron remained focused on the microfiche reader, oblivious to Sara's initial attempt to get his attention. Undeterred, Sara raised her voice, hoping to break through his concentration.

"Aaron, there's something here that I think you need to see," Sara repeated, her voice carrying an urgency that caught Aaron's attention.

Startled by the worry etched on Sara's face, Aaron abandoned the microfiche reader and hurried to her side. She gestured to the screen, her eyes wide with shock and confusion. Aaron leaned in to read the display, his voice trembling as he spoke the words aloud.

"On Friday, April 25th, Allison Baker, beloved child of Leon and Norma Baker, passed away unexpectedly. Funeral services will be conducted at twelve o'clock this coming Monday at the First Ionia Church," Aaron read aloud, his voice trailing off as the weight of the words settled heavily upon them.

The revelation left Aaron feeling as though he were made of lead, each step heavier than the last. Confusion clouded his mind, rendering him unable to form a coherent thought. Beside him, Sara seemed equally stunned by the discovery.

"We've got to talk to my parents. This can't be right. I have to know the truth," Sara whispered, her voice barely audible in the stillness of the room. "My parents never mentioned that they had a child before I was born."

The air around them seemed to thicken with unspoken questions, the weight of the unknown pressing down upon their shoulders. Aaron nodded, his mind racing as he tried to make sense of the newfound information.

"Yeah, we should... we should definitely talk to them," Aaron replied, his voice tinged with uncertainty. "There has to be an explanation for this."

Together, they made their way out of the records room, the journey back feeling longer and more uncertain than before. The once-familiar halls of the town hall now seemed foreign and foreboding, casting shadows that whispered of hidden secrets.

Aaron couldn't shake the feeling of unease that had settled in the pit of his stomach. The mystery surrounding Allison Baker's birth and death being kept from Sara loomed large in his mind, casting a dark cloud over their once ordinary lives. With each passing moment, the need for answers grew more urgent, propelling them forward into the unknown.

"Yeah, well, that article isn't the only thing we've got to ask them about. That isn't the only first born to have died unexpectedly. Over half of the obituary columns that deals with deaths on the day that you gave me are for first-born children. It seems that there is an epidemic in Ionia that affects the first born child of every family," Aaron said, his voice laced with unease.

Sara's hand flew to her mouth, stifling a gasp of shock that threatened to escape. It wasn't the revelation itself that stunned her, but the chilling implications that unfolded before her. With trembling fingers, she hastily typed a command into the computer, her heart pounding in her chest. The results appeared on the screen, confirming her worst fears.

Aaron's parents had only had two children, as far as he knew, and Aaron was the first-born.

"Aaron, you're the first born. You are the oldest child your parents had," Sara whispered, her voice trembling with emotion. Tears welled up in her eyes, blurring her vision as she struggled to make sense of the cruel twist of fate.

Aaron watched helplessly as Sara's composure crumbled, her sobs wracking her body with heart-wrenching intensity. He reached out to her, pulling her into a tight embrace as she buried her face against his chest.

Sara looked up at him, her eyes filled with fear and desperation. "Does this mean that this epidemic with the first born will affect you too? Are you going to leave me?" she pleaded, her voice cracking with anguish.

"I don't know, Sara. I don't know," Aaron murmured, his own voice thick with emotion. The weight of uncertainty hung heavy in the air, suffocating them with its oppressive presence.

Aaron's heart clenched at the raw vulnerability in her eyes, the pain mirrored in his own heart. He cupped her face in his hands, his thumbs brushing away her tears.

"I won't leave you, Sara. I promise," Aaron vowed, his voice steady despite the turmoil raging within him. "We'll find a way to figure this out, together. I won't let anything happen to us."

Their world had been upended in an instant, uncertainty looming large over their future. But in that moment, they clung to each other amidst the chaos of unsettling revelations.

Aaron's arms enveloped her, offering a sense of comfort amidst the turmoil of their thoughts. "I'm not going anywhere, Sara. I'll be with you for eternity," he whispered, the words a vow of steadfast devotion. Yet, beneath the reassurance he offered, a gnawing uncertainty tugged at his heart.

In truth, Aaron's mind raced with a myriad of fears and questions. The revelation that he was the first-born, coupled with the grim reality of the epidemic they were uncovering, sent a shiver of dread down his spine. If what they suspected was true, then the specter of an untimely death loomed over him, casting a shadow over their fragile hopes.

A new question pierced through his panic, demanding answers in the face of uncertainty. "What's the oldest that any of the children lived to? Can you get the computer to tell you that? You know, the average age that they died at," Aaron asked, his voice tinged with urgency.

Sara felt a surge of determination amidst her own rising panic. She didn't have an immediate answer to his question, but she knew they needed to uncover every piece of information they could. With steady hands, she formulated a query, her fingers flying across the keyboard in a blur of motion.

As the computer hummed with activity, Sara held her breath, willing it to yield the answers they sought. The screen flickered to life, displaying a series of numbers and statistics that danced before her eyes. She sifted through the data, her brow furrowed in concentration, until she found what they were looking for.

"The average age of death for the first-born children is..." Sara trailed off, her voice barely above a whisper as she read the chilling numbers before her.

Aaron leaned in closer, his heart pounding in his chest as they braced themselves for the grim reality that awaited them. The weight of their discovery hung heavy in the air, casting a pall over their hopes for a future together.

Sara took a deep breath, her voice trembling slightly as she spoke the words they both dreaded to hear. "The average age... is eight years old."

Eight years old. The average age of death for the first-born children was a stark and chilling reality, one that loomed over Aaron and Sara like a specter of dread.

Aaron's mind raced with a sense of urgency, a need to confront the truth that now lay bare before them. "We've got to talk to your parents now, Sara. This can't wait," he said, his voice tinged with a mixture of fear and determination.

Sara nodded, her eyes brimming with unshed tears as she grasped Aaron's hand tightly. The discovery hung heavy between them, driving them to seek answers from the one place they hoped could shed light on this dark mystery, Sara's parents.

With a shared sense of resolve, Aaron and Sara made their way to the door, their hearts heavy with the what they were about to confront. The journey ahead was uncertain, but they knew they could not turn back now.

As they stepped outside into the cool morning air, the sun cast long shadows across the quiet streets of Ionia. Each step brought them closer to the truth, to the answers they so desperately sought. And though the path ahead was fraught with danger that might be exposed when the truth was learned. They were resolved to face it together, united in their quest to unravel the secrets that had haunted their town.

14

Katherine parked the car she had borrowed from her aunt in front of her cousins' house, the familiar sight bringing a sense of diversion from the turmoil of her thoughts. She had been feeling lonely lately, the weight of her failed relationship smothering her like a heavy shroud. Coming here was an excuse, a way to distract herself from the memories that threatened to overwhelm her.

As she walked up to the front door, she could hear the faint sound of a television from inside. The sounds of canned laughter barely audible. Taking a deep breath, she knocked, the sound echoing through the quiet street. The door swung open, as Katherine waited. The door creaked open with a tired sigh, as if it had been waiting for this moment for far too long.

A musty scent, a blend of old wood and neglect, wafted out to greet her, wrapping around her like a forgotten memory. She was greeted by her cousin Michael.

Michael stood in the doorway, a tired smile on his face as he welcomed her inside. The foyer, once grand, now stood silent and dim, the faded wallpaper peeling at the corners. The air held a heavy stillness, as if time itself had settled in to rest. Dust danced in the weak light filtering from the television, casting a melancholic haze over the space.

"Hey, Katherine! I wasn't expecting you," Michael said with a confused look on his face. After a moment's awkwardness and hesitation, he gestured, ushering her into the house. "Come on in," Michael said, stepping aside to let her enter.

"Thanks, Michael," Katherine replied, offering him a small smile as she stepped inside.

Upon the worn welcome mat, there lingered traces of what could have been a vibrant home: a few cardboard boxes forgotten in a corner, the hallway a canvas of weathered photographs with faded smiles. Yet, these remnants only served to accentuate the emptiness that now pervaded the halls.

There was a peculiar sense of displacement in the air, as though the house itself longed to be filled with laughter and warmth once more. It seemed to ache for the sound of footsteps running down the hallway, for the echo of voices raised in conversation.

But instead, it stood in silence, a sentinel to forgotten dreams and faded hopes. It wasn't a house that repelled, nor was it one that welcomed with open arms. It simply existed, suspended in a state of quiet longing, aching to be more than just walls and a roof. Michael glanced around, his gaze lingering on the remnants of his family scattered about, a bittersweet smile tugging at his lips. "Welcome home," he said softly, the words heavy with unspoken memories.

Katherine hesitated, unsure of the muted welcome Michael seemed to offer. It wasn't that he appeared unwelcoming; rather, a palpable despondency hung heavy in the air, coloring the atmosphere with an unspoken heaviness.

Following Michael into the living room, Katherine settled onto the worn couch, observing the thoughtful furrow of his brow. The silence between them seemed pregnant with unspoken words, a tension that pulled at the edges of their get together.

Without preamble, Michael leaned forward, his voice carrying the weight of a heartfelt confession. "I've missed this place feeling alive," he murmured, his gaze fixed on a spot in the worn rug, as if searching for lost pieces of the past.

Katherine listened, her heart aching with the weight of his words. Michael's memories flooded back, of childhood laughter echoing through these now still halls, of games played long into the night. The house around them seemed to sigh, as if in agreement, a silent witness to the passage of time and the burdens it carried.

"I know it's not the same," Michael continued, his voice tinged with a mix of regret and longing. "But I can't help but hope that maybe, with you here, we can bring back some of that warmth."

The air between them crackled with unresolved emotions, a dance of hesitance and longing. Katherine reached out, her hand finding his in a silent gesture of understanding.

"How can I help you find it again," she whispered. "I just found out about you guys only so long ago. I hope that I can have a tight bond with you guys as my blood relatives." Her voice was promise and a plea.

"I guess that means we've got to see more of each other in the future then. You can't be a stranger to me," said Michael.

Katherine hesitated, sensing that Michael's invitation didn't quite extend to Aaron, still wrapped in the aftermath of their recent argument. Despite this, a fragile smile touched her lips as she responded, "I'd like that.

In that moment, amidst the faded grandeur of the living room, they forged a silent pact to breathe life back into the forgotten corners of the house, to fill its empty spaces with the echoes of their shared past. The house seemed to sigh in relief, as if finally acknowledging the possibility of renewal after years of quiet resignation.

Together, they sat in the dimly lit room, lost in memories and the promise of a future tinged with hope. Eventually, Michael excused himself, disappearing into the nearby kitchen. He returned moments later, a sense of purpose in his step, carrying two delicate glasses of wine. With a quiet grace, he handed one to Katherine.

"I hope you don't mind," he began, a small, almost shy smile playing on his lips, "I took the liberty of assuming that you drink."

Katherine accepted the glass with a grateful smile and a nod. "Thank you," she murmured, her fingers curling around the stem of the glass and her voice a soft melody in the quiet room.

Her gaze fixed on the crimson liquid swirling in the glass. The crimson liquid catching the soft light of the room. It was a dance of colors, a fleeting moment of beauty amidst the shadows of the evening. She brought the glass to her lips, taking a slow, thoughtful sip, savoring the rich, velvety taste of the wine.

She looked again into the glass. Lost in the mesmerizing patterns, Katherine found herself lost in a moment of quiet contemplation. Thinking of Brian and how things ended. The warmth of the wine spread through her, a comforting embrace that eased the tension in her shoulders. Her emotions shifted from hot to cold and then bitter resentment at his treatment of her. Her face betrayed her thoughts, leading Michael to speak up about his own thoughts.

"You know, Katherine, I've been feeling a bit... left behind lately," Michael began, his eyes fixed on a spot on the floor. "Sara gets to spend so much time with Alex, and I feel like I'm always on the sidelines."

Katherine listened intently, her heart going out to her cousin. She could easily guess that the bond between Michael and his brother Alex was strong, but she hadn't realized the depth of Michael's feelings of jealousy and loneliness.

"I miss him, you know?" Michael continued, his voice tinged with longing. "I wish things were different, that we could spend more time together like we used to."

As Katherine listened, a pang of empathy tugged at her heart. She could relate to the feeling of missing someone, of longing for a connection that seemed just out of reach. But as Michael poured out his heart, Katherine found her thoughts drifting to her own past relationship.

She remembered the way she struggled to get her her ex-boyfriend to understand her work, his immaturity glaringly obvious as their relationship progressed. It was a sore point, one that had ultimately led to their breakup. Katherine was grateful, in a way, that she had discovered his true nature before things had gotten too serious.

Lost in her thoughts, Katherine realized that Michael had fallen silent, his eyes searching hers for understanding. It was then that she realized he had no idea about her own struggles, about the pain she carried from her failed relationship.

"I'm sorry, Michael," Katherine said softly, her voice barely above a whisper. "I know how hard it can be to feel left behind."

Michael nodded, a look of gratitude passing over his features. "Thanks, Katherine. It helps to know but honestly, it still doesn't make it easy to deal with."

A heavy silence settled between them, the shared emotions drifting in the air. Katherine took a deep breath, steeling herself to share a piece of herself with Michael.

"I wish I had a sibling," Katherine said suddenly, surprising herself with the admission. "I'm an only child, as far as I know. The first born."

Michael's eyes widened in surprise, a flicker of understanding passing between them. In that moment, they both realized the depth of their shared loneliness, the longing for a connection that seemed just out of reach.

"I never knew," Michael said softly, his voice filled with empathy. "I guess we both have our own struggles, huh?"

Katherine nodded, a small smile tugging at her lips. "Yeah, I guess we do."

They sat in companionable silence, their shared confessions easing the burden of their loneliness. In that moment, Katherine felt a sense of kinship with Michael, a bond forged through shared pain and understanding.

As the evening wore on, they talked late into the night, sharing stories and laughter as they navigated the complexities of their emotions. They eventually finished the bottle of wine. And in that small living room, amidst the warmth of family and the comfort of shared confidences, Katherine found a sense of peace she hadn't felt in a long time. She realized then that, even though she may not have a sibling by blood, she had found a brother in Michael. And for that, she was grateful.

Michael cleared his throat, a subtle signal of his growing awareness of the hour. Evening had settled in deeply, casting a tranquil veil over their conversation. It seemed neither of them were quite ready to bid the night farewell, but responsibilities beckoned with the dawn. He glanced at the clock, noting the late hour, and a flicker of concern crossed his features.

However, another thought tugged at his mind, one born of care and consideration for Katherine's well-being. The idea of her navigating the roads after indulging in wine sat uncomfortably in his mind.

With ample space available within the quiet confines of the house, Michael contemplated the best course of action. It seemed logical, almost necessary, that she spend the night and leave in the morning. Gathering his resolve, he broached the subject gently.

"I don't think it's a good idea for you to be driving home after having a few drinks," Michael began, his tone gentle yet firm. "Besides, it's quite late now. We have plenty of room here, if you'd like to stay the night."

Katherine glanced down at the now-empty wine glass in her hand, contemplating his words. The warmth of the wine still lingered on her lips, a subtle reminder of the evening's indulgence. Placing the glass carefully on the coffee table before her, she met Michael's gaze with a soft smile.

"Yeah, I think you're right," she admitted, her voice carrying a hint of sheepishness. "I shouldn't be driving right now. Feeling a bit... tipsy."

Michael nodded in understanding, a sense of relief washing over him. "It's settled then," he replied, a gentle warmth in his voice. "You can stay here for the night. We've got a spare room all ready for you."

A sense of gratitude washed over Katherine, mingling with the lingering effects of the wine. With a grateful nod, she accepted his offer, feeling a sense of ease settle over her.

She rose from the couch, stretching her arms above her head. "Are you sure it won't be a bother to put me up for the night?" Katherine inquired, a note of uncertainty in her voice.

Michael stood as well, a reassuring smile touching his lips. "Not a problem at all," he replied, shaking his head. "You can stay in Aaron's room tonight. He's away for the weekend, so it's all yours."

With a nod of gratitude, Katherine followed Michael's lead as he began to ascend the staircase, the old wooden steps creaking softly beneath their weight. The upper hallway unfolded before her, revealing more of the house she had yet to explore.

They walked in companionable silence, the only sound the hushed echo of their footsteps against the polished floorboards. Michael paused at the door to Aaron's room, turning to face Katherine who stood behind him, curiosity flickering in her eyes.

"Alright," he said, gesturing towards the room, "this is where you'll be staying. Let me know if you need anything at all. The bathroom is just there," he pointed to a door a few feet away, "and my room is right next door."

Katherine nodded, a sense of gratitude warming her chest. "Thank you, Michael," she murmured, her voice soft in the quiet hallway. "I appreciate it."

A faint smile tugged at Michael's lips as he stepped aside, allowing her to enter the room. "Of course. Make yourself at home," he said warmly.

Katherine had been looking at the bathroom and considering the invitation to a shower before bed. She hoped that it would help to dispel some of the dizziness from the wine. "I'll take a shower and just take one of Aaron's shirts."

Michael nodded and started to walk off before turning back towards Katherine.

As Katherine disappeared into the bathroom, the soft click of the door closing behind her, Michael couldn't shake the feeling of responsibility that lingered in the air. He was sure she would be just fine but he felt somehow compelled to tell her about some of the odd occurrences that he had witnessed in the house when he was growing up. It wasn't that he felt there was a danger, that he knew of, he just felt a need to tell her that strange things had been known to happen so that if it did occur, she wouldn't freak out.

After stepping into the bathroom, Katherine reached out to start the water, the familiar sound of rushing water filling the room as it heated up. She paused, feeling the warmth seep into the tiled space, a comforting sensation against her skin.

Turning to step back outside, she glanced around the bathroom, her eyes searching for the towels and remembering that she needed something to change into from Aaron's room after her shower. Just as she reached for the door handle, she was surprised to find Michael standing in the hallway, his presence unexpected yet somehow reassuring.

"Oh, hey," Katherine greeted him with a small smile, a hint of surprise in her voice. "Didn't expect to see you here."

Michael returned her smile, though there was a shadow of concern in his eyes. "I just wanted to make sure you're all settled in," he explained, his voice soft in the quiet of the hallway.

Katherine nodded, feeling a wave of gratitude wash over her at his thoughtfulness. "Thanks," she replied, a genuine warmth in her tone. "I appreciate it."

Michael found himself speaking further before he could fully form the words. "You know, there have been some... unusual occurrences in this house over the years," Michael said, his tone careful and measured, trying not to alarm Katherine.

Michael watched as a flicker of curiosity and caution danced in Katherine's eyes, her expression a mix of intrigue and apprehension. He hurriedly continued, saying, "I just wanted to let you know that weird things have happened in this house."

Katherine still continued to look at him as before.

"It's not that I think there's any danger," Michael continued, wanting to reassure her. "But, well, I thought it might be best to let you know. Just in case."

Katherine furrowed her brow slightly, her curiosity piqued. "Weird things?" she echoed, a note of skepticism in her voice.

Michael nodded, a rueful smile tugging at his lips. "Yeah, really weird things."

"Like strange noises, lights flickering, that sort of thing?" Katherine asked, trying to downplay the eerie nature of the occurrences.

"I just didn't want you to be caught off guard if something... unexpected happens," Michael added, his voice trailing off.

Katherine took a moment to process his words, the faint sound of water running in the background adding a soothing backdrop to their conversation. She studied Michael's earnest expression, sensing the genuine concern beneath his attempt at nonchalance.

"Are you telling me the house is haunted?" Katherine asked, a playful smile gracing her lips as she took Michael's words as a jest.

"I'm serious," Michael replied earnestly, his tone tinged with a hint of concern. "I don't want to alarm you, but there have been a couple of occasions where a little girl appeared in the house. We don't know who or what she is, but she doesn't stay long, and there hasn't been anything else."

Katherine's smile faltered slightly, her playful demeanor giving way to a more contemplative expression. "Alright," she conceded, her tone carrying a hint of seriousness. "If you say so. I'll just stay in the room after my shower, then. Hopefully, I won't run into that ghost."

With that, Katherine turned to make her way to Aaron's room, Michael's words lingering in the air around her. She stopped just before entering the room. Over her shoulder, she called out to him, a note of assurance in her voice.

"Thank you for letting me know," she replied, her voice soft but steady. "I'll keep that in mind but I don't think I have to worry about a ghost, though," she said with a soft chuckle, her hand resting on the door handle. "I've had a guardian angel watching out for me my whole life."

With a nod of acknowledgment, Michael offered her a reassuring smile. "I'm sure you'll be just fine," he said, a hint of warmth in his voice. He hoped he hadn't alarmed her too much with his warning, but it felt better to have shared the information.

As she disappeared into the room, Michael couldn't help but feel a sense of relief wash over him. Despite his earlier reservations about alarming Katherine, he was grateful for her lighthearted response to his warning.

With a sigh, he turned and made his way down the hallway, the faint sound of running water drifting through the hallway accompanied by the sound of Katherine's humming drifting out from behind him from Aaron's room. As he settled into his own room for the night, the quiet of the house enveloped him.

Alone in the dimly lit room, Katherine took a moment to survey her surroundings. The room was cozy, with a neatly made bed and a scattering of Aaron's belongings lending a sense of familiarity to the space. She quickly found something to wear to bed in the dresser.

Her gaze drifted to the closed door of the bathroom, the promise of a warm shower beckoning invitingly. With a grateful sigh, she crossed the room and turned the handle, stepping into the small but well-appointed space.

As the warm water cascaded over her, washing away the remnants of the day, Katherine couldn't help but feel a sense of peace settle over her. The soft towels, the gentle hum of the old pipes, it all felt strangely comforting.

After her shower, clad in one of Aaron's oversized t-shirts, Katherine returned to the room feeling refreshed and more at ease. She sank into the soft embrace of the bed, the weight of the day's events finally catching up to her.

With a contented sigh, she closed her eyes, letting the gentle rhythm of the house lull her into a peaceful slumber. In the quiet of the room, amidst the faint scent of Aaron's cologne and the soft glow of the bedside lamp, Katherine drifted off to sleep, grateful for the unexpected refuge her cousin had provided.

15

Sara and Aaron had been waiting at her house for a few hours, the early afternoon sunlight filtering through the windows. Sara's parents were still at work, so they had the house to themselves. There was an air of anticipation between them, a list of questions hovering in the room like unspoken echoes.

They sat in the living room, surrounded by the quiet of the house. Sara fidgeted with the hem of her sweater, her mind buzzing with all the inquiries they had. Aaron, on the other hand, sat with a furrowed brow, lost in his thoughts.

"Did they know about the deaths of the first-born children?" Sara wondered aloud, her voice barely above a whisper.

"Why didn't they tell you about your older sibling?" Aaron added, his tone tinged with curiosity and a hint of frustration.

"And what about the ghost of the little girl?" Sara asked, her eyes flickering towards the hallway as if expecting to see her.

Aaron nodded in agreement, his gaze fixed on the door as if willing her parents to arrive sooner.

But amidst all these questions, Aaron harbored one that weighed heavily on his mind, one that felt deeply personal. How did all of these events, these family secrets, affect him as a first born?

Time seemed to stretch on as they waited, the tension in the room palpable. It was sometime after five in the evening when they finally heard the familiar sound of the car pulling into the driveway. Sara's parents were home.

The front door opened, and Sara's parents entered, their expressions bright and oblivious of the storm of questions waiting for them. They greeted Sara and Aaron with warm smiles, unwary of the inquisition that was about to unfold. Sara and Aaron exchanged a glance, a silent agreement passing between them. It was time to unravel the mysteries that had haunted them for so long.

"Mom, can we have a moment to talk? Aaron and I have some questions we'd like to ask you and Dad," Sara spoke up just after the front door swung open, revealing her mother.

Norma paused, glancing at Leon who had just stepped in behind her, a quizzical expression on his face. They exchanged a brief look, both curious about the nature of the conversation but ready to listen.

"Of course, sweetheart. Let's go to the living room," Norma replied, her tone gentle as she took Sara's arm and guided her towards the cozy space.

Leon followed behind, shedding his and Norma's jackets before joining the group in the living room. The air in the room seemed to thicken with anticipation as they settled into their respective seats. Aaron and Sara sat opposite Norma and Leon, their expressions a mix of determination and curiosity.

Now that Norma and Leon had settled into the living room, they were prepared for the conversation that awaited them. Norma took a deep breath, her eyes full of concern as she turned to Sara and Aaron.

"Alright, Sara. What's on your mind? Is everything alright?" Norma asked, her voice gentle yet filled with maternal concern. She could sense the weight of seriousness in the air, the anticipation of the questions to come.

Sara sat up straighter, her eyes locking onto her mother's with a mixture of earnestness and apprehension. "We've been thinking about some things... important things," she started, her voice steady despite the nervous flutter in her chest.

Norma's heart clenched at the serious tone in Sara's voice. She reached out to squeeze Sara's hand reassuringly, silently encouraging her to continue.

"Are you two doing okay?" Norma asked, shifting her gaze between the two of them.

Sara felt a flush of embarrassment color her cheeks. She hadn't intended to make her mother worry about her and Aaron.

"No, Mom," Sara started, her voice soft but earnest, "you've misunderstood. It's not about Aaron and me, it's about some things that have been happening, and have happened, here in Ionia."

Leon's expression darkened, a flicker of discomfort crossing his features. He could already anticipate the direction of the impending questions, and he felt a surge of reluctance to delve into these memories. He wasn't prepared to confront the difficult truths of the past, especially not with the two young adults seated across from him.

Norma sensed the tension in her husband immediately, the unspoken words heavy in the air. She reached out, her hand finding his, a gesture of reassurance and understanding. But even her calming touch couldn't hold back the words that spilled from Leon's lips.

"I'm not getting into this," Leon declared firmly, his voice edged with frustration. "I want nothing to do with it. I've given all I had to give, and I've carried the regret for a lifetime. I don't owe anyone an explanation for the choices I made." The bitterness in his tone was palpable, a reflection of the pain he still carried.

Leon made a move as if to rise from his seat, a clear indication of his desire to leave the conversation behind. But Norma's gentle hand on his stayed him, anchoring him to his place on the sofa. Her touch was a silent plea for him to stay, to weather this storm of emotions with them.

Sara and Aaron exchanged a bewildered glance, the heaviness of Leon's words settling ponderously between them. They had watched as Norma reached across, her hand gently enveloping Leon's, a silent plea for unity in the face of their shared history. Her touch was tender, a fragile bridge between past regrets and the uncertain present.

"I think it's time," Norma began, her voice barely above a whisper, "that we told them, dear. I can't do this alone. I need your help. Will you please reconsider and talk to them with me?" Her eyes, brimming with unshed tears, met Leon's, a plea for understanding and support.

Norma looked so bone-weary, so vulnerable in that moment. The past had etched lines of sorrow on her face, mirroring the burden that Leon carried. She had endured just as much as he had, forced to navigate the shadows of their shared history alone.

Leon felt a pang of guilt and helplessness wash over him at the sight of Norma's pleading expression. He couldn't bear to see her struggle alone, couldn't leave the two young adults in the dark about the secrets that haunted their town.

With a heavy sigh, Leon relented, his resolve faltering in the face of Norma's unwavering gaze. His shoulders sagged, the weight of his past mistakes pressing down on him like a leaden weight.

"Alright," Leon murmured, his voice tinged with resignation. "Alright, Norma. I'll talk to them with you."

Norma's eyes softened with gratitude, her hand squeezing Leon's in silent appreciation. She turned to Sara and Aaron, her expression a mix of sadness and determination.

"There are things about this town, about our past, that you need to know," Norma began, her voice trembling with emotion. "Things that we've kept hidden for far too long."

Leon looked from Sara to Aaron, his expression a mix of resignation and reluctance. It was clear that he was willing to cooperate, to answer their questions, but it was equally evident that he wasn't happy about it. He only did it out of necessity, out of the need to confront the past, and because Norma needed him by her side.

"You're not going to like the answers to some of your questions. I'll warn you of that right now," Leon said, his tone edged with a hint of solemnity.

Sara and Aaron exchanged a glance, a silent acknowledgment of the significance of their inquiries. Sara, gathering her resolve, took the lead after a momentary pause.

"Mom, why didn't you tell me about Allison?" Sara's voice wavered slightly, the name carrying unspoken pain.

Norma's breath caught in her throat at the mention of her first daughter's name. It had been a long and arduous battle to suppress the raw emotions that still lingered beneath the surface. She felt Leon's arm around her shoulders, offering a silent comfort and support.

Leon sighed heavily, feeling the force of decades of secrecy bearing down on him. He knew this conversation was inevitable, yet he couldn't help but dread it.

"It wasn't an easy decision, Sara," he began, his voice thick with regret and sorrow. "Your mom and I made a choice a long time ago not to tell you about Allison. We thought it wouldn't change anything. She was taken from us before she even had a chance to live."

Norma flinched at the mention of her daughter's name, her pain palpable. Leon instinctively drew her closer, offering what little comfort he could muster. "We didn't have a choice," he continued, his voice barely above a whisper. "We couldn't have stopped it, no matter how much we wanted to."

Aaron's voice broke the heavy silence that followed. "Who took her? And why couldn't you do anything?"

Norma's voice wavered as she struggled to find the words. "We loved her," she whispered, her eyes brimming with unshed tears and not really answering Aaron's question.

Leon silenced her gently, his gaze fixed on Sara and Aaron. "We were warned by our parents when we got married," he explained, his tone grave. "They told us that we would possibly lose our firstborn child as payment for something our ancestors did long ago. It was a debt owed to ensure the future of our town."

He paused, the weight of his words hanging heavy in the air. "We didn't know when or how it would happen, only that it would. And when the time came, there was nothing we could do to stop it."

As the reality of their town's past sank in, Sara felt a surge of anger and sadness wash over her. She couldn't comprehend the cruelty of the fate that had befallen her sister, the injustice of it all.

"How... how could they do that?" Sara whispered, her voice trembling with emotion. "How could they sacrifice an innocent child for the sake of... of their own greed?"

Norma and Leon exchanged a somber glance, the heaviness of the town's sins bearing on their hearts. Leon reached for Norma's hand, intertwining their fingers in a silent gesture of solidarity.

"We... we don't know, Sara," Leon replied, his voice filled with sorrow. "We... We've asked ourselves that same question a thousand times. But... but it's the truth. It's... It's what happened."

The room fell into a heavy silence.

Leon paused, the memories of that fateful night still vivid in his mind, the pain of loss raw despite the passing years. The ache of losing a child who had barely tasted life gnawed at him, a burden he carried silently.

He could still recall the disbelief that coursed through him when both sets of parents had sat them down, revealing the impossible truth. Leon had raged against their words, unable to accept the fantastical tale they spun. Norma, devastated by the news, had stormed out of the room, leaving Leon to confront their parents alone.

"I didn't believe them," Leon confessed, the weight of his words heavy in the air. "It was too much to accept, too unbelievable."

The memory of that night haunted him, the echoes of his anger and denial reverberating in his mind. He had threatened and shouted, demanding they leave his house and never return. Reluctantly, the parents had left, their faces etched with sorrow at Leon's refusal to believe.

It wasn't until the day before Allison's birth that Leon and Norma had come face to face with the truth. Precious, the harbinger of their sorrow, had visited them that night.

The house had been shrouded in an eerie silence as Leon and Norma settled into bed, ready to drift into sleep. It was then that the rocking chair, positioned in the far corner of the bedroom, began to sway gently.

A soft, childlike laughter filled the room, sending shivers down their spines. Leon and Norma, hearts pounding with fear and curiosity, watched in disbelief as the rocking chair moved of its own accord.

Frozen in terror, they could do nothing but stare as the figure of a little girl materialized before them. Her feet dangled a few inches above the floor, too short to reach the ground.

The child's eyes glowed with an otherworldly light, a fiery red that pierced through the darkness of the room. Leon felt a chill run down his spine as she spoke, her voice hauntingly familiar yet filled with an unearthly command.

"I want what is mine," Precious declared, her words echoing in the stillness of the night.

Norma went into labor unexpectedly, the pains seizing her with a fierce intensity. It was a tumultuous delivery, fraught with danger that threatened both her life and that of the unborn child. Blood, a stark reminder of the perilous situation, stained the hospital sheets.

The doctors, a flurry of urgency and whispered consultations, grappled with the gravity of the situation. They debated fiercely, each vying for the best course of action to ensure the survival of both mother and child. In the midst of the chaos, Leon stood by, his heart heavy with fear and helplessness.

As Norma's condition worsened, Leon felt a surge of panic rise within him. The world around him blurred, his thoughts consumed by the looming specter of loss. It was all too much to bear, and in a moment of overwhelming despair, he had to be sedated to quell the rising tide of emotion.

The doctors, their faces etched with determination, battled against the odds. They knew the grim fate that awaited the child, yet they fought with every ounce of their expertise to save both mother and newborn.

Sixteen agonizing hours later, Leon and Norma welcomed their first child into the world. Exhausted yet elated, they cradled their daughter in their arms, unwilling to be separated from her even for a moment. The air was thick with the weight of uncertainty, the knowledge of the looming threat that hung over their heads.

The doctors, though valiant in their efforts, could not approach the newborn without an air of trepidation. Even Leon and Norma's relatives, eager to celebrate the arrival of the newest member of the family, were kept at bay by an invisible barrier of fear.

For Leon and Norma, the joy of welcoming their child into the world was tempered by a deep sense of dread. They knew, deep in their hearts, that their daughter was not long for this world.

Morning broke, casting a harsh light on the grim reality that had unfolded during the night. Norma's cries echoed through the hospital, mingling with Leon's anguished sobs. Their loss pressed down on the whole town, a collective grief that seemed to settle over Ionia like a shroud.

Allison, their precious newborn, had not survived the night. Her tiny form lay still beneath the soft sheets of her crib, her eyes closed forever to the world.

Leon's grief turned to seething anger, a raging fire that threatened to consume him. He longed to strike out, to find something, anything, to blame. But there was nothing tangible to direct his fury towards. The object of his wrath was a malevolent force, a shadowy specter that had stolen his daughter away in the darkness.

"I wanted revenge," Leon admitted through gritted teeth, his voice laced with pain and anger. "I wanted to lash out, to hurt something. But there was nothing I could do. I felt utterly powerless."

The helplessness gnawed at him, a bitter taste in his mouth. The creature that had taken their child was beyond his reach, its insidious presence lurking in the shadows.

Aaron, still grappling with the enormity of the situation, pieced together the fragments of the story. "So, you're saying... this was something unnatural? A... a little girl?"

"Exactly," Leon affirmed, his voice heavy with the weight of the memories. He drew Norma closer to him

His jaw clenched in remembered fury. "Yes. She appeared to us that night... a child-like figure, but with eyes that burned like fire. You can't imagine what it was like," he continued, his voice trembling slightly. "We were lost, adrift in a sea of sorrow. We didn't know how to move forward, how to live with the emptiness that consumed us."

Norma, though her sobs had subsided, still bore the fresh anguish in the tracks of tears that stained her cheeks.

"The community rallied around us," Leon recounted, a hint of gratitude in his voice amidst the pain. "They told us to push it from our minds, to focus on the child we would eventually get to raise. They said that God would watch over Allison, that they had all endured the same heartache. It was the darkest secret of this cursed town, and we were thrust into its cruel reality."

The room fell into a heavy silence as Leon's words settled over them, the unspoken horrors lingering in the air.

Aaron, unable to contain his curiosity and frustration, pressed on with his questions. "But why stay? Why subject yourselves to this town and its... its curse?" His voice cracked with a mixture of anger and disbelief.

Leon met Aaron's gaze, his eyes tired but steely with resolve. "Because this is our home," he answered, his voice firm. "As twisted and haunted as it may be, it's where we belong. We couldn't just uproot ourselves, leave behind everything we've known. And... and we couldn't abandon the memories of Allison."

Norma's hand tightened around Leon's, a silent show of solidarity.

"We made a choice to stay," Leon continued, his voice filled with quiet determination. The room seemed to grow colder.

"What else were we supposed to do?" Leon's voice carried resignation. He held Norma a little tighter, feeling her tears still wet against his chest. "We had already lost our baby... and everyone kept telling us that the next one would be different. Healthy. Safe. They said it like it was some sort of guarantee."

The anger that had flared within Leon moments ago began to ebb away, replaced by a weariness that seemed to settle deep into his bones. He understood Aaron's frustration, remembering his own accusatory tone towards their parents when they had revealed the same horrifying truth.

"We were broken," Leon continued, his voice barely above a whisper. "Our only solace came from our family and friends, the ones who stood by us through it all."

Pausing to gather his thoughts, Leon fixed Aaron and Sara with a solemn gaze. He wanted them to truly grasp the gravity of what he was about to say next.

"You can't escape her," Leon's words hung heavy in the air, each syllable laden with a grim finality. "She knows when you try to leave... and she won't allow it."

A shiver ran down Aaron's spine, a chill of realization creeping over him. "So... You're saying she controls this town? That she keeps everyone trapped here?"

Leon nodded, the weight of the revelation settling heavily upon him. "Every road out of town... it leads you right back to where you started. No matter which direction you choose, you always end up back home. It's like she's... She's woven herself into the very fabric of this place."

The room fell silent, the gravity of their situation hanging over them like a shroud. The knowledge that they were trapped in a town haunted by an ancient, vengeful force was almost too much to bear.

And as they sat there, the walls seeming to close in around them, Aaron and Sara couldn't shake the feeling of being watched. The presence of Precious, that malevolent specter from the past, loomed over them like a dark shadow

The truth was clear now, undeniable in its horror. A chill crept up Aaron and Sara's spines as the realization dawned on them. The malevolent force that had haunted their town for generations was real, its hunger for innocence insatiable. The legacy of their town's dark past loomed large, casting a long shadow over their uncertain future.

Sara's brows furrowed, a mix of confusion and sadness crossing her features. "But why didn't you tell us? About... about all of this?" she asked, her voice barely above a whisper.

Norma's eyes widened in surprise, her mind racing as she processed the question. She exchanged a quick glance with Leon, seeing the flicker of concern mirrored in his eyes.

Norma took a deep breath, her gaze softening as she met Sara's eyes. "We... we wanted to," Norma began, her voice gentle yet laden with the burden of the truth. "It's something we hoped to protect you from, sweetheart. To shield you from the pain. We thought it was best to let the past rest, to focus on the present and the future," she explained, her voice filled with a mother's love.

Aaron jumped in, his voice firm as he voiced the questions that had been plaguing them. "You knew about the deaths of the first-born children?" he asked, his gaze unwavering as he watched for their reactions.

Norma's expression softened, a sad smile tugging at her lips. "We... we knew," she admitted, her voice barely a whisper. "But we never wanted to frighten you. We hoped you wouldn't have to bear the burden of this curse."

Aaron nodded, understanding dawning in his eyes. "And what about the ghost? The little girl?" he pressed, his curiosity getting the better of him. "I can't believe this is real."

Norma gently disentangled herself from Leon's protective embrace, her voice steady despite the uneasiness of their conversation.

"He's telling you the truth," Norma began, her gaze fixed on Aaron and Sara, her eyes reflecting the solemnity of their situation. "Let me tell you about the Jacksons. They found out they were expecting a baby, and they decided they had to leave town to protect their child. They packed up their car, determined to get out, but..."

Norma's voice faltered for a moment, the memories of that harrowing time etched in her mind. "They drove for days, only stopping for gas, but no matter which way they turned, they always ended up back here. Back in Ionia."

She shook her head, the sorrow evident in her eyes. "It nearly drove Sylvia out of her mind with fear. She couldn't sleep, couldn't eat... They finally gave up, and it wasn't until after the baby was born that they were able to leave. But by then... it was too late."

Leon's voice was heavy with regret as he continued the tale. "I haven't seen them since. Greg and Sylvia... they were good people. We grew up together, went to school together... They didn't believe the legends, the stories we were all told. But now... now they know. They know the truth."

The room fell into a thick silence, the history of the town suppressing everything like a suffocating blanket. The stories of those who had tried to escape, only to be drawn back by an unseen force, echoed in the air around them.

"And that's not all," Norma added quietly, her voice barely above a whisper. "There have been others... others who tried to leave, only to meet a similar fate. It's like... like she won't let anyone escape her grasp."

Aaron and Sara exchanged a glance, the reality of their situation sinking in with chilling clarity. Trapped in a town haunted by an ancient curse, surrounded by the stories of those who had tried—and failed—to break free, they knew that their only choice was to face the truth head-on.

But even as they steeled themselves for what lay ahead, the presence of Precious lingered in the air, a constant reminder of the malevolent force that held Ionia in its grip. And as they sat there, Aaron and Sara couldn't shake the feeling that their every move was being watched... and that escape, true escape, might be an impossible dream.

"The little girl you're asking about, her name is Precious," Norma stated solemnly, her voice carrying the weight of years of fear and uncertainty. "When you see her, there's no mistaking her. She's downright evil, to the very core of her being."

Aaron's brow furrowed in concern. "Where did she come from? And how do we get rid of her?"

Norma exchanged a glance with Leon, a shared look of resignation passing between them before Leon spoke up. "Many folks in this town have asked that same question over the years, and none have found a solid answer on how to rid ourselves of her. But if you're truly seeking the truth about her origins, about what she is... You'll find it in the records at the church."

He paused, the weight of their shared history heavy in the air. "The records are old, kept safe down in the basement. They hold the history of this town, the Christian names of every child ever born here."

There was a silent understanding in Leon's words, an unspoken acknowledgment that these records also held the names of those children who had met untimely ends, whose lives had been cut short by the sinister force that haunted Ionia.

Aaron and Sara exchanged a glance, a silent agreement passing between them. If they were to uncover the truth about Precious, about the curse that held their town in its grip, they would need to delve into the dark history that lay hidden within the church records.

As they sat there, the importance of their impending task settling over them like a heavy shroud, Aaron couldn't shake the feeling that they were embarking on a journey from which there might be no return.

Aaron mulled over the information shared by Leon and Norma. He knew it was time to make a decision; they had divulged as much as they could, leaving him with a sense of finality. There seemed to be a limit to what they were willing or able to reveal, and he wasn't sure he wanted to delve any deeper into the dark secrets of Ionia.

It was Sara who voiced the question that had been haunting Aaron's thoughts, a question he had been too afraid to confront. He hadn't even realized the question needed asking until Sara spoke up.

"Mom," Sara's voice trembled with uncertainty, "Aaron is the firstborn of the Smiths, right?"

Norma's eyes welled up with tears once more, her heart heavy with the weight of the truth. She couldn't bear to meet Aaron's gaze as she answered, her voice barely above a whisper.

"Yes, he's the firstborn," Norma's voice was heavy with burden, laden with sorrow. But she wasn't about to leave Sara hanging in despair. She quickly added, her voice filled with a reassuring tone, "We're gonna take good care of you, Sara. You'll be alright, and you'll find another man to love... if you lose Aaron."

Sara looked on the verge of collapse, the revelation hitting her with a force she hadn't expected. Meanwhile, Aaron, reeling from the news, rose as if to leave, his mind overwhelmed. Yet Norma's words pressed him back into his seat with a heavy thud. A chill seemed to seep into his bones, a coldness that settled deep within him, unforgiving and unyielding.

Gritting his teeth, Aaron struggled to keep his composure, the muscles in his jaw working furiously as he fought to process it all. Finally, his voice emerged, edged with a raw intensity, "Did my parents know about this? All about the events that have been happening in Ionia?"

Leon and Norma found themselves caught in a difficult dilemma, the revelation heavy on their shoulders. They shared a glance, silently communicating the misfortune of what they were about to reveal to Aaron, a boy they loved as their own. It was Leon who spoke, his voice carrying a mix of regret and empathy, though his eyes remained fixed on Sara.

"Yeah, they did, son," Leon's words hung heavily in the air. "We were hoping you'd be some kind of miracle, 'cause she ain't taken you yet. The oldest she's let any firstborn child get to was ten."

Aaron's world seemed to tilt on its axis. The anger boiled within him, an uncontrollable torrent lashing out at the room, at everyone present, even Sara, who sat stunned beside him. His hands gestured wildly, punctuating each accusation. "You all knew, and yet you didn't tell me," he seethed. "My parents knew, and they kept it from me. I could be torn away from everything I know and love at any moment, and none of you were going to say a damn thing."

His voice echoed through the room, then another realization struck him, a pang of guilt that twisted his gut. "You let Sara believe we had a future together, and now we're so tied to each other that it'll kill her if I die." His words hung in the air, a heavy silence settling over the room.

Leon sprang up from the couch, his temper flaring, ready to confront Aaron head-on. He took a step forward, only to be held back by Norma, her grip firm and determined. She pulled him back, straining against his anger-fueled momentum, keeping a physical barrier between him and Aaron. Leon's eyes blazed with fury, his emotions roiling within him.

"Now hold on, son," Leon's voice was sharp, his frustration evident. "There ain't no need for accusations here. Your poppa, he told us not to tell you a thing. I loved that man, respected his wishes. He didn't want you carrying the weight of something nobody could change..." Leon's voice trailed off, a bitter taste in his mouth.

But Aaron wasn't having it. His own anger surged to match Leon's, his voice rising to a shout, drowning out Leon's attempt to explain. "My poppa!" Aaron's words were a thunderous roar, filled with hurt and betrayal. "He didn't love me. He barely acknowledged I was alive. And now you tell me he didn't want me to know because he didn't want me to worry!"

The room crackled with tension, the strain of untold truths hanging ponderously in the air. Aaron's accusations echoed off the walls, vibrating in their intensity, each word a painful reminder of the fractures in his own past. Norma held onto Leon, her eyes pleading for calm, for understanding amidst the storm of emotions.

But in that charged moment, it seemed that understanding was a distant hope.

"That ain't no way to talk about your poppa," Leon's voice was gruff, his eyes flashing with a mix of anger and pain as he shook his fist at Aaron. "Your poppa loved you, son. Loved you in the only way he knew how, knowing he could lose you at any moment. Every time he looked at you, all he could see was his love and all he could feel was that emptiness eating away at him, knowing he was going to lose his firstborn child."

Aaron's gaze swept the room, his eyes filled with a seething mix of betrayal and anger. "Damn you. Damn all of you for what you kept from me, from Sara," he spat out the words like venom, his voice filled with raw emotion. "And damn my poppa too."

With a forceful stride, Aaron brushed past Leon, his jaw clenched tight with determination. He made his way towards the front door, his steps heavy with the crushing newfound knowledge and a burning rage. Sara's voice called out to him from behind, pleading and desperate, but he couldn't bear to face her, not now.

As he stepped out into the cool evening air, a storm of emotions raged within him. Anger, fear, and a sense of helplessness churned in his chest. He felt a fierce determination rising within him, a resolve to confront the unknown menace that threatened his very existence.

"I'll go down fighting," Aaron muttered through gritted teeth, his fists clenched at his sides. "I'll stop this damn thing, whatever it takes."

With a final glance back at the house, he set off into the night, his mind consumed with thoughts of revenge and justice, determined to rid the town of the insidious threat that had haunted it for generations.

16

Aaron's plans unraveled swiftly. His intention to head straight to the church, to delve into the records Sara's parents had mentioned, was thwarted. The church doors loomed shut for the night, a formidable barrier to the information he sought.

Dejection settled heavily upon him as he turned away from the closed church. Disappointment coursed through his veins, a bitter taste in his mouth. The urgency of his quest clashed with the reality of the locked doors; waiting until morning was now an inevitable delay.

With a heavy heart, Aaron wandered down the dimly lit street. His hands sought refuge in the depths of his pockets, shoulders hunched against the chill of the night. Uncertainty clouded his mind, leaving him adrift without a clear destination. Returning home was out of the question, thanks to his brother's unpredictable moods. As for Sara's house, the memory of his strained conversation with her parents lingered uncomfortably in his thoughts.

Several blocks passed in a blur of aimless footsteps, the world around him a muted backdrop to his swirling thoughts. Then, faint strains of music teased his ears, drawing his attention. Casting a searching gaze around, he realized a couple of bars lay nearby, their inviting glow a beacon against the cold and wind.

The decision was made in an instant, spurred by the need for shelter from the elements. Aaron veered towards the warm lights of the bars, a faint glimmer of relief mingling with the weight of his unresolved tasks.

Upon entering the nearest bar, Aaron paused to survey his surroundings. Seeking solace in solitude, he yearned for a corner where he could be left undisturbed with his tumultuous thoughts. His gaze swept over the dimly lit interior, searching for the most secluded spot the bar had to offer.

At the back of the establishment, a solitary table beckoned to him, shrouded in shadows. The feeble light struggled to pierce the gloom, casting a dismal aura over the seedy bar. Yet, to Aaron's relief, the darkness seemed fitting, almost comforting in its obscurity. Without hesitation, he made his way to the chosen table and settled into the worn seat.

His contemplative reverie was interrupted by the arrival of a lackluster waitress, her demeanor matching the dreary ambiance of the bar. With dingy brown hair framing a bored expression, she stood before him, gum smacking with each indifferent movement. Aaron couldn't help but note the absence of any hint of refinement in her attire.

Considering his options, Aaron decided it would be prudent to order a drink that would keep his wits about him. Glancing around at the less-than-respectable scene of the bar, he realized the wisdom in choosing a beverage that came in its own container, one that wouldn't lead to a hasty intoxication.

The atmosphere of the bar, far from respectable, bordered on dismal—a fact that Aaron deemed an understatement. Yet, in the midst of the questionable surroundings, he found a strange solace in the shadows and the anonymity they provided.

The waitress swiftly took Aaron's order and disappeared into the dim recesses of the bar. His hopes for a beverage neatly contained within its own vessel were dashed when he learned that the establishment only served drinks straight from the tap. With a resigned shrug, he awaited the return of the lackluster waitress.

Moments later, she reappeared, bearing a grimy mug filled with the sole offering of the bar—a lukewarm, flat concoction that tasted as though it had been dredged from the depths of an old boot. Aaron's disappointment was palpable, yet in that moment, he cared little for the quality of the drink. He accepted it with a nonchalant nod, slipping a few crumpled dollars across the table in exchange.

The waitress made a sluggish attempt to return his change, but Aaron waved her off with a dismissive gesture. The unspoken agreement between them was clear—neither wanted nor needed the fuss of small change.

Settling into the booth, Aaron sank into a brooding silence, his thoughts a tempestuous whirlwind of anger and frustration. His ire was directed at the world at large, but most acutely at the spectral figure of the little girl haunting the town.

Lost in his inner turmoil, he failed to notice the approach of another until a warm body slid into the booth beside him. Startled, Aaron's gaze was drawn to the woman who now sat beside him, her presence both unexpected and intriguing.

"Hello," a voice, sensuous and silky, whispered near his ear, sending a shiver down his spine.

Turning fully towards her, Aaron found himself ensnared in the depths of the most brilliant green eyes he had ever beheld. He was momentarily speechless, caught off guard by the striking woman before him. It was her—the redheaded girl from his dreams, the same ethereal presence he had encountered at his mother's funeral.

For a fleeting moment, time seemed to stand still as Aaron struggled to find his voice, his heart pounding in his chest. Here, in the shadowy confines of the bar, fate had woven their paths together once more.

"Who the hell are you?" Aaron blurted out before he could temper his words, immediately regretting the brashness of his tone. His abruptness caught even him off guard, a product of his foul mood that seemed to amplify in the presence of this unexpected visitor.

Unfazed by his rudeness, the woman's voice returned, laced with a hint of amusement. "It's nice to meet you too," she replied, her tone teasingly light. Ignoring his initial response, she extended her hand, slipping it effortlessly into his limp one.

Aaron couldn't help but notice the warmth and smoothness of her skin against his own. A hint of surprise flickered across his features as her hand remained firm in his grasp. Her smile, when it came, was a radiant burst of light in the dimness of the bar.

The brightness of her smile took Aaron aback, momentarily disarming him. Her porcelain skin, unblemished and unusually dark for a redhead, held a certain allure. High cheekbones accentuated her features, while her bright green eyes sparkled with an enigmatic charm. The sprinkling of freckles across her nose only added to her endearing appearance, contrasting with the richness of her complexion.

"My name is Katherine Morgan, but you can call me Katherine," she introduced herself with polite grace. "I noticed you when you came into the bar, though it seems I went unnoticed. I doubt you would have been so surprised to find me sitting here otherwise."

Turning towards the waitress, Katherine caught her eye and deftly signaled for a refill for Aaron and a drink for herself. With a smooth motion, she returned her attention to Aaron, her expression shifting to a more solemn demeanor.

"I wanted to offer my condolences for the loss of your mother," Katherine said sincerely, her gaze unwavering.

Though Katherine was eager to reveal her true identity to Aaron, she sensed his prickly mood and decided to hold off. Perhaps it was best to wait until he was in a more receptive state before dropping such bombshell revelations.

Aaron, for his part, was keenly aware of his ignorance regarding Katherine's identity. In truth, he didn't recognize most of the mourners at his mother's funeral, and the fact didn't trouble him.

"Thank you, um... Katherine," Aaron responded, genuine gratitude coloring his tone. "That means a lot to me."

He cleared his throat, straightening up in his seat as he sought to explain his earlier rudeness. "I didn't mean to be so abrupt; my mind is just... elsewhere right now."

Silence settled between them for a moment as Aaron studied Katherine, his gaze lingering on every detail of her features. He found himself captivated by her smile, the contours of her face, and the essence of her presence. It was as if he were comparing her to the memories of his dream—the same girl who had haunted his nightmares, down to the smallest detail.

The unsettling feeling of sitting next to someone he had only encountered in dreams lingered in the air, casting a surreal quality over their interaction. Aaron couldn't shake the uncanny resemblance, the eerie sense of familiarity that tugged at the edges of his consciousness.

Katherine arched an eyebrow inquisitively, puzzled by Aaron's intense scrutiny. "You seem to think you know me from somewhere," she observed, her tone a mix of curiosity and amusement. "I'm quite certain I would remember meeting you before. So, where do you think we've crossed paths?"

Aaron shook his head slightly, attempting to dispel the lingering remnants of that haunting dream. He couldn't afford to get lost in thoughts of that unsettling vision, especially not now. "I don't know you," he replied quickly, a hint of defensiveness in his tone. "I... must have mistaken you for someone else."

Taking a gulp of the tepid beer in a feeble attempt to divert his attention, Aaron nearly choked on the bitter liquid. He coughed, trying to regain his composure as Katherine watched with patient amusement.

Changing the subject, Aaron shifted the focus to her origins. "So, where are you from?" he asked, his words a tad rushed. "You're clearly not a local. I'm sure I would have remembered meeting such an..." He hesitated, the unspoken compliment hanging in the air. Aaron quickly backtracked, not wanting to come across as too forward. "I mean, someone as attractive as you would have caught my eye sooner," he finished awkwardly.

Realizing the potential misunderstanding, Aaron shifted slightly in his seat, putting a bit of distance between himself and Katherine. Thoughts of Sara flashed through his mind, grounding him in the reality of his feelings. He couldn't afford to get sidetracked by the allure of a stranger, no matter how captivating she seemed.

A delicate blush spread across Katherine's cheeks, the rosy hue standing out even in the dim light of the bar. "I'm here visiting my Aunt," she explained, her voice softening with a hint of embarrassment. "She knew your mother, which is why I was at the church earlier."

"I don't really know my aunt all that well, or the city for that matter," Katherine continued, her gaze shifting slightly. "So, I decided to spend the night exploring a bit before heading back."

Aaron listened, his mind racing with a mixture of confusion and apprehension. He glanced down at his now-empty beer mug, a sinking feeling settling in the pit of his stomach. He couldn't shake the nagging thought that Katherine might be about to suggest something he wasn't prepared for—a proposition perhaps. He was oblivious to the fact that they were actually related.

"Ah, I see," Aaron replied, trying to maintain a casual demeanor despite the turmoil in his mind.

As Katherine turned to scan the bar for the elusive waitress, Aaron took a moment to collect his thoughts. He hadn't expected this encounter.

"I was feeling a bit bored myself," Katherine continued, turning back to face Aaron with a small smile. "So, I thought I'd come down here to see what the town has to offer and maybe get to know some of the locals."

Aaron nodded, his mind still reeling from the unexpected guest at his table. He couldn't deny the flutter of curiosity that stirred within him, despite his earlier reservations. The circumstances of their meeting were far from ideal, but there was an undeniable pull, a desire to uncover the mysteries surrounding Katherine.

"Sounds like an adventure," Aaron replied, mustering a faint smile of his own. "Well, it's a pleasure to finally meet you, Katherine," Aaron managed, his greeting belated but sincere. The reality of Katherine's presence still felt surreal to him, a stark contrast to the ethereal figure that had haunted his dreams.

Sitting beside him, the girl from his nightmares seemed to exude a vibrant energy, her smile infectious. Aaron couldn't help but return the gesture, though his mind raced with a mix of disbelief and uncertainty. He couldn't shake the nagging suspicion that she might be flirting with him, adding to the already bewildering situation.

The fact that Katherine was sitting right there, tangible and real, only added to Aaron's confusion. He could almost reach out and touch her, the scent of her perfume mingling with the subtle hint of soap. She was no longer a figment of his imagination, but a living, breathing presence beside him.

Katherine tilted her head slightly, her curly red hair cascading in loose waves down her neck. Her gaze held a playful glint as she studied Aaron's reaction.

"You seem a bit unsure of what to make of me," she observed with a teasing smile, her eyes sparkling with amusement. She paused, waiting for a response that seemed to elude Aaron in his state of mild shock.

"Are you surprised that an attractive woman like me would show interest in you?" Katherine teased, her tone playful yet genuine. "Or maybe you find me too forward? I can tone it down if it makes you uncomfortable."

Katherine's words held a hint of jest, her playful nature shining through. She wasn't trying to flirt; it was simply a part of her personality to be light-hearted in conversation. However, she made a mental note that if things became too confusing or if Aaron seemed uncomfortable, she would reveal their familial connection later on.

Aaron blinked, caught off guard by Katherine's directness. He opened his mouth to respond, then closed it again, unsure of what to say. The sudden shift in the conversation left him feeling slightly flustered, though he couldn't deny the intrigue that flickered in the depths of his gaze.

Katherine chuckled lightly, her eyes twinkling mischievously as she turned and gestured playfully across the room. "I'll retreat to the safety of the bar and wait for you to muster up the courage to come chat with me," she teased, a hint of playful challenge in her tone. "But if my hunch is correct, I might be waiting all night."

Aaron felt a surge of both relief and apprehension as Katherine's playful banter lightened the mood. He finally found his voice, though it came out a bit hesitant. "You're probably right," he admitted with a sheepish grin. "I wouldn't have had the guts to approach you otherwise." Inwardly, he added, nor the desire.

The thought of mentioning his girlfriend crossed Aaron's mind fleetingly. He considered it for a moment, then dismissed the idea. It wasn't that he was worried about Katherine trying to steal him away; rather, he simply didn't want to divulge too much about himself to someone he barely knew. Trust didn't come easy, especially in these uncertain circumstances.

As Katherine let out a genuine laugh, Aaron couldn't help but feel a twinge of defensiveness, wondering if he was the source of her amusement. Before he could dwell on it, she placed a reassuring hand on his shoulder, her touch surprisingly warm.

"Don't worry," Katherine reassured him, her tone sincere. "I know you have a girlfriend. I'm not here to interfere with that. You just seem like a decent guy, someone I could get to know and feel comfortable around." She paused, her gaze meeting his with a sense of earnestness. "I wouldn't feel pressured to do anything I didn't want to with you."

Katherine's remark caught Aaron off guard, a flicker of discomfort flashing across his features. It felt as though she had peered into his thoughts, a notion that left him unsettled. Without thinking, he subtly shifted away from her touch, allowing her hand to slip from his shoulder. The last thing he wanted was any inadvertent intimacy.

"You make it sound like I'm as harmless as a chihuahua," Aaron retorted, his tone laced with a hint of defensiveness.

"Even small dogs bite," Katherine quipped back, a playful grin dancing across her lips.

Despite the initial unease, they continued their conversation, each eager to learn more about the other. As they exchanged stories and shared anecdotes, Aaron found himself gradually relaxing in Katherine's company. The tension that had lingered between them began to dissipate, replaced by a growing sense of ease and familiarity.

Unbeknownst to Aaron, the distance between them gradually closed once more, the barrier of caution melting away in the warmth of their interaction. Before he realized it, Katherine's hand found its way into his own, her touch gentle yet reassuring. Leaning in slightly, she shook his hand in greeting, the closeness of her proximity allowing the warmth of her presence to envelop him.

Their conversation flowed effortlessly, each sharing stories and anecdotes, delving into the depths of their lives to uncover hidden gems of familiarity. Aaron found himself gradually relaxing in Katherine's presence, the initial awkwardness melting away with each passing moment. Katherine was quickly coming to the conclusion that it was nearing the perfect time to tell Aaron of their familial ties.

Lost in the easy rhythm of their exchange, Aaron failed to notice the diminishing space between them. Before he knew it, Katherine was leaning in closer, her presence enveloped him, the warmth of her body seeping into his own in friendly companionship.

The dim ambiance of the bar, coupled with the effects of the cheap booze, created a cocoon of intimacy around them for their interactions. They continued chatting amiably, their voices hushed in the relative solitude of the booth. Aaron found himself playing the role of the attentive host, refreshing Katherine's drink with a smile.

In a moment of gratitude, Katherine leaned over, intent on kissing him on the cheek in gratitude for the drinks. Aaron turned towards her to respond to a question she had asked previously, only to find himself caught in a moment of unforeseen passion. Her lips met his own in a brief yet undeniable kiss, a collision neither had expected. Startled, Katherine's eyes widened.

Aaron felt awkward. In a heartbeat, he realized the mistake, the heat of embarrassment flushing his cheeks. Instinctively, he reached out to gently push her away, but in his flustered state, his hand landed in an unintended, awkward position.

"I... I apologize," Aaron stammered, his cheeks burning with embarrassment.

Katherine, equally flustered, quickly interjected, her voice filled with regret. "I'm sorry, I only meant to thank you for the drink."

Their eyes met in a moment of shared embarrassment and confusion. Aaron found himself unable to look away, his gaze locked with hers. It was then that Katherine noticed his gaze shift, his attention drawn to something behind her. Curious, she turned to follow his line of sight, her heart skipping a beat as she realized what had caught his attention.

Aaron's gaze shifted past Katherine, his eyes landing on the woman standing beside their booth. Tears brimmed in her eyes, her hand pressed against her mouth to stifle a sob that threatened to escape.

"Let me explain, Sara," Aaron blurted out, his words tumbling over each other in his haste. "Nothing happened. It was an accident."

Sara's reaction was swift and visceral. A shriek tore from her lips, filled with hurt and betrayal. "How could you do this?" she cried, her voice raw with emotion. "I hate you. Don't ever come near me again."

Stunned by her outburst, Aaron sprang to his feet, a desperate attempt to reach out to Sara before she could flee. "Sara, wait," he pleaded, his voice tinged with desperation. He struggled to come from behind the small table and reached out a hand to Sara, finally.

But Sara was beyond reason, her anger boiling over into a torrent of fury. "Get your damn hands off of me, you bastard!" she screamed, her words slicing through the air like a knife.

In her rage, Sara lashed out, her hand connecting with Aaron's cheek in a stinging slap. The force of the blow sent him staggering backward, tumbling unceremoniously into the booth. In a moment of unexpected chaos, he found himself landing directly in Katherine's lap, the weight of his body knocking the breath from her lungs.

"Ugghh," Sara grunted, her voice thick with pain and frustration. Without another word, she turned and bolted from the bar, her hurried steps sending chairs and stools clattering in her wake. Unhindered by the chaos she left behind, she rushed out into the cold night, the faint patter of rain echoing her tumultuous emotions.

Katherine watched Sara's abrupt departure, concern etching lines of worry on her brow. "Are you going to go after her?" she inquired softly, her gaze shifting back to Aaron.

Aaron listened to the distant sounds of a slamming car door and tires screeching on the wet pavement outside. "I don't think that will be necessary," he muttered, his voice heavy with resignation as he sat up in the booth.

Sensing his discomfort, Katherine slid closer, making room for him beside her. Her touch was gentle as she reached out, her fingertips grazing the side of Aaron's face where Sara's hand had struck. Aaron winced slightly at the contact, feeling the sting of the slap lingering.

With a concerned frown, Katherine dipped a napkin into a glass of water sitting on the table. Gently, she dabbed at the corner of Aaron's mouth, her touch surprisingly soothing. As she pulled the napkin away, Aaron saw a smear of blood on the white fabric, evidence of the force behind Sara's blow. He couldn't help but marvel at the strength hidden within her slender frame.

Katherine glanced around the dimly lit bar, her eyes lingering on the other patrons who pretended not to eavesdrop on their conversation. "So if you're not going to go after her, what are you going to do?" she prodded gently, her voice a soft murmur against the somber atmosphere.

Aaron remained silent, his gaze fixed on the door through which Sara had disappeared. Lost in his thoughts, he didn't notice Katherine's approach until she threw her arm around him, pulling him closer in a comforting embrace. She tenderly dabbed at the cut on his lip, the warmth of her touch a stark contrast to the cold turmoil churning within him.

"I'm going to sit here and get drunk," Aaron finally muttered, his voice tinged with resignation as Katherine finished attending to his wound and pulled away.

True to his word, Aaron proceeded to drown his troubles in alcohol. The initial mugs of beer were soon replaced by stronger, more potent spirits like whiskey. With each passing drink, he felt the weight of his emotions grow heavier, the haze of intoxication clouding his mind.

By the time the clock struck closing time at two in the morning, Aaron was thoroughly inebriated. His thoughts were a jumbled mess, his memories fading into a blur of confusion. He couldn't even remember why he had started drinking in the first place, lost in a fog of numbness and despair.

KATHERINE watched Aaron slump further into the booth, his disheveled appearance a stark contrast to the composed man she had met earlier. Guilt gnawed at her insides as she replayed the events of the evening in her mind. The accidental kiss, the shock on Aaron's face, and the subsequent unraveling of his composure—it all weighed heavily on her.

She couldn't shake the feeling of responsibility for Aaron's current state. If only she hadn't leaned in for that ill-fated kiss on the cheek. If only he hadn't turned towards her at that exact moment. The memory of their lips meeting briefly, the surprise and confusion that followed—it haunted her.

"Are you alright?" Katherine asked softly, her voice laced with genuine concern.

Aaron mumbled something incoherent, his words slurring together in a drunken haze. His eyes, usually sharp and attentive, now appeared glazed and unfocused.

Katherine sighed inwardly, her heart aching at the sight of him in this state. She knew she had to do something, but the question of where to take him loomed large in her mind.

She couldn't take him to her aunt's house; the thought of introducing him in his current condition was out of the question. And she doubted he would want to go back home, not after learning from Michael about the argument he had mentioned with his brother.

As for Sara, Aaron's girlfriend, Katherine had no idea where she lived. The mention of her name had sparked a flicker of discomfort in Aaron earlier, a hint of something unresolved between them.

With a heavy heart, Katherine made a decision. She couldn't leave Aaron here, alone and vulnerable. Despite the awkwardness of the situation, she knew she had to take care of him. She was his relative, a cousin, after all.

"Come on, Aaron," Katherine said gently, reaching out to touch his arm. "Let's get you out of here."

Aaron blinked up at her, confusion evident in his gaze. "Where... where are we going?" he slurred, his words barely intelligible.

"To a hotel," Katherine replied, her voice firm but gentle. "Just for tonight. You need some rest."

She helped him to his feet, his weight heavy against her as they stumbled out of the dimly lit bar. The rain had stopped by then. The cool night air hit them in a rush, clearing Aaron's head slightly.

They made their way down the deserted streets, Katherine supporting Aaron as they walked. Their footsteps echoed down the streets as they struck the still wet pavement. The silence between them was heavy with unspoken words, the events of the evening pressing down on them both.

Finally, they reached a small hotel tucked away on a side street. Katherine guided Aaron inside, the warm glow of the lobby a welcome relief from the chilly night air.

The receptionist was engrossed in a magazine, the blaring television in the background a mere afterthought. As Katherine and Aaron approached the front desk, the receptionist glanced up, her gum smacking in a steady rhythm. Aaron swayed slightly on his feet, prompting a curious glance from the receptionist.

She paused her reading, but not her gum smacking, and raised an eyebrow at them. "Can I help you?" she asked, her voice tinged with boredom.

Katherine ignored the uninterested demeanor, her focus fixed on the task at hand. "Yes, we need a room for the night," she replied, her tone steady despite the whirlwind of emotions inside her.

The receptionist nodded, typing away on the computer before handing Katherine a key card. "Room 204," she said with a polite smile.

Katherine thanked her and turned to Aaron, who was leaning heavily against the counter. "Come on, let's get you settled," she said, slipping her arm around his waist to support him. Aaron groaned in response.

They made their way to the elevator, the ride up feeling interminable. Aaron had seemed to develop a disconcerting tilt to his stance. Katherine felt Aaron's weight against her, the warmth of his body seeping through her clothes.

Finally, they reached their floor and stumbled down the hallway to their room. Katherine fumbled with the key card before finally managing to open the door.

The room was small and sparsely furnished, but it was clean and quiet. Katherine helped Aaron over to the bed, where he collapsed in a heap.

She sat down beside him, a flood of emotions washing over her. Guilt, worry, and a strange sense of protectiveness mingled together inside her.

"I'm sorry, Aaron," she whispered, her voice barely above a murmur. "I didn't mean for things to turn out this way."

Katherine couldn't shake the feeling that she was only causing trouble for those around her. Her once strong self-assurance took a hit, leading her to delve into a more introspective analysis of her actions and the impact they had on others. As she reflected, the weight of her decisions seemed to grow heavier, each moment replaying in her mind with vivid clarity. She had always prided herself on being careful and considerate, but tonight's events had shaken that belief to its core.

The accidental kiss with Aaron, the chaos that ensued with Sara's sudden appearance—it all felt like a series of missteps that she couldn't take back. Katherine had never intended to complicate Aaron's life or cause him any distress. Yet, here they were, tangled in a mess of emotions and misunderstandings.

By chance, she found herself stepping into that particular bar, her eyes landing on her cousin unexpectedly. The plan to meet him had been foiled by circumstances up until that moment, so she saw an opportunity to finally connect.

She had to admit to herself that there was a part of her that had been drawn to Aaron's enigmatic presence, his troubled aura stirring something within her. But now, faced with the consequences of her actions, Katherine couldn't help but feel a pang of guilt.

Aaron looked up at her, his eyes bleary but filled with a hint of something unreadable. "It's not your fault," he slurred, his words barely coherent.

Katherine shook her head, a tear slipping down her cheek. "I should've been more careful," she said, her voice filled with regret. "It was bad that your girlfriend had to show up when we had that accidental kiss."

Aaron reached out, his hand brushing against hers. "It's okay," he said softly, his touch surprisingly gentle.

They sat in silence for a moment, the weight of the evening hanging heavy in the air. Katherine couldn't shake the feeling of responsibility, the nagging thought that she had somehow caused all of this.

But as she looked down at Aaron, his eyes closed in sleep, she knew she had made the right decision. She would stay with him tonight, watch over him until morning came.

With a sigh, Katherine leaned back against the headboard, her hand still clasped in Aaron's. The steady rise and fall of his chest as he slept brought her a sense of peace, a reassurance that he was safe, at least for now.

ChatGPT

Katherine couldn't shake the feeling that she was only causing trouble for those around her. Her once strong self-assurance took a hit, leading her to delve into a more introspective analysis of her actions and the impact they had on others. As she reflected, the weight of her decisions seemed to grow heavier, each moment replaying in her mind with vivid clarity. She had always prided herself on being careful and considerate, but tonight's events had shaken that belief to its core.

The accidental kiss with Aaron, the chaos that ensued with Sara's sudden appearance—it all felt like a series of missteps that she couldn't take back. Katherine had never intended to complicate Aaron's life or cause him any distress. Yet, here they were, tangled in a mess of emotions and misunderstandings.

She had to admit to herself that there was a part of her that had been drawn to Aaron's enigmatic presence, his troubled aura stirring something within her. But now, faced with the consequences of her actions, Katherine couldn't help but feel a pang of guilt.

Sitting beside Aaron in the dimly lit hotel room, she watched as he slept, his features softened in repose. The rise and fall of his chest, the gentle sound of his breathing—it all served as a poignant reminder of the vulnerability they both shared.

Katherine reached out to brush a lock of hair from Aaron's forehead, her touch light and tentative. In this quiet moment, amidst the turmoil of the evening, she found herself drawn to him in a way she couldn't fully comprehend. He was one of the family that she had wanted to make a connection with and now she had potentially screwed his relationship up.

However, the events of the night had brought them closer together, forging a bond that was both unexpected and undeniable. As she sat there, lost in her thoughts, Katherine couldn't shake the feeling that Aaron would become an integral part of her life, his presence filling a void she hadn't realized existed.

With a sigh, Katherine leaned back against the headboard, her gaze lingering on Aaron's sleeping form. She knew that tomorrow would bring its own set of challenges and uncertainties, but for now, in this fleeting moment of quiet, she allowed herself to simply be.

The rhythm of Aaron's breathing filled the room, a steady and comforting presence amidst the chaos of their tangled emotions. In that moment, Katherine felt a sense of peace wash over her, a quiet acceptance of the events that had brought them together.

She couldn't undo the past, couldn't erase the mistakes she had made. But as she sat there, watching over Aaron as he slept, Katherine knew that she would do whatever it took to make things right. For him, for herself, and for the unexpected bond that had formed between them.

As exhaustion washed over her, Katherine closed her eyes, letting the darkness of sleep pull her under. Tomorrow would bring its own challenges, but for now, in this quiet moment, she allowed herself

17

Sara's emotions surged like a storm within her, a tumult of hurt and betrayal threatening to overwhelm her. Anger simmered beneath the surface, a volatile mix of emotions that left her feeling unsteady and lost. She was not accustomed to such intense feelings, unsure of how to navigate this unfamiliar terrain.

Tears cascaded down her soft cheeks, silent witnesses to the depth of her pain. With a muffled cry of anguish, she buried her face into a pillow, seeking some refuge from the storm raging inside her. The scream tore from her throat, raw and primal, muffled by the plush fabric of the pillow.

Exhausted from the outburst, Sara tossed the pillow onto her bed with a frustrated huff. She sank heavily onto the mattress, the bed squeaking in protest at the sudden weight. The room seemed to echo with the remnants of her anguish, the air heavy with unspoken words and shattered emotions.

A soft knock on the door pulled Sara from the depths of her grief, demanding her attention. She blinked back tears, her voice trembling as she called out, "Who is it?"

"It's your mother, sweetheart. Can I come in?" Norma's gentle voice filtered through the door, filled with concern and love.

Sara hesitated for a moment, her heart aching with a mix of emotions. She longed for comfort yet felt a pang of guilt for burdening her mother with her troubles. She attempted to brush away the tears streaming down her cheeks, but the effort was futile.

Her eyes were swollen, red, and nearly swollen shut from the force of her emotions. "No, I'm not alright," swallowing hard, she managed to choke out, her voice thick with tears. "Yes, you can come in."

As the door creaked open, Sara rushed forward, unable to contain the flood of emotions any longer. She threw herself into her mother's waiting arms, surrendering to the overwhelming wave of grief that consumed her. Sobs wracked her body, each one a painful reminder of the betrayal she felt.

Norma was stunned by the intensity of her daughter's emotions. Sara, usually so composed and reserved, was now unraveling before her eyes. The raw grief radiating from her was palpable, a tangible force that threatened to engulf them both. As a mother, Norma felt Sara's pain as if it were her own, the force of it pressing down on her chest.

Wrapping her arms tightly around Sara, Norma held her daughter close, offering whatever comfort she could with just the embrace. She murmured soothing words, her voice a gentle lullaby against the storm of Sara's emotions. With each sob that racked Sara's body, Norma felt her own heart break a little more.

Time seemed to blur as they clung to each other, mother and daughter bound by love and shared pain. The room was filled with the sound of Sara's ragged sobs, the only sound in the stillness of the night. Norma held on tight, offering silent strength and support.

Eventually, the tears began to subside, leaving Sara spent and exhausted. She sagged against her mother, her body trembling with the aftershocks of her emotional outburst. Norma held her daughter close, a silent vow to never let go.

Norma tenderly encouraged Sara to join her on the nearby bed. With gentle hands, she brushed aside pillows and stuffed animals, making room for them both. Sara, her emotions still raw and overwhelming, sank down onto the bed beside her mother.

As she settled in, Norma couldn't help but smile inwardly at her daughter's lingering touch of childhood innocence. Despite Sara's grown stature, the remnants of her childhood were evident in the way she interacted with the stuffed animals, moving them aside as if they were still an integral part of her world.

Sara leaned against her mother, seeking comfort in the familiar warmth of her presence. Norma wrapped an arm around her daughter, holding her close as they sat together on the bed. The room was quiet except for the occasional sniffle from Sara.

Norma waited patiently, giving Sara the space to process her emotions at her own pace. She knew that sometimes words were unnecessary, that the simple act of being there was enough.

Finally, after what seemed like an eternity, Sara attempted to speak. Her voice was hoarse from crying and her attempts ended up in unexpected huffs instead of words as she strained to try to not burst into tears again.

"I've never seen you this upset before, Sara," Norma muttered quietly, her voice filled with concern as she gently stroked her daughter's hair. "Please tell me what's wrong so I can try to help you fix it."

Sara found herself unable to speak, the weight of her emotions too heavy to put into words. Norma waited patiently, understanding that Sara needed time to compose herself. She knew she couldn't rush Sara's grief or lessen the pain until she understood its source. So, she sat there with her, offering silent comfort, gently wiping away the tears that streamed down Sara's cheeks with the hem of her blouse.

After a few moments, Sara managed to gather herself enough to speak, though her voice trembled with emotion. "I don't know how to say it, Mom," she began haltingly. "I saw Aaron... I am through with him... it's done."

Norma's heart clenched at her daughter's words, confusion clouding her expression. Without knowing the specifics of what had happened, Sara's statement was like a puzzle with missing pieces. She felt a surge of fear at the thought of Aaron having hurt her daughter in any way. After all, Aaron was not just any boy to Norma; he was like a son, someone she had hoped would one day become family.

Aaron and Sara, in Norma's eyes, were meant to be together. Their personalities complemented each other in countless ways, and Norma had often pictured a future where they would wed, creating a beautiful life together. It was hard for her to fathom what could have gone so wrong between them.

Sara buried her face in her hands, unable to meet her mother's eyes. The pain of betrayal cut deep, leaving her feeling raw and exposed. Norma placed a comforting arm around her daughter, pulling her close in a protective embrace.

"What has he done, child?" Norma asked finally, her voice trembling with a mixture of fear and concern.

Sara hesitated, her emotions crushing down on her chest. She wasn't immediately forthcoming, unexpected reluctance catching her off guard. There was a part of her that dreaded speaking the words out loud, as if by doing so, she would make the painful truth all the more real.

For Sara, admitting what had happened meant facing the possibility that her relationship with Aaron might be irreparably broken. She loved him with all her heart, and the thought of him betraying her trust was almost unbearable. Aaron had always been the epitome of sincerity and love in her eyes. It was hard to reconcile the image she had of him with the reality she had witnessed.

"What has Aaron done, Sara?" Norma asked again, her voice soft but insistent. "Sweetheart, I need you to tell me what happened. I can't help you unless I know."

Sara took a deep breath, steeling herself to recount the painful events of the night. "I went out to look for him when he didn't come back," she began, her voice trembling with emotion. "His house was empty, Michael wasn't there either, so I drove around, searching for him everywhere I could think of. Finally, I found him at the third bar I checked."

She paused, the memory of that moment threatening to overwhelm her. The sight of Aaron, entwined with another woman, was seared into her mind like a brand. She felt a fresh wave of tears welling up, but she fought to keep her composure.

"I saw him kissing another woman, mom," Sara confessed, her voice heavy with shame. There was a weight of undeserved guilt in her tone, as if she bore the blame for Aaron's betrayal.

Norma was speechless, her mind struggling to grasp the enormity of what Sara had just revealed. She stammered a few times before finally closing her mouth, unable to articulate the disbelief and shock that coursed through her.

"Did you ask him what was going on?" Norma managed to ask, her voice barely above a whisper, the question hanging heavy in the air.

Sara turned to her mother, her eyes ablaze with a mixture of hurt and anger. "What do you mean, did I ask him what was going on?" she retorted sharply. "He was kissing another woman, Mom. What else is there to ask?"

Norma shook her head, feeling a sense of helplessness wash over her. She hadn't meant to upset Sara further, but her words seemed to have had the opposite effect.

"I didn't mean to upset you, Sara," Norma said softly, her voice filled with remorse. "But didn't you try to find out what was going on? Did you ask him why he was with her? If he had been drinking and not in his right mind? So much has happened tonight, and both of you have so much to come to terms with."

Sara's anger softened slightly, replaced by a deep sadness that seemed to weigh heavily on her shoulders. She had replayed the scene over and over in her mind, each time hoping for a different outcome.

"I... I didn't ask him anything," Sara admitted, her voice barely audible. "I couldn't. I was... I was so shocked, Mom. I couldn't believe what I was seeing."

Norma reached out, taking Sara's trembling hands in her own, offering what little comfort she could. "Oh, sweetheart," she murmured, her heart aching for her daughter's pain. "I can't imagine how much this must hurt. But you need to talk to him, Sara. You need to find out the truth, no matter how painful it may be."

"Are you trying to justify what he did?" Sara's voice cut through the heavy air, filled with a mix of pain and accusation.

Norma felt a pang of guilt at Sara's words. She realized that her attempts at comforting her daughter were falling short, perhaps even fueling Sara's anger further. She needed to approach the situation from a different angle, one that might offer Sara some clarity and relief from the tumult of emotions.

"I'm not trying to defend him, Sara," Norma said gently, her voice tinged with empathy. "I just wanted you to consider everything before you make any decisions. I love you, and I love Aaron too. I can't imagine he would intentionally hurt you like this. Think about the love you both share, the history you've built together. This... this is a shock, I know. But don't let it destroy everything you have."

Sara's gaze diminished slightly, her demeanor visibly softened, the anger in her eyes giving way to a glimmer of uncertainty and pain. It was as if a weight lifting off her shoulders as she leaned into her mother's comforting embrace. Her once ragged breaths steadied, finding a rhythm more akin to calmness than the storm of emotions that had engulfed her moments before. She had been with Aaron for so long, and their relationship had weathered its share of storms.

"I'm sorry I got upset, Mom," Sara whispered, her voice tinged with vulnerability. "I'm just... confused, and... hurt right now. I love you."

"I love you too, Sara," Norma replied, her voice tender and full of reassurance. "I always have, and I always will. I'll protect you with everything I have."

Norma gently pulled back, her hand reaching up to brush away the tears that still lingered on Sara's cheeks. A faint, weary smile crossed Sara's face—a small glimmer of hope amidst the pain.

Norma could sense that Sara was slowly beginning to find her footing again, but she knew the road to healing would be long and arduous. Aaron's actions had shaken the foundation of their relationship, leaving behind a trail of questions and hurt.

As Sara settled into a momentary calm, Norma's thoughts turned to Aaron. He had a lot of explaining to do—not just to Sara, but to Norma as well. The betrayal Sara had described cut deep, leaving Norma with a sense of hurt and disappointment as well.

With a firm resolve, Norma knew that Aaron would need to work hard to earn back their trust. His actions had consequences, not just for Sara, but for their entire family.

But for now, in this moment of shared love and understanding, Norma held her daughter close, offering silent support and unwavering love. Together, they would navigate the turbulent waters ahead, drawing strength from each other along the way.

18

Beneath the ancient stone foundations of the church, a crypt-like labyrinth sprawled in silent darkness, Precious stood facing the fireplace, her back to the rest of the room, the warm glow of the dying embers casting shadows across the dusty space. Three figures milled about aimlessly, their restless energy palpable in the stagnant air. Lesser angels who had chosen to fall with Kafziel. They longed to escape the dreariness of the room, to distance themselves from the imposing figure that loomed in the corner—Marcus, a demon in the guise of a man, who hovered over Precious like a shadow.

Paziel, Thaniel, and Lazuriel were drawn to Precious and now bound by the same fate that held her captive. Unlike Precious, they remained beings of the immaterial world, their essence trapped in the mortal realm. Their wings, darkened because of the fall from grace, rustled softly against their backs, the sound reverberating off the walls of the confined space.

"Put your wings away," Precious commanded sharply, her voice cutting through the stillness. "The noise disturbs me."

"Why do we wait here? What is the purpose of it all, Precious?" Paziel's voice carried a note of impatience, his wings twitching with restlessness.

"Silence," Precious replied, her tone eerily soft yet commanding. "Your incessant chatter grates on my nerves." Her gaze remained fixed on the dying flames, her thoughts veiled behind a mask of indifference.

Lazuriel proved to be less easily subdued than Paziel, his defiance echoing Paziel's earlier sentiments. "He's right, Precious. Why do we linger here? Why do we subject ourselves to the presence of that... thing?" He pointed accusingly at Marcus, who only responded with an oily smile, his eyes glinting with amusement.

"QUIET!" Precious's scream filled the chamber, reverberating off the stone walls with such force that dust rained down from the rafters, falling like a slow, mournful and discolored snow, before settling to the floor. The outburst silenced the three lesser angels, their expressions a mix of fear and subservience. "I tire of your incessant questions. You will do as I command, and nothing more, as long as you are in my presence," Precious declared, her voice dripping with authority.

With an air of controlled anger, Precious made her way to the chair she preferred, the sound of her small shoes clicking sharply against the stone floor. Her steps were measured. She clasped her hands behind her back. The tension was evident in the tightness of her fists, betraying the simmering anger beneath her calm facade.

"Where is my Katherine?" Precious's voice was soft, a deceptive calmness masking the turmoil within her. Her eyes trailed around the space. Though her words were spoken softly for herself, they carried a weight that filled the chamber, each syllable heavy with unspoken urgency. It was a question that had echoed in her mind, haunting her thoughts in moments of silence and not meant to be uttered at that time.

At her side, Marcus slid closer, his hand reaching out to touch her shoulder. But Precious recoiled at his touch, a shudder of revulsion passing through her. His oily voice whispered in her ear, filling her with a creeping sense of unease. "Katherine is with the boy now. She does your bidding."

"What do you know of my bidding?" Precious's voice was sharp, cutting through the room like a blade. Her gaze turned dark until Marcus took a small step back.

Precious turned and sat down. Her eyes were on some distant place, beyond the confines of her present location. "Aaron", she whispered almost reverently, carefully.

Marcus was observant to a fault. He picked up on the unintended utterance by Precious. "He is the key," Marcus murmured to himself, his voice a seductive whisper.

His murmuring caused Precious to recall her place and she looked at Marcus questioningly, wondering if her internal musing had been overheard.

"Let me help you with whatever your plans are, Precious. Together, we can achieve greatness," said Marcus, one of his hands across his chest and the other extended in offering to her.

Precious recoiled, pushing Marcus's proffered hand away with a look of revulsion. "I have no need for your assistance, demon. My path is my own." But beneath her defiance, a seed of doubt lingered. Marcus had glimpsed her desires, her weaknesses. He knew too much.

Marcus almost let his anger get the better of him. His face twisted, just a brief second, into something hideous and inhuman. The smile returned quickly, in the blink of an eye, seeming as if it had always been there planted on his face.

Precious turned away from him and cursed as she tried to stretch. "Damn this flesh. It is so confining and uncomfortable."

"I know your thoughts, little one," Marcus's voice oozed with dark promise as he leaned closer. "Your flesh speaks to me, even when your mouth remains silent. Let me quell those feelings."

Precious gazed at Marcus with a mixture of disgust and fear, Precious's eyes flashed with anger. "You disgust me, beast. I want nothing to do with you."

But Marcus only smiled, a knowing gleam in his eyes. "You've been in this form for so long, you feel the weakness of the flesh," he taunted, his words a twisted melody of temptation.

"You overstep, Marcus," Precious said, her voice laced with warning. "You have no idea," she hissed, her eyes blazing with an otherworldly light. "The danger you are in, the fire you stoke with your careless words. Tread lightly when you speak to me."

Marcus slipped around to stand in front of Precious. He squatted down and placed his hands on her knees. "I know your thoughts, little one."

The other angels, sensing her unease, gathered around her chair protectively. Paziel straightened her dress, Thaniel smoothed her hair, and Lazuriel showered her with affectionate kisses.

Precious basked in their adoration, even as a pang of longing tugged at her heart. She yearned to shed this mortal guise, to embrace her true form once more.

"Tell me why, Precious. If you are so unconcerned about what your flesh wants, then tell me what I can do, that they can't, to help you." Marcus indicated the three angels hovering around Precious.

The accusations hung heavy in the air, a palpable tension that crackled with unseen energy. "You know nothing of me," Precious's voice was a cold whisper, her eyes flashing with barely contained fury.

"Don't I?" Marcus retorted, his smile twisted in what was supposed to be a sardonic look but came across as something more sinister. "You've been in this form so long that you feel the weakness of the flesh. I saw your eyes moisten and felt your flesh quiver when you thought of Aaron."

With a sudden surge of rage, Precious rose from her chair, her wings unfurling from her back in a sweeping display of power. "You are repugnant, Marcus," Precious's voice was a deadly whisper, her eyes burning with a fierce intensity. "Leave me now, all of you. I must be alone."

"You treat us like we are nothing but air and all we ever wanted to do was serve you, Kafziel," Lazuriel said. She, most of all, was the closest to Precious.

Thaniel and Paziel stood close by Lazuriel. Precious knew that they felt the same but wouldn't voice their opinions, instead, deferring to Lazuriel and letting her talk for them.

"You love the girl Katherine more than you love us and you look at the boy Aaron with some kind of unknown hope. You promised the town that they would lose the first born of their family lines. They have been nothing but a distraction to you since they were conceived," Lazuriel said.

"They are both first born children but he and she, as first born of their line, have lived for so long," Thaniel said.

Paziel moved forward towards Precious. "We have seen you brooding over there in your chair for days without end in all of these years. Tell us why, Precious. Tell us why you sit and wait and do nothing."

"I don't owe any of you an explanation for what I do. Now leave!" Precious boomed. The room seemed to tremble with her fury, the very air charged with electricity. The lesser angels seemed to fold into the shadows and disappear. With a silent nod, Marcus retreated. He raised his hand and disappeared in a noxious plume of smoke smelling of wormwood and pitch.

Alone in the echoing chamber, Precious stood, her form a silhouette against the dancing flames. The weight of her power hung heavy in the air, a dark and brooding presence that seemed to fill the very walls themselves.

And so, in the depths of the crypt-like labyrinth beneath the ancient church, Precious stood alone, her heart filled with a tumultuous mix of desire and fury, her dark thoughts a haunting echo in the silent darkness.

ALONE for once, Precious relished the solitude that enveloped her. Focusing her thoughts, she conjured a mental image of Katherine, and there, in a dimly lit hotel room, the young girl materialized before her. Precious shifted her presence to be near her.

Neon lights from the establishment's sign outside filtered through the window, casting a feeble glow across the space. Despite the poor illumination, Katherine's sleeping form lay clearly on the bed, serene in her slumber. Taking a seat nearby, Precious watched over her ward, feeling a bittersweet mix of calm and longing. An uncomfortable urge to unfurl her angelic wings tugged at her, but she suppressed it, the mortal confines of the body she resided in restraining her ethereal essence.

Being near Katherine eased the frayed nerves of Precious. Lost in the tranquility it offered, she was sharply reminded of the fragility of this peace—ephemeral, liable to vanish in an instant, unlike the eternal serenity of her heavenly realm. Unaware of her impact, Precious remained lost in her thoughts.

Meanwhile, Katherine stirred, sensing a subtle shift in the room's atmosphere. Battling the remnants of sleep, she blinked her heavy eyelids open to find Precious seated across from her. The warmth of her guardian angel's smile greeted her, bringing a sense of comfort.

Pleased at Katherine's awakening, Precious spoke softly, her voice carrying a gentle warmth, "You have found your family, I see." Her eyes swept over the figure of Aaron, sprawled on the bed nearby. "He's quite handsome, and I believe you two would get along perfectly." With these words, Precious rose from her seat, drawing closer to Katherine's bedside, her presence radiating a protective aura.

Slightly taken aback by the unexpected presence of her guardian angel, Katherine's surprise softened into a warm smile as she reached out to embrace her. "Kafziel, I didn't know that you were here watching over me," she murmured softly, a sense of comfort enveloping her.

In this moment, Katherine was the only being allowed to address Precious by her angelic name without correction, a silent understanding between them. Precious, in her mortal form, let this familiarity linger, a small concession to the bond they shared.

"I am always watching over you," Precious replied with a gentle smile, her gaze lingering on Aaron's sleeping figure nearby. There was a knowing look in her eyes, a silent acknowledgment of the complexities of mortal lives.

Katherine's attention shifted back to the bed where Aaron lay, his form still and unconscious. Turning to Precious once more, she spoke with a hint of ruefulness, "It isn't what you might think. Aaron had an argument with his girlfriend, and I couldn't leave him in that state." Her voice carried a note of concern, tinged with regret. "He was rather drunk," she added, her words trailing off as she glanced back at Aaron, a mixture of emotions playing across her features.

After a brief pause, Katherine turned her gaze back to Precious, her expression tinged with apology. She felt a weight of responsibility for Aaron's current state and the fact that he now shared the night with her instead of his girlfriend. "I know he's family," she began softly, her voice filled with sincerity, "I can feel it in every fiber of my being. I've never felt as close to anyone as I do to Aaron and his brother, but I can't shake this feeling that my presence here in Ionia is a mistake."

Though seething with anger, Precious masked her emotions well. "Do not burden yourself with such thoughts," she replied calmly, her voice betraying none of the fury bubbling beneath the surface. "Stay with your family as much as you can. As for Aaron, I will see what the future holds for him."

Katherine remained hesitant, her doubts lingering like shadows in the dimly lit room. She was unsure about allowing her guardian angel to intervene in this matter, uncertain of the consequences. However, she trusted Precious implicitly, knowing that her guidance had never led her astray before.

Noticing Katherine's lingering uncertainty, Precious gently probed, "Have I ever led you astray, Katherine?" Her voice was soothing, reassuring.

After a moment of contemplation, Katherine spoke slowly, her words filled with hesitation, "No, you haven't." She paused, her thoughts swirling with conflicting emotions. "But I don't want to jeopardize what Aaron has with his girlfriend. I inadvertently gave her reason to suspect something between us, and before Aaron could explain, she left."

The weight of the situation hung heavy in the air, the tension palpable between the two figures in the dimly lit room. Precious listened intently, her expression unreadable as Katherine voiced her concerns and fears. This delicate balance of familial bonds and unforeseen complications left the room charged with uncertainty, awaiting the resolution that fate would inevitably bring.

Precious offered a reassuring smile, her eyes filled with unwavering confidence. "Don't worry. I believe everything will fall into place. Since the day we first met, you've longed to uncover the mystery of your family. Now that you've found them here in Ionia, trust in fate's guidance. Have faith that all will unfold as it should."

Katherine returned the smile, a sense of gratitude warming her heart. She embraced her guardian angel once more, feeling the comforting presence envelop her. With a gentle kiss on Precious's cheek, Katherine bid her goodnight.

Settling back beside Aaron in the dimly lit room, Katherine found solace in his familiar presence. As sleep began to claim her, she nestled as close to her cousin as she dared, the bond of newfound family strengthening her resolve. Despite her lingering doubts, she couldn't deny the warmth of familial love that now filled her heart.

Closing her eyes, Katherine drifted into slumber, a faint smile on her lips. She knew there might be challenges ahead, uncertainties that could stir trouble. Yet, guided by her guardian angel's words, she held onto the belief that family would weather any storm together. With this thought in mind, she surrendered to the peaceful embrace of sleep, trusting in the journey that awaited her.

MARCUS followed the fading figures of the lesser angels into a dimly lit room, his steps echoing off the stone walls as he materialized and walked towards them. Anger simmered beneath his skin, a seething resentment towards the treatment he received from Precious burning within him.

There was something that bothered him. In the conversation that had followed between those lesser angels and Precious, Marcus had caught wind of something that he had not previously known. Just a bit of information that seemed incongruent with what he had already gathered about this coven of angels.

Paziel, Thaniel, and Lazuriel seemed to be lost in their own conversation, ignoring Marcus's presence in the room with them. Marcus neared them, as he neared them, their conversation stopped. He could tell that they were upset to have been banished from Precious's presence along with him. Their stares in his direction did little to hide their dislike of the demon.

Marcus came to a stop facing the lesser angels, his eyes flashing with barely contained fury as well as curiosity. "What did you mean by that statement?" he demanded, his voice a low growl that filled the chamber.

The three fallen angels exchanged glances that showed they didn't understand what Marcus was asking after, their darkened wings rustling softly against their backs. Paziel stepped forward to address Marcus.

"What are you talking about?" Paziel asked carefully, not knowing what Marcus was asking after and being cautious less what he revealed be something that Precious did not want known to others.

Marcus was being careful not to offend the angel's sensibilities and to keep him talking so that he could learn more. He cautiously asked, "I'm asking about that promise that you mentioned. I did not know that Precious had done such a thing."

The cautions Marcus had employed served him well. "You heard right, demon," Paziel began, his voice tinged with bitterness. "Precious made a promise centuries ago when she was burned at the stake. She vowed that the town of Ionia would lose the firstborn of their family lines."

Marcus's eyes widened in disbelief, his features twisted into a mask of shock. "Why would she do such a thing?" Marcus asked.

Thaniel stepped forward, just a step closer towards Marcus but keeping his distance from the repugnant being. "She inhabits the body of a first born of Ionia."

Lazuriel spoke next. "When the town cursed her and burned her at the stake, she spoke out in anger, cursing them for their actions."

Some things were beginning to make sense for Marcus. Just a few of the pieces had fallen into place for him. He looked between the three angels, regarding them with narrowed and suspicious eyes. From what he knew, Precious had never taken the lives of any child in the town. That left only one possibility.

"And you have been fulfilling this prophecy all these years?" Marcus asked, his voice barely a whisper.

Thaniel, his expression grave, nodded solemnly. "Yes, we have," he admitted, his voice filled with resolution. "We assumed her form and acted in her stead. We have taken the lives of the firstborn children of Ionia, following Precious's promise."

A cold chill settled over the chamber as the revelation of the angel's actions hung heavy in the air. Marcus paced the room, his mind reeling with the implications of their revelation.

"Why? Why would Precious make such a vow?" Marcus's voice was filled with confusion, his eyes searching the faces of the lesser angels for answers.

Lazuriel, her voice barely above a whisper, spoke up from the shadows. "She was want to ease the suffering of the parents of the child by taking it's form but the parents rejected her, not knowing that it was Kafziel seeking to ease their suffering at the loss of the child that was no longer Precious." she explained, her voice filled with sorrow. "And in her anger, she made a promise that should be fulfilled."

Their words settled heavily upon Marcus, a sense of understanding creeping over him. "And Aaron? Katherine?" he asked, his voice barely a whisper.

Paziel, his gaze somber, replied. "They, too, are firstborn children," he revealed, his words heavy with meaning. "But we have left them untouched, for Precious seems fixated on them. We feared drawing her attention to our actions."

A sickening realization dawned upon Marcus, the pieces of the puzzle falling into place with horrifying clarity. "You have been killing innocent children," he whispered, his voice filled with disbelief.

The chamber fell into a heavy silence. Marcus turned to the lesser angels, his eyes blazing with a firery glee.

"This is interesting," he declared, his voice ringing with satisfaction. "Innocent lives taken in the name of Precious's folly."

With a determined stride, Marcus stormed out of the chamber, his mind racing with plans to put an end to the dark prophecy that had plagued Ionia for centuries.

Alone once more, the lesser angels exchanged uneasy glances, their hearts heavy with guilt. They knew that their actions had caused untold suffering, their souls tarnished by the darkness of their deeds.

In the depths of the crypt-like labyrinth beneath the ancient church, a sense of foreboding settled over them like a shroud. The time had come to confront their sins, to right the wrongs they had committed in the name of a misguided promise.

And as Marcus set forth on his mission to confront Precious and put an end to the darkness that had plagued Ionia for far too long, the lesser angels braced themselves for the reckoning that awaited them. The truth had been unveiled, their secrets laid bare in the silent darkness of the crypt. It was time to face the consequences of their actions and seek redemption for the lives they had taken.

19

Aaron awoke to a splitting headache, a relentless throb that seemed to echo the pounding in his temples. His memory was a jumbled mess, shards of last night's escapades cutting through the haze. What stood out vividly, however, was the image of the redheaded girl nestled beside him in the rumpled sheets. A surge of panic washed over him, mingled with confusion. What had he done?

Fragmented scenes from the bar flickered in his mind like a poorly spliced film reel. Something about Sara's place, a blurry exit, and then... nothing but a gaping void. The forgotten hours settled heavily upon him as he glanced at the sleeping figure beside him, her tousled hair a stark contrast to his mounting dread.

"Oh, no," Aaron groaned, the realization hitting him like a ton of bricks.

With hesitant fingers, he drew the sheet over her, a feeble attempt to shield her slumbering form. Gently, he reached out and shook her shoulder, whispering her name in a voice thick with regret until she stirred from her sleep.

Katherine blinked away the remnants of sleep, her eyes squinting against the morning light filtering through the curtains. With a tired yawn, she pushed herself upright in bed, the sheet slipping down to her lap, revealing her t-shirt-clad figure. There was an air of casual ease about her, as if being so underdressed in front of him was of no consequence.

Glancing over at Aaron, she furrowed her brow at the confusion etched on his features. "What is it?" Katherine inquired, her voice still thick with sleep. "What's on your mind, Aaron?"

Aaron wasted no time with pleasantries, his urgency cutting through the grogginess of the morning. "What the hell did we get up to last night?"

Katherine's expression shifted to one of bewilderment. It was clear Aaron was missing a crucial piece of the puzzle, though what it was eluded him. Initially, she had been as clueless as he seemed, her sluggish brain slow to catch up with the present. However, as awareness dawned, her confusion gave way to a quizzical look directed at him.

Aaron's impatience was palpable as he waited for her response, his mind racing to fill in the blanks of the forgotten night.

"What are you talking about?" Katherine mumbled, her voice thick with remnants of sleep as she rubbed her eyes.

Aaron fought to keep his frustration in check, his patience wearing thin beneath the weight of unanswered questions. "Did anything happen between us last night?" he pressed, the urgency clear in his tone.

A mischievous glint sparkled in Katherine's eyes as understanding dawned on her. With a playful smirk, she decided to draw out the moment, relishing in Aaron's discomposure. "Hmm, like what? Are you asking if we had a wild romp?" she teased, her smirk widening at his evident distress.

Fully in control of her faculties now, Katherine could sense Aaron's tension, though she couldn't resist teasing him a bit longer. With a theatrical flourish, she pulled back the sheet, revealing her t-shirt and panties-clad form, contrasting with Aaron still fully dressed in his pants.

"You can relax, Aaron," she reassured, her voice flat but with a hint of amusement. "No need to worry. It's kind of hard to get up to anything with a guy when he's still in his jeans. I may be good, but I'm not that good," Katherine quipped, the teasing lilt in her voice finally breaking through the tension.

"I'm going to hop in the shower and get dressed. Feel free to join me if you dare," Katherine quipped, her tone playful. Of course, she wasn't serious—this was her cousin, after all. But Aaron was just too easy to tease, and she couldn't resist the opportunity to rib him a bit.

Aaron, unaware of Katherine's jest, declined with a puzzled shake of his head.

"Suit yourself," Katherine chuckled, her eyes dancing mischievously. "But you might want to wash the sleep from your eyes and tame that bushy hair of yours. There are new toothbrushes by the sink. And, well," she wrinkled her nose dramatically, "after last night, I suggest you use it." The lingering scent of alcohol clung to Aaron, a reminder of the revelries of the previous evening.

With a teasing smile and a casual wave, Katherine sauntered towards the bathroom, leaving Aaron to ponder her playful banter.

Sitting on the edge of the bed, Aaron felt a rush of embarrassment wash over him. He'd leaped to conclusions upon waking, assuming the worst when he saw Katherine beside him in bed. It hadn't occurred to him in his rush to uncover the events of the night that he was still fully clothed.

Feeling like a complete fool, he rubbed a hand over his face, trying to shake off the remnants of confusion and embarrassment. The realization slowly dawned on him that perhaps he had jumped to conclusions too quickly.

The bathroom door stood ajar and Aaron hoped it wasn't a silent invitation left in Katherine's wake. She hadn't bothered to check if it had properly latched to the frame, too caught up in her playful banter with Aaron. From his vantage point in the room, Aaron could hear the sound of running water as Katherine hummed a familiar tune, her voice surprisingly melodious against the backdrop of the shower's steady stream.

As the melody drifted through the crack in the door, Aaron couldn't help but admire her carefree attitude. Here she was, humming away without a care, unbothered by her modest attire in the presence of someone she hardly knew. It was a refreshing contrast to his own awkwardness.

With a resigned sigh, Aaron made his way to the sink in the small cubby beside the bathroom. He reached for the toothbrush, hoping fervently that the toothpaste and mouthwash would do their magic to mask the lingering scent of alcohol that seemed to permeate the room every time he opened his mouth.

As he scrubbed at his teeth, trying to banish the aftertaste of last night's revelry, Aaron couldn't shake the throbbing ache in his head. The hangover was settling in like an unwelcome guest, squeezing his temples in a merciless vise grip. He knew there was little he could do to dispel it, aside from the futile hope that the morning routine would bring some relief.

Aaron carefully avoided glancing towards the direction of the shower, a sense of propriety guiding his movements. Swiftly, he finished his morning rituals and moved back to the bed, eager to put distance between himself and the situation that still hung in the air like a lingering fog.

Patiently, he waited for Katherine to finish her shower. Soon enough, she emerged from the bathroom, wrapped snugly in a towel that clung to her dampened skin, her hair trailing droplets of water.

Meeting Aaron's gaze, Katherine was greeted with a direct question that cut through the morning haze. "How did we end up in bed together last night?" Aaron asked, his tone a mix of confusion and embarrassment.

A mischievous grin tugged at the corners of Katherine's lips, though she suppressed the urge to burst into laughter at the earnestness in Aaron's expression. It was almost comical, considering nothing untoward had transpired.

"You stumbled in, completely out of it," Katherine explained patiently, her amusement evident. "I tried to get you to move, but you were dead weight. So, I did the decent thing—I took off your jacket, covered you up, and then had to decide between a night on that uncomfortable chair or sharing the bed with you."

Aaron's hand found its way to his forehead, a groan escaping him as he processed the information. He shook his head, immediately regretting the motion as his headache protested. Sheepishly, he looked at Katherine, his embarrassment palpable. "You must think I'm a complete mess," he muttered.

Katherine's gaze drifted down to her modestly wrapped form, her shoulders lifting in a casual shrug. "Oh, I've seen worse," she quipped, a playful glint in her eyes.

"You obviously have no problems being so vulnerable in front of a stranger," Aaron stated while regarding Katherine's current state of dress.

Katherine's gaze dropped to survey her attire. "You don't like what you see." She turned around slowly as if on the runway aggravating Aaron to the point of distraction.

"Yeah, but the problem is, I don't want to see it." Aaron turned his head.

Katherine shrugged nonchalantly. "This much isn't so bad. Besides, I'm a lingerie model. But don't worry," she added, stepping aside to gesture towards the bathroom, "I have no intention of being naked in front of you."

A blush tinged Aaron's cheeks at her remark, his discomfort evident. "Right, of course," he stammered, taking the hint. "Yeah. I'll just... go freshen up in there. Can you please have something on by the time I'm done? I'll be out soon," he said, quickly making his way into the bathroom, leaving Katherine to her privacy.

As he closed the door behind him, Aaron couldn't help but let out a nervous chuckle. This unexpected morning had certainly taken an interesting turn.

As Aaron contemplated the delicate balance of what was said, a silence settled on him. Thoughts of his girlfriend lingered at the periphery of his mind, a reminder of the complexities of his current predicament. Yet, after the events of last night, he harbored little hope that Sara would want anything to do with him again. The guilt rested unbearingly on him, a nagging presence he couldn't shake.

He longed to explain, to make amends with Sara. The desire to talk to her, to see her if possible, gnawed at him with an insistent urgency.

An hour later, Aaron and Katherine finally emerged from the hotel room, the morning's revelations still lingering in the air. Aaron couldn't help but marvel at the intricate dance of preparations Katherine went through before they could leave. It was a peculiar fascination he'd always held about women—how effortlessly they could turn the simplest of tasks into an elaborate ritual. He chided himself for the sexist thought, knowing it was unfair to generalize, yet Katherine seemed to embody the stereotype in a way that amused and frustrated him simultaneously.

Their destination was a park, a serene oasis amidst the bustle of the city. Katherine had insisted on the visit, eager to witness the autumn leaves in their vibrant hues as they clung tenaciously to the branches. She skipped a few steps ahead, her mood seemingly buoyant despite Aaron's somber demeanor.

The wind danced around them, teasingly tugging at Katherine's full-length skirt as she moved gracefully through the park's winding paths. She pulled the collar of her light jacket tighter around her neck, a futile attempt to ward off the brisk chill in the air.

Meanwhile, Aaron trailed behind, lost in his thoughts. His mind was a jumble of conflicting emotions, the guilt of the previous night's events still fresh in his mind. As they strolled through the park, he couldn't shake the feeling of being adrift, caught between the desire to make things right with Sara and the inexplicable pull of Katherine's teasing allure.

With each step, his decisions pressed upon him, a reminder of the web he found himself entangled in. As they walked on, the park's tranquility offered a fleeting respite from the storm of emotions swirling within him.

Unlike Katherine, Aaron found himself ill-prepared for the chill that swept through the park. In his hurried departure from Sara's house the night before, he had left behind his heavier jacket, now sorely missed. The thin windbreaker he wore offered little protection against the biting wind, its promise of warmth a cruel tease. His discomfort was palpable, though it wasn't just the weather that left him feeling miserable.

Watching Katherine dance about with a carefree abandon only served to underscore Aaron's sense of longing. The absence of Sara loomed large in his mind, a gaping void he couldn't ignore. The ache of missing her was immeasurable.

Determined to bridge the distance, Aaron resolved to call Sara at his earliest opportunity. He needed to hear her voice, to explain, to apologize, to feel some semblance of connection amidst the turmoil of emotions swirling within him.

An hour passed, marked by the rhythmic crunch of fallen leaves beneath their feet as they wandered through the park. Aaron's exhaustion crept upon him, his steps growing heavier with each passing moment. Finally, unable to match Katherine's boundless energy, he sank down onto an empty bench, the weariness settling deep into his bones.

The park had warmed slightly since their arrival, the sun casting a gentle glow over the landscape. Katherine paused in her lively antics, turning to regard Aaron with an amused twinkle in her eyes.

"Could you do me a favor?" Katherine asked, her voice light with amusement.

Aaron let out a weary sigh, feeling the weight of fatigue pressing down upon him. He mustered a polite nod, willing himself to be cordial despite his exhaustion. "What do you need?" he replied, his voice tinged with weariness.

With a swift movement, Katherine reached into the pocket of her jacket, retrieving a camera that she then pressed into Aaron's hands. Without hesitation, she tugged him up from the bench, taking his place with an easy grace.

"Take a picture," Katherine commanded, her voice playful yet insistent.

The request seemed simple enough, a mundane task in the midst of their park excursion. But as Aaron raised the camera to his eye, ready to capture the moment, a sudden rush of memory blindsided him. The dream—no, the nightmare— crashed over him like a relentless wave, squeezing his chest in a vice-like grip, stealing the air from his lungs.

Before he could fully comprehend what was happening, Katherine was on her feet in an instant, her hands reaching out to steady him. "Are you alright, Aaron?" she asked, her concern evident as she guided him back to the bench.

In a haze of confusion and panic, Aaron found himself sinking onto the bench once more, his head spinning as Katherine let him lay in her lap. The world seemed to tilt and blur around him, the sense of déjà vu overwhelming in its intensity. He felt as though he was being dragged back into the nightmare, the images and emotions threatening to consume him whole.

"Stop," Aaron cried out, his voice raw with desperation. He clutched at his head, willing the nightmare to release its grip on him, to let him be.

His sudden outburst startled Katherine, her eyes widening in shock. Hastily, she moved to free her lap from Aaron's head just as he reached out, grasping onto her jacket lapel with a surprising intensity. He clung to her as if she were the only solid ground in a tumultuous sea, his grip fierce and desperate.

For a few heart-pounding moments, Aaron was lost in the grip of the nightmare, the world spinning around him. But gradually, as he clung to Katherine, he felt the panic recede, the nightmare loosening its hold. Slowly, his breathing steadied, and the world came back into focus.

As the last tendrils of the nightmare faded, Aaron found himself still clinging to Katherine, his heart pounding in his chest. Embarrassment flooded through him, and he released his grip, pulling back slightly.

"I-I'm sorry," he stammered, his voice hoarse with emotion. "I don't know what came over me."

The nightmare had seized Aaron in its merciless grip, catching him completely off guard. What should have been a simple task—taking a picture—had transformed into a harrowing journey through the haunting visions of his dreams. The entire first portion of the dream had played out in a mere fraction of a minute, each moment etching itself into his consciousness with startling clarity. The experience shook him to the core, leaving him reeling in its wake.

"I'm sorry, Katherine," Aaron managed again, his voice trembling with the remnants of fear. "I... I had a nightmare. It felt so real." He struggled to find his bearings, his gaze searching hers desperately for some semblance of reassurance. "I didn't know what was happening."

His words hung in the air, the effects of the nightmare still lingering between them. Aaron needed to ground himself, to confirm that he was indeed awake and that the horrors of his dreams had not followed him into reality. "Am I... awake?" he asked, his voice tinged with uncertainty.

Katherine regarded him with a mixture of concern and confusion. Aaron appeared awake, his eyes wide with fear and confusion, yet the surreal experience they had just shared defied explanation. "Yes, you're awake," she replied shakily, uncertainty coloring her tone. "But... are you going to be alright?"

The question hung between them, laden with unspoken fears and uncertainties. Katherine couldn't shake the unease that settled in the pit of her stomach, a nagging sense that something wasn't quite right. Aaron's sudden and intense reaction had shaken her to the core, leaving her grasping for answers in the midst of the surreal moment.

As they sat there, the park around them seemingly holding its breath, Katherine couldn't help but wonder what other secrets lay buried within Aaron's troubled mind. The unspoken lingered in the air, a silent understanding passing between them as Katherine grappled with the unsettling aftermath.

Aaron's head throbbed with the remnants of the recurring nightmare, his mind still reeling from the haunting images that had always plagued him. With a frustrated shake of his head, he tried desperately to banish the visions that clung to the edges of his consciousness. Taking a moment to gather his thoughts, he surveyed the disarray of emotions and confusion that seemed to surround him.

"Yeah, I think so," Aaron finally managed, his voice strained with the effort of steadying himself. "Can you... help me up?"

Katherine nodded, her own hands trembling slightly as she reached out to assist him to his feet. The shock of the moment lingered in the air between them, a tension that neither knew quite how to dispel.

"What kind of nightmare can you have while awake?" Katherine asked incredulously, her voice betraying a hint of unease.

Aaron met her gaze, uncertainty flickering in his eyes. He knew he had to explain, to make her understand, or risk losing her to the unsettling darkness that had enveloped him. The fear he saw reflected in her eyes spurred him into action.

Taking a deep breath, Aaron began to recount the fragments of his dream, each memory vivid and unsettling. He spoke of the eerie familiarity of the dream, the sense of foreboding that had always gripped him. And then, with a sense of reluctance, he told her about the redheaded woman—the woman who bore an uncanny resemblance to Katherine herself.

As he spoke, the tension within him seemed to lift slightly, the act of sharing his fears and uncertainties offering a small measure of relief. Yet, with each word, the realization of the strangeness of it all settled upon him like a heavy cloak.

Katherine listened intently, her eyes widening with each revelation. The resemblance to the mysterious woman in Aaron's dream left her unsettled, a shiver running down her spine. Yet, despite the unease that gnawed at her, she remained by his side, her presence a comforting anchor amidst the tumult of emotions.

When Aaron finally fell silent, the park seemed to hold its breath, the quiet of the moment broken only by the rustling of leaves in the gentle breeze. A silence hung between them, full of unspoken questions and uncertainties.

"I... I don't know what to make of it," Aaron admitted, his voice barely above a whisper. "But... thank you for staying."

Katherine took in Aaron's story with surprising grace, considering the unsettling possibility that the woman in his dreams could very well have been her. As they sat together on the bench, the tension of the moment seemed to ease, melting away into an easy conversation that flowed between them effortlessly.

When Aaron recounted the details of his haunting dream, he found himself opening up to Katherine in a way he hadn't expected. The nightmare seemed to lessen with each word, the act of confiding in her offering a strange sense of relief. What surprised Aaron the most was Katherine's unwavering belief in his story, her acceptance devoid of any hint of skepticism or condescension.

"What does this thing that comes after me want from me?" Katherine asked after a moment, her voice filled with a mix of curiosity and concern.

Aaron shook his head, a frown creasing his brow. "I don't know," he admitted, his voice tinged with frustration. "I've never been able to figure it out. I don't even know if you're the redheaded girl from my dreams."

Katherine looked skeptical, her gaze piercing as she regarded him. She had no doubt in her mind that she was the woman in his dreams, despite Aaron's uncertainty. Instead, she focused on another detail from his narrative from what he had told her of the discussion with Sara's parents.

"You were headed to the church last night, weren't you?" Katherine queried, her brow furrowing in thought. "Did you find what you were looking for?"

Aaron shook his head, a sense of disappointment shadowing his features. "No," he replied with a sigh. "The door was closed. I didn't even get a chance to go inside."

A flicker of determination crossed Aaron's expression as he looked around, a newfound resolve taking hold. When his gaze met Katherine's once more, there was a spark of something new, an unspoken challenge.

"I was thinking... maybe we could go there now," Aaron suggested tentatively, his voice tinged with uncertainty.

Katherine's eyes widened in surprise, the suggestion catching her off guard. Yet, without hesitation, she nodded eagerly. Her decision was made in an instant, fueled by a desire to help Aaron in any way she could.

"Let's go," she exclaimed, a hint of excitement in her voice.

"We can cut across the park and be at the church in about twenty minutes," said Aaron.

With a shared sense of purpose, they rose from the bench with a newfound determination. They set off through the park, the path ahead filled with the promise of answers and the possibility of unraveling the mystery that had plagued Aaron's dreams.

IT didn't take them quite twenty minutes to traverse the park and reach the church, but the urgency in Aaron's steps made the time seem irrelevant. He was driven by a need to uncover the mysteries that had eluded him—about the little girl, about the town, about everything that had been kept hidden from him by his parents and Sara's parents.

As they pushed open the heavy doors of the church, a wave of solemn tranquility washed over them. The interior was bathed in the soft, multicolored hues of sunlight filtering through the towering stained glass windows that adorned the east and west walls. Each pane depicted a different scene from biblical tales, their vibrant colors casting dancing reflections on the polished wooden floors.

The rows of pews stood in silent vigil, leading the way toward the pulpit that awaited at the front of the church. The seats were covered in rich burgundy velvet, their surfaces smooth and inviting under the fingers. It was as though they whispered tales of prayers and hymns sung in hushed reverence.

At the center of it all, the pulpit stood as a beacon of light and faith. Candles were fitted in their stanchions of majestic brass candelabras. A mellow scarlet sash adorned the table before the pulpit, its embroidered borders of heavy gold thread shimmering in the gentle light. The sash, with its ornate design and intricate details, seemed to hold centuries of history and tradition within its folds.

It was clear that the church was preparing for the upcoming Sunday service, every detail meticulously arranged with care. The heavy gold tassels of the sash brushed against the floor, a symbol of the reverence with which the sacrament of Holy Communion was held.

For a moment, Aaron and Katherine stood in awe of the solemn beauty that surrounded them. The air was thick with the scent of polished wood, beeswax from the past burning of candles, and a faint hint of incense lingering from past services. It was a sensory overload, the sights and smells weaving together to create a tapestry of sacredness.

Their footsteps echoed softly against the stone floors as they wandered down the aisles, pausing to admire the intricate carvings on the wooden pews, the delicate stained glass windows that bathed the interior in a kaleidoscope of colors.

Aaron took a hesitant step forward, drawn toward the pulpit as though by an invisible force. He reached out, his fingers grazing the smooth wood of the table where the scarlet sash lay. It was cool to the touch, the intricate embroidery rough against his skin.

"I wonder..." Aaron murmured, his voice barely above a whisper as he traced the golden threads with his fingertips. He couldn't shake the feeling that there was something here, something hidden beneath the surface waiting to be discovered.

Katherine stood beside him, her gaze sweeping over the majestic beauty of the church. She could sense Aaron's curiosity, his eagerness to unravel the mysteries that lay within these sacred walls. There was a shared sense of purpose between them. She wanted to help Aaron find answers to his questions.

Aaron glanced around, noting the absence of anyone to greet them. "I need to speak with Father Gordon," he said mainly to himself, his voice firm with determination. He hoped fervently that the priest would be in, ready to assist him in his quest for answers.

Aaron strode purposefully towards the rear of the church. There was a sense of urgency driving him. Katherine followed closely behind him. Aaron could sense the tension in her, a quiet unease that mirrored his own. He wondered briefly what could be troubling her, but his thoughts were consumed by the task at hand.

With each step, Aaron's heart hammered in his chest. The memories of his mother's funeral, held in this very church, lingered at the edges of his mind. He felt a pang of sorrow and longing, the loss heavy upon him.

Glancing back, Aaron saw Katherine trailing behind him, her expression unreadable. He offered her a reassuring smile, hoping to ease whatever apprehension she might be feeling.

As they reached the back of the church, he turned his attention to the door that led to Father Gordon's office, his heart pounding with a mixture of anticipation and apprehension. This was the moment he had been waiting for, the chance to talk with Father Gordon and delve into the church's records and uncover the truth.

The rich scent of mahogany filled the air. The wood was warm to the touch as Aaron rapped lightly on the door, the sound echoing in the quiet hallway. He waited anxiously, his heart racing as he hoped for a response. To his relief, a voice from within called out, granting them permission to enter.

Pushing open the door, Aaron stepped into the office, followed closely by Katherine. The room was cozy and inviting, the walls lined with bookshelves filled with leather-bound tomes and religious artifacts. A large wooden desk sat at the center of the room, its surface cluttered with papers and inkwells.

Father Gordon sat comfortably behind his desk, the familiar collar of his calling a symbol of his lifelong dedication to the people of Ionia. His years of ministry had woven him deeply into the fabric of the town, each moment spent tending to the spiritual needs of its residents. He looked up from his papers, warmth spreading across his face as he recognized Aaron, one of his most cherished sons.

"Aaron!" Father Gordon's voice boomed with genuine affection as he rose from his chair, arms outstretched in a welcoming embrace. He enveloped Aaron in a paternal hug, planting kisses on both of his cheeks. The genuine joy in his eyes reflected the bond they shared, a bond that had weathered the trials of time.

Turning his gaze to Katherine, Father Gordon's expression softened with curiosity. He extended the same warm greeting to her, though he couldn't hide a hint of unfamiliarity. He had not seen her before, and the absence of Sara by Aaron's side did not escape his notice. However, he chose to let the matter lie for the moment, focusing instead on the reunion before him.

"Please, have a seat," Father Gordon gestured towards the chairs scattered around the cozy office. Aaron and Katherine settled onto a plush love seat, while Father Gordon took his place in the high-backed chair across from them.

"It warms my heart to see you, Aaron," Father Gordon began, his voice a mix of joviality and concern. "I couldn't help but worry after what happened at your mother's funeral. How have you been? You look... better." There was a genuine concern in his tone, a deep-rooted care for the well-being of those he considered family.

Aaron nodded, a grateful smile playing on his lips. "Thank you, Father," he replied, his voice tinged with emotion. "It's been a difficult time, but I'm managing."

Aaron's smile, though polite, held a tinge of restraint—a mere facade to conceal his troubles. He ran a nervous finger along his cheek, his unease noticeable in the air around him. The was on his mind, casting a shadow over the otherwise warm reunion.

"Yes, Father," Aaron finally replied, the words coming out with effort. The memory of the funeral scene lingered like a specter in his thoughts, a scene he wished fervently to bury in the past.

Father Gordon's eyes softened with understanding as he glanced between Aaron and Katherine. He had sensed the underlying tension, the unspoken burdens that each of them carried. For a moment, he hesitated, choosing his words carefully before speaking.

Katherine, ever perceptive, caught the brief hesitation in Father Gordon's expression. With a gentle grin, she sought to ease the atmosphere, to make herself more approachable to the kindly priest.

Father Gordon cleared his throat, his eyes crinkling at the corners with a gentle warmth. "What can I do for you and your young friend...?" He trailed off, a subtle invitation for Aaron to introduce Katherine.

Realizing his oversight, Aaron felt a flush of embarrassment color his cheeks. He glanced apologetically at Katherine before turning back to Father Gordon.

"Her name is Katherine Morgan," Aaron stated firmly, his tone leaving no room for further questions. The mention of her name brought with it a rush of memories, a reminder of the tangled web of emotions that still clung to him from the previous night. "I met her just last night, and I would rather not discuss anything else about it."

Father Gordon nodded understandingly, his gaze softening with empathy. He could sense Aaron's unspoken troubles, the lingering pain that seemed to color his words. "Of course, Aaron," Father Gordon replied gently, choosing to respect his wish for privacy.

The thought of Sara, and why she wasn't there, was present within Aaron's thoughts. It presented as a silent reminder of the fractured relationship that now lay between them.

Realizing that dwelling on the past would only hinder their progress, Aaron straightened in his seat, his resolve firm. It was time to focus on the task at hand, to delve into the mysteries that had brought them to the church in the first place.

Aaron continued, his voice steady. "I came to ask you a favor. I need to know if I could look over the church records. In particular, I would like to see the history of the town, if that's possible."

Father Gordon's response was swift and accommodating. his eyes brightened with interest at Aaron's request, a spark of curiosity igniting within him. The church records held a wealth of information, a treasure trove of history that few had the opportunity to explore.

"Ah, the town's history," Father Gordon mused, his voice tinged with excitement.

The church records were not kept under lock and key; there was no reason to withhold them from Aaron's inquiry. Besides, Father Gordon found himself pleasantly unoccupied for the day, with only minor church duties awaiting his attention. The prospect of sharing the company of the two young adults seemed far more appealing.

"Of course, Aaron," Father Gordon replied warmly, a genial smile gracing his features.

"Thank you, Father Gordon," Aaron said gratefully, his voice filled with genuine appreciation. "This means a lot to me."

"Well, I see no reason not to grant your request," said Father Gordon as he stood up. "Please, follow me to the church library."

With that, Father Gordon led the way, his footsteps echoing softly against the polished floors of the church. Aaron and Katherine followed closely behind, their curiosity piqued by the promise of history waiting to be uncovered.

As they walked, Father Gordon cast a casual glance over his shoulder, his curiosity getting the better of him. "May I inquire as to what sparked this sudden interest in the town's history?" he asked, his tone laced with genuine curiosity.

Aaron paused for a moment, taking in the grandeur of the church library as they arrived at their destination. The library was a marvel in itself, its spaciousness belying the unassuming exterior of the church. Two levels made up the main portion of the library, with the second floor extending into the basement from the floor that they entered on, hidden from view.

"It's quite impressive," Aaron remarked, his eyes roaming over the rows of towering bookshelves that lined the walls. The air was thick with the scent of old paper and leather bindings, a comforting scent that enveloped him in a sense of nostalgia.

The walls were lined with shelves filled with old books and relics of times long past. Dust motes danced in the shafts of sunlight that filtered through a small window, casting a warm glow over the ancient tomes.

Aaron felt a shiver of excitement run down his spine as he reached out to touch one of the dusty volumes. The leather was worn and cracked with age, the pages yellowed and fragile beneath his fingers. It was a treasure trove of forgotten lore, a glimpse into the history of the town and its people.

Turning his attention back to Father Gordon's question, Aaron settled himself at a small wooden reading table situated on a far wall across from the stairs. Katherine took a seat beside him, her eyes alight with curiosity.

"I've heard a few troubling tales, particularly concerning the firstborn children of the town," Aaron explained, his voice carrying concern. The tranquility of the moment shattered as Father Gordon's complexion visibly paled, a reaction that caught Aaron off guard. Undeterred by the sudden change, he pressed on. "Lately, I've been haunted by visions of a young girl. I can't place her origin or identity, but I sense she's tied to the mysteries of Ionia."

Father Gordon's reaction was immediate and unsettling. He brought a hand to his mouth, crossing himself in a gesture of both fear and reverence. With a trembling hand, he pointed towards a distant bookshelf, his voice barely above a whisper. "All the answers you seek... they should be found there. But do not speak of this matter again, nor of that child, that... abomination," Father Gordon's agitation was perceivable, his voice strained with an urgency that sent shivers down Aaron's spine. "I can offer no more aid in this affair. Find your own way out when you're done; I won't return."

With that, Father Gordon turned abruptly, his swift departure leaving a stunned silence in his wake. He didn't spare a backward glance as he exited the room, his footsteps echoing down the corridor.

Katherine and Aaron exchanged bewildered looks; Father Gordon's reaction hung in the air.

"What was that all about?" Katherine asked, her eyes still fixed on the doorway through which Father Gordon had disappeared.

Aaron could only shake his head in bewilderment, the puzzle of Father Gordon's cryptic warnings swirling in his mind. "I have no idea," he replied, his voice tinged with a mixture of confusion and unease. "But it seems we've stumbled upon something much darker than I anticipated."

Together, they rose from their seats, the atmosphere of the library suddenly oppressive around them. The ancient tomes lining the shelves seemed to whisper secrets of the town's past, their pages filled with untold stories and hidden truths.

As they made their way towards the indicated shelves, uncertainty hung heavy on their shoulders. Whatever mysteries awaited them in the history of Ionia, it was clear that they had only just begun to scratch the surface.

20

Katherine regarded Aaron with a furrowed brow, her expression mirroring the confusion swirling within her. She sensed that Aaron himself was grappling with the unsettling encounter they had just experienced, so she refrained from pressing further. Instead, she kept her questions to herself, allowing Aaron the space to lead the way in their investigation—it had been his idea to delve into the church records, after all.

Despite her silence, Katherine's mind buzzed with intrigue over Father Gordon's cryptic behavior. The abruptness of his departure and the intensity of his warnings left her curious, though she couldn't quite grasp the reasons behind them.

Aaron, on the other hand, found himself consumed by curiosity, the scene with Father Gordon replaying in his mind like a persistent whisper. A part of him yearned to confront the priest, to demand answers to the questions that gnawed at him. Yet, a deeper instinct told him to focus on the task at hand.

Resisting the urge to dwell on Father Gordon's enigmatic words, Aaron redirected his thoughts to the purpose of their visit. The mention of the "abomination" and the connection to the little girl haunted him, driving him to seek answers within the church's ancient records. He believed that these records held the key to unraveling the mystery that had gripped Ionia.

"I think we should start with the oldest records," Aaron suggested, his voice tinged with determination. "There might be something in there about the town's early history, about the families who first settled here."

Katherine nodded in agreement, her curiosity piqued by the prospect of uncovering the town's secrets. Together, they made their way to the towering shelves that housed the ancient tomes, their spines cracked and worn with age.

Aaron wandered to the closest shelf, his fingers trailing along the stiff spines, leaving a faint trail in the settled dust. With a casual air, he plucked a book from its resting place, the cover coated in a layer of neglect. Lazily, he leafed through its pages, the contents unfamiliar and seemingly unrelated to their quest. Frustration gnawed at him as he returned the book to its dusty perch, realizing its irrelevance.

Beside him, Katherine moved gracefully, her fingers skimming over the multitude of ledgers lining the shelves. She cast a glance at Aaron, noting his uncertainty and the furrow that creased his brow. It was clear he didn't know where to start.

"Why don't you tell me the date you're looking for?" Katherine suggested, her voice soft with reassurance. "They seem to be organized in chronological order."

Aaron's brow furrowed in thought as Katherine's suggestion settled into his mind. It seemed almost too simple, yet he couldn't deny its logic. His mind raced back to the snippets of information he and Sara had unearthed from the records at city hall. One particular detail stood out amidst the faded ink and weathered pages.

Without hesitation, he reached for one of the earliest sets of ledgers, the leather cover worn with age. With a soft thud, he placed it on the table to his left, the slightly musty scent of old paper rising around them. Taking a seat, he ran his fingers over the crumbling pages, feeling the weight of history beneath his touch.

"If memory serves me right," Aaron began, his voice low as he turned the yellowed pages, "the city of Ionia was founded in the early seventeen hundreds." His eyes scanned the faded script, searching for the information he sought. "According to the records at city hall, the early deaths of first-born children didn't begin until the middle of the seventeen hundreds, some thirty years or so after the town's founding."

Katherine listened intently, her eyes flickering with curiosity as Aaron spoke. She watched as he traced his finger along the lines of text, his expression focused and intent. There was a determination in his gaze, a fire burning bright despite the weight of the revelations they were uncovering.

As Aaron delved deeper into the ledger, Katherine decided to join him, pulling up a chair beside him. The worn wood creaked softly beneath her weight as she settled in, the leather of the chair cool against her skin.

Aaron muttered to himself, his voice barely audible as he turned the fragile pages of the ledger. Each rustle of paper seemed to echo in the quiet library with centuries settling around them like a heavy shroud. He scanned the faded ink, his eyes flickering with determination.

It took three complete ledgers before his finger finally landed on a passage of significance. His brow furrowed in concentration as he read aloud, his voice tinged with a mixture of shock and disbelief.

"It says here that the city was experiencing a low birth rate," Aaron murmured, his finger tracing the faded words on the page. "Infant deaths were becoming abnormally common. Only one out of every five births actually survived..."

Aaron shook his head, his mind reeling at the thought of so much loss and suffering. "That's... That's crazy," he finally managed, his voice barely above a whisper.

Katherine leaned in closer, her eyes scanning the passage with a thoughtful frown. "That's not necessarily surprising," she offered, her voice calm and steady. "In those days, it was common for children to die at birth. The lack of modern medicine at that time... it was a perilous time for infants."

Aaron glanced at Katherine, a sense of urgency in his gaze as he pointed to the particular paragraph in the ledger. He wanted her to see the information for herself. With a silent nod, Katherine leaned in closer, her eyes scanning the faded ink with a furrowed brow.

As Aaron turned the page, his heart skipped a beat at the unexpected discovery. Nestled within the folds of the ledger lay a small, weathered journal, its leather cover worn with age. It was a thin volume, almost unnoticeable if not for the twist of fate that had led him to this exact page.

Carefully, Aaron lifted the journal from its resting place, his fingers trembling slightly with anticipation. The leather was soft beneath his touch, the ties worn but still intact. Despite its simplicity, the journal held an air of elegance, a relic of a time long past.

Gently, Aaron untied the leather bindings, taking care not to damage the fragile pages within. As he opened the journal, the scent of old paper and ink filled the air, a tangible reminder of the history contained within its pages.

The handwritten words were neat and precise, each letter etched with care. Aaron's eyes scanned the pages, his heart racing with each revelation. An initial scan indicated that the journal spoke of the burning of witches, rituals performed under the light of the full moon, and offerings made to some unknown entity.

"What is this?" Aaron murmured, his voice barely above a whisper.

Katherine leaned in closer, her eyes wide with a mixture of fear and fascination. "It seems to be some sort of... diary," Katherine said, her voice filled with awe.

VERILY, I am known as Father Henry, and this day marks the 15th of August, in the year of our Lord 1781. A mystery shrouds the recent events that have befallen our once fair city. Alas, we are powerless to save the lives of many of our tender children; they depart this world unexplained, either at birth or in their earliest days. The mothers, too, are taken from our midst, ushered into the embrace of our Lord, may they find solace in His eternal arms.

I have beseeched the heavens, seeking a revelation of God's divine plan for our afflicted township. We cannot endure this plight much longer. Should we persist upon this path, our once thriving township will surely cease to be ere the turn of the century.

ON THIS 23RD DAY OF November, in the year of our Lord 1791, I continue this journal, wherein I recount the events that have led us to our lamentable state. Only one blessed birth graced our township in the summer of 1781, and we christened her Precious, for she was indeed a treasure to us all. The very hope of our beloved settlement, she brought joy to every heart within these humble abodes.

Yet, alas, on the occasion of her tenth year upon this earth, Precious fell grievously ill. We, poor souls, were helpless in the face of her malady. Every remedy known to us was attempted in the desperate bid to restore her to health. Yet, it seems not the hand of God that intervened in our pleas, for the once merry child now wanders among us as a specter of her former self.

Fear grips the hearts of our township's folk at the mere sight of her. Her own parents, in the throes of hysteria, insist that this is not their daughter. They whisper that the true Precious perished with her sudden affliction, and that which now inhabits her fragile frame is an unnatural spirit. I have attempted to console them, to counsel them in their distress, and I have conversed with Precious herself. Yet, I must confess, dear journal, that the child we once adored no longer dwells among the living. Who or what she has become, I dare not speculate, but this much I know: she is lost to us.

ON THIS 15TH DAY OF January, in the year of our Lord 1792, I found myself in conversation with Elbert, the father of Precious, regarding the tragic event that has befallen our midst. His dear wife, Racheal, departed this world in an untimely manner, her life claimed in the silent hours of the night. Evidence points to a somber conclusion: she met her end upon the stairs of their dwelling, ensnared in the clutches of sleep's deceptive embrace.

Yet, to my dismay, Elbert harbors suspicions darker still. He is firmly convinced that his own flesh and blood, his daughter Precious, played a hand in this dreadful affair. Nay, more than that, he fears she harbors intentions against his very life.

Oh, the child is undeniably peculiar, of that there can be no dispute. But could she, in her tender years, be capable of such a heinous act as the cold-blooded murder of the one who cradled her in infancy? I dare not venture into the realms of conjecture. Yet, this much is clear: if swift action is not taken to address this dire situation, the good folk of our town may be driven to take justice into their own hands. The specter of vigilante justice looms ominously on the horizon.

ON THIS 4TH DAY OF April, in the year of our Lord 1792, dark accusations have been levied against Precious, casting shadows upon her very soul. Whispers drift through the air, tales of her consorting with the infernal powers that dwell beyond the veil of our understanding. She is said to wander the wooded realms that encircle our township, accompanied by three mysterious figures, cloaked in the shroud of anonymity.

These figures, strangers to our eyes and our knowledge, are rumored to be a witch and two warlocks, their presence a stain upon the sanctity of our humble abode. As for Precious herself, I have borne witness to her conversations with entities beyond the mortal realm. A fallen angel, I would deem it, though not the Fallen Angel of scripture.

Yet, to bring forth such revelations is to court peril of the gravest nature. The flames of suspicion burn brightly in the hearts of our community, eager to cast blame upon any who dare tread the shadowed path of the occult. Should I dare to speak of what I have seen, I too risk the stake and the pyre, condemned as a consorter with witches and the devil.

Fear grips my heart, not only for my own mortal safety but for the eternal soul of Precious. The townsfolk, their minds inflamed with righteous fervor, speak of seizing her this very night, holding her captive until the dawn's first light. May the mercies of God descend upon her soul, for in these dark times, divine grace is our only solace.

ON THIS 5TH DAY OF April, in the year of our Lord 1792, tragedy has once again cast its somber shadow upon our beleaguered township. The passing of Precious' father, Elbert, came as little surprise to those who knew him best. A man given wholly to the indulgence of spirits, his constitution was weakened by the ceaseless consumption of potent liquors.

The good folk of Ionia, in their grief and confusion, have turned their accusatory gaze upon the dark figure of Precious, as they have come to dub her in whispered tones. This morning, she was taken into custody, her fate now entwined with the cruel machinations of our fearful populace.

The pall of death hangs heavy upon us, for the discovery of Elbert's lifeless form in his bed has left a chill upon our souls. I beheld his countenance in death, marred by an expression of profound shock. A sight such as this gives rise to unsettling doubts within my breast, doubts that whisper of unseen hands at play in the affairs of mortals.

In this hour of turmoil, the city council has convened, beseeching my aid in a most dire task. They bid me examine the child, Precious, seeking out any trace of demonic influence that may linger within her fragile frame. Their hearts heavy with the weight of potential injustice, they seek absolution for their souls, fearing the condemnation of an innocent to the flames of righteous retribution.

Thus, the wheels of fate turn evermore, propelled by the fear and uncertainty that now grip our once tranquil hamlet. May divine providence guide my hand in this solemn endeavor, for the fate of Precious hangs precariously in the balance, a pawn in a game of shadows and whispers.

UPON THIS 15TH DAY of April, in the year of our Lord 1792, the trial of the unfortunate child has drawn to a close, though not without leaving a lingering pall of unease upon our stricken township. The proceedings unfolded at a pace that none could have foreseen, revealing truths more harrowing than any dared to imagine.

It is now evident, beyond the shadow of a doubt, that the innocent form of the child is ensnared by an unholy and unnatural spirit. Such power emanates from her, a force that defies the bounds of mortal understanding. Yet, despite the potency of this malevolent presence, she remains bound by the flesh, a fragile vessel for forces beyond her ken.

I, for my part, stand aloof from the grim deliberations of the town council, for I hold no belief that the expulsion of this dark entity can be achieved through the barbarous act of burning the child at the stake. Such a course of action smacks of folly and desperation, born of fear rather than reason.

In a gesture both poignant and perplexing, the child bestowed upon me a locket, a keepsake from her mother's hand. She spoke in cryptic tones of a need for its safekeeping, hinting at a longing for the home from whence she came. Her words, laden with enigma, leave me confounded, for I cannot fathom the depths of her sorrow or the nature of her yearning.

Thus, I confine my musings to these hallowed pages, inscribing my doubts and fears in ink that may one day bear witness to the grim tale that has unfolded in our midst. I pray unceasingly for divine guidance, beseeching the Heavenly Father for insight that may yet illuminate the path before us. Yet, alas, my entreaties fall upon silent heavens, and I am left to counsel my troubled flock in the shadows of uncertainty and dread.

ON THIS 20TH DAY OF April, in the year of our Lord 1792, I find myself compelled to set down the dire events that have transpired in our once peaceful township. The toll of sorrow weighs heavy upon us, for in the span of mere days, several esteemed members of our town council have met their untimely demise.

The necessity of recounting this dark narrative cannot be overstated. It is a solemn duty, a burden I bear with a heavy heart, that the full truth of our plight be known to those who come after us.

Precious, that accursed child of darkness, was brought forth to the stake following the sudden passing of the fourth council member. The noonday sun bore witness to the grim proceedings as she was bound to the pyre, left to endure the agonizing hours until the veil of dusk descended upon our anguished township.

Throughout the day, she ranted and raved with a fervor that struck terror into the hearts of all who beheld her. The good folk of Ionia, in their desperation, implored her to repent, to cast off the shackles of her infernal alliance, and to seek solace in the merciful embrace of the Lord above. Yet, she met their entreaties with naught but scornful laughter, a mirthless echo that chilled the soul.

As twilight descended, casting its somber shroud upon the land, the tinder was kindled, and the flames leapt forth with a voracious hunger. Precious, clad in her simple, white Sunday dress, stood amidst the inferno, her visage untouched by the searing heat. The fabric of her gown caught alight with an unholy ease, the flames consuming her flesh with an unyielding voracity.

Not a cry of pain escaped her lips, only the haunting echoes of her laughter reverberated amidst the crackling of the flames. In that harrowing moment, she spoke words that chilled us to the very marrow of our beings.

She cursed us, her voice carrying upon the wind like a harbinger of doom. She spoke of retribution, of a dark and terrible vengeance that she would wreak upon our hapless township. She vowed to claim the firstborn of every house, a grisly tithe for the life we had taken from her. With a voice that seemed to echo from the depths of the abyss itself, she damned us for our love turned to ashes, for the dreams we had shattered, and for the innocence we had stolen.

In that fateful hour, she declared herself the harbinger of our undoing, a specter of wrath unleashed upon a world that had forsaken her. As the flames consumed her form, her laughter mingled with the crackling of the pyre, a haunting dirge that echoed long into the night.

May the Lord above have mercy upon our wretched souls, for we have unleashed a darkness upon the world that shall never be forgotten.

ON THIS 30TH DAY OF June, in the year of our Lord 1805, I pen what shall surely be my final entry in this tattered journal. Precious, that spectral specter, haunts us still. She shan't be parted from our wretched souls, for we are bound to her by a cruel twist of fate.

No refuge can we find, no solace in flight, for all paths lead inexorably back to Ionia, that cursed crucible of our misfortune. The heavens themselves have turned a cold gaze upon us, forsaking us for the heinous transgressions we wrought upon Precious, staining our hands with the crimson mark of sin.

Under cover of night, she descends upon us like a malevolent wraith, stealing the very breath of life from our cherished offspring. What we once held dear, our firstborn, now serves as a bitter reminder of our folly, a source of unending sorrow.

Those fortunate souls spared her cruel embrace are left as hollow husks, drained of vitality, their life essence stolen away by her insatiable hunger. There are times when the missing child is naught but a haunting absence, a whispered memory that fades with each passing day.

Our firstborn, once the promise of our legacy, are now condemned to an untimely demise, and we are powerless to prevent it. I have gazed into the abyss of her dark eyes, beheld the twisted visage of the Dark Daughter, that abomination born of our sins.

She regales me with tales of celestial strife, of angels locked in furious battle amidst the hallowed halls of heaven. Her words are a blasphemous symphony, a twisted narrative of divine apathy. She speaks of a God who has turned a deaf ear to our pleas, a God who chooses to ignore our anguished cries.

But I know now what must be done to break this accursed cycle, to banish her from our midst. I have unearthed the ancient rites, the forgotten incantations that can pierce her veil of darkness. It is a perilous path I tread, fraught with danger and uncertainty.

Yet, in the face of such unspeakable evil, I am resolved. I shall confront the Dark Daughter, armed with the knowledge of ages past. I shall wield the power of forgotten lore, invoking the forces of light to vanquish this malevolent spirit that plagues us so.

May the heavens grant me strength, may the angels lend me their divine protection. For I shall venture into the heart of darkness itself, to confront the evil that lurks within and without. And in so doing, I shall redeem our souls from the abyss, and bring an end to the reign of terror that has befallen our fair township.

Let this be my final testament, my solemn vow. I go now to face the Dark Daughter, to do battle with the forces of darkness. Pray for me, dear reader, for I embark upon a quest from which there may be no return.

TURNING eagerly to the next page of the journal, Aaron anticipated the revelation promised by the priest—an answer to the enigma of Precious, a solution to rid themselves of the Dark Daughter. However, his hopeful anticipation quickly turned to disbelief as he found nothing of the sort. The remaining pages of the journal lay blank before him, a stark and perplexing contrast to his expectations. Three untouched pages, devoid of any inked secrets, offered no clues to unravel the mystery. There would be no easy resolution to this intricate puzzle.

Fury surged within Aaron, a hot, searing anger directed at himself, the town, and the seemingly useless journal. With a growl of frustration, he rose abruptly from his seat, his fingers clenching into fists around the journal. In a burst of pent-up emotion, he hurled the small diary across the room, the satisfying thud against the far wall doing little to ease his mounting frustration.

"What the hell are we supposed to do now?" Aaron's voice echoed through the empty room, his tone laced with desperation and anger. His hands trembled with the intensity of his emotions, uncertainty gnawing at his mind like a relentless beast. His troubles bore down on him, leaving him adrift in a sea of unanswered questions.

His thoughts immediately turned to Sara, her presence a beacon of comfort and solace in the chaos that surrounded him. In that moment of turmoil and uncertainty, he longed for her embrace, the warmth of her love offering a fleeting respite from the overwhelming tide of emotions threatening to consume him.

The room fell silent, save for the faint rustle of pages as the journal lay discarded on the floor. Aaron stood there, a turbulent storm of emotions roiling within him, unsure of what to do next. The mystery loomed large, its shadow stretching across the room like a specter of the unknown.

With a heavy sigh, Aaron sank back into his chair. He knew he was merely scratching the surface of a much deeper, darker truth. His challenge lay in finding more of the answers.

As the wave of anger receded from Aaron, it left behind an overwhelming sense of exhaustion and numbness. Wearily, he glanced towards Katherine, only to find her trembling uncontrollably, tears streaming silently down her cheeks. The raw fear in her eyes tore at his heart, aching with the knowledge that he could offer little in the face of her terror.

"What's wrong, Katherine?" Aaron's voice was gentle, filled with concern as he settled beside her, his arm instinctively wrapping around her trembling shoulders. He pulled her close, offering what little comfort he could in the midst of their shared turmoil. Katherine clung to him tightly, her grip unyielding in its desperation.

"Why are you shaking? Why the tears?" His questions hung in the air, heavy with worry and a deep-rooted need to protect her from whatever haunted her. Gently, he brushed away her tears, his touch gentle against her dampened cheeks.

Katherine struggled to find her voice amidst the storm of emotions that threatened to overwhelm her. Her words came out in a shaky whisper, barely audible above the soft rustle of their breathing.

"I... I'm scared, Aaron," she finally managed, her voice trembling with emotion. "I don't understand any of this. The journal, the... the darkness that's talked about seems to linger around us. It's... It's too much."

Aaron's heart clenched at her words, a fierce protectiveness rising within him. He shifted closer, his gaze locked with hers as he tried to offer some semblance of reassurance.

"You're not alone, Katherine," he murmured, his voice filled with quiet determination.

Her tear-stained face turned towards his, their breath mingling in the close proximity. In that moment, time seemed to stand still, their shared fear and uncertainty making the air heavy.

"What's going on, Katherine?" Aaron asked again, his voice a gentle plea for her to share the burden that she had.

"I... I don't know what to do," Katherine's voice wavered, her admission heavy with emotion. "My mother was born here, but I was raised elsewhere. After my mother passed away, a foster family took me in. And... I was their first child too." Her gaze dropped to her lap, hands gripping her head as if trying to contain the whirlwind of thoughts.

Katherine's revelation hung suspended, the silence thick with uncertainties. In the recesses of her mind, the image of the little girl from the journal danced like a ghostly apparition—an unsettling reminder of her own past.

"That can't be right," Katherine whispered to herself, the words barely audible. "The little girl described in the journal reminds me of my guardian angel," she thought to herself.

Suddenly, she turned towards Aaron, the movement so abrupt it startled him. "I came to this city to find my relatives," Katherine blurted out accusitorily, her eyes wide with a mixture of fear and disbelief. "That includes you, Michael, and my aunt from my father's side."

"What?" Aaron's voice was filled with incredulity, his mind struggling to process the revelation. "We're... We're related?"

"That's what you're focusing on?" Katherine's frustration bubbled to the surface, her hand waving dismissively at Aaron. "Your mother and my mother were sisters," she explained, her words coming out in a rush. "I'm your cousin, Aaron."

The words were like an invisible thread linking their pasts. For a moment, all Aaron could do was stare at each Katherine as the revelation began sinking in.

Aaron's mind raced, thoughts swirling with the implications of this newfound family tie. He looked at Katherine, seeing her in a new light—no longer just a new companion but now a blood relative, bound by the ties of shared ancestry.

"I... I don't know what to say," Aaron finally managed, his voice tinged with a mixture of surprise and wonder. "I had no idea." His thoughts drifted back to the night previous and the events that led to Sara's misunderstandings.

"That would have been helpful to know last night, Katherine. Why didn't you tell me until now?" Aaron's voice held a hint of frustration, his brow furrowing with a mix of concern and confusion. Despite the urgency of their situation, he couldn't ignore the feeling of being left in the dark.

Katherine met Aaron's gaze, her eyes reflecting a tumultuous mix of emotions. "What does that even matter now?" she asked, desperation creeping into her voice. "I was my parents' only child," she emphasized, the weight of uncertainty heavy in her words. "What's going to happen to me?"

Unspoken in her words was the realization that she knew Precious. The name had stirred memories deep within her, memories of a companion who had been a constant presence throughout her life. She couldn't bring herself to voice the fear that gnawed at her—a fear that her cherished companion might be entangled in the dark mysteries of Ionia.

"What am I supposed to do, Aaron?" Katherine's voice trembled, her eyes pleading for answers she wasn't sure existed. "I can't just ignore this..."

Aaron's heart ached at the desperation in Katherine's voice, his mind racing. He reached out, taking her hand in his, offering what comfort he could.

"I don't know, Katherine." Aaron rose from his seat, his gaze locked with hers as he pulled her gently to her feet. Uncertainty flickered in his eyes, mirroring the tumult within her. "I know as much about this as you do. I want you to go back to the hotel, lock the doors. I'll call you as soon as I can," he suggested, recalling that she had mentioned renting the room for two nights, just in case he had nowhere else to go.

"There's someone I need to see," he added, a sense of urgency tingeing his words.

"You're leaving me?" Katherine's voice trembled with a mix of fear and desperation, her eyes pleading for reassurance.

"I have to go see Sara. I need her... I need to talk to her, let her know what I've found," Aaron explained, his voice softening with a hint of regret as his hand swept to indicate the journal they had just read.

Katherine's frustration boiled over, her emotions swirling in a storm of anger and hurt. With a sudden movement, she pushed Aaron's hands away from her shoulders and turned to leave the library, her steps echoing with determined purpose.

"Go to your precious Sara. I don't need you," her voice rang out, laced with bitterness and wounded pride. "I can take care of myself. I'm leaving this town, and I'm not coming back."

As Katherine stormed out, her words were like a bitter echo of the rift that had formed between them suddenly.

"Damn," Aaron muttered under his breath, his heart clenching tightly because of the fractured bond. He watched her retreating figure, a pang of regret piercing through him. He gripped his chest tightly. For a moment, he stood there, torn between the urgency of his mission and the ache of leaving Katherine alone.

Aaron hesitated, torn between following Katherine and staying behind. Despite the urgency of the situation, he couldn't ignore the nagging feeling that he hardly knew this girl. Right now, informing Sara of what he had discovered felt more crucial, no matter the possible connection he shared with Katherine.

He could have asked Katherine to come with him but he had no idea how Sara would react. He decided that he would explain things to Sara first and then introduce her to Katherine but the way things were now, it wasn't likely to happen.

"Katherine, wait!" Aaron called out, his voice echoing in the quiet library. He watched as she continued to walk away, her steps resolute and unfaltering.

"Don't you remember what we just read in the journal?" Aaron's words fell on deaf ears as Katherine remained steadfast in her stride, ignoring his plea.

"If Precious doesn't want you to leave Ionia, then you won't be able to go anywhere," Aaron's voice carried a note of urgency, a sense of foreboding creeping into his tone.

But Katherine seemed determined to ignore him, her pace quickening as she approached the library door.

"Listen to me, Katherine!" Aaron's voice rose with desperation, a last attempt to reach her.

Yet, it was too late. With a final glance over her shoulder, Katherine disappeared through the library doors, leaving Aaron standing alone in the silent room.

With a heavy sigh, he turned back to the journals spread out on the table. Despite the turmoil of emotions, he knew that he had to find Sara, had to tell her what he had uncovered.

With a determined set to his jaw, Aaron gathered the journals and put them back on the shelves where he had gotten them from. As he worked, he couldn't shake the feeling of loss that clung to him like a shadow.

Finally, Aaron crossed the room slowly, his eyes falling on the diary he had thrown in frustration. Kneeling down, he retrieved the worn leather-bound book, dusting off its cover with care. He tucked it securely into his pocket.

Taking one last look around the library, Aaron couldn't shake the feeling of being watched, of unseen eyes studying him from the shadows. A shiver ran down his spine, but he pushed the sensation aside, dismissing it as mere paranoia.

With a determined stride, he made his way to the library exit, the heavy wooden doors creaking softly as he pushed them open.

From the shadowy corner where he had been lurking, Marcus emerged. He had witnessed the scene unfold, adding a little more to his store of knowledge. Knowledge was power, and Marcus craved it like a starving man. His lips curled into a sinister smile as he thought of the redheaded girl, tears streaming down her face. He imagined her in agony, her delicate flesh torn and bleeding. The desire for violence burned within him, a dark and twisted craving.

Precious was beyond his reach, too powerful to touch. But Katherine, dear Katherine, was another matter entirely. A wicked gleam danced in Marcus's eyes as he entertained thoughts of the unspeakable acts he longed to commit upon her. A bead of drool escaped his parted lips, a grotesque testament to his twisted desires.

Meanwhile, Aaron passed by Father Gordon's closed study door, the sense of unease settling over him and refusing to let go. After the disturbing encounter with the priest, Aaron decided against attempting to bid farewell. Father Gordon's cryptic warnings still echoed in his mind, warning him away.

Resolving to leave the church behind, Aaron stepped out into the fading daylight, the warmth of the setting sun washing over him. The diary in his pocket felt heavy. It served as a grim reminder of the secrets he had uncovered.

The town felt like it was cloaked in an eerie silence. The air seemed heavy with the promise of an impending storm. Aaron couldn't shake the feeling of the town seemingly holding its breath, waiting for some unseen event to unfold. But Aaron pressed on. He had to find Sara.

21

F ather Gordon watched Aaron's departure from the church through the expansive window of his office. The young man had paused at the door, a moment pregnant with unspoken words. Desperation tinged the priest's heart; he yearned to reach out, to offer aid, but the shadow of Precious loomed large, casting a chilling pall over his resolve. What could he possibly do to thwart the plans of this dark daughter? It seemed an insurmountable task, a battle against forces far beyond mortal ken.

He turned slowly from the window, his head hanging low and shaking from side to side as he moved towards his desk. As he grappled with his thoughts, the door to his study creaked open slowly. A small figure emerged, the twisted smile upon her pretty, cherubic face sending shivers down the priest's spine. Her eyes gleamed with malicious intent, a dark mirth dancing within their depths.

"Father Gordon," Precious spoke, her voice dripping with venom, "Are you contemplating ways to halt my plans? How quaint. But know this, dear priest, you are powerless against me. I will weave my designs unabated, and neither you nor any mortal soul can impede my path."

The priest's heart clenched at her words, a mixture of fear and determination coursing through his veins. A false bravado. The air in the room seemed to thicken with her presence, suffocating in its malevolence.

"Child," Father Gordon's voice was a low rumble, edged with a hint of defiance, "You may think yourself beyond the reach of mortal intervention, but there are forces greater than you can fathom. The light will always find a way to pierce the darkness, even in the darkest of nights."

Precious's laughter echoed through the study, a chilling sound that seemed to reverberate off the very walls. "Oh, dear Father," she taunted, "Your faith is admirable, but ultimately futile. Your words will fall on deaf ears."

Father Gordon's lip curled in disdain at the abomination that inhabited the innocent facade of a little girl before him. "Leave my office at once and return to the tomb that awaits you deep beneath this church," he commanded, his voice a mix of authority and disgust.

But Precious, ever defiant, stood her ground with an unsettling calmness. "I pray daily to the Heavenly Father above," Father Gordon continued, his words laced with fervent hope, "that He may rid this town of your darkness and forgive us for the sins we have unwittingly unleashed upon the innocent."

To this, Precious responded with a peal of mocking laughter, her small hands rising to cover her mouth as if to stifle the mirth that bubbled within her. The sound echoed off the walls of the office, filling the air with a chilling merriment.

"Oh, Father," Precious spoke, her voice dripping with malice disguised beneath a facade of innocence, "Your prayers are as futile as your commands. I shall depart from this place, but know that it is of my own accord, not because of any feeble attempts to sway me."

With that, she turned on her heel, the echo of her laughter trailing behind her like a haunting melody. Her footsteps echoed through the halls of the church, a chilling reminder of the darkness that now lurked within its sacred walls, waiting within the foundation of this sacred place.

Left alone in his office, Father Gordon bowed his head in silent prayer, his heart heavy with the weight of the darkness that surrounded him. "Heavenly Father," he whispered, the words a desperate plea for guidance and protection, "grant us strength in this time of trial. Banish this dark daughter from our midst and bring light back to this hallowed place."

As he prayed, the sound of Precious's laughter seemed to fade into the distance, replaced by a solemn silence that hung heavy in the air. The priest's prayers filled the room, a beacon of hope in the face of encroaching darkness. For in this battle against the forces of evil, faith was his only weapon. And so, he prayed on, his voice rising in fervent supplication to the heavens above.

THIS is the scene where Samael tells Father Gordon to look for something to connect Precious to the material world even though Marcus has already done this. Father Gordon asks how he knows this and says that he was just recently told this but doesn't understand what's meant by it. Samael refers to their conversation about an object imbued with celestial power. Father Gordon is then told that Precious is the angel known as Kafziel and she must be stopped. Father Gordon was unaware of Precious's status as an angel and thought that she was a demon. This is also the scene where Father Gordon asks who Samael is and thinks that he is Satan/Lucifer. Samael explains who he is and the difference between him and Satan/Lucifer/The Morning Star, etc. Samael makes reference to their past discussions about angels and celestial beings and sin and then clarifies that angels are exempt from sin but are still punished if they go against God's will. He explains where the misconception about Satan began and that Satan isn't actually the name of an angel but the term used for any action that they do by instruction from God that tempts man.

Fear and confusion still lingered heavy in the air as Father Gordon sat hunched over his desk, his hands hovering hesitantly over the worn pages of his Bible. Precious' departure had left him shaken, her words echoing in his mind like a haunting refrain. He bowed his head in prayer, seeking solace from the malevolent presence that seemed to linger long after she was gone.

It was in this fragile moment of vulnerability that a soft knock on the door frame jolted him from his reverie. Samael stood there, a silent figure in the doorway, his presence both reassuring and unsettling.

"Is it a bad time?" Samael's voice was gentle, a hint of concern underlying his words.

Father Gordon straightened in his chair, the weariness in his eyes masked by a facade of composure. "No, no, please come in," he replied, his voice more steady than he felt.

As Samael entered the room, an unspoken tension hung between them, the priest's unease palpable in the air. Yet, there was also a sense of curiosity, a desire to unravel the mysteries that seemed to surround this enigmatic figure.

"What brings you here, Samael?" Father Gordon asked, his voice betraying a hint of apprehension.

Samael's gaze met his, a silent understanding passing between them. "I have come to offer clarity in the midst of confusion," he replied cryptically, his words carrying a weight of ancient knowledge. And with that, the room seemed to hum with an energy both ominous and electrifying.

Samael's voice was calm, yet tinged with a sorrowful wisdom that seemed to echo through the room. "Father Gordon, what you know as 'Precious' is not what she seems," he began, his eyes holding a depth of knowledge that sent shivers down the priest's spine. "She is Kafziel, a fallen angel who once stood among the celestial hosts."

Father Gordon's brows furrowed in disbelief, his mind struggling to grasp the enormity of Samael's words. "No... no, that cannot be," he protested, his voice filled with a mix of fear and denial. "Precious is evil incarnate. A bane in this world, bringing darkness." But Samael's gaze remained unwavering, as if peering into the depths of Father Gordon's soul.

"Angels are supposed to be good," said Father Gordon.

"Angels are neither good nor evil, Father," Samael replied with an apologetic tone full of sorrow.

Father Gordon seemed a bit confused. There were too many events that had happened recently that he was still struggling to get his thoughts around. Regardless, he pressed on, asking, "But how can angels be considered neither good nor evil? They are the epitome of goodness, aren't they?"

Samael smiled gently. He moved further into the office and took a seat in the chair stationed before Father Gordon's desk. Crossing his legs, his hands found a resting place atop his knees.

"My friend," he began again, "goodness and evil are concepts that belong to the realm of humanity, tied to choices and their consequences. Angels, on the other hand, are bound by a different nature."

"You mean they are above such moral distinctions?"

Samael nodded in agreement. "Precisely. The capacity for sin does not burden angels, as servants of the divine. Sin is a uniquely human trait, a test of faith and resolve. Angels cannot bear sin because it is not within their nature to do so."

Father Gordon's fear had long receded as the conversation wore on. His attention was focused solely on the refined man before him. "But what about the Fallen One? Wasn't his rebellion a sinful act?"

"Defiance is a grave transgression against the divine order, but it is not a sin in the sense that you understand it," said Samael. "Angels, though free from sin, can still face divine retribution for actions that challenge God's will. Their nature is one of obedience and service, not of moral judgment."

Father Gordon couldn't just readily accept that explanation. "If that's the case, how could the angel of light, turn against God? It seems so contrary to everything I know."

"What you perceive as rebellion may, in fact, be a part of the divine plan."

Father Gordon's eyes widened. "You mean God intended for the angel of light to fall?" he asked incredulously.

"If," began Samael while stressing the word, "a particular angel did fall, as you believe, that angel's rebellion would not be a surprise but a necessary step in the unfolding of His plan. My Father's omniscience allows Him to see all possibilities and outcomes."

Father Gordon paused, allowing a silence to gather in the room. He stroked his chin with his hand. When he spoke again, it was more to himself than to anyone in particular. "But why would God create an angel destined to rebel against Him?"

Father Gordon looked up from his reverie into Samael's eyes. There seemed to be more to this man than initially met the eye.

"How do you know this?" the priest finally asked, his voice barely above a whisper, a glimmer of doubt beginning to take root in his heart.

Samael's lips curled into a knowing smile, a hint of sadness in his eyes. "I have walked the realms between heaven and earth for eons," he replied, his voice carrying the weight of centuries-old truths. "I have seen the rise and fall of angels, the weaving of destinies. It is my burden to know."

The words hung heavy in the air, leaving Father Gordon with a chilling realization that the world he thought he knew was far more mysterious and dangerous than he could have ever imagined. His heart pounded in his chest as he stared into the eyes of the enigmatic figure before him. Everything about Samael seemed otherworldly, from the ethereal glow that now surrounded him to the sense of ancient power that emanated from his presence. The priest's mind raced with the realization that this being, whom he had taken for a man seeking guidance, was something far beyond human.

"You... You're not human," Father Gordon whispered, his voice barely above a breath. "You're... Satan, Lucifer himself." The words hung heavy in the air, carrying the weight of centuries-old fears and beliefs. But to his surprise, Samael's lips curled into a knowing smile, revealing a glint of amusement in his eyes.

"Ah, Father Gordon," Samael replied, his voice a gentle whisper that seemed to echo through the room. "I am not the devil you fear. I am correctly called Samael, the Angel of Death."

The words sent a chill down Father Gordon's spine, as he realized that the truth of this encounter was far more complex and unsettling than he could have ever imagined.

Father Gordon's hands trembled as he clutched the worn Bible in his grasp, flipping through the pages with a fevered intensity. His mind raced with verses and prophecies, seeking validation for the truth he dared not admit.

"It's all here," he murmured to himself, the words of ancient scripture seeming to leap off the page. "The fallen one, the deceiver, the adversary... it can only be him."

Motivated by fear and a desperate need to make sense of the impossible, Father Gordon pieced together a narrative of biblical literalism and motivated reasoning. Every mention of darkness, of temptation, of the angel who fell from grace, seemed to point to one undeniable conclusion: Samael was the devil incarnate.

The priest's heart sank with the weight of his discovery, the realization settling like a heavy stone in the pit of his stomach. With a trembling voice, he raised his eyes to meet Samael's gaze, conviction burning in his soul. "You are... the devil," Father Gordon declared, the words a desperate plea for confirmation of his beliefs, no matter how terrifying they may be.

"You, an educated man, devout in his priesthood, would utilize biblical literalism and motivated reasoning to come to a conclusion such as that?" Samael asked pointedly. "I am not the devil you think I am."

Father Gordon appeared inflexible in his assertions. "Given what you say might have validity," he said doubtfully, "how can it be proven?"

It was some time before Samael spoke again. He stood gracefully and walked towards the middle of the office. He turned back to face Father Gordon. Digressing, Samael delved into a discourse on cosmology.

"Did you know that in days of antiquity, the planet Venus was regularly observed in the heavens easily with the naked eye? A name was given to this bright speck in the sky. As a name for the planet in its morning aspect, "Lucifer" or Light Bringer. For the planet in its evening aspect is "Noctifer" or Night-Bringer."

Father Gordon nodded, not sure where Samael was going with this speech. He calmed down enough to at least hear the man out.

This was but the beginning of Samael's discourse. He turned and walked to the other side of the small office, gazing at the books lining a simple shelf there. His hand roamed slowly, almost hypnotically against the fine leather bound casements containing who knows what words without looking within. The spine's letterings were well worn on some works and not clear enough of the entirety of the contents on the rest to give someone an idea of what inspiration lay within.

Turning, he continued. "In the Book of Isaiah, the king of Babylon was condemned in a prophetic vision by the prophet Isaiah and is called Helel ben Shachar. The title refers to the planet Venus as the morning star, and that is how the Hebrew word is usually interpreted."

"I understand that, but what are you getting at?" Father Gordon asked. It had indeed become easier to talk to Samael in the last few moments. Even after his assertion of who he was, Father Gordon felt no fear of the man as he had expected and initially done.

"Oh, how could Satanial fall at that time when it was also claimed that God punished Satan, or Lucifer, for not bowing down to Adam after He created man? How could his fall have occurred before Isaiah when Isaiah was not born upon the earth with Adam and Eve and only but later in time was he here?" Samael asked.

Father Gordon spoke not. It wasn't the time for him to ask or answer questions so he allowed Samael to continue.

"Isaiah spoke of the Babylonian kings. There has never been a rebel angel cast down from heaven, nor will there ever be. Fallen angels have made their choice to do so, but is it even freewill in the face of the Father?"

Samael waited, not for a response from Father Gordon but giving the man enough time to take in what he was saying. He slowly approached the desk again in the meantime.

"In history, satans are angels whose role it is to test the faithfulness of humans. They act out God's will. When the prophet Jesus of Nazareth was tempted to sin, an angel did it at the command of God. The name satan is but a name for a collective of angels whose job it is to tempt man into sin. This understanding has since fallen into inequity and many have forgotten for what it was. The angel's true name is Satanail."

"Well isn't he the ruler of hell?" asked Father Gordon.

Samael shook his head no. "The angel Mastema commands demons, not some Satan or Lucifer as you would believe. Also, the Chief Angel and Prince of the World, is identified as Metatron. You would know him better as the Arch-angel, Michael, the true bringer of light, my arch enemy and nemesis."

"Then who punishes the sins of man?" Father Gordon asked.

Samael didn't waver from the answer nor wait long to answer the question. "I do."

This revelation caused Father Gordon to lean back in his chair.

"Although I condemn the sins of man, I remain a servant of my Father. I appeared in the Garden of Eden and engineered the fall of Adam and Eve, however, the serpent is not my form, but a beast I rode. The Fifth Heaven is the realm of divine justice, purity, and the harmonious balance of cosmic forces. It is seen as a realm where the justice and righteousness of God are upheld, and where celestial beings carry out their duties in accordance with the divine will."

"But you don't seem evil," Father Gordon said softly.

Samael returned to his seat. "My role as an angel of light or darkness can vary widely depending on the need. I am a complex figure, embodying both light and darkness, and associated with various roles such as angel of death, ruler of the fifth heaven, and accuser of humans."

Father Gordon's mind reeled with the weight of Samael's revelations, his thoughts racing to make sense of the unimaginable truths laid bare before him. Yet, amidst the shock and disbelief, fear did not take hold. Instead, a steely resolve settled in his heart as he grappled with the newfound knowledge.

"If Precious is indeed a fallen angel," he began, his voice steady despite the tremor in his hands, "how can we rid the town of her malevolence?"

Samael regarded him with an unreadable expression, the ancient wisdom in his eyes speaking volumes. "There may be a way," he replied cryptically, his words hanging in the air like a whispered promise of hope.

Father Gordon leaned forward, his gaze intent as he listened to Samael's counsel. Samael asked after his remembrance of their previous encounter and conversation. The mention of their previous conversation about celestial objects of divine power sparked a flicker of recognition in his mind.

"Is there such an object here?" he asked, his voice filled with a mix of determination and desperation. Samael nodded solemnly, a ghost of a smile playing at the corners of his lips.

"Somewhere, hidden in the shadows, lies an object of great value to Precious. It contains a part of her celestial gifts from the time when she was still a true angel," he explained.

Father Gordon looked up, a mix of desperation and hope in his eyes. "But, Samael, if you are the Angel of Death, can't you do something about Precious... about Kafziel?" His voice quivered with the weight of his plea.

Samael's expression softened, a deep sadness shadowing his eyes. "Oh, Father Gordon," he began, his voice carrying a mournful tone. "I am bound by a duty that transcends even familial ties." A sense of forelorn resignation settled over him as he continued, "Kafziel is trapped in the form she is in. She needs to be released. I can do no harm to my sister, nor can I intervene where no divine directive guides me."

The weight of his words hung heavy in the air, the realization of his limitations evident in his demeanor. Samael looked down briefly, gathering his thoughts before meeting Father Gordon's gaze once more.

"It is not my place to intervene in this trial," Samael finally said, his voice carrying a sense of solemn resolve. "This trial must be finished in the hands of mortals, for it is your world, your choices, that will shape the outcome."

With that, Samael stood, the weight of his presence lifting as he made his way to the door. "Search for it, Father Gordon," he urged, his voice carrying the weight of centuries-old wisdom. "Only then may you find the key to rid this town of her darkness." And with a final nod, Samael departed, leaving Father Gordon with a newfound sense of purpose and a daunting quest ahead.

FATHER Gordon made his way down the worn, dusty path to the forgotten mausoleum hidden beneath the ancient church. Past the library, where the town's records lay dormant in aged tomes, and beyond the hallway leading to Precious's dwelling, he ventured into a realm known only to those privy to the town's darkest secrets.

Standing before the weathered, dust-laden doors, Father Gordon hesitated. Beyond these doors lay the chamber that held the only body ever interred beneath the church—a desperate attempt to contain the evil that now plagued the town. The mortal remains of the Dark Daughter of Ionia lay just beyond, a mere ten feet away, yet it felt like an insurmountable distance to the priest.

A tumult of emotions raged within him, a fierce battle between fear and guilt. Fear of what awaited him behind that door warred with the guilt of years spent in passive acceptance of Precious's presence. Prayer had been his only weapon, and now, faced with the tangible reality of the crypt, he grappled with the weight of his inaction.

With a silent prayer on his lips, Father Gordon found the strength to overcome his fear. It was the guilt that remained, a heavy burden that clung to him like a shroud. Closing his eyes, he drew in a deep breath and reached out, his trembling hand grasping the tarnished handle of the ancient door.

"What should I fear?" Father Gordon thought to himself, a quiet confidence settling over him. "God is on my side, and what lies ahead is nothing but ashes and dust."

Even Precious, with all her dark power, would not venture into this chamber. The memories it held, of what she once was in her human existence, kept her at bay. Father Gordon's conversations with Samael had sparked an idea—a search for some physical relic tied to Precious's ancient past.

With a reluctant creak, the door swung open, protesting loudly against its neglect. Light spilled into the chamber from the outer hallway, casting a pallid, grey hue instead of the usual ominous darkness.

While electricity had long since found its way into the other parts of the building, this room remained untouched by modernization. It was a deliberate choice, a conscious decision made by those who knew of the Dark Daughter's resting place. None dared to disturb her tomb, fearing the wrath of her malevolent spirit.

The workers, wise to the superstitions of the town, avoided this chamber as if it were cursed. The church leadership, aware of the tales that swirled around the Dark Daughter, saw no need to extend the electrical wiring to this forsaken corner of the building.

Stepping into the dimly lit room, Father Gordon felt a chill creep up his spine. The air was heavy with the scent of age and decay, the silence broken only by the soft whisper of his footsteps on the ancient stone floor.

The walls stood bare and lifeless, devoid of any comforting images of heaven. No one had felt the inclination to adorn these stone confines, not for the soul of the lost child whose remains lay beneath the church. To remember her, to acknowledge her existence—such thoughts seemed foreign, unwelcome. In truth, no one would have ventured into this tomb regardless.

Father Gordon stepped forward, his heart fluttering with a blend of trepidation and an odd, lingering fear from childhood, a fear of the dark that should have faded with age. Yet, here he was, braving the silence of a chamber untouched by human presence for years.

His hand trembled slightly as he retrieved a flashlight from his pocket, casting its beam around the barren space. Dust danced in the light, disturbed from its long slumber.

As he moved further into the chamber, a sense of solemnity settled over him. This was a place forgotten by time, a sanctuary untouched by the living. Yet, it held a weight—a burden of history and secrets long buried.

Father Gordon knew, deep down, that he need not fear the spectral presence of Precious. She would never tread into this sacred space; that much was certain. The day they laid her remains to rest in the sarcophagus, she made her stance clear.

The priest recalled tales of the eerie calm that had settled over the town when they extinguished the flames that consumed her mortal form. Ashes and bones, that was all that remained of the once powerful Dark Daughter. They could have let the wind carry her remnants away, yet they chose to entomb her, sealing her fate along with her curse. The bitterness of that decision lingered in the air, a bitter reminder of the town's past sins and the weight of their consequences.

Father Gordon brushed off the lingering fear that clung to him like a spectral shroud. A chill wind whispered across his spine, making him shudder involuntarily. He knew he shouldn't be here, in this forgotten chamber beneath the church, yet an insistent curiosity drove him forward. There had to be something, some overlooked clue left behind by his ancestors, something that could help him confront the demon child that plagued the town.

Setting his flashlight on an outcropping shelf, its beam casting eerie shadows on the stone walls, Father Gordon steeled himself for what lay ahead. The meager light would have to suffice as he began his survey of the room, starting with the unassuming sarcophagus that held the remains of the Dark Daughter.

The sarcophagus offered little in the way of clues. Plain and unadorned, its surface bore no markings or inscriptions, as if its occupant needed no introduction. Disappointed but undeterred, Father Gordon shifted his focus to the task at hand.

With a deep breath to steady his nerves, he examined the top of the sarcophagus, searching for a means of access. It took him a few moments to realize that it was a simple slab of granite, lying heavy and immovable. If he was to uncover the secrets hidden within, he would have to move it himself.

An hour of exertion followed, each moment a test of his resolve. The slab proved obstinate, unmoved by his efforts. Sweat beaded on his brow as he strained against the unyielding stone, muscles protesting with each futile attempt. Yet, with determination etched on his face, Father Gordon persevered. It was no easy feat.

Twice he had ventured out, determined to find something—anything—that could pry open the stubborn lid of the sarcophagus. The last time, he returned with a crowbar salvaged from the dusty corners of the church's maintenance shed. With a grunt of effort, Father Gordon wedged the bar into the slender opening he had managed to create over the course of an hour. He braced himself, muscles straining as he pushed and pulled, each movement a battle against the unyielding stone.

Finally, with a mammoth heave and a series of grunts, the lid began to slide aside, revealing the unexpected within.

What lay before him defied all expectations. No sane mind could have predicted this. Instead of mere ashes and bone fragments, the sarcophagus cradled the form of the most exquisite child he had ever seen. She appeared as though in peaceful slumber, yet Father Gordon, peering at her intently, knew this was no ordinary rest.

Her skin, like porcelain, glowed softly in the dim light of the chamber. Lustrous blond hair cascaded around her, framing a face untouched by the passage of time. She seemed suspended in time, as if the decay of death had never touched her.

Despite his hesitation, a sense of awe and curiosity overtook Father Gordon. He reached out tentatively, fingers brushing against the smooth cheek of the girl before him. To his astonishment, her skin retained a warmth, a pliancy that echoed the living. It was as though she had only just slipped into slumber, her form preserved in an eerie state of eternal rest.

For a moment, disbelief warred with wonder within him. The reality of what he touched sent a jolt of fear through his veins, and he recoiled as if burned by an unseen fire, his hand snapping back as if stung.

Father Gordon crossed himself slowly, his fingers trembling in a feverish prayer. As he turned away, disbelief gnawed at his senses. It couldn't be true, and yet, here lay the evidence before him. The ghost of Precious haunted these halls, a truth as undeniable as the girl's serene form resting in the sarcophagus.

His heart ached for the innocent child she had once been, before the darkness claimed her. Yet, he shook his head, dragging himself back from the brink of pity.

This body, this vessel that now held the specter of Precious, was not the same as the little girl he remembered. He steeled himself against the urge to weep for the twisted fate she now endured. Long ago, a child in his congregation had posed a question that echoed in his mind: "Does God love the devil?" And Father Gordon had answered, "Yes, He does. God's love is boundless, embracing us all, even the fallen ones."

Now, those words held a weighty truth. He didn't pity Precious; he loved her, in the way that only a servant of God could.

A glimmer caught his eye in the dim light of the chamber, drawing his attention back to the body before him. Kneeling down, Father Gordon inspected the delicate necklace of light gold adorning the girl's neck. It was barely noticeable, a whisper of adornment against her pale skin. He would have missed it entirely if not for the subtle reflection that caught his eye.

Fearful of disturbing the illusion of slumber, he reached out with trembling fingers, tracing the cool metal of the necklace. Despite the lifelike appearance of the girl, he knew she was beyond the touch of the living. Precious had left this world long ago, leaving only this fragile shell behind.

With a gentle tug, Father Gordon felt the delicate chain give way, breaking at the slightest pull. In an instant, the body before him crumbled to dust, leaving him stunned and gasping in astonishment. His eyes fell upon the gold chain clutched in his hand, its charm revealing a small portrait of the child's mother.

Kneeling amidst the remnants of what had once been Precious, Father Gordon pondered the significance of the necklace. There had to be something about this simple chain that had preserved the girl's body in such a state of near-perfection.

The idea churned in his mind, twisting and turning until clarity struck him like a bolt of lightning. It wasn't magic embedded in the chain, as he had first thought. No, there was a deeper meaning, something he couldn't quite grasp.

Examining the cameo closely, Father Gordon furrowed his brow in concentration. The image seemed to hold no secret, no clue to unraveling the mystery that surrounded Precious and her cursed existence. Despite that, Father Gordon believed in what he had been told by Samael so he took the locket with him.

Determined to find answers, Father Gordon carefully tucked the chain into his pocket, the weight of its discovery heavy against his chest. He retrieved his flashlight, its beam cutting through the darkness of the crypt, and made his way out.

His thoughts raced as he decided to go towards Sara's house. To his understanding of her character, she was proficient in matters beyond the ordinary. Sara possessed a gift for piecing together puzzles that eluded even the most astute minds.

As he walked, the weight of the necklace pressed against him, a tangible reminder of the task that lay ahead. There was much to uncover, much to understand about the tragic tale of Precious and the secrets that lay buried beneath the old church. And Father Gordon was determined to unveil them, one piece at a time.

22

Sara's demeanor was far from welcoming as Aaron stood outside her home, his breath ragged and sweat glistening despite the chilly night air. Behind the closed screen door, she stood with arms crossed, a clear message in her posture that his presence was unwelcome.

"Can I please come in and talk to you, Sara?" Aaron's plea carried a sense of urgency.

Sara shifted her weight, spreading her feet and tilting her head slightly. Her expression remained stern, signaling to Aaron that a mere request wouldn't suffice.

"Sara, please," Aaron continued, desperation creeping into his voice. "I ran all the way from the church. I found something, something about that girl. She was real, Sara. Alive. And now... now she's something else, haunting this town."

The door inched closed as Sara's patience waned, her voice cutting through the chilly air. "I don't care, Aaron. You hurt me. I don't know if I want to see you again. Maybe your new girlfriend wants to hear your tales. As for me, I don't need the pain."

With each word, the gap between them grew wider, both physically and emotionally. Aaron could feel the weight of his actions pressing down on him, the regret heavy in his chest. But he couldn't leave, not without making her understand.

"Sara, please," he pleaded once more, his voice cracking with emotion. "I made a mistake. But this... this is bigger than us. I need your help. Please."

Sara hesitated, the door pausing in its closing motion. Her eyes, filled with a mix of hurt and uncertainty, met Aaron's pleading gaze. For a moment, time seemed to stand still between them. Only a moment passed before she resumed closing the door after giving him a final, fleeting glance.

"Don't go, Sara. Please, I need you," Aaron's voice cracked with emotion, tears streaming down his cheeks. "I didn't do anything with her. I love you."

But Sara had already closed the door, cutting off any chance of communication. Aaron's pleas fell on deaf ears, the wooden barrier a stark reminder of the distance between them.

"I love you, Sara," Aaron's cries echoed in the empty porch, desperation clinging to each word. "You're everything to me. I would never hurt you."

Collapsed on his knees, Aaron sobbed, his chest heaving with the weight of his emotions. The cold seeped through his clothes, chilling him to the bone as he knelt there, alone and broken.

With a deep breath, Aaron gathered what little remained of his pride and rose to his feet. He knew he couldn't stay here, exposed to the elements and his own anguish. The street lamps cast feeble light on the darkening road, the town shrouded in a cloak of gloom that mirrored his mood.

Struggling against the chill, Aaron made his way to the corner of the street, where he hailed a passing taxi. He needed to find warmth, both for his body and his shattered heart. The town offered little solace, its familiar streets now suffocating in their familiarity.

As he settled into the back of the cab, Aaron's mind raced with uncertainty. Where could he go now? The hotel seemed like the only option, Kate's room the only refuge he could think of. But would she even want him there after the way he had left her, chasing after a ghost of his past?

Leaning back in the worn seat, Aaron left a note pinned to Sara's door, a feeble attempt to explain his sudden departure. His heart ached with the weight of his actions, the consequences of his choices crashing down on him with each passing moment.

The taxi pulled away from the curb, the town slipping away into the darkness behind him. Aaron couldn't shake the feeling of loss that gripped him, the ache of a love lost and the uncertainty of what lay ahead. All he could do now was wait, wait for the hotel to come into view, and wait for whatever fate had in store for him next.

KATHERINE paced back and forth in her small hotel room, the journal's revelations pressing heavily on her mind. It was impossible to reconcile the dark history she had just found out with the loving, protective presence she knew as Precious. Precious had always been her guardian angel, her unwavering protector in a world that had often been harsh and unforgiving.

Orphaned as a child, it was a journey across the country to Ionia to visit her blood relatives that had brought her face to face with the unsettling truths in that old journal.

But Precious had been there through it all. She had comforted Katherine when she was a confused child grappling with being alone in the world. She had been the one to dry Katherine's tears when her first boyfriend had broken her heart in high school. Precious had always been a constant, a source of unwavering love and support.

Yet, the journal painted a different picture—a tale of darkness and evil that seemed impossible to square with the Precious she knew. Why would the priest who wrote those words lie? It was a question that gnawed at Katherine's mind, a puzzle she couldn't solve.

Amidst her confusion and worry, one thought loomed large in Katherine's mind: she was the first-born in her family. She had learned this from her aunt Megan and Precious had told her so as well. If the journal's accounts were true, then Katherine should have met a grim fate long ago. Aaron was a first-born. He was still alive. The uncertainty of her own fate weighed heavily on her heart.

Unable to bear the burden of these thoughts alone, Katherine longed to turn to Precious for answers. But fear held her back. What if the journal was right? What if Precious wasn't the loving guardian she believed her to be?

With a heavy heart, Katherine sank onto the edge of her bed, her mind spinning with doubt and fear. The truth seemed elusive, and the thick darkness of the night outside mirrored the turmoil within her soul. She couldn't shake the feeling of impending doom, the sense that her life was balanced on a knife's edge.

As she sat there, the only sound in the room was the steady tick of the old clock on the wall. Katherine knew she needed answers, but she was afraid of what she might discover. In that moment of uncertainty, she could only wait.

Every time Katherine whispered the name "Precious," it was as if she could summon the angel herself. From childhood to the present, that was how it was. She remembered Precious' words, spoken with certainty before Katherine left for Ionia—that she would find a new family here. Meeting Aaron had seemed like the start of that new chapter, but now, with the chilling revelations of first-born deaths, everything felt uncertain.

Lost in these troubling thoughts, a gentle knock on the door broke Katherine's reverie. She hastily wrapped the hotel housecoat around herself and approached the door, peering through the peephole. To her surprise, there stood Aaron, looking utterly forlorn and out of place. He seemed like a stray caught in a rainstorm, a sight that stirred conflicting emotions within her.

Despite the lingering animosity she felt toward him for his lack of comfort during their last encounter in the church's library, Katherine sighed and opened the door.

"What's going on, Aaron?" Katherine asked, her voice tinged with weariness. "Why are you here?"

Aaron looked forlorn. His eventual downcast eyes and silence spoke for itself.

"Come in. You know where everything is," she muttered wearily, stepping aside to let Aaron enter. "You've managed to ruin my day already. You were right—I couldn't leave town. No one was willing to go at this hour, and I couldn't just take my aunt Megan's car without permission."

"I'm sorry to hear that," Aaron replied genuinely, his expression reflecting remorse. "I was hoping I'd find you here though. Sara wouldn't even talk to me."

Katherine led the way back into the modest hotel room, the tension palpable between them. She sank into a chair, the weight of the day's revelations pressing down on her. Aaron hesitated for a moment before taking a seat opposite her on the bed, his gaze troubled.

Moments later, Aaron flopped down wearily, his hands tucked beneath his head. Exhaustion weighed heavily on him, pulling at his eyelids, yet sleep eluded him. The events of the day had left him in a tangled mess of emotions, especially his tumultuous encounter with Sara.

"I don't know what to tell you. I'm sorry for bringing all this trouble into your life," Katherine muttered, her voice laden with a mix of frustration and fear. She stood and crossed over to the bed. She settled down beside Aaron, drawing her knees up to her chest.

"I'm scared, Aaron. I don't know where to turn or who to trust. And my aunt isn't even in town to help."

Katherine hesitated, the urge to call out to Precious for guidance flickering briefly in her mind. But as quickly as it came, she dismissed the thought. She couldn't trust Precious anymore, not after the revelations of the day. The ghostly presence that had been her constant companion seemed suddenly ominous, its intentions shrouded in mystery.

"It's okay, Katherine. I'm scared too," Aaron replied softly, his voice filled with genuine concern. He sat up and enveloped Katherine in a comforting embrace, holding her close. She turned to meet his gaze, finding solace in the warmth of his eyes. In that moment, she realized how much she cared for Aaron, this newfound relative who had become a pillar of support.

With a surge of emotion, Katherine leaned in and pressed her lips against his cheek, a fleeting yet tender kiss. It was an expression of familial affection—nothing more. A silent acknowledgment of the bond they shared amidst the chaos surrounding them. As they parted, Katherine felt a bittersweet pang in her heart, knowing that this moment could never be more than a cherished memory. She turned in his arms until her back was against him and leaned in closer.

"I'll do whatever I can to help, Katherine," Aaron whispered, his voice barely above a murmur. "We'll figure this out together."

Katherine nodded, her eyes glistening with unshed tears. For now, in the safety of Aaron's arms, she found a fleeting moment of peace amidst the storm. Together, they would face the mysteries of Ionia, determined to unravel the dark secrets that threatened their lives. And in that quiet embrace, they found a strength they never knew they possessed, ready to confront whatever darkness awaited them.

UNBEKNOWNST to Katherine and Aaron, four shadowy figures slinked from the dim recesses of the room, emerging stealthily from near the closet. A soft, sinister voice shattered the fragile peace of their embrace, plunging Aaron and Katherine back into the stark reality of their perilous situation. "You should be afraid," Marcus sneered, echoing Aaron's earlier admission of fear.

Seating himself casually in a nearby chair, Marcus drew back the curtain just enough to cast a sinister glance out into the inky darkness beyond. He paid no heed to the two trembling figures on the bed, their fear palpable in the air.

Closing the curtain, Marcus turned back to the pair. His eyes lingered on Katherine, taking in her vulnerable form as her housecoat slipped open, revealing her bare legs. Marcus felt a twisted desire stir within him, a hunger for something more than mere fear.

"You've played your part well, Katherine," Marcus lied smoothly, his words dripping with deceit. "You've delivered the boy to us, just as Precious desired."

A malicious grin spread across Marcus's face as he continued, his voice oozing with malevolence. "Precious has no desire for my touch, and I have no interest in the boy. But you, my dear Katherine, you will serve my purposes quite nicely."

The air in the room grew thick with tension as Marcus's dark intentions hung heavily between them. Aaron clenched his fists, his jaw set in defiance, while Katherine's heart raced with a mix of fear and revulsion. They were trapped, at the mercy of this sinister figure who seemed to relish in their terror.

Aware of the deadly consequences if he dared to lay a hand on Aaron or Katherine, Marcus cunningly left the task to his companions. The three angels—Paziel, Thaniel, and

Lazuriel—moved with eerie grace, gliding soundlessly across the room as if borne on the whispers of shadows. Their silent advance sent shivers down Katherine's spine, rendering her immobile with fear.

"I've informed them of your presence, Katherine, and of Precious's intentions to abandon them for you," Marcus taunted, his voice dripping with malice as he indicated the approaching angels. "They were ignorant of your existence, unaware of Precious's favor toward you. But now, they despise you, and they've agreed to my suggestions of ridding Precious of your presence. Oh, and I must say, you look positively delectable." Marcus was referring to her looks as well as the palpable fear oozing from her.

As Thaniel drew near Aaron, her ethereal robes billowing softly as if moved by unseen currents, she cast an admiring gaze upon him. "Ah, now I understand why Precious covets you so," she cooed, her voice saccharine sweet. With delicate fingers, she traced a path across Aaron's chest, gently drawing him away from Katherine, while Paziel and Lazuriel closed in.

"But we cannot allow you to stand between us and Precious," Thaniel murmured, her voice laced with a sinister edge. "She is ours, and we are bound to fulfill her wishes."

Katherine could do nothing but watch in horror as Thaniel's soft touch ensnared Aaron, pulling him further from her grasp. The room seemed to pulse with malevolence as the angels closed in, their intentions dark and insidious. Aaron's eyes darted between the menacing figures, his heart pounding in his chest as he realized the peril they were in. They were at the mercy of these otherworldly beings, pawns in a game they could not hope to understand.

Aaron felt powerless against Thaniel's enchantment. Her touch seemed to draw him in, pulling him away from Katherine despite his feeble attempts to resist. He reached out for Katherine, but Thaniel intercepted his hand, guiding it to rest against her own chest, a deliberate barrier between him and any thoughts of escape. Meanwhile, Katherine reached out to him, only to find herself ensnared by the cold, ethereal touch of Paziel and Lazuriel. They caressed her hair with unnerving tenderness, their presence sending shivers of fear down her spine, a response she couldn't control.

Thaniel, Paziel, and Lazuriel, driven by their unyielding devotion to Precious, sought to please her in every way. But in recent times, Precious had seemed to cast them aside, her attention focused elsewhere—on Aaron and Katherine.

Marcus, consumed by his seething hatred and lust for Precious, watched the scene unfold with a twisted sense of satisfaction. He had persuaded the angels to accompany him on this ominous visit to Aaron and Katherine, knowing full well the power he held over them because of their misplaced desires of pleasing Precious and being the center of her attention. Denied the object of his desires—Precious herself—he turned his malevolent attention toward destruction, toward those who stood closest to her.

In this cruel act of vengeance, Marcus found an outlet for his rage, frustrations, and dark desires. He could have sated his twisted cravings with any mortal, but these two—Aaron and Katherine—were a direct link to Precious, and harming them was his bitter retaliation against the one who had captivated his dark heart. The room, once a sanctuary, now crackled with malevolence, a stage for the unfolding tragedy orchestrated by forces beyond mortal comprehension.

As Marcus stood, his demonic wings unfurled from his back, casting a sinister shadow across the room. With purposeful strides, he glided towards Katherine, his intent unmistakable.

Paziel and Lazuriel, indifferent to Katherine's fate and driven by their desire to reclaim their once cherished roles in Precious' life, positioned her before Marcus, following his dark command.

Meanwhile, Thaniel held Aaron in a spellbound trance, his will subdued under her enchantment. Helpless and weakened, Aaron could do nothing but watch in horrified disbelief as the nightmare he had long dreaded unfolded before his eyes, the scenes from his haunting dreams now a chilling reality.

Katherine trembled violently, her heart torn between conflicting emotions. Part of her screamed to flee, to escape the monstrous presence drawing closer, while another part quivered in paralyzing fear. Marcus, his touch chillingly gentle against her skin, cupped her cheek in his clawed hand. Her fiery red hair cascaded over her shoulders, her chest heaving with ragged breaths as terror gripped her in its icy hold. She fought against the overwhelming fear, her entire being reduced to a quivering, helpless mess before the looming threat of Marcus.

Fear had been the only force that kept Katherine rooted in place, but as Marcus's hand made contact with her cheek, the spell shattered. With a violent scream, she broke free from the grip of the angel beside her and lashed out, her nails clawing at Marcus's face with desperate fury. Marcus, taken by surprise, reacted swiftly, delivering a brutal backhand that sent Katherine hurtling across the room like a discarded toy. She collided with the wall with a sickening thud, her body crumpling to the floor in an unnatural, lifeless heap, her eyes staring blankly ahead.

With an almost casual stride, Marcus crossed the room to loom over Katherine's prone form, a sneer of contempt twisting his features. He prodded her motionless body with the tip of his shoe, a cruel mockery of indifference. "I didn't hit you that hard," he muttered, his voice tinged with derision. Growing impatient, he delivered a harsh kick to her side, the force of it causing her body to jerk unnaturally. "Get up, girl!" he bellowed, his voice reverberating through the room like a thunderclap.

But Katherine remained still, her form limp and lifeless on the ground. It was then, as he lifted her lifeless body, that Marcus's realization struck like a physical blow. He stared at her pale, unmoving face, her head lolling awkwardly to the side. His mind struggled to comprehend the finality of death that now enveloped her. A guttural, primal scream of anger tore from his throat, echoing through the empty room in a haunting lament for the life he had just extinguished.

Aaron's body trembled with the urge to collapse, every fiber screaming for release, yet he remained frozen in place, trapped in the nightmare that now unfolded before his eyes. It was the dream, that same haunting vision that had plagued him in the park, come to life once more. But this time, there was no awakening at the brink of terror, no escape from the gruesome reality playing out before him. He was utterly powerless, gripped by a paralyzing dread that rendered him immobile.

With a sickening sense of helplessness, Aaron bore witness to Marcus's frenzied brutality. The once lifeless body of Katherine became a canvas of horror as Marcus, consumed by rage and madness, tore her limb from limb. Each sickening rip and tear echoed through the room, mingling with the anguished cries that tore from Aaron's throat, though no sound escaped his lips. He could only watch in mute horror as crimson streams of blood painted the walls, a grotesque tableau of violence and despair.

And then, in a final act of depravity, Marcus defiled what remained of Katherine's broken form, desecrating her with his vile act. Aaron's mind reeled, the sheer horror of it all threatening to overwhelm him. His vision swam, the room spinning in a sickening dance of gore and madness. The metallic tang of blood filled his nostrils, mingling with the stench of death and decay.

Unable to bear another moment of the grotesque spectacle, Aaron's consciousness flickered and faltered. Darkness crept at the edges of his vision, threatening to consume him whole. With one last desperate struggle against the encroaching oblivion, Aaron's world dissolved into blackness, and he knew no more.

23

Aaron's eyes fluttered open, the remnants of the nightmare still clinging to his senses like a suffocating fog. His heart was hammering in his chest with enough force that he could hear it echoing in his head. For a moment, he lay there, disoriented, unsure of where he was. Then, as the memories of the dream flooded back, he jolted upright.

Beside him, Katherine slept soundly, her chest rising and falling in a steady rhythm. Relief washed over him like a cool wave as he realized that the events within his nightmare that he had taken as reality had been just that—a twisted figment of his imagination.

But then, his gaze fell upon the figure seated across the room, bathed in the dim light filtering through the curtains. It was Precious.

The presence of the little girl seemed to emanate a calm yet solemn energy, her form ethereal in the shadows. Aaron's breath caught in his throat as he watched her, the weight of her gaze heavy upon him.

"Leave, Aaron," Precious's voice echoed in the stillness of the room, her tone firm yet filled with an underlying urgency. "Take Katherine and go. You are not safe here."

Aaron's heart pounded with a mix of fear and confusion. He wanted to ask questions, to demand answers, but something in Precious's demeanor stopped him. There was a gravity to her presence, a sense of imminent danger that made his blood run cold.

With trembling hands, Aaron reached out to shake Katherine awake. "Katherine," he whispered urgently, his voice barely above a hoarse murmur. "Wake up, we need to leave."

Katherine stirred, her eyes fluttering open as she gazed up at Aaron with bleary confusion. "Aaron? What's wrong?" she asked, her voice thick with sleep.

"We have to go," Aaron insisted, his urgency growing with each passing moment. He glanced back at Precious, who nodded in silent confirmation of his words.

Fear flickered in Katherine's eyes as she registered the seriousness in Aaron's voice. Without hesitation, she scrambled out of bed, hastily pulling on her clothes, shoes and jacket.

As Aaron waited, having taken significantly less time than Katherine to get ready to leave, it became apparent to him that Katherine hadn't registered the presence of Precious. Aaron thought that was intentional on the part of their intruder. As they made their way to the door, Aaron couldn't shake the feeling of being watched. He cast a wary glance over his shoulder, his heart skipping a beat as he caught sight of the scene behind them.

There, in the dimly lit room, lay the dismembered corpse of Marcus, a grotesque tableau of violence and death. The three angels from Aaron's nightmare stood motionless, their ethereal forms casting eerie shadows against the walls.

Realization dawned on Aaron like a bolt of lightning. The events of his nightmare had not been mere figments of his imagination—they had been a twisted premonition of what could have been.

Aaron was given even more impetus to make their exit from the hotel room a reality. "We need to go, now," Aaron urged, his voice strained with urgency as he pulled Katherine towards the door.

Together, they fled the hotel room, the memory of the nightmare still fresh in his minds. As they stepped out into the cool night air, Aaron couldn't help but glance back one last time.

In the darkness of the room, Precious stood vigil, her gaze fixed upon the gruesome scene before her. With a silent nod of farewell, she vanished into the shadows, leaving Aaron and Katherine alone in the empty hallway. The corpse of Marcus seemed to dissolve of its own accord.

Breathless and shaken, they made their way down the deserted corridor. The nightmare had passed, but its echoes lingered, a haunting reminder of the darkness that lurked in the shadows.

"What's the rush?" Katherine asked breathlessly. Aaron had taken her hand and was hurrying the two of them out of the building.

As they reached the exit, Aaron paused, turning to Katherine with a solemn expression. "We can't stay here," he said quietly, his voice filled with determination. "We need to go, before it's too late." He glanced back at the building and his body shook.

Katherine nodded, seeking not to question Aaron's hurried actions. She felt that he would reveal to her later his urgency in making them leave so late in the evening. Together, they stepped out into the night that seemed to be reluctant to relinquish its hold on the world so that those that inhabited the world could face a new day.

Aaron couldn't help but consider that somewhere, in the darkness beyond, Precious watched over them, her silent presence a reassurance that there was still the unknown to be faced.

With nowhere else to turn, Aaron led them to his house, a knot of apprehension coiling in his stomach at the thought of facing his brother after the night's horrors. Yet, there seemed to be no alternative, no sanctuary other than the familiar walls of his home.

Grateful that the hour was still early, shrouded in the predawn hush, Aaron hoped his brother would remain undisturbed in slumber.

After stealthily checking on his sleeping brother and confirming his continued rest, Aaron returned to the living room where Katherine awaited him, her eyes heavy with the weight of exhaustion.

"Why did we have to leave the hotel room so early?" Katherine asked, her voice laced with weariness as the lingering tendrils of sleep tried to pull her back under.

Aaron hesitated, grappling with the desire to shield her from the full weight of their grim reality. The truth of his nightmare, the specter of Katherine's recent ordeal, hung heavy between them. Instead, he chose a simpler explanation, a veil of half-truths to ease her troubled mind.

"I just didn't feel comfortable there anymore," Aaron replied, his voice steady despite the turmoil roiling within him. He studied Katherine, her drowsy demeanor a stark reminder of the harrowing events they had endured. "Go upstairs to my room. Get some rest."

He moved to offer directions, but Katherine forestalled him with a gentle interruption, her hand rising to stifle another yawn. "No need for directions. I know the way," she murmured, her words muffled by the press of her palm against her lips.

Aaron watched her ascent, a flicker of curiosity tempered by exhaustion flickering within him. How did she know the layout of his home? It seemed a trivial question amidst the chaos that had engulfed them, and he let it slip away, allowing Katherine to retreat to the refuge of his room.

Alone in the dimly lit living room, Aaron found himself restless, unable to succumb to the beckoning call of sleep. The events of the night played on an endless loop in his mind, a haunting chorus of horror and despair. He paced the familiar confines of his home, each step echoing in the silence of the early morning, his thoughts a tumultuous whirlwind of fear and uncertainty.

After a relentless tide of adrenaline-fueled wakefulness carried him through the late evening, Aaron finally yielded, settling onto the couch. Though he had no intention of succumbing to sleep once more, exhaustion tugged insistently at his eyelids.

Moments later, against his own will, his head lolled to the side, and the gentle cadence of snores filled the quiet room.

AARON'S heart leaped to his throat as he found himself sitting in a pool of something wet and sticky. The sensation of warmth seeping away slowly registered in his foggy mind. With a sickening dread, he turned over and was met with the vacant stare of Katherine's severed head.

For a moment, sheer horror threatened to overwhelm him. His mind screamed in denial, refusing to accept the grisly reality before him. Pushing himself up on his elbow, Aaron forced himself to confront the scene. The sheets were smeared with blood and tattered bits of flesh lay scattered around the bed.

A surge of panic shot through him. He knew he had to get out of there, away from the macabre tableau, before anyone discovered the horrifying aftermath of what had happened. Fear clawed at his chest as he imagined the questions, the accusations that would come if he was found in this state.

With a sudden jolt, Aaron snapped out of the nightmare that had held him in its grip. His head spun as he realized he was still on the couch, his body drenched in a cold sweat. The dim light of the room offered little comfort as the remnants of his dream clung to him like a suffocating fog.

Desperation flooded him. He couldn't stay here, couldn't risk falling asleep again and being trapped in the twisted world of his nightmares. With trembling hands, he pushed himself to his feet, his mind racing with frantic thoughts of escape. How could he explain this to anyone? How could he make them understand the horrors he had witnessed, both real and imagined?

Aaron rubbed the sleep from his eyes with the back of his hand, the lingering remnants of his nightmare clinging to his waking thoughts. He grimaced and looked down at the shirt clinging uncomfortably to his skin. With a resigned sigh, he peeled off his sweat-soaked shirt, feeling the clammy fabric stick uncomfortably to his skin. Tucking it under his arm, he knew he couldn't bear to wear it any longer.

Stepping out onto the front porch, Aaron welcomed the cool embrace of the early morning air on his naked chest. The early morning air was a welcome reprieve, the cool breeze offering a brief respite. The familiar route of his morning run beckoned, offering a temporary respite from the turmoil swirling inside his mind.

With a determined stride, Aaron set off in the direction of his usual running route. The empty streets stretched out before him, the early hour ensuring that he encountered few souls along the way. The deserted back streets provided a fleeting sense of escape. It was a futile attempt to outrun the darkness that pursued him.

As he ran, thoughts raced through his mind, a jumble of fear and confusion. It took nearly two hours of pounding the pavement before he found himself back at his home, standing on the front lawn, uncertain of his next move. He struck out on his route twice.

Aaron hesitated to disrupt the fragile peace of the morning. He debated whether to intrude into a home that was his as well as Michael's. He felt uninvited, knowing full well that Michael was likely still angry with him and didn't want him there. But the overall situation pushed aside any hesitation. Michael and Katherine were likely still asleep. Both were still unaware of the horrors that had unfolded in Aaron's mind.

Turning his thoughts to Sara, Aaron felt a pang of uncertainty. The thought of seeking solace from her crossed his mind, but he quickly dismissed it. Their last encounter had ended on a sour note, and he doubted she would welcome him with open arms. Still, he knew he needed her, needed someone to share the burden of his nightmares.

Aaron knelt beside the low brick wall lining the sidewalk to the front door, his fingers fumbling behind a loose brick until they closed around the small brass key he sought. It was a key he never expected to need again, his early morning runs having long been a thing of the past. But the nightmare that now seemed to be his waking reality had shattered that plan entirely.

With a click, the door yielded to the key, allowing Aaron to step into the dimly lit house. His first stop was the kitchen, where a half-eaten sandwich, likely Michael's forgotten dinner, sat on the table, a gathering place for flies. The sight turned Aaron's stomach, a wave of nausea threatening to overwhelm him. It struck him as absurd that a plate of food covered in flies could elicit such a physical reaction, while the horrors of his nightmare had left him strangely numb.

Shaking off the unsettling feeling, Aaron pushed the thought aside, his focus squarely on getting Sara to his side as quickly as possible. He pulled out his phone and dialed her number, the urgency evident in his actions. Sara answered after the second ring, her tone cool and distant, betraying her displeasure at the unexpected call.

"What is it, Aaron? What do you want? Wasn't it enough for you to be turned away from my house earlier?" Sara's voice crackled with anger, cutting through the line.

"I need you now. Come over to my house as soon as you can, it can't wait and I won't take no for an answer," Aaron's words rushed out before Sara could interrupt.

"Aaron, it's just now six thirty in the morning," Sara protested, the early hour evident in her tone.

"Sara, I need you more now than I've ever needed you in my life," Aaron responded without hesitation, urgency lacing his voice.

Sara felt the weight of his plea, the raw emotion reaching through the phone. Despite their past, she knew she couldn't ignore his call for help. There was a vulnerability in his voice that stirred something within her.

"I'll be over as soon as I can," Sara promised, her tone softening before she hung up the phone.

Aaron felt a wave of relief wash over him. He had no doubt that Sara would come to his aid, especially now when he needed her more than ever. If anyone could help him hold onto his sanity, it was Sara.

After clearing the dishes from the table, Aaron ran water into the sink to wash his face, the cool water soothing against his skin. Drying his face with a dishtowel, he replaced it on the rack before heading to his room for a shirt. Despite not living at the house full-time, he still kept some clothes there. Careful not to disturb Katherine, he returned to the kitchen and prepared to wait for Sara.

As he sat down at the table, Aaron nearly leapt out of his skin at the sight of who was already waiting for him.

"I'm relieved to see you're still alive. My fledglings, and the demon that spurred their hasty actions, have been dealt with. I was deeply troubled to discover what he might have done to my beloved Katherine if I hadn't intervened. I made sure that demon paid dearly," Precious spoke, her voice holding a strange mix of innocence and cunning.

Aaron couldn't help but wonder who the real demon was in this situation.

AARON slouched in the chair opposite Precious, his gaze fixed on her in speechless disbelief. He didn't want to be in her presence, but denying the reality of her existence wouldn't change anything. She was there, and he had to accept it, no matter how unsettling it felt.

Desperate for answers, Aaron mustered the courage to speak. "What are you? Why are you here?" he asked, his voice tinged with a mix of fear and curiosity.

Precious couldn't help but smile at his question. "First things first. My three little fledglings were acting against my wishes. They've done things..." Her voice trailed off, her eyes drifting away as if she were gazing into some unseen distance. For a moment, she seemed lost in thought, a faint tremor passing through her before she refocused on Aaron with a sly smile. "They really messed up my plans, but I'm not worried. I have an eternity to ensure I get what I want," Precious replied.

She swung her legs childishly, the tips of her shoes barely brushing the floor. Folding her hands neatly in her lap, she continued to speak, her gaze shifting between her hands and Aaron's face. The baby blue satin ribbon sash around her waist seemed out of place, a stark contrast to what Aaron had learned of her.

"As for what I am, you could say I'm an Angel," Precious revealed, her gaze fixating on Aaron once more.

Aaron shot her a dubious look, skepticism etched on his face.

"Don't look surprised; I am a true angel of the choir of Cherubs. I am not as powerful as an angel from the choir of Seraphim, but I am just below that," Precious whispered, her voice carrying an unsettling weight.

"If you're an angel, then why are you doing this?" Aaron questioned, his confusion evident.

"Why?" Precious hissed vehemently, her eyes flashing with anger. "You ask me why? I do it because I can. I hate you and everything about you. Humans with their dear souls trying to imitate what you can never be. You took my God away from me, and I hated you for it," she finished, her voice laced with bitterness.

Aaron was taken aback. "What are you talking about?" he asked, trying to make sense of her words.

"I was one of God's most trusted angels. He spoke to me as He spoke to no other, and then when He created the heavens and the earth, He took to looking after His children on the earth and He didn't speak to us anymore. I haven't spoken with God for so long that I have forgotten what it was like," Precious explained, her voice filled with a haunting sorrow.

"That couldn't have been our fault. Why didn't you ask God why He didn't speak to you anymore?" Aaron inquired, attempting to grasp the depths of her anguish.

"I tried. We all tried. We fought war after war with those angels who didn't question His aloofness, trying to get Him to see us, to acknowledge us as He did in the beginning before you humans. We only received banishment for our pain. Those who fought on the side of the Most Beloved Angel were sent from heaven without preamble," Precious recounted, her voice carrying the weight of centuries of anguish.

As Aaron continued to question Precious, he found his fear of her diminishing. She remained imposing, yet a sense of understanding began to bloom within him.

Precious rose from her seat and approached Aaron, her eyes captivating him with their deep blue hue. In those eyes, he thought he glimpsed a faint reflection of the magnificence of heaven itself. But when she saw his wonder, she turned her gaze away.

"You don't realize how alone and afraid we were. God gave us minds to think for ourselves but made us so that we worshiped Him.

We were without God after you creatures came and nothing that we did could bring Him to glance at us or even speak to us. I tried for thousands of years with no success. Then it came to me, He thought that His precious humans were more important than the angels who did nothing but worship Him and He cared for them so much more than us angels, so I would study them and find out why," Precious explained, her voice a mixture of sorrow and resentment.

She walked over to another chair at the dining table, where Aaron had hung his jacket and forgotten about it. From one of its pockets, she retrieved an object that Aaron had overlooked. With a casual flick of her wrist, she tossed a small leather-bound book onto the kitchen table. It skidded to a stop in front of Aaron's hands.

"You've read the tale. You know what happened. I heard their cries to heaven when the little girl first fell ill. I went to her bedside and I watched over her. I called to Him myself, asking that He spare the little girl. He didn't answer the call, so when her little soul left the body, I decided to save the people from their pain and get His attention by becoming one of His favorite humans," Precious explained, her voice heavy with emotion.

"You still didn't get God's attention, did you?" Aaron questioned.

"No. I didn't," Precious hissed, her anger palpable. "He turned His eyes away from me. In all of His magnificence, He only had time for watching His precious humans. He didn't have time for me. He didn't have time for anything to do with me, or the confusion that He caused the other angels true to the Most Beloved Angel's cause. He didn't have time to save that little girl."

There was a moment of silence, but Aaron could feel the turmoil simmering within Precious, ready to boil over.

"How could God not have time? He is God!" Precious exclaimed, her voice laced with malice.

Precious slapped the book off the table in a fit of anger. It hit the far wall and fell to the floor, where it remained, ignored by both of them.

"I raged against Him, and I desired to destroy one human after another. I was willing to do anything to get Him to notice me once more. The people of the town saw me for what I was, and they destroyed me, but because I was..." she drifted off. "Am," she corrected, "an angel, I couldn't die. I was trapped in this form because the human form that held me died before I could escape it," Precious explained.

"That explains why you are in the form of a little girl, but it doesn't explain what you want from me or what you needed poor Kate for," Aaron remarked.

"Don't you see? I can't get out of this form because I died as a human," Precious said quietly, as if that would explain everything.

Aaron was even more confused, a fact not lost on Precious.

"I needed the perfect host in order to get out of this form, and from there I can exit the host and be a true angel again," Precious clarified.

"What does that have to do with me or anyone else?" Aaron retorted, his anger overcoming his fear of her.

Precious's hand slammed down on the table with a loud thwack. Her face contorted in anger, a sneer curling the side of her lips up, making her appear even more malevolent than before—if that was even possible.

"Your ancestors, your brother's ancestors, Katherine's ancestors, and that girl named Sara's ancestors," Precious began, pointing towards Sara's house when she mentioned the girl. "For decades, I waited for a reincarnation of the parents of this body. The exactness of what this little girl's parents were. Any of the four of you would have been able to father or mother the host that I needed. I would have succeeded if it hadn't been for Marcus figuring out my plan and disrupting it. You, Michael, Sara, or Kate were to be my saviors and have the child that I would become. You would become the loving parents that gave birth to this body I inhabit, and once I was reborn as your child, I would be able to leave this cursed form," Precious explained, her voice seething with bitterness.

Aaron was horrified at the thought of being a parent to this... thing that appeared human. He shivered uncontrollably, his back spasming. Another thought struck him, one concerning the curse that was said to be on the town.

"What of the other first-born children then? Why did you kill all of them?" Aaron demanded, his voice tinged with accusation.

"What need did I have for doing that? They are nothing to me," Precious replied in disbelief.

"But for centuries, the firstborn children of Ionia have been dying," Aaron pressed on. "You swore on the fire that you would take the firstborn children."

"I had to fulfill my own prophecy?" Precious stated flatly. "I don't even know what you're talking about."

Precious made a move toward Aaron, and he jumped up from his chair, instinctively trying to keep her away from him. She ignored his accusation, deeming it insignificant and not deserving of a proper response.

Her eyes were unfocused even as she looked at Aaron. She began a rambling tirade.

"You have intrigued me through all of these years. There were times when I felt that you were no longer useful to me, and I would have left you alone then. You were safe from harm— at least from me. I needed you, Katherine, Michael, or Sara to have the child with, possibly something else, I don't know. I could do nothing to you; I thought it was your mother that was doing it, but I was wrong. I find myself in a peculiar predicament. I am finding it difficult to get to you now, but that shouldn't be. I still don't know what it is that is keeping me from harming you," Precious said, her voice laced with frustration and confusion.

"Maybe it's because God is preventing you from destroying any innocent lives," Aaron suggested, his voice filled with a mix of fear and conviction.

Precious laughed bitterly, her demeanor shifting to one of horror. "All of those murders were committed by my fledglings in my name," she admitted, aghast at the revelation. "Marcus. He admitted it before I killed him. I never asked them to do that."

"You're still evil, despite that. God is likely stopping you," Aaron retorted, his voice firm with conviction.

"You are wrong. I would know if God was intervening, and as I told you before, God doesn't care enough about you, me, or anyone else to intervene on their behalf. Remember what I told you about this child whose body I inhabit?" Precious insisted, her voice carrying a chilling certainty.

As she continued to move slowly towards Aaron, he felt a surge of panic and bolted for the living room, only to find her there, around the corner, waiting for him with an eerie calmness. Aaron skidded to a halt, his heart pounding in his chest. His jaw dropped in shock, not because of the presence of Precious, but because Sara was standing behind her, wielding a fire poker in her hand.

Sara called out something that Aaron couldn't understand, her voice filled with a mix of fear and determination. Precious turned, her expression shifting from calm to surprise as she caught sight of Sara's weapon. Aaron's stomach churned with a sickening dread as he heard the sharp crack of the fire poker connecting with Precious' head.

24

The phone rang once. Sara wasn't in the mood to answer it. She thought that she should pick up the incessant device and stop the annoying ring.

She reached across her bed to pick up the phone but not before noting that it was from Aaron. She thought it was Michael calling but she couldn't figure out why he would call her. "What is it, Aaron? What do you want? Wasn't it enough for you to be turned away from my house earlier?" Sara asked angrily. Aaron's voice was the last thing she was expecting to hear and even though she was mad at him, she was glad to hear him.

"I need you now. Come over to my house as soon as you can, it can't wait and I won't take no for an answer," Aaron said quickly.

Sara's heart clenched at Aaron's urgent plea, a knot of worry tightening in her stomach. The phone felt heavy against her ear, each word from Aaron's trembling voice sending shivers down her spine. The weight of his need settled on her shoulders like an invisible burden she couldn't ignore.

She pulled the phone away from the side of her face and looked at the time, her gaze flicking to the glaring 6:30 AM in red digits. The early morning light filtering through her window seemed harsh, uninviting, as if the world itself mirrored her apprehension. "Aaron, it's just now six thirty in the morning," Sara protested.

"Sara, I need you more now than I've ever needed you in my life."

Sara knew she wasn't going to say no. It just wasn't in her to abandon Aaron when he sounded as if he needed her so much. "I can't just sit here," she muttered to herself. "I'll be over as soon as I can," Sara said.

Hanging up, she stood motionless for a moment, feeling the weight of the impending journey settle on her shoulders like a heavy cloak. She had to get ready to leave. Her mind raced with a thousand questions, doubts clouding her thoughts. But beneath it all, a fierce determination burned—a determination born from her love for Aaron, a love that refused to yield to fear.

Slipping on her shoes and grabbing a light jacket, she decided against changing out of the pajamas she had worn to bed. It wasn't as if she hadn't been underdressed like this before at Aaron's house. Heart racing, she made her way down the stairs.

As Sara swung open the front door, her heart skipped a beat. Father Gordon stood on the porch, his hand frozen mid-knock, surprise mirrored on both their faces.

"My dear girl, I'm glad I caught you," Father Gordon said, his tone urgent. "I need to find Aaron; I want to ask him about what he found in the church library."

Sara, itching to push past the Father to reach Aaron, suppressed her impatience. She hadn't known Aaron had gone to the church; he hadn't had the chance to mention it when he stopped by her house earlier that evening. She hadn't given him the time.

"Aaron isn't here, Father Gordon. He's at his house, and I think he's in trouble. He called me just a moment ago and asked me to come over," Sara replied, glancing in the direction of Aaron's house.

Father Gordon followed her gaze to the Smith's house, sensing the darkness shrouding it. No matter how much he wanted to speak with Aaron, he couldn't bring himself to approach that house. He knew he was powerless against that malevolence. He couldn't quite pinpoint why he felt the urge to ask Aaron about what he had discovered. An instinctual need to deliver the locket he had found to Aaron prompted him to hand over the necklace to Sara instead.

"Take this; it was hers before she was burned. I think it's important," Father Gordon said, referring to Precious. He turned to leave but stopped abruptly, then turned back to find Sara right on his heels.

"It just occurred to me that if Precious is as potent a spirit as I suspect, there won't be much in this world to contain her," Father Gordon continued, his voice grave. "According to what I've been told, if a spirit inhabits a living body, it can supplant the original soul. Should the body perish, the spirit becomes trapped—neither able to ascend to heaven nor descend to hell as its deeds dictate."

"If Precious chose to possess a living body, she'd have the ability to leave earth behind. Yet, she remains trapped, stuck in an eternal, unyielding form," Father Gordon explained, his voice tinged with unease. "I retrieved that necklace from her grave, and I won't delve into what I witnessed there. But I believe this necklace is a tether to her past self, a possible means to vanquish her."

Father Gordon seemed on the verge of sharing more, his gaze piercing into Sara's eyes. However, he chose to hold his tongue, a somber expression on his face. With that, he turned and left, his silence more poignant than any words could convey.

Sara stood on the walkway, her gaze fixed on Father Gordon's retreating figure as he made his way down to his car. The engine revved, and soon he disappeared into the night. In her hand, she tightly grasped the necklace he had given her, raising it to examine.

It was a simple thing, unassuming. How could this small object possibly hold the key to defeating Precious, the formidable entity?

Summoning her courage, Sara clenched her fist against her chest. With a determined step forward, she moved to leave the house, only to find herself enveloped in darkness. Confusion clouded her senses as she looked around, yet amidst the obsidian void, she could still feel her own presence and discern the outline of the landscape.

As she took a moment to survey her surroundings, Sara realized the world hadn't plunged entirely into darkness. Instead, it seemed to have faded into a gray-scale, devoid of vibrancy and any apparent signs of life save for her own.

Sara caught a flicker of movement ahead, a form materializing from the surrounding darkness. She squinted, trying to make out the figure. Slowly, the shape of a slightly built man emerged, hands casually tucked in his pockets. With each step, his presence seemed to solidify, illuminating the dim world around her, revealing more of his features.

The man appeared to be in his mid to late thirties, exuding an air of elegance with a gentle smile gracing his features. His hair, longish and swept behind his shoulders, was neatly pulled back behind his ears. He wore a well-fitted dark gray suit that complemented his demeanor.

"What...?" Sara started, her gaze darting around before settling back on the person before her.

"It's alright. You're safe here," the man spoke gently, his voice a soothing presence. "I simply wanted to have a chat with you."

Sara's gaze sharpened as she studied the man before her, her focus drawn to a subtle movement just behind his back. And then, she saw it—wings.

"Who are you?" she asked, her voice barely above a whisper.

The man's smile widened, his features softening even more. Tilting his head to the side, he regarded her with a curious glint in his eyes.

"You see them, don't you?" he replied, his voice gentle. "You can see where we are, can't you? Only a select few can perceive this realm we now inhabit."

Sara, her heart pounding, ignored Samael's question, her mind reeling with the sight of the wings behind him. Instead, she repeated her query, her voice trembling with both fear and fascination.

"Who... who are you?"

"Samael," the man answered simply, his expression serene despite the gravity of his revelation. "I am Samael, the Angel of Death."

Shock reverberated through Sara as she struggled to process the weight of his words. The Angel of Death stood before her, a being of both light and darkness.

For a moment, panic threatened to overwhelm her, but then a steely resolve settled within her. She turned her gaze towards Aaron's house, a sense of protectiveness surging through her.

"Are you here to take Aaron from me?" Sara blurted out, her voice wavering with a mix of desperation and defiance. "You can't have him. I won't let you take Aaron from me."

Samael regarded her with a mixture of amusement and admiration. "You're rather brave, Sara," he remarked, his tone gentle. "But fear not, I have no intention of taking Aaron. I simply came to see you, and now that I have, I must leave."

With that, Samael turned, his figure disappearing into the encroaching darkness. As he walked away, he raised a hand in a farewell gesture, his voice carrying back to her on the whisper of the wind.

"Hurry, Sara. Get that necklace to Aaron."

Left to decipher Samael's cryptic words on her own, Sara wrestled with the urge to call out to him, demand an explanation. Yet, Aaron waited for her, his need pulling at her heartstrings. She couldn't leave him in this time of darkness and uncertainty.

With determination, she crossed the yard separating the houses in quick strides. As she approached Aaron's home, a palpable sense of malevolence hung heavy in the air, the same darkness that had driven

Father Gordon away. Despite her hesitation, Sara pushed open the front door, stepping into the ominous shadows of the house.

Uncertainty gripped her as she stood in the dimly lit foyer, her eyes scanning the darkness for any sign of Aaron. The air in Aaron's house felt suffocating, each creak of the floorboards echoing like a sinister whisper.

Sara's grip tightened on the locket, Father Gordon's whispered hope now her only anchor in the swirling darkness. Each step into Aaron's house felt like a plunge into the unknown, the air heavy with unseen whispers and the weight of malevolence.

The creak of floorboards beneath her feet echoed like a sinister chorus, urging her to turn back. But Sara pressed on, her heart hammering in her chest, a mix of fear and fierce determination propelling her forward.

As Aaron's voice, tinged with unease, drifted from the kitchen, Sara's senses sharpened. She knew she was not alone—felt the weight of unseen eyes upon her, the oppressive presence of Precious lurking in the shadows.

A chill raced down her spine as she heard another voice—a child's voice, haunting and unfamiliar. It filled the air with a sense of dread, each word a whispered threat that sent shivers down Sara's spine.

Clutching the locket tightly, Sara fought the rising panic threatening to overwhelm her. She could feel the weight of unseen forces bearing down on her, the darkness pressing in from all sides.

But amidst the suffocating fear, a fierce protectiveness surged within her—a love for Aaron that refused to yield to the darkness. 'No,' she whispered, her voice a defiant whisper against the ominous silence.

With a swift turn, Sara's gaze locked on the fireplace, the fire poker resting among the shadows. In that moment, it became a weapon of defiance, a symbol of her unwavering resolve.

'I think you lost this,' she spoke sharply, her voice ringing out in the dimly lit room. With a swift motion, Sara hurled the locket towards Precious, the small object glinting in the dim light.

The little girl turned, her eyes widening in surprise as the locket flew through the air. Sara closed her eyes, a silent prayer on her lips, as she felt the weight of the fire poker in her hand.

You can't have him. You can't take my Aaron.

With a resolute swing, Sara felt the fire poker connect with something solid. The impact reverberated through her body, the dull thud echoing in the room.

She didn't see the exact moment of impact, but Sara knew she had struck Precious. The weight of her actions settled heavily on her shoulders, a mix of fear and fierce determination coursing through her veins.

The darkness seemed to recede, a faint glimmer of light filtering through the shadows. Sara stood amidst the aftermath, her chest heaving with exertion, her eyes fixed on the fallen form of Precious.

In that moment, she knew—she would do whatever it took to protect Aaron, even if it meant facing the darkness head-on.

25

The force of Sara's strike sent Precious hurtling across the room, her body tumbling like a discarded rag doll. Blood seeped from the gash at the back of her head, staining the floor beneath her.

Aaron swiftly moved to Sara's side, gently prying the fire poker from her clenched fingers. He held it tightly, a determined glint in his eyes, as he grasped both of Sara's hands firmly in his own.

Meanwhile, Precious struggled to her feet, shock etched across her face as she touched the wound on her head. Her fingers came away slick with blood, a disturbing contrast against her pale skin. A twisted smile curled her lips, mingling disbelief with a growing sense of malevolence.

"This is impossible," Precious muttered between breathless laughs, her voice tinged with hysteria. "I am an angel. No one has ever drawn blood from me before. Many have tried, and all have failed. I don't know how you managed it, but now I will have to end you all."

"You're no angel," Sara retorted, her voice unwavering with defiance. "You're just a frightened, angry little girl with demonic powers."

At Sara's words, Precious let out a piercing scream that reverberated through the house, causing both Sara and Aaron to wince in pain. The air around them crackled with an otherworldly energy as Precious unfurled her wings, the dark feathers casting a sinister shadow across the room.

With a sudden motion, she swept her wings forward, creating a powerful gust of wind that knocked Sara and Aaron off their feet, sending them sprawling to the ground. The very walls of the house seemed to tremble as Precious spoke, her voice echoing with an eerie resonance that shook the very foundation of their reality.

Turning away from Sara and Aaron, who now lay sprawled on the ground, Precious faced another figure in the room. An angel stood before her, his majestic wings spread wide, the dark gray feathers emitting a faint, ethereal glow. He was a vision of beauty, reminiscent of the celestial hosts and the harmonious choirs that sang in the heavens above. Yet, for Precious, this reminder brought no joy; it only stirred unsettling memories.

"What do you want here, Samael?" Precious hissed, her voice laced with a mixture of defiance and unease.

Samael's smile remained serene as he crossed the room, his wings gracefully folding behind his back as he approached a nearby couch. With a fluid motion, he seated himself, a picture of ease and nonchalance.

"Please, continue," Samael spoke calmly, his voice carrying a hint of amusement. "I did not come to intervene, only to observe. Without divine commandment, my hands are tied, as you well know."

As Precious moved closer to Samael, her own wings rustled nervously behind her. She could feel the weight of his presence, the aura of power that emanated from him. Samael was among the most formidable of the angels, known for his role as the Accuser of Israel, possessing strength equal to that of Michael, the Defender of Israel.

Her voice quivered slightly as she repeated her question, her eyes locked with his. "I'll ask you again, Samael. What do you want here?"

Samael crossed his arms casually, raising one hand to inspect his fingernails with a nonchalant air. His voice, soft and soothing, cut through the tense atmosphere of the room.

"You understand the intricate dance between causality and fate, don't you?" Samael remarked, his gaze shifting between Precious and the two mortals, Aaron and Sara. "That is what has brought me here."

With deliberate slowness, he extended a finger, pointing first at Aaron and Sara, then directing his focus towards Precious.

"Their fate," Samael's finger lingered on Aaron and Sara, "and your causality, Kafziel," he continued, his tone measured. "They do not align."

"Bah, be gone from me. I don't want you here," Precious spat, her voice laced with frustration.

Ignoring her dismissal, Samael remained steadfast, his presence commanding attention.

Sensing the urgency of the situation, Precious turned her attention back to Aaron and Sara, her eyes gleaming with malice.

"I will rid myself of you two once and for all," she hissed, a dark energy pulsating around her. "I will show you who the most terrifying angel truly is."

Aaron, already gripped with terror, could barely stand, the weight of Precious's words and the presence of Samael crushing down on him. Beside him, Sara trembled with fear.

As Sara sat there in the tense air of the room, a realization washed over her. She was facing a being of immense power, yet one trapped within the form of a child. The sight of Precious, with all her anger and malice, housed in such an innocent guise, struck Sara with an unsettling truth.

In that moment, as she stared at the child-like figure before her, Sara saw a reflection of herself as a child when she wanted attention. But now, as she truly looked at the small, trembling form of the girl, Sara couldn't shake the feeling that she was acting out in a way that mirrored the very body Precious inhabited. She saw a lost soul, trapped in a cycle of fear and resentment.

The realization hit her like a wave crashing against the shore. She was behaving like a child throwing a tantrum, seeking attention, demanding validation. Sara then found a sliver of courage within her to speak out.

Sara's voice, though trembling with emotion, held an unmistakable resolve as she spoke to Precious. "You have no idea what true fear is," she began, her gaze unwavering despite the turmoil within her. "You believe yourself to be terrifying because you think God has forsaken you."

With deliberate grace, Sara rose to her feet, her eyes locking with the intense gaze of Precious. In that moment, she saw not just a powerful being, but a soul burdened by anger and pain.

"Are you so certain that He is blind to your actions?" Sara's words cut through the tension of the room, her voice carrying a weight of conviction. "Do you truly believe that this is not all part of His grand design? You are deceiving yourself, Precious. God sees all, even in the darkest of moments." Sara paused for a second, her gaze swiftly taking in Precious from top to bottom. Her lip curled in disgust. "I pity you."

Beside her, Aaron stood, his expression a mix of fear and determination.

With a swift movement, Precious closed the distance between them, her presence looming over Sara and Aaron. They instinctively crouched toward the floor, fear palpable in the air. She stood above them, just inches away, her wings folded against her back as she peered down at them from the guise of a ten-year-old girl. The absurdity of the situation might have struck them, if not for the imminent danger that surrounded them.

"I don't need your pity, mortal," Precious hissed, her voice dripping with venomous disdain.

Aaron hesitated, weighing the risk of his plan against the peril they faced. Sara, sensing the opportunity, kept Precious distracted with her words, allowing Aaron the moment to act. With a sudden resolve, Aaron lunged forward, the fire prod held like a spear before him. Precious, weakened by her earlier injury and the distraction of Samael's presence, was too slow to react.

The fire prod found its mark, piercing the small form of Precious. A sharp, agonized scream tore through the room as Aaron stood over her, breathless and trembling.

"You cannot destroy me," Precious gasped, her voice strained with pain. "I am an angel, and already I feel my power increasing to compensate for what you've done."

"Don't deceive yourself, Kafziel," Samael's voice cut through the chaos, his tone calm yet authoritative. "Lies do not become you. Acknowledge your defeat and come with me."

The room fell silent, the weight of Samael's words hanging heavy in the air. Sara and Aaron exchanged a glance, a mix of relief and uncertainty washing over them. They waited, their breaths held, as Precious lay on the ground, her form trembling with pain and the realization of her own vulnerability.

"Stop calling me by that damned name!" Precious's scream echoed through the room, her voice filled with raw anguish and defiance.

Aaron glanced over at the well-dressed man sitting calmly on the couch. Despite his harmless appearance, Aaron knew better than to underestimate him. Samael's presence, though composed, carried an undeniable weight of authority.

Meanwhile, Precious coughed hoarsely, blood and spittle staining her soiled dress as she struggled to rise. The fire prod had pierced her heart, but she had not been slain as Aaron had hoped. With a grim determination, she pulled the rod from her chest, dropping it to her side with a chilling resolve.

Sara, moved by a mix of compassion and sorrow, knelt beside Precious's broken form. Her eyes, filled with love and empathy, gazed down at the fallen angel.

"You claim that God has forsaken you," Sara began, her voice gentle yet firm. "But perhaps it is you who have turned away from Him. Even now, His love surrounds you, despite all that has transpired. If you truly desired to return home, to find solace in His presence, all you needed to do was ask for forgiveness."

Tears welled in Sara's eyes as she spoke, her heart heavy with the weight of the moment. "But pride, Precious. It was pride that clouded your judgment, that stood between you and redemption. Pride, a deadly poison to you, held you captive for so long."

As the words hung in the air, a heavy silence settled over the room. Sara reached out a hand, hesitating for a moment before gently resting it on Precious's trembling shoulder.

"There is still time, Precious," Sara whispered, her voice filled with hope. "It is never too late to seek forgiveness, to find peace in His love. Will you let go of your pride and accept His grace?"

Precious listened intently, her eyes narrowing with a mix of curiosity and defiance. Every word Sara spoke seemed to sear into her, leaving an indelible mark on her consciousness.

"How did you do this to me?" Precious demanded, her voice strained with a mixture of anger and disbelief.

Sara, feeling a weight of sorrow and exhaustion settle upon her, cast her gaze around the dimly lit room. Her eyes fell upon the small amulet and chain, glinting faintly in the subdued light.

"I don't know," Sara admitted quietly, her fingers tracing the delicate curves of the locket. "Perhaps it was God's intervention. Perhaps it was love from your mother." Her gaze lingered on the locket, a sense of reverence in her eyes. "My love for Aaron, our love for each other, it kept you from harming him."

A flicker of something akin to amusement crossed Precious's features. "I don't have a mother," she retorted sharply, her voice tinged with bitterness. "You forget, I am an angel."

Samael, who had been silently observing, finally spoke, his voice carrying a weight of finality. "You are no longer an angel, Kafziel," he stated firmly, his gaze unwavering. "The moment you took on that form, you began a transformation into mortality. You assumed the life of that child as she passed into the arms of heaven. Though you may still possess remnants of your angelic powers, you are more mortal now than you have ever been. You brought about your own downfall."

With a solemn nod, Samael rose from the couch, his expression a mix of sorrow and resignation. He approached Precious, standing tall over her broken form. Aaron and Sara watched in a mix of dread and fascination as Samael regarded her with a mixture of pity and regret.

"You destroyed yourself," Samael murmured, his voice barely above a whisper. Without another word, he turned and walked away, his footsteps fading into the silence of the room.

Alone with Precious now, Sara felt a surge of conflicting emotions. Pity, sorrow, and a lingering sense of fear mingled within her. With a heavy heart, she spoke softly, her voice carrying a gentle yet firm command.

"Go away, Precious," Sara said, her eyes filled with a mixture of sadness and resolve. "It is time for you to leave this place, to find peace wherever you may."

In the midst of her agony, Precious momentarily lost track of her surroundings. The searing pain tore through her chest, a stark reminder of the mortal wound that now consumed her. Life ebbed away with each passing moment, yet strangely, she found a sense of peace settling over her. Anger and bitterness drained from her body as she resigned herself to the inevitable. Through the haze of pain, she could hear the distant echoes of celestial hymns, the anthems of heaven calling out to her once more.

Heaven's gates stood before her, a vision of beauty and serenity, yet they remained closed to her. Precious knew she was not destined for those hallowed halls. Another path awaited her, one veiled in mystery and uncertainty.

Meanwhile, Sara watched as Precious faded before her eyes, the once formidable being now reduced to a fading specter. "All you needed to do was seek forgiveness," Sara murmured softly, her voice filled with a mixture of sorrow and compassion. "You could have been home, at peace. But you chose a path of anger and pride."

The room fell silent save for the sounds of Precious's labored breaths. Sara's gaze remained fixed on the diminishing figure, her heart heavy with the weight of the moment.

"If you had only understood," Sara continued, her voice carrying a note of regret. "My love for Aaron, our love, it was a bond blessed by God Himself. It kept you at bay, weakened your hold on us. Love, true and unwavering, was our shield against you."

Aaron, standing beside Sara, looked down at Precious's writhing form with a mix of pity and disdain. "You are a sad creature," he said, his voice tinged with sorrow. "I hope you rot in hell."

Sara bowed her head, a tear trailing down her cheek. In that moment of quiet reflection, she offered a silent prayer for the troubled soul of Precious, hoping that somehow, in the vastness of eternity, she would find the peace that had eluded her in life.

Precious coughed, her body wracked with the effort. Weakly, she beckoned Aaron closer, her voice barely a whisper. Reluctantly, Aaron leaned in, his expression a mix of apprehension and resignation.

"Come closer, Aaron," Precious rasped, her voice filled with a haunting urgency. As Aaron leaned in, she gently wrapped her arms around his neck, pulling herself up with what little strength remained within her fragile form.

"I loved you too. I also loved Katherine," she murmured, her words barely audible. "I needed you and her. I was becoming more mortal with each passing day, unable to conceal my longing for either of you to have a child any longer."

With a fragile yet determined resolve, Precious pressed her lips against Aaron's, a final gesture of love and regret. The taste of blood lingered on his lips as she kissed him, a bitter reminder of the fate that awaited her.

"I'll give you a token before I go," Precious whispered as she pulled away, her eyes searching Aaron's for a fleeting moment of understanding.

Aaron watched, a mix of sorrow and disgust swirling within him, as Precious spoke of the darkness that awaited him.

"This is far from over," she warned, her voice filled with a haunting certainty. "You will never be the same, Aaron. Darkness will follow you, both from the depths of hell and the shadows of heaven. You will have power over them, and it will consume you. You will watch all that you love wither and die, while you remain unchanged."

The weight of her words hung heavy in the air, suffocating in its inevitability. Aaron, his patience at an end, turned away from her ramblings. With a sense of finality, he reached for the fire prod, its metal gleaming in the dim light.

"You have caused me nothing but grief," Aaron muttered, his voice filled with a quiet rage. "I will not follow your path into damnation."

With a swift, decisive motion, Aaron plunged the fire prod back into Precious's ruined body. She screamed in agony, the sound echoing through the room until it was abruptly silenced.

"Be glad that Sara has pity for you," Aaron spat, his disgust palpable. "For I have none. I will seek forgiveness before it is too late, and I will not be consumed by the darkness that you have wrought."

With those final words, Aaron withdrew the fire prod, leaving Precious's lifeless form crumpled on the ground. The room fell silent, the weight of their ordeal settling heavily upon them as they stood amidst the remnants of their battle.

Sara, her eyes filled with a mixture of sorrow and relief, reached out to Aaron, her hand trembling in his. Together, they stood in the quiet of the room, their hearts heavy with the weight of the past and the uncertain future that lay ahead.

The sound of slow, deliberate clapping filled the room, drawing Sara and Aaron's attention towards the kitchen doorway. There stood Samael, his presence commanding yet strangely alluring.

"Nice speech. I must say, I admire you, boy," Samael remarked, his gaze flickering towards Precious's lifeless form with a rueful shake of his head. "I'll be seeing her soon enough."

With a measured stride, Samael approached the young couple, his movements graceful and enticing. He regarded Aaron with a curious gleam in his eyes.

"You are a remarkable young man," Samael murmured, his hand reaching out to rest on Aaron's chest. "I see why she loved you. Why not work for me? I could offer you rewards beyond your wildest dreams."

Aaron, unaware of the being he was facing and the immense power he possessed, brushed Samael's hand aside with a determined glare. "Never," he stated firmly, his voice filled with a steely resolve.

Samael's expression shifted, a hint of disappointment flickering across his features as he realized Aaron was not easily swayed. He turned his attention towards Sara, a calculating gleam in his eyes.

"I have other ways to persuade you," Samael began, his voice low and persuasive as he moved closer to Sara. However, before he could take another step, Aaron grabbed him by the arm, his grip firm and unyielding.

"Don't even think about it," Aaron warned, his voice laced with a cold intensity that surprised even himself. He felt a surge of unfamiliar strength coursing through him, an almost primal force that seemed to emanate from deep within.

Samael regarded Aaron with a mixture of surprise and curiosity, his eyes narrowing slightly. He could sense the raw power radiating from the young man, a power that was both fascinating and dangerous.

"Very well," Samael conceded, his tone tinged with a hint of amusement.

Samael, taken aback by the audacity of a mortal daring to threaten him, locked eyes with Aaron, searching for any hint of hesitation or fear. What he found instead surprised him. In the depths of Aaron's gaze, he glimpsed a resolve as unyielding as steel. A flicker of amusement crossed Samael's features as he leaned in closer, scrutinizing the young man.

"You have some fire in you, boy," Samael chuckled, a deep rumble of laughter echoing through the room. "I'll leave you two be for now. But mark my words, you tread a dangerous path when you challenge me. I've faced beings far mightier than you and lived to tell the tale."

With a final lingering look at Aaron, Samael turned towards the lifeless form of Precious, his demeanor shifting to a more somber tone.

"There are lessons yet for you to learn," Samael mused, his voice carrying a weight of ancient wisdom. "But we will meet again, of that I am certain. When you are ready, call upon me, and I will come."

As he approached Precious's body, Samael's form seemed to blur, his hand passing through her flesh as if it were mere mist. With a graceful motion, he drew forth a translucent figure—a small girl with delicate wings, her form shimmering in the dim light of the room.

"Come, Kafziel," Samael began, his voice softening with a touch of sorrow. Then, as if struck by a sudden realization, he corrected himself. "Sister."

Gently, Samael cradled the ethereal form of Precious in his arms, a tender expression softening his features. He brushed her hair back from her face, his touch gentle and loving.

"I will bear your burden," Samael murmured, his voice filled with a mixture of compassion and regret. "Though you can never return to the heavens, I will find a place for you to rest. You have suffered enough."

With a final, sorrowful glance towards Aaron and Sara, Samael offered a small, wistful smile. In that fleeting moment, Aaron thought he caught a glimpse of unshed tears in the angel's eyes—a rare display of emotion from one so ancient and powerful.

Samael approached Aaron with deliberate care, cradling the fragile form of Kafziel tenderly against his chest. The love he held for his sister was palpable, evident in every gentle movement. Reluctantly tearing his gaze away from her face, he spoke softly.

"Here," Samael said, his voice filled with gentle warmth. "This is yours."

With a careful motion, he began moving to place Kafziel into Aaron's arms. Aaron hesitated before accepting her. He stared at the small, ethereal form, his expression a mix of confusion and disbelief.

"And what am I to do with this?" he asked, his voice barely above a whisper as he fought to keep his arms to his sides.

Samael regarded Aaron with a patient gaze, as if expecting him to understand. "She is yours," he replied simply.

"Mine?" Aaron echoed, still grappling with the idea.

A soft smile played on Samael's lips as he looked down at Kafziel in his arms. "She is one of my siblings, younger than me by far. Love her. Right now, this is the best thing I can do for her... and for you."

Aaron's mind raced with questions, his heart heavy with the weight of everything that had transpired. "How can I do that? How can I offer her love... after everything that's happened because of her?"

Samael met Aaron's gaze, his eyes holding a depth of wisdom that seemed ancient. "Love does not come without a measure of poverty," he said, his voice gentle yet firm. "Sometimes, we are called to give more than we thought possible, especially when love is needed most."

Slowly, tentatively, Aaron opened his arms to receive Kafziel's fragile form. He looked down at her closed eyes, her breathing shallow and steady. The wounds that had marred Precious's body seemed to have vanished now that her angelic essence was separate.

"Kiss her forehead gently," Samael's voice broke through Aaron's thoughts, "and give her the love she needs right now."

In that moment, Aaron felt a surge of reluctance. He wanted nothing more to do with angels, with Precious, with any of it. Glancing back at Sara, Aaron found her watching the scene with a thoughtful expression. She offered a shrug, as if to say, "What else can we do?"

Aaron hesitated for a moment, then leaned down to press a gentle kiss to Kafziel's forehead. A sense of warmth and peace washed over him, a feeling of connection to this fragile being in his arms.

"I will return soon," Samael's voice sounded from behind Aaron.

As Aaron turned back to speak to Samael, he found that the angel had vanished, leaving behind only the faint echo of fluttering wings in the quiet room. Aaron sighed heavily, feeling the weight of responsibility settling on his shoulders.

He looked upwards towards where the second floor of the house was. Beyond that ceiling, Michael and Katherine were probably still sleeping, unaware of what had transpired. He turned and smiled softly at Sara. Whatever awaited them, he knew he was not alone.

Six months had drifted by since the night of Precious's demise. In the aftermath, Aaron and Sara had brought Kafziel to Sara's home, yet the child vanished into the night, leaving only questions in her wake come morning.

The following day, Aaron and Sara sat down with Michael and Katherine, recounting the harrowing events that had unfolded. At first, Michael, lacking firsthand experience of the confrontation, hesitated to believe, but the memory of his mother's encounters with Precious years ago lingered in his mind, pushing him to accept the truth. For Katherine, the revelation was a difficult pill to swallow—her lifelong guardian angel harboring a dark side unbeknownst to her. She chose to internalize her shock, quietly accepting the unsettling reality.

In the days that followed, Aaron and Sara found themselves settling into the familiarity of his parents' home. Michael, with a heavy heart, expressed his intention to accompany Katherine back to her own home, leaving the house in their care. The town's chief of police, understanding the gravity of the situation, posed a few necessary questions but ultimately granted the couple peace. Having lost his own child to the curse that plagued the town, albeit not at the hands of Precious as widely believed but by the trio of angels that trailed after her, the chief felt a sense of relief at her demise. He adeptly managed to cloak the details of the incident, sparing Aaron from undue worry.

In a somber procession, the chief and a handful of town members laid Precious's body to rest, mingling what remained of her ashes with her physical remains. It was an oddity, merging the tangible with the ethereal, but it was the final act in a centuries-old saga. Precious was finally granted peace, her turbulent existence finding closure at last.

Aaron found himself standing in the main bedroom of the house, a space they had meticulously cleared of his parents' belongings months earlier. Despite the sense of home they had cultivated here, an unease lingered within him, a persistent feeling of unfinished business gnawing at his thoughts.

His gaze drifted out of the large bay windows, offering a view of the tranquil street outside. Yet, the tranquility of the scene did little to quell the restlessness brewing within him. It had been with him for months now, an insistent whisper in the back of his mind that refused to be ignored.

Startled by the sound of footsteps behind him, Aaron turned to find himself face to face with Samael, the angelic figure he had encountered during the tumultuous events of the past. Beside him stood Kafziel, still in the guise of the young girl but appearing less foreboding than before, her hand firmly clasped in Samael's.

The sudden appearance of the two figures sent a jolt of surprise through Aaron, causing him to instinctively take a step back. "What the... why are you here?" he blurted out, his voice betraying a mixture of confusion and apprehension.

"I told you we would meet again," Kafziel spoke up, her voice surprisingly calm and composed.

Samael, ever the enigmatic figure, cast a brief glance at Kafziel before addressing Aaron. "I have something for you," he began, his tone measured and deliberate. "Something you seemed to have lost."

Aaron's brow furrowed in confusion, his eyes flickering between Samael and Kafziel. "Lost? What do you mean?" he asked, the unease within him growing palpable.

"She sought asylum and rest with me until the time was right," Samael explained, gesturing towards Kafziel. "Consider it a gift, and perhaps a warning."

A sense of realization dawned on Aaron as he comprehended Samael's words. Kafziel, the enigmatic presence that had slipped from their grasp, had found refuge with the angelic being before him. The weight of the situation settled heavily upon him as he grasped the significance of her return.

"Don't lose her again," Samael's voice carried a solemn tone, a hint of warning beneath the surface. "You will need her in the future."

The gravity of Samael's words hung in the air, casting a shadow over the room. Aaron's mind raced with questions, the implications of Kafziel's return stirring a whirlwind of emotions within him. As he looked upon the young girl, her gaze steady and resolute.

"What do you mean?" Aaron demanded, his voice edged with frustration and confusion.

Samael continued to move with a deliberate grace, leading Kafziel towards the bed and seating her gently on its edge. Turning back to face Aaron, he spoke with a solemnity that caught Aaron's attention.

"There is more to all of this than what meets the eye," Samael began, his gaze unwavering. "My Father assigned me a role in the celestial heavens, and that is what I must fulfill until the end of time. But you, Aaron, you also have a role in this world. I thought it best to inform you before circumstances made it clear. Consider it a gift of knowledge."

"I don't want anything from you," Aaron retorted, a hint of defiance in his voice.

"You've already received the true gift long ago, when you entered this world," Samael replied, his tone measured. "I am simply here to shed light on it."

"Then speak your piece and leave," Aaron said, gesturing towards Kafziel with a sense of unease. "I want nothing to do with you or her again."

Samael glanced briefly at Kafziel before turning his attention back to Aaron. "I was created to gather and aid souls in redeeming their sins," he explained, his voice carrying a weight of ancient wisdom. "It is a role I fulfill with purpose. Just as I have mine, you have yours."

"And what is that?" Aaron asked, his curiosity piqued despite himself.

"It's not a simple answer," Samael replied, his gaze steady. "Contrary to what many myths and doctrines may suggest, I do not perpetrate evil for the sake of it. I serve to punish sins with the aim of achieving redemption. Your experience with Kafziel has prepared you for the role that awaits you."

Aaron's mind whirled with questions, the implications of Samael's words sinking in. A sense of unease settled over him, mingled with a growing understanding of the weight of responsibility that now lay on his shoulders.

"What do you mean by 'prepared'?" Aaron pressed, his voice tinged with a mixture of apprehension and curiosity.

Samael regarded him with a thoughtful gaze, as if weighing his words carefully. "Your encounter with Kafziel has shown you the depths of darkness and the strength of light within you," he explained. "It has opened your eyes to the complexities of the human soul and the choices that shape our paths."

Aaron felt a shiver run down his spine, a sense of foreboding creeping over him. "And what am I supposed to do with this... knowledge?" he asked, the weight of uncertainty heavy in his words.

"Use it wisely," Samael replied, his voice carrying a note of caution. "You have a role to play in the balance of this world, a path to walk that will test your resolve and your faith."

"You're talking in circles, and you're making the hairs on the back of my neck rise," Aaron said, his hand instinctively cupping the nape of his neck. "None of this is making sense. What exactly is this role or job you keep mentioning?"

"I'll reveal it all in due time, but let me pose a question to you first," Samael replied calmly. "Have you sensed that things are amiss of late?"

Aaron hesitated, a furrow forming on his brow. "Yes, but... what does that have to do with anything?"

"What you've experienced is an awakening," Samael explained, his gaze steady. "You've become attuned to the realms between heaven and hell that exist right here on Earth. You have brushed against the celestial, and in doing so, you've become sensitive to the presence of demons and fallen angels."

Aaron's eyes widened in disbelief. "Wait, what?"

"That's your gift, Aaron," Samael continued, a faint smile playing on his lips. "It has awakened within you, and now you have a purpose—a duty to fulfill. And this girl here," he gestured towards Kafziel, "this redeemed fallen angel, she will assist you in this task. Consider it a parting gift."

With that, Samael's form seemed to shimmer before he vanished from sight, leaving Aaron standing there, bewildered and grappling with the weight of his newfound knowledge. The room fell silent, save for the faint rustle of fabric as Kafziel shifted beside him.

As Aaron processed the gravity of what had just been revealed to him, a sense of apprehension mingled with determination settled over him. The world around him seemed to shift, taking on new layers of meaning and mystery.

"I... I don't understand," Aaron muttered to himself, his gaze fixed on Kafziel.

But there were no answers forthcoming, only the quiet presence of the girl beside him.

Sara was at the back of the house, tending to the small garden she had lovingly planted at the start of spring. The gentle melody of birdsong accompanied her, and she hummed softly to herself, savoring the simple joys of the day. With the fall semester looming ahead, she and Aaron had decided to relish these precious moments of respite, cherishing the time as a soon-to-be-married couple.

As she tended to the blooms, a faint whisper of unease tugged at the edges of Sara's mind. At first, she dismissed it as nothing more than a trick of the wind, until Aaron's voice shattered the tranquility.

"Sara!" The call sliced through the air, laden with an unfamiliar hoarseness that sent a jolt of fear coursing through her.

Without a second thought, Sara dropped the hoe she held and raced towards the house. Her steps echoed through the kitchen, urgency lending wings to her feet as she dashed into the living room. Heart pounding, she thundered up the stairs, each step a frantic beat of worry.

As she reached the doorway of the main bedroom, Aaron's voice, strangled with pain, reached her ears once more. "Don't come in here!"

But it was too late, her momentum carrying her forward despite his warning. Sara burst into the room, her eyes widening in shock and disbelief at the scene that unfolded before her.

There, in the dim light of the room, were wings—magnificent and ethereal—protruding from Aaron's back. Her gaze shifted, locking onto the form of a smiling little girl, a haunting familiarity stirring within her.

"Precious?" The name escaped her lips in a breathless whisper, the realization hitting her like a thunderbolt.

Time seemed to stand still as Sara stood frozen in the doorway, the weight of the truth crashing down upon her. Her screams pierced the air, a cacophony of fear, confusion, and disbelief echoing off the walls of the room. It felt like an eternity before the sound faded, leaving only a heavy silence in its wake.

Trembling, Sara could only stare, her mind reeling with questions that begged for answers. The world around her had shifted irrevocably, and she was left to grapple with the unimaginable truth that now stared back at her with innocent eyes.

explicitus est liber

explicitus est liber

---⌘---

https://writingfortheworldpress.com

Also by J. A. Springs

Chronicles of Cosmic Realms
Shadows of the Forgotten Void

elctrcsheepdrmwrks (Electric Sheep Dreamworks)
Blurred Vision
Fractured
Zero One

Essays in Systems and Being
Essays in Systems and Being

The Absurdities Anthology
How Not to Find Your Local Weed-Man

The Gifted
The Untamed Force
Next Exit

The Shepherd Series
The Bad Shepherd
The Good Wolf

Standalone
Sundrops
Behind the Red Door
Boundless Fragments: A Collection of Novellas and Short Stories
Fragments of Forever

Watch for more at https://authorjasprings.com.

About the Author

I'm J. A. Springs.

Father of six wonderful children. I served twenty years on active duty, living around the world and experiencing things I never imagined I would. I spent time in societies and countries I once couldn't have envisioned as part of my future. I've done a lot—and still not enough.

These days, I live quietly, accompanied by my cats, music, and an interest in writing that consumes me. I've been writing seriously since 2021. I never set out to write in a particular genre—it made more sense to write around them instead. As for goals? There aren't many. Enjoy the first cup of coffee in the morning and see what the day brings.

Read more at https://authorjasprings.com.

About the Publisher

LLC. Lancaster, PA

www.writingfortheworldpress.com

Read more at https://www.writingfortheworldpress.com.